Samuel Norvell Lapsley

Life and Letters of Samuel Norvell Lapsley

Missionary to the Congo Valley, West Africa, 1866-1892

Samuel Norvell Lapsley

Life and Letters of Samuel Norvell Lapsley
Missionary to the Congo Valley, West Africa, 1866-1892

ISBN/EAN: 9783744758222

Printed in Europe, USA, Canada, Australia, Japan

Cover: Foto ©Raphael Reischuk / pixelio.de

More available books at **www.hansebooks.com**

LIFE AND LETTERS

OF

SAMUEL NORVELL LAPSLEY,

MISSIONARY TO THE CONGO VALLEY, WEST AFRICA.

1866 – 1892.

———————

RICHMOND, VA.:

WHITTET & SHEPPERSON, PRINTERS, TENTH AND MAIN STREETS.

1893.

This is
Inscribed to
The dear little Mother,

From whom our boy
Learned his earliest lessons of entire
Devotion to God and duty;
Whose beautiful life, and gentle
And wise words were as an inspiration,
Ever inciting and guiding him,
In that life of consecration,
Some pictures from which,
These pages seek
To portray;

PREFATORY NOTE.

WITH the exception of the memoir and closing chapter, this book is made up of extracts from my son's letters and diary, beginning February 26, 1890, the day he left New York, and ending March 17, 1892, a few days before his death.

For the better parts of the memoir and the editing of the letters from May to July, 1890, we are indebted to his brother, R. A. L., who would gladly and efficiently have done more of this labor of love had not his time been constantly occupied as an evangelist elsewhere.

We have a continuous diary and also contemporaneous letters, and I have selected from one or the other, as seemed best, in order to give briefly a clear and connected view of his journeyings and labors, and of the countries and peoples among whom he went.

In his daily intercourse with people of divers tongues, he acquired polyglot capacities and habits which naturally show themselves in his familiar writings, in editing which an effort was at first made to translate or substitute the strange words that occur with others. This was found undesirable, in place of which I give here a little glossary showing the meanings of those most commonly occurring; in addition to which, it is well to be forewarned that almost every place and person has at least two names: *e. g.*, Leopoldville is known also as Kintamo; Bwemba, as Chumbiri; Luluaburg, the farthest point east to which he journeyed, is called also Malange; and Underhill, where he died, is known as Tunduwa, etc., etc. And there are no established rules of spelling, and hence we must not think it strange to find the same word written by him in different ways at different times.

As an example of the strange mixing of languages, see the diary March 25, 1891, chapter VII., and note.

J. W. L.

ANNISTON, ALA., *August*, 1892.

CONTENTS:

GLOSSARY.

BA.—A prefix signifying people, as "Bakongo" the Congo people. But in speaking of *individuals* among the tribes around Luebo, the prefix "Mo" is used, as Chinyama of the Bakete tribe is called a "Mokete," etc.

KI.—A prefix signifying tongue or speech, as "Kikongo" the language of the Congo people.

BENA.—Sometimes written simply "B," a town or village.

BULA MATADI.—Literally, rock breaker; the name given Stanley by the Africans; applied now to all State officers, soldiers and employees.

CHIMBEC.—A house.

CHICOT.—A whip, cat o' nine tails.

CHOP.—Noun and verb. Food and to eat.

COWRIES.—Shells, used in currency.

DASH.—Noun and verb. A present, and to give.

KWANGA, or QUANGA.—The native bread.

MUNDELE.—White man.

NGUVO.—Hippopotamus.

NTAKU.—A small brass rod, about a foot long; the currency.

NYAU (pronounced Neyou).—Elephant.

PALAVER.—Any sort of interview, talk, controversy, contention, war.

SABBY.—To know.

CHAPTER I.

MEMOIR.

A T Underhill, an English Mission Station, near the foot of the Cataracts of the Congo, on the 26th of March, 1892, a young soldier of the Cross put off his armor and entered into rest. He had been in the dark continent nearly two years, and had not completed his twenty-sixth year when he was called to his high reward. It might seem that his life came to an untimely end. But since the days of the martyr Stephen, our Lord has often taken honor to himself from those who, at the very threshold of a career of richest promise, have laid down their lives for his sake. Thus at the head of the roll of Scottish martyrs stands Patrick Hamilton, who suffered at the stake when but twenty-four, accomplishing more by his death than he could by the longest life, although he was learned, eloquent, and of the blood royal of Scotland: and in these latter days David Brainerd, Henry Martyn, Allen Gardiner, Hannington, Keith Falconer, and many more have thus glorified their Master in an early death. To these names of blessed memory we may now add that of another, whose brief life these pages record.

SAMUEL NORVELL LAPSLEY

was born in Selma, Alabama, April 14th, 1866. He came into life with the inestimable advantage of pious parentage and a godly ancestry. He was the third son of James Woods Lapsley and Sara E. Pratt, his wife: he an elder in the church, and both of them children of Presbyterian ministers. On his father's side the blood was that of the Scotch-Irish and Scotch, who came to the Valley of Virginia over one hundred and fifty years ago; he being descended from Michael Woods, of Albemarle, an Irish immigrant, who came up the Valley in 1734; his son-in-law, Joseph Lapsley, coming by way of Pennsylvania a little later, and also from Andrew Woods, of Botetourt, and Mary Ponge, his wife, and counting among his ancestors in the last century the Moores, Rayburns, and Armstrongs, who came into the Valley country when it was a wilderness.

His father's father was the Rev. Robert Armstrong Lapsley, D. D., of Nashville, Tenn., a name still greatly revered through Tennessee and Kentucky. And in the old cemetery at Nashville, over the grave of his father's mother, Catherine Rutherford Lapsley, is an inscription telling of her pious life and triumphant death, and of her descent from Samuel Rutherford, of the Westminster Assembly. Her father was John Moore Walker, son of Joseph Walker, for thirty years a trustee and treasurer of Washington College, now the Washington and Lee University. Joseph Walker's wife was Jane Moore, an aunt of Mary Moore, the heroine of the little book in our Sunday-school libraries, *The Captives of Abbs Valley*.[1] How the name and character of the brave old Covenanter, Samuel Rutherford, has been held in reverence, is observable from the constant recurrence of his name and that of his wife, Catherine, in the families of his descendants. An instance is that of Samuel Rutherford Lapsley, an uncle of the subject of this Memoir (and for whom he was named), his father's youngest brother, who, in his twentieth year, got his death wound in the front of the battle at Shiloh, April, 1862, struck down with the colors of his regiment in his hands.

On the mother's side the lineage was drawn from New England and the Georgia low-country. His mother's father, the Rev. Horace Southworth Pratt, was from Connecticut, but spent his life in Georgia and Alabama, dying while professor of *Belles-lettres* in the University of Alabama, in which office he was succeeded by his son, Rev. John W. Pratt, D. D., afterwards pastor of the Presbyterian Church in Lexington, Va., and of the Second Church in Louisville, Ky. His mother's mother, Isabel Drysdale, was of an old loyalist Episcopal family of the low-country, to which the late Bishop Drysdale, of Louisiana, belonged. Rather than rebel against King George, they fled to the Bahamas, where Mrs. Pratt was born. She was equally eminent for piety, literary taste, and business capacity. For many years a widow, she managed well her children's education and pro-

---

[1] Mrs. Kay, our venerable aunt, says: "The book, *Captives of Abbs Valley*, omits one thing that my mother used to tell. She said, as the Indians were taking Cousin Mary away, that she caught up her Bible and carried it with her through her long captivity, and when she was at last released and came back to live at Grandma Walker's she still had that Bible. Grandma was quite a match-maker, and thought very highly of preachers. She married Cousin Mary Moore to the Rev. Samuel Brown, and among their children were five preachers, one of whom was the Rev. Dr. William Brown, of Richmond. She married her daughter, my Aunt Peggy, to Rev. Samuel Houston. Their son, Rev. Samuel Rutherford Houston, was missionary to Greece, and his daughter, Janet, is now a missionary in Mexico."

perty, and also found time to write and publish a number of books for children.

These brief references to an honored and faithful ancestry are worthy of record, showing the value of family religion, coming down from generation to generation, and testifying to the faithfulness of a covenant-keeping God.

The power of religion was early manifest in the life of our young missionary. He was admitted to the communion of the Selma Church, in which he was born, on the 16th of April, 1876, having just passed his tenth birth-day. And like the Lord Jesus, he "went about his Father's business" at an early age; for, only two years later, he acted as superintendent of a Sunday-school for the negroes in the little church built by his father and uncles at Vine Hill, their country home, twenty miles north of Selma. The school was, in fact, managed by his grand-aunt, Mrs. Elsie M. Kay, but he did his part in a quiet and efficient manner. Mrs. K. says, "I well remember the first meeting, when Sam had to open the school with prayer and say a few words to the crowd that filled the church. He was badly frightened, and came near breaking down once, but he looked toward me and caught my eye, went on and got through nicely. Among the pupils was William Clark, the blacksmith, a colored Baptist preacher, who often stopped over after school to discuss with us some troublesome points of doctrine. I remember Sam's sedate manner as. pacing up and down or standing before William, he would say, 'But, Uncle William, what does Paul say about that?' And he then would quote to him the Scripture."

At the outset of his career he was, like his Master, subjected to great temptations and conflicts. which continued for years. It was a very common thing for him to come late at night to the bedside of his father and mother, and tell them of his agony of trial from doubts and fears and evil thoughts; sometimes it almost seemed as if his mind would give way under the pressure of these terrible conflicts; and it is highly probable that some of these siftings of Satan continued in his later years, and helped to wear him away, even though latterly he said but little of it to human helpers.

All kinds of knowledge he carefully gathered and readily assimilated. He very early learned the geography of the heavens, and could call the stars and constellations by their names; and crossing the Equator in May, 1890, he observed and wrote of the new acquaintances he was making among the stars looking down from the Southern sky.

He had a wonderful love and talent for music; and we hardly know when he began to get melody from the piano and organ. Very often from the little church at Vine Hill would be heard late in the night the tones of the organ, as the boy, all alone in the darkness, played over all he could think of, one piece gliding into another, and now and then strange new chords, his own improvising, floating out upon the night air.

Many in different parts of Alabama remember the fair-faced youth, who during a summer vacation was with the Synod's evangelist, leading with the voice and organ the music of the great congregation gathered under "The Presbyterian gospel tent." In his diary are African boat songs, written down carefully, the notes for each part being given, all being caught by him as they fell from the lips of his wild Bayansi boatmen, in his canoe trip in January, 1891, up the Kassai and Duma.

In his final preparation for college, he was privileged to receive instruction from an eminent scholar and divine, the Rev. James A. Waddell, D. D., of Virginia, who preached and taught in the Vine Hill Church in 1880-'81. The mutual esteem and affection of teacher and pupil was exceedingly interesting; and Dr. Waddell ever spoke of him as the most brilliant pupil that he had ever had.

He went to the University of Alabama in the fall of 1881, entering Sophomore, and graduated at the head of his class in the summer of 1884; each of the three years having ended with his taking the highest stand in his class, though that honor was sometimes divided with others. He assisted his brother James in organizing the Young Men's Christian Association at the University. It was said in Tuscaloosa that, while some of the faculty and city pastors were consulting and arranging to get prepared a constitution and by-laws for organizing a Christian association among the students, the "Lapsley boys," who had just entered, and did not know what the elders were doing, had quietly gone ahead and organized it. Of course, an innovation in the direction of religious life among the students did not pass unchallenged, and some of the usual results ensued, but courage, tact and good temper enabled them to carry everything through quietly.[1]

During his senior year (not yet eighteen years old) and the year afterwards, he was employed at the University as an assistant professor, and he was elected for the third time in 1886, but declined the appointment, being afraid that the easy, quiet college life, surrounded by books and pleasant congenial friends, would draw him away from his purpose to enter the ministry. But he left in Tuscaloosa a name and history such as few have made for themselves.

The President of the University,[2] conversing with the writer in 1884

[1] See a reference to this in a letter to his brother J., May 3, in Chapter IX.
[2] Hon. B. B. Lewis.

or 1885, quoted approvingly the opinion of one of the most judicious of the faculty, to the effect that no one superior to Sam had been graduated from the University since the war. Another,[1] now a member of the faculty at Vanderbilt, writes from Dresden, Saxony, speaking of him as the "brilliant, the heroic, the beloved member of our class." Another[2] member of the University faculty writes, "Sam came as near following in the footsteps of his Master as any man of ancient or modern times." Another class-mate,[3] now *en route* for a mission field in Japan, writes, "Sam's death was to me the voice of God calling me to a nobler life. Would that I had entered the service as early as he!"

He was cadet captain of one of the companies comprising the corps of University cadets; and when the Alabama cadets took the prize at the great competitive drill at the New Orleans Exposition in 1885, he expressed a pardonable pride at their success, recognizing in some of those winning the prize boys whose thoroughness and accuracy in soldierly accomplishments were results, in part at least, of his long and careful drilling.

The scholastic year, 1885-'86, was spent at Union Theological Seminary, Virginia. A letter from there telling of his work in the neighboring country says, "His zeal made him go into every home, good and bad, and even the old 'Hardshells' loved him, and one gave him the wood for this same chapel; another, a Methodist, would help him in carpenter work, and two men, who each 'had killed his man' in drunken carousal, would go to hear 'the little preacher' when they would never listen to others. One man that Sam was interested in was about to leave the neighborhood, and had sent his family away, leaving him alone in a big comfortless house. Sam came by my house on his way there. We expostulated, telling him it was too cold, and the man had only one quilt left in his house I can now bring back his merry laugh: 'I am not going there to sleep or eat either; I want to talk with Ransom.' He wouldn't take or let me send him any comforts." She says, "he came back the next morning bright and happy, and being made to tell, it was learned that the fare was 'cold cornbread ash-cake,' and the bed the floor, with the single quilt for their cover and a stick of wood for a pillow; but he said, 'I had a good talk with Ransom.'" "That man," she says, "lives now and will thank him some day for pointing his way to heaven. My husband says, 'tell his mother his was the most devoted spirit I ever knew, and now he is tasting his reward.'"

---

[1] Professor John Daniel.   [2] Colonel R. A. Hardaway.   [3] Rev. H. G. Hawkins.

Another writing from Hampden-Sidney says, "I have thought of him so often lately, and more than once thanked God that I have known a man capable of such noble self-abnegation."

The summer of 1886 was spent, under direction of the Presbytery of North Alabama, in ministering to the church at Decatur and the neighboring churches in the country south of Decatur, Hartsell, Somerville and Fairview. His first appearance at one of his appointments in the country was on foot, having walked the greater part of the way from the railroad. He found the family with whom he was to stay all in the wheat-field, and at once set in and worked with them till they were through. A strong attachment sprung up between him and these good people in the hill country, and when the summer was over he was unwilling to leave them unsupplied with preaching. The people at home were anxious to have him with them, and asked him to come back to Vine Hill and spend the year teaching the home school. He had been away constantly for four or five years, and must soon go again and for good, and he was yet young enough to spare a year with those dearest to him, and so he was persuaded to come, his brother James, who was just out of the Seminary, going to supply the churches in North Alabama.

But even now he was not willing to enjoy the rest afforded him. The Second Church in Birmingham was ministered to by Rev. James Watson, an old and valued friend of his father and grandfather, who was now quite infirm from age and long service. Mr. Watson and the church asked him to come up and preach for them; and so, instead of resting, he went at the end of each week, a distance of seventy-five miles, and preached and visited among the people, and then returned to his school on Monday. When the summer came on and the school session closed, he gave all his time to the church at Birmingham. It was very hard work, and his health seemed at one time to be endangered by it, but he suffered no permanent injury; and he formed there some of the warmest and closest friendships of his life. One of his Birmingham friends[1] writes, May 20th, 1892: "I did not try to restrain the tears this morning as we gathered around his picture and looked in his lovely face; and on 'Children's Day' the address was devoted in part to him and his work. To-night at our church we are to have a memorial service. Our people of his day love him and cherish his memory."

In the fall of 1887 he went to McCormick Seminary, Chicago, hoping to gather and absorb in the great western metropolis varied

[1] Dr. E. H. Sholl.

and useful lessons, not to be found in books anywhere. In the summer of 1888 he preached at Royalton, Minnesota, returning to Chicago in the fall, and graduating in the spring of 1889. We have few memorials of his life during these two years; but a letter from one,[1] whose friendship he gained there, contains the following suggestive sentences: "I never came in contact with a young man who came so close to my heart as he did. I loved him and have followed him with the most tender and intense interest. Dr. and Mrs. Herrick Johnston were deeply touched with the news of his death, remembering him as they did with so much interest. Dr. Halsey has always had such an affectionate interest in Sam, both while here and since he left, and has often talked with me of him. Last night he said he had expected him to be read of by and by as we read of Livingston now. Three things he said impressed him so much as showing his character and purpose: First, that he should go to Africa; second, that he should go unmarried; third, that he should go with a colored man. He said he seemed to be so long-headed and far-seeing, and he could only wonder why such promise was interrupted."

A class-mate,[2] writing from Utah Territory, says: "We were associated in the opening of the Chicago City Mission Work, which is now the Olivet Presbyterian Church. I was named as leader in the mission. Sam never failed me, never; and I believe the success of that movement was, under God, due more to his efforts than to those of any other one engaged in it." Speaking of the meetings held in their rooms, after returning from the mission work, this brother adds: "Two traits stood out prominently, faithfulness to duty, and loyalty to home; there was always a petition for the dear ones at home. There was no high-wrought feeling, but we had a sense of being in the presence of a soul, with face set like a flint to gain 'the power of his resurrection in the fellowship of his sufferings.'"

In the spring of 1889 he returned home, the family having meantime moved up to Anniston; and from his return till the departure for Africa, in February, 1890, he was engaged mainly among the poor and neglected, whose homes are clustered around the work-shops, factories and furnaces in West Anniston, where his brother Robert was pastor of a new-built church. This brother gives the following account of his life during these months:

"Sam had been appointed by the Home Missions Committee of Tuscaloosa Presbytery to supply for the summer a group of churches

---

in Hale county, Alabama. At my earnest solicitation he gave up this appointment and came to Anniston to spend the summer with me, working partly in a mission of the West Anniston Church, and partly in the mission of the First Church at Glen Addie (another suburb of Anniston). He gave the Sunday mornings to Glen Addie, and the afternoon and night to Washertown, as the West Anniston Mission was familiarly known, from the first of May to the middle of November, 1889. The immediate results of his work were the organization of the Glen Addie Mission into the Anniston Third Church, with thirty-three members, and an addition to the West Anniston Church through the Washertown Mission of almost an equal number; and beneath this numerical result, striking as it is, was an impression for time and eternity upon these two communities rarely ever achieved by any man in so short a time.

"In the Washertown neighborhood particularly little short of a social and religious revolution was effected. For the first time in the lives of the poor people in that spiritually neglected locality, there came into their homes, ate at their tables, and walked with them on their streets, one who bore the manifest image of the Lord Jesus; and the results were very much like those which followed the footsteps of the Master himself. He was specially successful in individual cases. He more than once quoted to me, 'Who will bring me into the strong city? Who will lead me into Edom? Will not thou, O God?' And he would then say, 'Edom is C.'s boarding-house in Glen Addie, and M. S.'s house in Washertown.' The conversion of the individual last named was given him as one of the most signal triumphs of his work. This man was, upon his own oft-repeated confession in our meetings after his conversion, one of the worst of sinners. He was a man of strong character, carrying under a rough and careless exterior much capacity and kindness. Sam wisely selected him as the centre and leader of influence in the neighborhood. He hated Sam's coming to his house, and left messages with his wife (which she never delivered) forbidding his coming again. Sam would come and take meals with him, ask a blessing at his table, have prayers with his family, the host outwardly polite, but inwardly rebelling against it all. The first strong impression on this man's soul was made as he came home one evening through the pines, and saw a man kneeling behind a tree. He drew near to see the sight, and found Sam on his knees, who arose and came forward saying, 'I am glad to see you, I was praying for you'; and then he made him sit down as he read the Scriptures to him. He says Sam got him to service first by meeting him on the railroad-track, some distance from his house, as he came home wet and muddy from his work. (To give the incident in his own words.) 'I wasn't a studying about him when he stepped out from behind a box-car, and says he, "How do you do." "Well enough," I answered him, as short as pie-crust. He said, "Are you going home?" "Yes," said I as grum as I could. "I am going that way," said he. I didn't say nothing, didn't countenance him no more an' if he was a dog, but he went on with me, talking pleasant and friendly, took supper at my house, and after supper said, "You know you promised me to go to church to-night: it's about time we were going." I couldn't think of no excuse to get out of it, and he started on and held the gate open for me to go before, and there was nothing for me to do but to go along with him. And next night I joined the church, and have been following Jesus ever since.' Other like cases occurred, all showing the same unwavering purpose and consecration, together with a manifest enjoyment of the service, that at once lessened the hardship and increased his power for good.

"During the last protracted meeting at Washertown, when most of the fruits of his work there were gathered up, and which continued four weeks, he took his valise over to our little Mission Chapel, made his toilet and did his studying there (he preached twice a day for the whole four weeks), and took his meals and slept among the people. In this connection he once quoted to me the remark of a friend at McCormick Seminary, who was remonstrated with for going down to · live in the slums of Chicago, where he had his Mission Chapel, and made the quaint rejoinder that, 'he had noticed that the Lord Jesus while here among men did not come down from heaven every morning bringing his dinner with him and go back every night.'

"So thoroughly was his house to house visitation accomplished that, when he resigned the Washertown work into my hand, he gave me from memory a map of the entire district, with the name of the family and the religious character of the inmates of every house.

"I had confidently looked forward to the time when he would have carried out on the banks of the Congo the lessons learned at his Master's feet in this Anniston Mission work, and a more conspicuous and far wider harvest of souls would have been his. The Lord willed it otherwise. For that very reason it will be a comfort to know that he went to the foreign field, where his work was to end so soon, wearing a crown of souls already won for Jesus at home."

To some there seemed an incongruity between him and his work. He was essentially a scholar, with a mind and manner and appearance

showing innate refinement and high culture, yet his life was mainly
devoted to labors among a class of people wholly different, and he was
eminently successful with them.   An explanation of his success is
given by his uncle, R. L., in these words: "The trait which this early
departure emphasizes is his consecration; honest, thorough consecration.   He did not have the traits to influence the poor and low, but he
did influence them everywhere, because 'he gave himself for them.'"

But there was nothing of the ascetic about him.   We would have a
very imperfect idea of his life if we kept out of view that part of it
exemplified by a picture at home, which presents him in the centre of
a group of handsome young men and maidens, all seated on the ground
and garlanded with flowers; or if we forget how he enjoyed and made
others enjoy social and home pleasures and recreations, the song, the
ringing chorus, and all the games and merry makings, characteristic of
a really happy home life.   And mention also should be made of that
sunny humor which was so bright a feature of his character.   The
surface of a deep and singularly consecrated life was rippled over con-
tinually with a genuine appreciation of all that was happy and mirth
provoking.   None that knew him can ever forget the bright glow of
his countenance, and the flash of his blue eyes accompanying some
playful sally of an ever ready wit.   From his childhood he had the
faculty of extracting some quaint or odd experience and amusing
application out of almost every book he read and new acquaintance
he made; and his sober earnest work among the poor was lit up by
the keenest yet kindliest appreciation of the oddities and humorous
peculiarities constantly cropping out in a society freed from constraints
and conventionalities.   Those who have read the letters and journal of
his African labors will feel better than can be described the charm
which this never failing humor imparted to all his writings, especially
to those written currente calamo, as his letters were, for the eyes of
loving friends; and not the least valuable lesson of his life is the teaching this gives us, that genuine and exalted piety may form the warp and
woof of one of the sunniest characters ever known.

And he was equally free from enthusiasm as from asceticism.   His
final course was chosen and determined on after long and deliberate
consideration.   Before he left McCormick Seminary he had thought
much of his duty to become a foreign missionary, and there was in
his mind an inclination toward Africa as the worst field and the most
needy, and hence the one calling most loudly for help.   Then, the
General Assembly, in 1889, concluded to establish the Congo Mission.
Some one must go, and yet none seemed willing to offer for it.   He

had reason to believe he was fitted for the work, and he knew that he was willing to give himself up to it, if such was God's will. There were no counter calls or conflicting duties, and the way seemed open, so he offered himself to the cause in these words:

"ANNISTON, ALA., August 5, 1889.

"REV. M. H. HOUSTON, D. D.,

"Secretary of Foreign Missions, Nashville, Tenn.:

"REVEREND AND DEAR SIR: I hereby ask to be sent by your Committee as your missionary to the Congo Valley, in Africa. I do so because it is my desire and conviction that I should preach Christ to the heathen, and for several reasons I want to go to Africa, if God and the church permit me.

"Yours in Christ's work,

"S. N. LAPSLEY."

After due consideration his offer was accepted, and Presbytery met at Anniston, December 4th, 1889, and ordained him for the work; and the Rev. W. H. Sheppard, a colored member of the Presbytery of Atlanta, a highly approved graduate of the Institute at Tuscaloosa, offered, and was accepted also.

Just prior to leaving for Africa they together visited the churches, and deeply interested audiences gathered to bid them good-bye, at Selma, Anniston, Birmingham, Nashville, Louisville, and Washington. Being given a private interview at the White House, the President expressed his warm sympathy and interest, and had Mr. Blaine to give letters to our Ministers abroad; kindly reminding us also, that in these days of electricity and steam a foreign mission was not so far away as in the olden time. At the mission offices in New York and Boston such advice and information as was to be had was freely given. Friends everywhere gave and did what kindly solicitude could do, to prepare and provide them for their long journey; but the sad hour of departure came, and the steamer *Adriatic* sailed with them from New York, on Wednesday, the 26th of February, 1890.

A few months after their departure "Home letters from S. N. L.," which give account of their journey from the day they left New York till they reached Africa, were printed and circulated privately; and from time to time there have appeared in the newspapers extracts from his letters and diaries, which have been read with great interest, and have evoked frequent requests for publication of more of his writings. Since his death these requests have been more urgent, and to his friends it has been presented as a duty to the cause we all love, "That some connected account of his life and work should be published."

One judicious friend[1] writes, "I believe it would be blessed as no other missionary literature would be, and it may be that thus God will make most use of the noble young life laid down so soon." Another[2] writes from the far West, "I had often told our children of his brave and consecrated spirit shown in his undertaking that great difficult and dangerous work. . . . Many feel deeply interested in knowing all the facts, and a Memoir would be used to inspire the children of many a Christian family with a deep devotion to the Master's cause." Another[3] says, "The effect of this sacrifice will be to stir in many hearts the impulse to say, 'Here am I, send me.'" Another friend suggests that the publication would be "the surest means of perpetuating the influence of his short but devoted life."

In following these suggestions, the constant effort is to let the subject of these memoirs speak for himself, the letters and diaries being followed as closely as practicable, and with a minimum of editorial interference with the original text.

The "Home letters" are reprinted with a few additions and some notes taken from his contemporaneous diaries. Then follows the account taken from his letters and diary of the progress from the coast up to Stanley Pool, the long foot and hammock journey of two hundred and thirty miles; and after that comes an account of the trip up to Bolobo, and then back and down the caravan foot-path, hunting for carriers to go to the interior; and then the expedition in open canoes up the Kassai and Duma and back to the Pool; and then the journey on the Steamer *Florida* up to Luebo; and then the account of the settlement at Luebo, and the trip to Luluaberg; and then the last journey back to the coast where all his toilsome wanderings ceased.

Thus we give all that we know of him during these last busy years till the end came, and the circumstances of his death are told in the words of the kind friends who were with him in the final hours.

---

[1] Rev. D. C. Rankin, Nashville.   [2] Rev. J. J. Read, Indian Territory.
[3] W. S. Plumer Bryan, D. D., Cincinnati.

ORIGINAL PREFACE TO "HOME LETTERS."

Anniston, Ala., *July* 1, 1890.

NUMEROUS kin people and friends have asked to read these letters, and they have gone around, and have become worn and scattered until, that we may preserve them and also gratify many to whom the writer is dear, they have been printed.

The selection of a site for the Congo Mission was, by the Committee, devolved upon the missionaries, and necessary information to enable them to select judiciously was best obtained in Brussels and London. The Court of Leopold, King of the Belgians, is the centre of political and commercial influence in the Congo Free State ; and the most successful mission work there has its centre at Harley House, East London. Dr. H. Grattan Guinness was met in Boston, and gave a kind invitation and introduction to his wife, who, in his absence, is managing affairs at Harley House. In Washington in addition to formal letters from the State Department, most influential and kindly commendation was obtained to parties having influence in Brussels. And the first news of the visit to the Continent was in a letter from General Sanford to Senator Morgan, forwarded to us here. Extracts from which are as follows :

BRUSSELS, *March* 21, 1890.

DEAR SENATOR MORGAN : I have your good letter by the hand of Mr. Lapsley; or rather he sent it to me from London. I wrote to him to come over, and I have put him in communication with the Congo people, who will see that he is well treated and have all possible facilities for carrying out his mission. He is indeed a very young man for such a work, but all I see of him pleases me and inspires confidence. . . . . He is bound not to suffer at the hands of our people there. I'll see to that. Your letter was so good that I sent it yesterday to the King for his perusal. I will try and secure him an audience of his majesty a little later. . . . .

Truly yours,

H. S. SANFORD.

And the last letter we have from Europe, was one to General Sanford, written a few days before sailing and forwarded to us, as follows:

51 BOW ROAD E. LONDON, *April* 5, 1890.

MY DEAR SIR: Your kind letter of the 2nd inst, came duly to hand. Accept my thanks for the letters of introduction to your Congo friends. I am sure they will be of great service to me. We are to sail about the 15th, the *Afrikaan* being delayed as you predicted she would be. My outfit and stores have already been forwarded and are to-night, I suppose, crossing to Holland.

I have received from M. Van Eetvelder a letter of introduction to the Governor-General, enclosed in a very kind note. I shall not forget that I owe this and my other favors in Brussels to your kind offices. I hope that I may have the opportunity to show my appreciation and that you will command me. I am with sincere regard,

Yours very truly,

S. N. LAPSLEY.

GENERAL H. S. SANFORD,
Hotel De Bellevue, Brussels.

THE HOME AT ANNISTON.

CHAPTER II.

"HOME LETTERS FROM S. N. L."

FEBRUARY 26 TO APRIL 22, 1890.

STEAMER ADRIATIC, *February* 26, 1890.

MY DEAR PAPA AND MAMMA: To-day has been a perfect day so far as smooth sea and cloudless sky could make it, and now the moon is out, just past its second quarter, so that we shall have moonlight all our voyage.

My stateroom looks much like a home—a sort of home now. I have it to myself, and that means more room than in 314 Gilsey House. Still I wish I might spend to-night as near you as I have these last pleasant days; and 314 Gilsey House seems very pleasant in memory now. Here I have an opposite berth for a table, and an upper berth for a rack, or else I may have it taken out. My coats and hats hang on nails, my toilet articles are unpacked and stowed in sight and reach, and then with seat and washstand, I have six feet by five to spare. I am writing on my Glen-Addie portfolio. I have met two pleasant English gentlemen, one a Wesleyan minister and the other a Church of England clergyman.

I felt as I never had in my life, when I saw you walk out of sight in the great shed. I thought I saw you again on the Battery, and waved, and ran, and tried to see better, but lost you. I didn't know how much I loved you till to-day. I want a chance again to show you both how much; but I shall try to honor you by being a good man, by getting over the faults that you know, and filling the place God has put me in, as you have shown me how.

There are some very sick people aboard now I think, but I don't laugh at them—it don't look funny, and it don't feel very

25

funny, as both Sheppard and I can testify. I got squeamish in the stuffy saloon at lunch, and a "cigarette young man" set me off about an hour and a half after, so I had a typical case about half or three quarters of an hour. Since then, except in places where I smell cooking, etc., I am quite at ease. I hardly expect either of us will suffer.

I don't think you heard any whistle from our steamer this morning, the tug whistled, and I thought—they are saying, "There's the steamer!" The tug left us to ourselves before we passed the Battery. Then about twelve miles out, I calculated, the pilot dropped off, and rowed over to the pilot yacht, that stood off about five hundred yards, leaving us to the light-house above, the sun by day, the moon and stars by night. I thought that my piloting henceforth must be from the lights above. Do you remember, Mamma, we sang "pilot me" at Mr. Moody's meeting? Well, I must find Sheppard for prayers, and say good night for this first day's journal. Tillie and Isabel, part second.

Your loving son,   SAM.

February 28.—*The diary has this:* "Enjoy my Bible a good deal. Read Hannington. What a brave man! . . . Jesus and Paul avoided needless peril. Wisdom of a serpent often enabled Livingston to pass through savages unharmed and unharming. Let this Book be my 'time book'; God the time-keeper."

SATURDAY, March 1.

TILLIE AND ISABEL, DEAR LITTLE GIRLS: You want to know something of our voyage, I suppose. Well, I did not enter into it with much zest, I confess; seeing the last of Mamma and Papa was about all I could think of for the first day—still there was much to see. Two steamers started out with us, and the race would have been very interesting if we had been nearer together; but before night they were out of sight. About 4 P. M. we passed the great *Teutonic* outward bound—she is a monster, more than twice the weight of the *Adriatic*. We ran up a signal flag of enquiry, and she replied with a string of little flags, blue, red, red-white and blue, roan, brindle and brick dust. I suppose, and I think our captain understood by them whether there had been storms or icebergs, fair or foul winds,—I didn't. We whistled with our three-headed whistle, there rose a column of steam by the *Teutonic's* forward stack; then after a still minute the deep response came to us across the rippling water, and we passed on our ways. Thursday was rough, and I found it more salubrious in my berth, after an unpleasant experiment at breakfast. Friday and to-day were nice again, as I am quite easy with only the ordinary rocking. The white gulls follow us way out here 900 miles from New York. I can't divine the attraction, but they are beautiful; once in a while they take a rest on a wave, then up and on again.

It is strange to wake at night and listen, not quite recognizing the new world I am in, swash-sh-w-wash against the sides, on my little windows, port holes they call them; then from the heart of the big mass, the big thump of the steady pulse, felt rather than heard—I like it. First night I was waked by the big whistle. I jumped up to see if a steamer was in sight—saw nothing. Again and again the big toot, till I thought of the fog whistle, and understood the warning to any stray vessel to keep out of our way. To-day we passed the Grand Banks; we had fog again; and to-night at dinner we almost stopped. About nine to-night we passed three icebergs, one a monster, then a wide ribbon of ice, "pancakes," about two miles long by fifty to a hundred feet wide. There is the whistle again. The fog has settled down, and we are stock still, afraid to move lest we hurt some fine iceberg; what a pity that would be!

The boat's people are very fine for their places. The purser is a bright, quick, gentlemanly fellow. He said, speaking of Sheppard—"I had a fellow last trip who grumbled at a negro whom we had—I bounced him. If a man acts the gentleman we make him have a good time, white or black." So Sheppard is very politely treated. The bedroom steward on my side is very kind, and understands what is needed when people are a little under the weather. The stewardess shows a striking family likeness to Her Majesty, the Empress of India, in face and figure; so she is a comely matron. The table is very good. To-day for dinner we had a rabbit soup (under a *nomme de plume*), bass, fillet of beef, goose or mallard duck, charlotte (which was blanc mange), lemon ice, coffee, with two or three alterations each course.

There are no good looking ladies on board, or only one medium face. Everybody is just getting about now with ease; but I don't expect to get acquainted with any of the ladies. There is a good elder from a London Presbyterian Church here on his way home from Honduras. He is co-elder with Dr. Oswald Dykes, who is now principal of Regent College (Presbyterian). Mr. Brodie (Scotch, I am almost willing to bet,) is acquainted with a Tuscaloosa friend of Jimso and mine, now living at Balize, British Honduras, Frank P. Watrous by name. I have his picture at Anniston, a peculiar looking fellow, but quite a gentleman. The whistle blows every minute, and by the echo we know there are icebergs near and in what direction. We are creeping along like a man in a dark room, with rocking chairs in it too—four knots an hour.

Nappy time—good night.

I do wish you could see the waves and the spray. I could watch it a mouth "steady," I believe.

SUNDAY, *March* 2.—*The diary says:* "A poor Sunday. Slept late and otherwise dawdled. Not allowed to go to steerage. Much time wasted in unprofitable discussion on Episcopacy and Presbytery."

MONDAY EVENING.

DEAR NORVELL: I wish you could come aboard for awhile this evening, what a fine time you would have! There isn't a cloud in sight hardly, and that clear sunshine makes the water clear, deep blue. The wind is quite on a lark, so we roll half over on one side, then the other, and go diving head foremost for a change. Its a lively trip to walk around the deck. Sometimes a big wave jumps up as high as the upper deck, that wets folks on the lower deck you may be sure. It didn't keep me from playing a new game on deck to-day. We have a broad platform, about three by four, built sloping a little toward the front, and a few inches from the floor. It is divided into twelve squares, and the game is, to pitch little iron weights into the squares, so they will lodge there. Each player takes his turn, throwing all five weights, aiming first for square one, then two, etc.

Whichever player has first lodged a weight in each square in order, has won the game. I am in the saloon writing to you, and they are setting the two long tables in the middle for supper; they call it dinner, you know, like hotels. There are pineapples and nuts and oranges on, and the napkins look much like they expected a birthday party. Two curious things: there are boards all around the table, fastened so as to stand three inches and keep things from jumping into our laps. Above hang broad boards with deep notches in their edges to hold wine glasses, little red and blue, and clear ones. I don't use them, but many of the gentlemen do. The chairs are screwed down of course, and the seats arranged to turn.

DEAR RUTHERFORD: I think you would like to know something about our trip; I know you would have found much that was interesting in to-day's happenings.

Well, before I got up, I am sorry to say, a big whale paid us a visit, and played fire-engine at a great rate. That probably meant that he was a little shocked at our looks and ways. About ten o'clock a big steamer passed about four miles south of us. An old sea captain aboard pronounced it a Cunarder, because her mainmast had yards, or I think that was why. At twelve the captain (our vessel's captain I mean) took his sextant and chart up on the bridge (that is, a platform across the upper deck, about ten feet long, at the forward end of the deck), and the reckoning for the day was taken. He found we were on latitude, 44°, 45′; longitude, 37°, 18′; and had run since yesterday noon, 328 miles. We were then about 43° north latitude and 40° west longitude. We have to get to about 52° north latitude, I think, and 3° west longitude. We are already a good way north of the latitude of New York and about 1,708 miles away. That leaves 1,200 yet to Liverpool. The passengers watch very eagerly for the charts to be posted, showing our progress, and lively guessing as to the number of miles, begins early in the day. We had raw, cold weather when we passed the Grand Banks of Newfoundland. You see the icebergs come cruising down there as spring opens, and the chill in air and water is so great, that we could almost tell how far off they were by the thermometer. But yesterday and to-day we have been in the Gulf Stream, and that insures us mild weather until we reach England.

About twelve to-day we enjoyed a pretty sight—a fine sailing vessel with all sails standing out against the sky about five miles, I suppose, South of us. At three, a very large steamer passed us on the North side not more than a mile off. We sent up a long string of bright little flags. She answered with some other signals, I couldn't see what at the distance, but the officers told us it meant that she had left Havre on Saturday. It was a great big steamer, with two fat smoke-stacks, one behind the other, red with a black ring around their tops.

We don't expect now to get to Liverpool before Saturday evening; maybe will be too late for the tide to take us over the bar, and have to wait till morning.

I wish I could see you and Norvell and have a good game of marbles; and I wish you could take my trip, or rather one of your own like it, you would enjoy it, I am sure.

I know you are having lots of fun, saying I am sea-sick, but you are much mistaken. I was sick last Thursday, but I lay in my berth and read, and so Friday morning I was quite well again.

You can't guess what they call those side guards that keep the dishes from jumping off the table, so I'll tell you. They are "fiddles."

We had a strange sort of church on Sunday. The hymns and tunes were new, and the prayers were all read out of a book and there was no sermon at all. Not a word spoken except the announcement of the collection—all read. That's the Episcopal way; sometimes they have no sermon, you know.

You are going to write to me arn't you? I can't answer often, but I will sometimes. You and Norvell and Robin write to me, and I'll tell you some wonders.

P. S. Anything about home you write will be pleasant to me, and I want to make a bargain with you, I am going to pray for you every night, and you for me.

WEDNESDAY.

DEAR KATTY: A very pleasant day has closed with us, though you are just coming home from school about now.

How late does that make it with me? There's an arithmetic problem for you. We are now 29° West of Greenwich, or a little less than that, now 29° at noon. We have climbed up to 48° North latitude. There has been little wind for two days, hardly any at all to-day. So we had made 342 miles by to-day, 12 M., and were very proud; that is 14 better than yesterday, and that 12 more than any other day. We had a sea almost smooth all day, and that is about as good as if we had a good wind behind us, because we can run by steam faster than any ordinary wind, and so it is not needed, in fact hardly any help. We do not hope now to reach port before Saturday morning, because we lost so much time during the fog off the Grand Banks. There we ran only three or four miles an hour and spent our steam tooting that wretched fog horn. That was from Saturday noon to 4 P. M. Sunday. But you are tired of so much sea talk, I know. I won't show off my bearings any more.

One thing that would get you I know, unless you have amended one of your little ways you had when I was at home. Our steward is quite an enthusiast for early rising, and has a little dodge to wake us up. You can hear in any room whatever is going on all along the passage. So he calls in quite an audible tone to some imaginary passenger: "So you saw the man-of-war just passing now, did you?" or "If you will go aloft you'll see two polar bears on the nearer of two icebergs." All of which is meant to tempt us up on deck. He has a new dodge every little while. But it is getting old now, and does little good.

Goodnight. Write me a letter soon, little woman.

Diary, March 6.—"Bull a good game. Glad I had grit enough to hold out and beat the English parson. I have not worked well— not a bit of work for sinners. Jesus help my traitor-heart truly to renounce sin and take up the testimony to thy love!"

FRIDAY, *March* 7.

DEAR MAMMA: Mails are about to close and start back from Queenstown, so a good-bye note to you will close my diary for the voyage. I enclose the daily bulletin and map. We expect to land Saturday afternoon and spend Sunday in Liverpool. I shall try to hunt up the friends I have letters to·on Saturday afternoon, as that may direct my Sunday movements.

I was vaccinated four days ago, but don't know yet whether it will take. I have studied my photography "quite a little," as these people say. I think I shall learn to make fair views without great loss of time; shall probably have too much spare time before I get to work, for a while.

On the whole, my time has been very pleasantly spent, but I have accomplished much less than I hoped. Besides the home letters, one to Zaidee, and one to Aunt Elsie, I hoped to have done a piece for the *Observer*, which may sound a little like something you heard at Anniston Sunday morning.

I am sorry to say nothing is accomplished that I know of for the passengers, cabin or steerage, and most of them are irreligious. I shall know better how to proceed the next time, I hope. There are men here from every quarter of the globe. There is a fellow-voyager who is bound for the gold fields of South Africa, one who has lived on the Gold Coast (above the Congo, you know), one from Jamaica, one from India, and so on.

Our circle of congenial companions has become distinct, and it is very pleasant. Mr. Windsor, the churchman, is more jovial than devout in his ways, but may be more solid than he'll have us think. Elders Brodie and McMurtrie, both Scotch, the former now of London, the latter a Baltimore ship-builder, are quite interesting. Yesterday Mr. McM., "the parson," and I played. The good elder would throw into the B. at the top and have to take ten off, so it got to be quite a joke. That is a different game from what I told Norvell about, played though with the same board and weights. In this we play into any square we want to, or can add up the numbers printed on squares we land in, deducting ten when a weight lands in one of the top course of squares, and playing for one hundred.

The other night when we were just half way, Mr. McMurtrie broke out suddenly, when we were trying to stand erect in the rolling cabin, "Well, we're half seas over to-night!" and wondered why we laughed. It is well that we know that he never takes any spirits.

It was quite crisp and cool after we got on the ocean, very chilly in the iceberg region, but since then we have forgotten overcoats and strolled about with coats unbuttoned.

To-day's excitements are two steamers, a shoal of porpoises, and just now a cry of land! and through the misty distance we see what is supposed to be Cape Clear, on the Irish coast. Whether we shall get a glimpse of the ever-green fields on which the Irish bulls flourish is very doubtful. We are still far from land, running parallel with the coast, not towards it.

Mr. Brodie came up to-day with Psalm xxxii. 8, "I will guide"—for me. At Aunt Maria's Saturday night we sang, "There is a scene where spirits blend," you know the rest. I often think of it. I want you to know a text that did much to keep me from evil at Tuscaloosa, you sent it to me once in a letter, "All thy children shall be taught of the Lord; and great shall be the peace of thy children."

From Liverpool next. I am in perfect health. That is my blessing.

H. M. S. "ADRIATIC," FRIDAY NIGHT.

DEAR ISABEL: I enjoyed your letter to New York very much indeed. I am especially glad of the movement towards Glen-Addie. I take this as an answer to my prayers for the Third Church. I hope to see Mrs. Stevenson's people on Sunday. We shall reach Liverpool to-morrow afternoon, at four, it is likely.

Give my love to all at Mrs. F.'s and to all my friends who you think would like to hear from me. Land is in sight a few miles off. Hills in South Ireland.

I enclose our bulletin for each day of the voyage. I expect it will interest you.

Fast-net Light-house sixty miles from Queenstown is now in fine view.

Now a flash light-house is in sight, flashing out after a minute's darkness. It flashes eight times, then goes out again.

It is recognized by this number of flashes. A captain knows it as soon as he counts its flashes.

The saloon is almost too pleasant now to be a nice writing

place. A good voice is just now singing "Good bye Summer," our Tosti, you know. One good song follows another.

Good bye letters! it is.

I am writing a pleasant farewell to a friend in Birmingham. But now good night.

LETTERS FROM ENGLAND.

LIVERPOOL, SATURDAY NIGHT, 3–8.

MY DEAR TILLIE: We finished our trip very merrily this evening. Had to pass through the Custom House at once on landing. We waited comfortably in a warm room for the baggage to be got up to the inspection room. Then as soon as I could get my turn each bundle was opened; I had seven with the trunk, and it corded in memory of Rob.—about forty feet of grass rope. The porters next seized us and our things, taking time to ask where we would go, and to demand their fixed fee 1s. 6d. The cab took us to our hotel, the Shaftesbury, where we are comfortably fixed. As to Sheppard, the English don't notice at all what seems very odd to us. He is very modest, and easy to get along with; also quite an aid in sight-seeing, and in anything else where I need help. He took a jaunt in the neighborhood to-night, and came in quite full of the sights— the railway coaches opening at the sides, and the market— "such a market!" The Shaftesbury hotel (named for the Earl of Shaftesbury) is a temperance hotel, which means even more than the name implies. Everything is quiet, prices are reasonable, and it is like a family; prayers are held every evening. It is not a cheap house though. Though plain, everything is more than neat; cooking is homely and good tasting, and provision plentiful. Comely maids, with snowy aprons and caps and curtseys, always suggested in their air of serving you, wait on the Coffee room, and seem to run the house; men are in the minority.

I have not seen Mr. Franklin's people nor Mrs. Stevenson's yet. I may not until Monday. I expect to be in London Monday.

36 BEDFORD PLACE, LONDON, W. C.

MY DEAR MAMMA: To-day about two o'clock we reached the city and proceeded to find lodgings. Mr. Brodie, my Scotch friend, now a London merchant, kindly directed me to a good place near this. It was full. "I might try 51, across the street, and say he sent us." Full there. "Try 5." Five sent us to 36, just across Russell Square, and 36 we found was willing to take us at 2 pound 15 a week for us both, two rooms fourth floor; breakfast and seven o'clock dinner. Lunch we must find. It is a place for young men in business down town, and there are seven young men beside us. The house is a roomy one in what used to be the fashionable part of the city, very near where the shops and business begin. I don't know yet whether it shall be my address or not; I will decide to-morrow. Address care of Dr. Guinness till I can get you word to the contrary.

We had the pleasure of keeping our party together in Liverpool, and four of us came in the same carriage to-day to town.

Yesterday we attended the Cathedral in the morning and another Episcopal Church at 6:30. Both services were quite spiritual and pleasant. But I felt as if this noble church were bound hand and foot with red tape, and a napkin about its mouth, so that they heal the wound slightly.

The trip to-day was delightful to me. I saw the Manchester canal, that is to give Liverpool's prestige to Manchester, by taking the cotton right to the factories.

I saw the famous school towns of Rugby and Harrow, and I saw the English landscape, one continuous meadow, literally— now all green except where it is laid off by the early ploughman into the evenest of furrows. Cozy old villages, all the houses of a rough brick or stone, tiled or thatched, or covered with thick slate, and all over ivy in some places:

> "Meadows trim . . . .
> Shallow brooks, and rivers wide,
> Towns and battlements, it sees
> Bosomed high, in tufted trees:

and many an old church with several different but ever recurring kinds of architecture, that of our Grace Church being most common.

I enjoyed it all immensely. I had to postpone my visit to Liverpool friends till later.

Providence is still helping me in a wonderful way. Mr. Brodie will introduce me to Mr. Whyte, a most influential Presbyterian in the city, and a man of great spirituality. Of my plans, more anon.

I must write some other letters to-night. My pen is wretched, as my baggage is still at Euston Station about a mile away. I am waiting to see Mrs. Guinness and other friends, and so find out where I can most conveniently locate before I take it out. The station is in the city, you understand, but quite a way off. I am very thankful for help thus far, and "He who has been mindful of us will bless us." It helps me no little to know you are all praying for us day and night.

HARLEY HOUSE, BOW ROAD, E. LONDON,
WEDNESDAY EVE., *March* 12.

DEAR PAPA: Yesterday and to-day have proven days of great blessing to us in our enterprise. On Monday we only got our bearings. Tuesday morning I presented my letter to Mrs. Guinness, and on her hearty invitation that I should stay there, I accepted her kindness. I then met Sheppard by appointment at noon at Mr. Brodie's office. Mr. B. took me to see Mr. Robert Whyte, a warehouseman and supplier of fancy goods and of many other things; using a four-story building in his great business, in the heart of London. Mr. W. was cordial to me as Mr. Brodie's friend and as a missionary. He offered to take me to meet North London Presbytery at quarter to five. He also intimated that though his business was wholesale, he might be able to supply me with all I needed.

Mr. B. then asked his advice about my money, and the result was, that I was introduced to the National Bank of Scotland, No. 37 Nicholas Lane, Lombard St., by Mess. Whyte and Brodie. The polite manager undertook my business very readily; as I signed his book, he said, "Wherever you were, you learned to write" (we had been talking of my American birth and Scotch extraction). This was rather a new compliment! I put £600 on a deposite account to draw interest from date and £112 on current account and took a check-book. Coming out and finding Sheppard we walked through the Royal Exchange and found a lunch in a court not far off. I think I gave away a shilling too much on tip, by missing count of change.

Then I looked around the Mansion House, walked a little down Victoria street and back, and took a front seat on top of a bus going from the Bank down Cheapside, Ludgate Hill, and the Strand to Charing Cross and back. I can't tell you how I felt on turning a corner to see filling the whole prospect between the opening houses, a grand dome rising on a mass of stone graced with columns and relieved with smaller towers. If it were not so beautiful, I should be afraid in its presence. Soon after St. Paul's was passed, I saw the Law Courts, which is a very striking grove of light turrets, rising from a long mass of columned, arched and blackened stone, pierced by many gates; a light spire over-tops the pile. The whole way is rich with old buildings, many of whose names had associations for me. Looking casually to the right side, I saw, "Tickets for H. M. Stanley's Lecture at the booking office." It was Exeter Hall, the temple of Evangelicism. Stopping on the return trip, I found Stanley will lecture here soon, date not fixed.

To the Presbytery with Mr. Whyte by underground railway. Met there Mr. John McNeil, the young Scotchman, Pastor of Regent square, one of the great preachers of London; the most popular just now, I think, yet quite faithful and simple; just a great man, that explains it. I also met Dr. Fraser, Dr. Monro Gibson (of Chicago once) and several gentlemen of influence. I met too, Dr. Matthews, of one of the Executive Committees, who already knew us by name and had written congratulations to his friend, Dr. Houston, at Nashville. Introduced to Presbytery—which so took away my breath, that in reply to the kind speech of the moderator, said something which was not English, nor sense, I fear, and sat down.

Dr. Matthews took me from Mr. Whyte and we went to Dr. Alexander's, near my quarters at that time. This gentleman is doing a private mission work in the slums, of his own means, and has gathered a little seminary of young men around him, whom he trains in his mission, and at his house, and keeps them at the Presbyterian College; boarding them himself.

Among them is one who is going to Africa, and is looking for a place, a fine young man. He had also a young man who knows the Congo; and Sheppard, Dr. Matthews and I, are to meet this young man Friday, in Dr. Alexander's parlor.

Established at Harley House to-day. I find a party is preparing to sail April 15, for the Congo. They have all their arrangements to make. So I can learn just what they think necessary; indeed can doubtless buy with them.

I am writing in the room of a Mr. Sully, a jovial fellow, who has lived in Missouri, and ran an engine on a Chicago road, and who goes to run the new steamer, the *Pioneer*, of the Balolo mission. He will show us after 9 : 30 supper (?) to our lodgings in the neighborhood.

The people are kindness itself. A fine lot of boys in the Institute, of great cordiality and equal delicacy. One of them, pick of the seniors, is going out April 15. Three Swedes are going to their mission (Cataract region) same time. What a chain of Providences! "According to the good hand of my God upon me."

Our expenses here will be light, about one pound a week each, liberal estimate. I think our board is kindly furnished us at cost price, and rooms six shillings apiece per week. I have hopes of leaving some money here, perhaps a considerable sum. Isn't that good?

I think Mr. Whyte will be the man to do my buying for me. He is a famous business man, and equally prominent church leader. His solicitor told Mr. Brodie that Mr. Whyte usually saw through a point of business as quickly as the solicitor himself. He is very influential in Presbyterian circles, as I already see.

Your letters written the day I left have just reached me. I hope my good news will help you and Mamma to bear the great sacrifice the Master has asked of you. I feel as never before, the daily answer of your prayers for me.

MY DEAR MAMMA: I am very busy, but must try to get you a line to-night. To-day I got detailed list of all I shall need. It will be under $300 for each one of us, and we have $3,500 in bank to draw on. Many needed things are in my trunk, thanks to your foresight, if Papa and I did laugh at you. I think I may get Mr. Whyte to buy for me, so as to get in connection with English Presbyterians. A Presbyterian elder is a good and useful agent to have, especially when his business abilities are exceptional. Lunched at Dr. Alexander's to-day with Dr. Matthews, Secretary of the Presbyterian Alliance, and Mr. Smith, of the Congo Mission. Found several things new and important. Dr. Matthews took us to the Houses of Parliament, St. Margarets, Westminster and the Abbey, all near together. I'll tell you about it later. How I was moved over the blue-stone slab on which the brass letters inlaid tell that LIVINGSTONE lies beneath, you must imagine. I felt a similar emotion, but less deep, standing before Havelock, Nelson, and Gordon, in Trafalgar Square.

I want you to think about the marvelous providences that have brought me here, and what I have experienced in London—the succession of coincidences that have favored me lately. I know it will encourage you. "Hath been mindful." "Will bless." But I am very slipshod and dilatory still. If I were as deeply possessed by my mission as I should be, it would not be so. Pray especially for me to be strengthened with might in the inner man, that I may receive grace to be faithful!

My lodgings are exceedingly nice, a widow and her young son and two grown daughters. Don't get alarmed on the last score; but they are all very nice and really pious. The house is very comfortable and nicely furnished—though the six shillings per week is an object to them. I am in marvelous health, and think with much love and longing of you and all the loved ones at home.

P. S. The double New York and Hartford letter received with great appreciation.

COTTAGE GROVE, BOW ROAD,

LONDON, *March* 15, 1890.

DEAR KITTEN: I am writing in a cozy little sitting-room, where I stay, near the Institute for training missionaries, where I board and where you write to me. It is a very nice place. Three stories, and a basement wide and long enough for two medium-sized rooms, and a hall and stair alongside of them, not a big house by any means. But it is wonderfully neat and comfortable. Willie Short and his sister, Addie, are sitting by the same fire—she is sewing across the table from me, and he is learning his Sunday-school lesson. Just 4:20, Saturday evening, the clock says. The room is papered nicely and tastefully, and hung with quite a pretty lot of small paintings and illuminated texts. The piano and tables in the room, and the desk, sideboard, and sofa in the little front parlor are very pretty; the chairs look comfortable, and are upholstered with good brown leather. My room upstairs is as complete. The walls there have promise texts hung all around; they helped me much one day I was in a difficulty, so I consider them old friends now. I go up to Harley House to my meals, and often sit in the library there, or in one of the boys' rooms, to read or write. How many times do they eat in a day would you guess?—exactly four, not exactly four either, for I notice sometimes a "threepence worth" of sweet biscuits makes a fifth bait for some of the hearty fellows. My friends, the Shorts, are getting quite friendly indeed. They are very anxious to make me feel at home. Every night when I come in from supper (almost ten o'clock!) we sit up and talk till—later than we should. Every morning Willie brings me my shoes blacked, and a pitcher of hot water for shaving; then, just before I start out, a cup of hot tea; the English customs, you see.

Time to stop now. Good bye.

I know by the strange way our Father is helping me here in our work, that you are praying for me.

Your loving brother,　　　　SAM.

Diary, Sunday, March 16.—"To Mr. Spurgeon's. Three floors. Pulpit on 2nd floor. Mr. S., medium height, portly, slow almost, with age and weight. Deep melodious voice. Bunyanic, homely English (learnt from old Puritan divines). Often epigrammatic and figurative. Uses 'Thou.'"

LETTERS FROM BRUSSELS.

ENGLISH HOTEL, 44 RUE DE BRABANT,
BRUSSELS, March 21.

DEAR ROBIN: You see I am on new ground to-day. Last night

about 7 o'clock I walked over to the elevated station (five minutes from my lodgings in " Mile end "), and in ten minutes was in the city at the central station (they don't say *depot*) of the Great Eastern. Buying a second-class return ticket for Brussels, I got into the express for Harwich; at ten I got on the steamer *Ipswich*, got my supper and went to bed; waking up this morning to see that we were steaming up the Scheldt. We reached Antwerp about ten, and passed the old city of Mechlin at eleven. There I saw the old double, square Cathedral tower. The clock is curious. The dial is a great gilt rim, twice as big as our windmill wheel, fixed outside the tower. Great gilt bands passing over it. I couldn't make out the time; it was a mile from where I passed.

This is rather out of the region of dikes and wind-mills, though I saw many low embankments, about three feet higher than the marks the tide had left. The regulation wind-mills were on every side. Some have great brick towers; some seem to stand on four legs and have a long wide ladder up to the room, making the tail to the queer "varmint."

You would have been interested in the fortifications of Antwerp. The old wall (I think there was one) is replaced by a huge earthen mound, thirty feet high, with lines of heavy guns along the crest. Passing through a tunnel to the inner side we see that the mound covers a great brick wall, with large rooms all along for men and ammunition, as I suppose. I have just bought a map of Brussels, and shall proceed to explore a little, and finally call on General Sanford, whom I have come to see. I hope to go over to Rotterdam on my way back and see the steamer *Afrikaan*, in which I am to sail about April 9.

Your loving cousin, SAM.

BRUSSELS, SATURDAY, *March* 22.

DEAR PAPA : I came over yesterday in response to a letter from General Sanford. I am in a quiet English hotel, near the Station du Nord, by which I entered the city. Before I saw General Sanford I had time to see something of this historic city. The Cathedral (?) Church of St. Gudule is very beautiful, indeed the finest I have seen, to my taste. The Hotel de Ville attracted my interest by the busts in relief of Charles the Bold, his daughter Mary, the heiress of Burgundy, Maximilian, Charles the V., Philip II., and several others of the rulers of other days. The Hotel de Belle Vue, where General Sanford lives, is on the site of the palace of Charles V. Brussels is like Washington, a place to spend money. The people's faces are very interesting, and the blouse and the wooden shoe, no longer universal among the poorer class, attracted my attention at once.

General Sanford received me very kindly indeed. He had sent a copy of General Morgan's letter of introduction to King Leopold, so we went over to the palace and inscribed my name on his register with my address, in case he wants to see me. At noon I called again and met Lieut. Thys, of the great Congo Company. He will give me letters of introduction to Boma. The Russian, Turkish and Portugese ambassadors were also there.

To-day I have met several more of the Congo dignitaries through General Sanford, and am assured of transportation being furnished (@ 30 f per carrier) up to the Pool. I am also invited to consult these gentlemen on several matters I need to know. So my mission here is a success already, how great, depends. I see God's hand wonderfully in it all. I am booked to sail by the Steamship *Afrikaan* from Rotterdam April 5,–10, date not certain. My affairs are in the hands of Whyte, Ridsdale & Co., Commission Merchants, 75 Houndsditch, London. They buy, pack and ship for five per cent., allowing me all trade and cash discounts.

I am in haste for mail.

BRUSSELS, RUE DE BRABANT, 3 P. M.,
SUNDAY, *March*, 23.

MY DEAR MAMMA: To-day has been full of you somehow; your letters have come to my mind and I have read them over; the "good bye" verse and hymn are transferred from the little paper (it is getting worn now) to my memory, and to my heart too. I am quite sure I have experienced it somewhat at least, and my Bible reading has been very sweet. I finished the hundred and nineteenth Psalm. It amazes me. I once

thought it hardly much more than a sacred literary curiosity.
Now it is a mine. "I have found great spoil," as one verse
says. Another verse in it came to my notice. It is on one of the
illuminated cards in my room in London, at Mrs. S.'s. You'd
like to hear all of them, two I forgot, but the rest are, "We
love him because he first loved us"; "I will never leave thee
nor forsake thee," and "Thou art near, O Lord." (Psa. cxix.
vs. 151.)

I am writing in the *Salle à manger* of a quiet little hotel right
at the station where I take the train for Antwerp. I began while
waiting for my dinner. Now I am just through that necessary
evil, have gone through a dozen raw oysters, and cups of good
tea—four! You see, I pay for a pot, and I must "get what's
coming to me." That's why I ate all the rolls also.

Now, as I write, you are all going to Sunday-school, or about
beginning. Mr. Williams is reading from Gospel Hymns No. 5.
I hope it is a bright day, and that you all have your heart-
windows open, to know and believe the love God hath to us. I
am very happy to-day, and though I long after you all, it doesn't
distress me. My prayer and my hope is, that we may all get all
there is in religion, joy and great power ("all that is coming to
us"). Just when you got up this morning, if you were up by
quarter to six, I was being ushered into the *Palais du Roi*,
relieved of my overcoat and umbrella by half a dozen liveried attendants, and directed to the great stair and up to the ante-room.
There a decorated official received me, and found enough English to let me know I had five minutes to wait, my time was
11:45. By the way, I was terribly scared by this gentleman.
He was so much gilded (and so was the room) that I thought
I was in the royal presence. He made things worse by two
profound bows, before he opened his lips, his heels cracked
together, and his spurs rattled smartly as he did it. He didn't
find out my mistake.

After ten minutes (it seemed so at least), my courage now
come back, I was ushered into another great room, and heard a
kind voice from the middle of it, "Good morning!" I was
reassured, and after a respectful bow, I advanced and took the
hand extended to me. He said, "you asked to see me?" I

told him my business, whom I represented, the Presbyterian body in the United States, what I meant to do, and our plan of working with a combined white and colored force.

He warned me of the entire rudeness of the country, commended our plan of beginning on a small scale, until the tide comes in on the completion of the railways, then enter on that tide. "The Congo has a future," he said. "I cannot believe that God made that great river, with its many branches all through the land, for any lower purpose." He explained that if American negroes came, they must not hope to remain a separate colony, distinct from the State, but become citizens of the country and obey its laws. He also warned me of the danger of wine drinking in Africa. About my location, he recommended the Karsai, "I would advise, I would ask you not to go to the Ubangi yet; we cannot protect you, if you go so far from our stations." He said he admired the Americans, and wished his people to learn from our amazing progress. "Our people are slow," he said.

The king asked my age, and said he was glad I had begun the work of Christ so soon. I quite forgot he was a Catholic or a king, when he spoke with so much apparent sympathy of my mission. After half an hour's talk he asked me if I wanted to speak with him of anything else, and said he "felt sincerely," and if you will allow me, "warmly interested in my mission, and was glad to see a young man show 'so much courage, enterprise and Christian pluck.'"

King Leopold is tall, erect and slender, a man, I should say, forty-seven years of age; no, not so much. His hair, rather thin and gray, he parts a little to the right of the middle; his beard is long and fine, turning a little gray. His eyes, soft and clear, blue I think. His expression is very kind, and his voice matches it. He wore a dark green military frock coat, epaulettes and sword, with no star or decoration whatever. His manner is both bright and gentle, and his English is full, ready and expressive.

I may be mistaken in my description; I was of course highly strung in such a presence, and may have seen incorrectly.

I wonder at his kindness and freeness in talking with me, and questioning me, for I was not well-dressed nor courtly in manner, and worst, I had no special business with him, and I wonder now how God has so changed the times that a Catholic king, successor to Philip II., should talk Foreign Missions to an American boy and a Presbyterian.

I treated him just as I would any man I thought good and great. I asked nothing of him but his protection. What will come of my visit I do not know. I prayed long last night before I saw that it was my duty to go on Sunday. The character of the interview satisfied me that it was altogether right.

General Sanford has been very kind indeed. He is a zealous Congo man, not a visionary, for he has large interests there. He treats me as if I were on his business; directs all my movements, takes me to see everybody of importance to me, and claims from them in his own and General Morgan's name their good offices for me. He is quite free in his suggestions to me: "If you go to the king, you must have a top hat."[1] So I proceeded to have a tall silk hat, reflecting that Nehemiah would doubtless have had one, and a swallow-tail coat too. As my interview was to be in the morning, I deferred the dress-coat until my purse is more replete with shekels.

I wore Gus Hall's shoes, Birmingham pants, Chicago coat, "Famous" collar, Brussels hat, Rogers, Peet & Co.'s gloves (you bought them), and cravat of sister Gene's make. Be sure to tell her! I should like to have been somewhat better arrayed "among those that wear soft clothing," but the money can be better used just now in medicine, tea and jam, beads, etc.

I have placed the most difficult orders for my outfit; tools, stationery and medicines. Eatables and barter are simpler. I hope to perfect these lists by conferences with African people to-morrow. At nine I have an engagement with M. de La Fontaine, head of the great Dutch trading company of Rotterdam, and hope for a very fruitful interview.

I wish we each had a set of Sir John Bennett's clocks, showing the comparative time of Congo and Anniston. When you are at

---

[1] In the diary he says, General S. also said, "I made Henry Ward Beecher get a top hat."

prayers in the morning I shall be enjoying a midday rest, reading, fiddling, photographing, writing home. When you sit down about 9 o'clock to read your Bible, I shall begin the latter and shorter half day's work. When Papa comes to dinner (1:30), I shall be adjusting the musquito bar around my early couch. We shall, God willing, reach Banana by May 10th, at the farthest.

Good bye! God be with you and supply my place, and give more than I could of peace, and joy, and hope.

BRUSSELS, March 24, 1890.

To the Ladies of the Glen Addie Aid Society:

MY DEAR CHRISTIAN FRIENDS: I take a chance I have wanted ever since I last was with you, to tell you how I have felt your true kindness to me during the months we worked together for Christ. To-day, alone in a great foreign city, unable to speak for Christ in the strange tongue these poor people speak, I am glad to write to Christian friends at home. While you were worshipping God to-day, I passed a great church with a lofty gilded dome and many little towers, and over the doorway I saw an image, graven in stone, of the Virgin Mary. Right by the church in the same square were merry go-rounds and swings of curious make, all crowded full of people. I suppose a thousand people, most of them children, looking like our own Sunday-school children, were busy at play or at buying and selling toys and candies. Right under the eaves of their church! And no wonder! for that church teaches them no better. I am glad my own friends and loved ones are in a happier land, but I wish I could do something to show these Belgians a happier and better way. I have been often in your homes, in spirit I mean, since we had our good-bye meeting. I pray for you all often, together and singly by name. I feel sure that my prayers and yours will be richly answered, and that in your church work, and in your families, and in your own Christian experience God will encourage you, and fill you with grateful praises for special blessings. As Joseph said to his brethren and friends at his death, I say to you by faith, "God will surely visit you."[1] I hope that you will expect this. Expect and pray that God will convert

---

[1] This little church has prospered in the midst of great financial distress.

people, even those you have almost despaired of. And I hope that the band of Christian workers in the Third Presbyterian Church will embrace all the ladies in the church. If any are apt to be sometimes careless, and not regular in the attendance on service, a visit from two or three of the ladies would help to win them back. I know you could do it, not in the spirit of fault-finding, but of love, and show them that they are missed and the church cares for them.

A little system about this, and an understanding after each service that each missing one shall be found before next time, and agreeing as to how the visiting is to be divided out between the ladies, wouldn't this insure our little church a full and regular attendance of its members? I only suggest this. I am sure your good sense and energy can find the right way, very likely a better one than this, if you consider it together. And I hope that the few of our ladies whom sickness, or absence or other causes kept away from church, are again regular attendants, or soon will be by your prayerful efforts.

I especially send my Christian love to the two ladies who last joined us, and commend them to the sympathies of you all.

My request for you, you will find in 2 Thess. iii. 1, and Eph. vi. 18, 19; my wish for you in Romans xv. 13.

Your friend always,
SAMUEL N. LAPSLEY.

Diary, March 25.—To U. S. Minister (Mr. Terrell's), and left my letter and card. Then to the Egmont and Hoorn Memorial. A neat little park or garden. In the centre above a fountain stand Egmont and Hoorn in their sixteenth century dress, each with an arm about the other and the inscription is: "*Comptes d' Egmont et Hoorn.*" "Condemned by the unjust sentence of the Duke of Alva and beheaded at Brussels, ——, 1568." I feel much as I did standing under Havelocks: "Your bravery will not be forgotten by a grateful country." Or Nelson's, "England expects," etc., and Gordon's,

> These monuments "all remind us we can make our lives sublime,
> And departing leave behind us, foot-prints on the sands of time."

STEAMSHIP AFRIKAAN, *April* 20, 1890.

MY DEAR MAMMA: You have wondered why I have been so long silent.

The last week in England was very busy indeed, from early

morning until I tumbled into bed, rather later than you would
have liked, maybe. But I got all my business done economically,
and I think satisfactorily.

My friends were very kind. Their kindness touched me very
deeply.

I think Mr. Whyte, my agent, will be a valuable friend. He
is a very prominent Christian and Presbyterian as well as a
capital business man. The boys at Harley House were very
kind and cordial as we left them. Indeed, they laid themselves
out to make us welcome all the time we were there.

My friends at 20 Cottage Grove, where I had my room and my
home, seemed to regret my departure as if I had been their own
kin. I may tell you of a kind thing they said. They said:
Hebrew xiii. 2 applied to them now. I saved that up for you.
It was a delightful home for me. The house was holy. Such
depth and simplicity of piety I rarely meet. They took me to
their church. Archibald G. Brown, their pastor, was quite kind
too. The last Saturday night he had Sheppard and me, Sully
and Scannell (of the Congo Balolo Mission) on the platform with
him at the prayer meeting. He said perhaps the people could
best pray for us if we prayed for what we wanted. So, though
I did not like the plan quite for myself, we led in turn, and a
thousand Christians joined in our petitions for a good work on
the Congo. A large basement was literally packed from back
to desk, aisles then filled with chairs. It was a wonderful meeting, and every week it is the same. I had Miss Millie Short to
send Rob some of Mr. Brown's year books. He and his work
are quite after Rob's heart, I know.

Miss Millie is a devoted Christian, regularly employed by Mr.
Brown as a missionary, besides office work. She has one street
in the slums, which she tends as her own patch in the vast field.
The Shorts did everything they could, more than I could allow
without protest (ineffectual!) to make me comfortable.

Willie came up with my hot water for shaving in good time;
then as he started for the city, and I for Harley House for
breakfast, I could smell a fragrant cup of English tea coming
up stairs and maybe a "hot X bun" at Good Friday time,
or a nice bread and butter to prepare for going out in the
cold.

I enjoyed the religious life of London Christians. There is in those I know a rare acquaintance with the Bible, letter and spirit, and a delightful acquaintance with the Saviour. Much is said of the Spirit's presence and aid.

Last Sunday I went to hear Rev. John McNeil, the young Scotchman, who fills the leading Presbyterian pulpit here. There were about one thousand two hundred in the great central hall, Holborn, mostly Scotch; he gave us a good sermon indeed, on Rev. xxii. 17. I walked there and back, about six miles both ways, to find nice tea, bread and butter waiting for me before going to church at half past six.

Of Monday and Tuesday I have a very misty idea, so exceedingly full of business was I, though the really essential part was quite finished two weeks ago. I went twice to the Royal Geographical Society, took lunch Monday with Mr. Whyte in an old-fashioned English chop-house. Monday night I sent Sheppard ahead with Sully to Rotterdam. Tuesday night my friends, Mr. Ellis and Willie Short, put me on the train for Harwich. Harritch, they call it!

Mrs. Banks, of the A. B. M. U., was starting back to Equatorville, and Miss Dalgarno and Mr. Scannell were going to reinforce the Congo Balolo Mission.

Their friends, some fifty strong, filled the platform and sang hymns of encouragement as we left old England.

Scannell was very sick in the "Ipswich" from Harwich to Rotterdam, so I had my hands full. I learnt my trade as a sailor very effectually on my way from New York, so I can help the new hands.

After a few hours in Rotterdam, we took the tender down the Maas, some miles again to the Steamship *Afrikaan*, which lay near the river mouth. It was nearly night before we got started. After a quiet sleep we rose Thursday morning to see the chalk cliffs of Dover, gray and white mixed now, but bright enough to give Albion her name. Under our field-glasses the castle on the hill, and the town lying back in a valley which leads to the beach, with the great long buildings which line the cliffs for a great distance each way, shone out finely. I was shown Shakes-

4

pear's cliff, where he is said to have written many of his plays.
It suits King Lear very well.

Our party is a very pleasant one indeed. The majority are
Swedes, of the new Evangelical Church. Their piety is most
refreshing. They seem as if they only lately heard the story of
Jesus, and had not got used to the new joy and wonder. Such
charming simplicity and earnestness! Two of them learn English very readily, and speak with an accent that reminds you of
a sweet little child learning its first words. One of them, a
young lady, on her way to her betrothed at Mukinbunga, was
in here a minute ago to remonstrate against my writing here in
the saloon, instead of staying on deck with the rest. She would
do for the "Viking's Bride" in Longfellow, quite pretty and
clever. Miss Dalgarno is a young Scotch woman, having the
size, shape and accent of Aunt E. She knows her Bible. She
has already been to Kaffir land, and now is going to keep Miss
DeHails company in Balolo land. She wears a blue flannel
Deaconess dress (uniform at the ladies' department, Harley
House), with blue bonnet, and wide collar with cuffs outside the
dress. Her plump, vigorous figure, crowned with a mass of red
hair in the blue bonnet, makes quite a striking figure.

Mrs. Banks is a typical English lady, quite sweet, delicate,
with a remarkably developed piety. Her delight in Christ and
in missionary work is very refreshing—not that I ever heard
her speak of it. It is only a flavor to all she says and does.
She has left her little girl in England with her mother and sister
and goes back to help Mr. B. You would wonder that so slight
and delicate a woman could do good work on the very outposts
of the A. B. M. U. I pray that her slight, frail form may be
God-kept amid the hardships and pestilence of the Congo.

Sully is a good, hearty fellow. He has spent many years in
America, and now goes out as engineer on the new Congo-
Balolo boat, *Pioneer*. Scannell is a true, brave, gentle English
boy. It is remarkable that he and several others of our party
come from families only recently religious. He shows the same
sweetly simple faith and love. He and several of the Swedes
are still half in bed, lounging around, heavy-eyed and silent.

All are longing for Madeira, whither, we hope, Wednesday will bring us.

You see the *Afrikaan* is a trader, with limited passenger accommodations; our saloon and cabins altogether about the size of the hall and parlor at home (I'd like to be there a little while). To make matters worse, our Dutch fellow-passengers, though sleeping in a forward cabin, can come into ours and smoke, polluting the atmosphere still more. I wonder I have been so well. To-day (Monday, April 21st,) we feel the change of climate most pleasantly, everybody is about, and most of us are quite bright. Yesterday we had service on deck; just a little prayer-meeting; but it found one of the passengers. He is a young man from Rotterdam, whose mother, brother and cousin came to the *Afrikaan* to say "good-bye" to him, a distressful good-bye it was.

He is of a pious Mennonite family, and is going at nineteen to be a trader on the Congo. Three weeks ago his brother, a Mennonite preacher, baptized him. I am glad to see that the impressions are still fresh. He and an officer in the Belgian army are my instructors in French. They speak no English, and are quite patient as I stumble ahead with my poor French.

To-day (Wednesday) we near Madeira. The rocky island of Ponte Santo is in sight on the left, and Madeira in full view on the right as we sail around to the harbor. The sick are quite well again. We are very thankful. Our prayer-meetings are quite refreshing, and the passengers are asking us to come and hold them where all can sing. I desire a full preparation of heart before I leave this vessel, that the work may be begun aright. Several of the passengers are becoming interested in you. Particularly the Scotch maiden, and the sweet little English woman, who has taken your place for the time. We had a new game last evening: saying texts around, going down the alphabet. It is wonderful how the hap-hazard clustering of pious words strike one! I shall not forget Mrs. Banks saying: "I love my Master, I will not go out free!" I hope in a few weeks to get a batch of sweet home letters. They are exceedingly delightful now. I believe from them that you have already been blessed in giving me to Christ. Good-bye, dear Mamma, with a heartful of love to all of you, and two for yourself.

Your loving son,   SAM.

CHAPTER III.

FROM BANANA TO LEOPOLDVILLE.

MAY 9 TO JULY 18, 1890.

FIRST DAYS ON THE CONGO RIVER.

ON the evening of May 9th, we saw the light on Shark's Point, the hooked promontory that forms the southern lip of the mouth of the Congo. At midnight we were at anchor (and some of our number were actually fishing!), in the river itself. At daylight on Saturday, May 10th, we could see before us on the north bank the sand point of Banana, a pretty picture, the rows of long, low houses dressed in white, even to the roofs, peeping through green shrubbery, with cocoanut palms waving over all, so green and warm; and the broad river, dim, misty, with dark green banks beyond.

Then came the first boat alongside, with its crew of half-clad Africans, just like our own darkies; it made me feel quite at home to see them, muscular, active, rather slight than big, and with faces I liked to watch. It was pleasant to hear them sing, as a boat crew rowed Sully, Sheppard and myself to the shore. The "stroke," a fine-looking fellow, took the verse and the rest joined heartily in the refrain. The words were simple sounding and musical; the syllables are so many and quick that the rhythm is marked and carries you along with it. The tones are weird and strange. I liked it. Mrs. Banks told me afterwards that they were improvising right through, praising the white man and promising themselves that he would give them a "dash."

Arrived on shore, some of our party (seven Swedish, six English, and two American missionaries) found both pleasure and sadness awaiting them. The young Swedish girl, who had come out with us, found her betrothed waiting for her on the

52

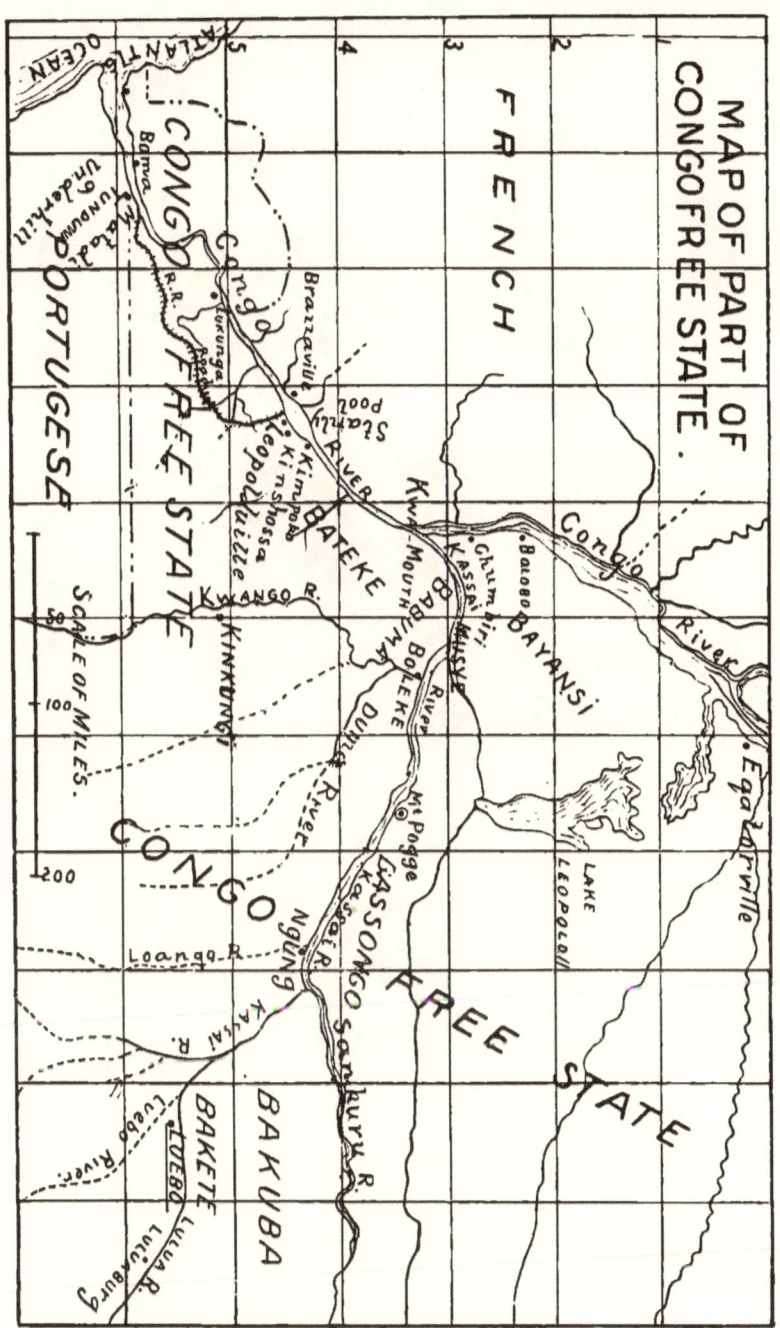

MAP OF PART OF CONGO FREE STATE.

beach; but their happiness was tinged with sorrow by the news he brought of the death of one of the Swedish mission up the river. We had a little meeting in one of their rooms in the afternoon, when we prayed for the young couple, just after the young gentleman had put on, in our presence, the ring she had brought him (she had hers already). Afterwards sixteen of us missionaries bowed in united prayer for the poor black people to whom God had brought us.

The groups of natives along the wharves and around the factories, which make up the town of Banana, gave us our first glimpses of African costume. Most of the men wear a simple breech-cloth, to which Sunday adds, in some cases (as we saw next day), a cane and a smashed derby hat. The women are much more decently and gracefully attired, in wide, gay colored bandanas, secured below the shoulders, and falling in drapery very picturesque and graceful.

How the scenes shift in this country! After a quiet Sunday in the company of fellow missionaries, Monday morning finds Sheppard and me in a native canoe, going up Banana creek (as big as the Alabama river, by the way,) to visit Miss Kildare, Bishop Taylor's lone lady missionary. Our pilot was George McGill, of Virginia, and Liberia, trained by Bishop Payne, of Richmond, once a missionary of Bishop Taylor's, who quit self-support and is out of favor with his former colleagues, but who still claims to be a worker for Christ. Our oarsman was a native convert, a pupil of McGill, Malafine by name. We started off to Nitambe's, Miss Kildare's station, in a long, narrow canoe, dug out of a large hard-wood tree, each of us on a box, and a big water bottle with a derby hat on top between us, and the paddlers standing in the prow and stern.

The water is a clear tea color, many big fish playing in it, frequently so near the boat as to splash water all over us. The river is lined with mangrove swamps, their matted roots in the water and dark green foliage above, and branches shooting out in every direction; many horizontal branches grown to trunks and resting on great roots in the water look like so many giant devil's horses.

Malafine, our oarsman, is a most interesting study. He has a

Testament (English), and is proud of it; knows something of it
too.   He describes his conversion in this one pungent sentence
of Kruboy English: "First time fit to drink Malafu (native
wine), now no drink."   This Kruboy English, by the way, is a
queer feature of West coast life, the *Lingua Franca*, known all
along the line.   It is a perverted English, seasoned with bad
French, with no inflection, and very limited vocabulary, one
word being made to do duty for ten kindred shades of meaning.
It is strange how many natives know it.   The Fiote people
often answer *Ki-fiote* with Kruboy English.   Even the state
officials and traders who know no English speak Kruboy.

The Kruboys themselves are Guinea negroes imported for
work for which the Congo natives could not be relied on.   They
are brought down from the coast above the Congo in large
numbers, and this accounts for the wide prevalence of Kruboy
English.

Miss Kildare was glad to welcome us; a white face must have
been a pleasant sight to that one woman alone among the
heathen.   She is a genuine heroine, full of faith and courage.
Her material surroundings are pleasant enough however.   She
lives in a corrugated iron house, built high enough for a good
room beneath, with a cool porch in front, a clean, nice yard on
one side of the house, and a great, thick-growing baobab or
calabash tree, seven feet in diameter on the other.   She owns
ten acres of land around her house, on which palms, plantains,
guavas and coffee trees flourish.   We went on beyond the mission station to the native village, where we saw our first live
African king, his royal highness, Domgele, imposing, deliberate,
wrapped in a toga like a Roman senator, and walking with a
royal reed studded with brass nail heads.   He knew a shilling
when we gave him one, and sent his Prime Minister for a present
in return, which when brought, was found to consist of three
eggs!

We did not dine with his Majesty, however, but came back
to Miss Kildare's for lunch, and had canned mutton, stewed,
canned apples, good bread and tea.   Then we started back down
the tide.   We saw two crocodiles, plenty of big fish, and a fish
fence one hundred yards long stretching around a point in the

river. Pretty soon Banana hove in sight, looking, with its white roofs and flags here and there, not unlike a big circus! And our third day on the Congo is over, a most pleasant and valuable day, for which we thanked God and took courage.

The missionaries here say that the Congo natives have learned the important lesson of discrimination between the missionary and other white men. Since Stanley, the State officials, and even the white settlement here, is called *Bula Matari* (Stanley's native name; it means breaker-of-rocks, from his road-making achievements!) White man is *mundila;* the missionary is *mundila-nzambi,* "God's white man"; or, sometimes, *nganga-nzambi,* "God's medicine man." If a party of white men approaches a lower Congo village the cry goes round: "Who is coming?" Answer, "*Mundila.*" "What mundila?" Answer, *Mundila nzambi;*" then out they all come to talk to and welcome the traveller. But if "*Weh! Bula Matari!*" then "*Sh-sh!*" And whiz they all go to hide in the long grass!

We are very much interested in two little *Fiote* boys, who are here in charge of a Swedish missionary from the up country. They sing gospel hymns very sweetly in their native *Ki-fiote.* One of them, Kiananna, had his teeth filed sharp like a saw for fighting, before he knew Christ. Now he is in training to preach Jesus among his own people.

May 20th, 1890. At six in the morning, a hurried breakfast, and we are off for Boma. Mr. Skaep (Swedish missionary), sick with fever, is carried by hammock along the beach; we take a row-boat from the hotel pier. A crowd of darkies line the doorway and porches of the hotel looking out for "dash." (They didn't all get it.) Our luggage is put in a long dug-out by the posse of porters, and follows us as we glide along the various piers and the hulks that line the shore of Banana Creek, and soon we clamber up the sides of the steamer *Morian.* There is the characteristic singing, with its complicated rhythm and half-concealed melody, as the "boys" windlass in the anchor. Then we go out of Banana, chasing the little French steamer, *Prince Baudoin.*

The banks of the great river are most interesting. Sometimes there is a full, deep, dark forest, mangrove or large trees with creepers and undergrowth, dense and impenetrable; or there is a lighter, more oriental growth, the feather-duster palm, high as a pine tree, against a rich forest hill, with low, fern-like palms lining the water side. Here and there is a strip of beach, then, clear, open land against the water, lined with six-foot water grass. This grass is a beautiful green. As we crossed the river to Scotchman's Head on the south bank (Banana you remember is on the north bank) the lead was plied steadily, the boy in front reporting the depth in a curious monotone. Both banks are in good sight, though far off sometimes; the river probably not as big looking as many other rivers. (It is really three to seven miles wide.) This is partly due to the large islands which so stop the view that you cannot guess where the course is going to be. We skirted one many miles long. We found the main channel near the hills on the south bank; the wide forest swamp on the north bank, with the net-work of creeks intersecting it, hid the hills until a long way up, where both banks converge to the deep Congo gorge from Boma to the falls. When we met the hills near Boma, we found them yellow with sere grass (it is winter now), red clay showing here and there, the gulches still green with tropical vegetation; finally, big sand rocks stand out. "Fetish Rock" impressed me particularly, abruptly ending a hill which juts out into the river. Here we bid good-bye to the sea-loving mangrove.

Boma is quite a town, and makes a most refreshing contrast to squatty little Banana point. The river as you come up seems to end in a nice harbor, almost round; the hills encircle it cup-like. At the far side on the slopes, Boma's white roofs dot the green. We find there a place of comfortable Dutch houses, each with its full garden of rich, new flowers and fruits. A swift, deep stream rushes in front. Across the river, on the island that here divides the Congo, is a striking green mound, like a Rhine hill.

There are some things in Boma which the African traveller would hardly expect. First, there is the hotel, a highly ornamental two-story building, tiles and hard-wood finish inside, verandas around each floor outside; an iron fence with brick curbing around the grounds. The eating is excellent—"good chop," as the Kruboys say; we had to pay for it, too. Then, in the second place, there is not a dummy line and electric lights, exactly, but there is a narrow-guage railroad, with a real live locomotive pulling two small coaches up the steep slope to the government bureaux. When you are waked in the morning by the shrill whistle, and look out to see the engine puffing out of a new car shed, pulling the coaches up the hill, you almost forget that you are in Central Africa.

The town of Boma consists, first, of a row of establishments stretching out for a mile along the river bank, six large trading houses, each with a considerable station of three to six good houses and sheds. Next from the river front is the hotel already described; then come the local government offices (City Hall and Police Court). Back of these latter, a row of houses is gradually extending towards the plateau, whither the railroad and good walks already make way. On this plateau, along a semi-circular avenue, well-shaded and graded on the edge of the hill, are the church (Catholic of course), the Court of Justice, the offices and residences of the officials who govern the Congo Free State. These buildings are neat and substantial, some of wood, whitewashed, many of ornamental galvanized iron. Near the government offices, across the hollow beneath the hill, is the great shed where some four hundred native soldiers are daily drilled, making a gay spectacle in their red coats, blue trousers and white crossbands. At the end of the shed are the " fortifications," a red clay breastwork, surmounted by a half dozen small cannon.

There is a large Catholic mission station on the hill between the English trading houses and the rest of the town.

Street scenes in Boma are a strange medley. Here in the market you see side by side, piles of rice, palm-nuts and pea-nuts, with rolls of matting, bunches of bananas and bottles of spirits. Yonder is a man carrying a piano-stool to the shop for mending. Here is a rough and tumble fight over a bag of sugar. Over there is a native tying in his pannier a demijohn of rum. At the factory door yonder they are having a " drink all round," and here are boys passing with a bottle under the arm. In the midst of this turmoil, imagine my feelings at hearing an African singing:

"Not one day of service give him,
Lay no trophy at his feet."

There is always somebody bathing in the river. One morning I saw a whole company of black soldiers taking their bath. They were all in at once, then the bugle sounded, splash! scamper! and in a moment here they came marching by in their red, white and blue.

There are crowds of imported workmen. They live in separate quarters according to nationality, Kruboys, Accras, Loangas, Kabindas, Liberians, Sierra Leone men. The soldiers have their barracks, they are Bangala.

These imported workmen raise a question which is a "live issue" among Christian men out here. If they won't work, or are rebellious, or insolent, shall they be coerced with the lash? Mr. Weeks (B. M. S., Tunduwa Station), says, "Yes." Mr. Clark (A. B. M. U., Palaballa Station), says, "No, it is wrong. But as they can't be managed any other way, don't get them." But if you don't get them, you don't get any work done, for the Congo native is above work. And so you don't get any houses built, nor any fields planted, and there the matter stands. The Liberians and Sierra Leone men who speak English, complain bitterly of their treatment by white men, other than missionaries. They say they suffer here, are called *canaille*, bushmen, etc. A mechanic gets, besides his pay, rations of one bottle of rum and a cup of rice. A common laborer gets just one half of this. If he wants fish or fruit, he has to sell rum for it. We held a meeting for the English-speaking blacks at Boma, with about forty of them present. They sung English hymns fairly well, but like our home Africans are "too superstitious." Sheppard preached to the Sierra Leone men at Matadi, after which they spoke to him freely of their condition. One of them said, "No good here for Sierra Leone man; plenty sick, too much flog."

Before leaving Boma I had a pleasant interview with Governor Coquilhat, the official head of the Free State. I found him very bright and clever, at the same time unaffected and exceedingly kind to me, with no "put on" about him. He offered me his map, from which I got the valuable details needed about the regions we are to consider in the location of our mission, particularly the altitudes throughout the southwest section of the Congo region.

I could not but be sorry for his physical condition, almost used up with one of Africa's scourges, chronic dysentery.

We spent the time from May 22 to June 17, moving back and forth from Boma to Tunduwa, getting ready for our trip further up the river. We formed most pleasant and useful acquaintanceships with the missionaries at Tunduwa and Palaballa Stations, but I must reserve an account of our visits to these interesting points for another letter.

TUNDUWA AND PALABALLA.

From May 22d to June 17th, we made Tunduwa our headquarters, paying occasional visits to Boma, Matadi, Palaballa and other points in easy reach. This stay of nearly a month at this point may seem a long delay to one unacquainted with the difficulties of African travel. It will be recollected, however, that here the navigation of the lower river comes to an end; and from this point to Stanley Pool, where the upper river is reached and navigation again resumed, a distance of two hundred and thirty miles, you have to go afoot. There is not so much as an ox or mule in all this Congo region; the railroad commencing at Matadi, one mile above Tunduwa, is only finished two miles as yet; all your goods and you yourself, if you cannot walk, have to go on the back of the native or imported African. And as we were arranging for the transport of the supplies upon which our future subsistence depends, it took some time before the needful arrangements were complete.

We consider this time well spent, however, outside of making the arrangements just alluded to. We were able by intercourse with experienced missionaries, to get a valuable insight into ways of living and working and travelling here. We made many valuable acquaintances, one of them was that notable character in these parts, *African fever*. It was a special mercy that we both had it here at Tunduwa among kind and experienced friends. We are not so apt to have it soon, and will understand it somewhat when it does come again. I had it several times before I found it out, I believe now, and finally the temperature ran up to one hundred and five degrees, which is right hot. I did not mind it much, however, as it went away in twelve hours after taking my bed. Still it might have had a very different termination with either or both of us.

It was only a mile from here at Matadi, that this same fever cut short the life of that young girl, a Swedish missionary, whose death we heard of as we landed at Banana Point. She was on her way to the river, to take steamer for Europe; there to be married to a fellow missionary who had preceded her to the old country. Through unwise exposure in walking from Palaballa to Matadi (she unfortunately missed her way and was much delayed in the great heat) she took a fever which shortly proved to be of the violent hematuric type. A few hours was enough; the temperature ran up to one hundred and ten degrees, and when evening came, she "fell asleep."

Frequent trips back and forth have made us quite familiar with this lower part of the great river. Its course is very much like a rail fence—six panels from Boma to Vivi. Each stretch is like a good-sized bay, no way out is to be seen. The deception is enhanced by the clearness of the atmosphere, which makes the hill in front seem nearer than it really is. It is almost impossible for the eye to judge any distances in this country.

The power of this river impresses me more every time I look at it. When it turns Tunduwa Point it gets a current in the mid-stream like a mill tail, forming an awful whirlpool, where Sheppard took a good spin one day when out on the river. One of the singular features of this mighty stream is the up-current, due perhaps to the depth and over violence of the river here. If you know where to look for it, there is almost always a strong current up stream, somewhere between bank and bank, when the main current is so strong that only a most powerful steamer can breast it; this is most fortunate, if you are rowing up the river. Going down stream, however, it plays strange pranks with those ignorant of it. I have seen canoes carried up, when the rowers were pulling down stream with all their might.

THE CEMETERY AT UNDERHILL.—From Photo.

"A little back, in the hollow of the hill, are the graves of the men who pioneered this work. A sacred spot."—Page 61

A few words on the localities around Tunduwa, or Underhill. (Tunduwa, is the native; Underhill, the English name). Tunduwa is on the south bank of the Congo, some twenty or thirty miles (air line) from Boma. Just up the river, around the bend on the north bank, is Vivi, so graphically described in Stanley's *Founding of the Free State.* Opposite Vivi, on the same side with Tunduwa, but higher up, is Matadi, the head of navigation and terminus of the great Congo railway, now building. Ten miles back of Tunduwa and Matadi, on a lofty hill which overlooks the entire country, is Palaballa. As we come up the river to Tunduwa Point, we see on the hill jutting out into the river the neat line of white houses, which forms the Tunduwa (or Underhill) Station of the Baptist Missionary Society (English). Below the mission station on the river bank is the group of gray corrugated iron storehouses, in one of which the Baptist Missionary Society receives and stores its goods from steamers. The Swedish Missionary Society and the American Baptist Missionary Union are granted space for the same purpose, on Baptist Missionary Society ground.

A little back in the hollow of the hill are the graves of the men who pioneered this work—a sacred spot!¹ The mission station, originally down here on the beach, has been moved to the healthier locality on the top of the hill, and is approached by an admirable stone walk, five feet wide, built out of the stone only too abundant, just at hand. The climb of one hundred and fifty feet is made in a zig-zag of six sections, so that the ascent is just perceptible. Arrived at the top, we find a row of four excellent frame houses, roomy and substantial to look at. Good stone walks connect them; flowering shrubs, quick-growing shade trees, and tropical fruits, aloes, cactus, custard-apples, limes, oranges and pine-apples are flourishing around them. We found in Mr. Weeks, the principal missionary in charge of the station, a friend and valued helper in forwarding the business necessary to our onward movements.

On May 26th, we took a trip (a ten-mile walk up the mountain) from Tunduwa to Palaballa. We were up and off before breakfast, a boy, carrying my valise on his head, following behind. The path is ten miles long, up and down hill, and the

¹ His own resting place "till He come."

ascent is between one and two thousand feet. The road is only half wide enough for one, the bush and grass closing over it in spite of hundreds passing every week. It is as rough as can be, with holes washed in it and covered with stones, big and little, smooth and sharp. At one point the path winds around the mountain, with a towering cliff above, and a precipitous chasm beneath. The hills seem solid rock, first flint, then sandstone, broom sedge over all, with scant bush, which looks like the mockery of an orchard. Many a valley between the hills, however, is full and running over with rich, green trees, clad with creepers flowering red and white.

The boy took his time following us. I could see my valise moving uncertainly through the grass far below us. We met two caravans at the M'Pozo river, one going each way, most of the loads in crates, the carriers' own make. At last, near the top of the hill, we saw palms in the distance, then a house, then M'Palaballa!

This is the first station on the Congo of the American Baptist Missionary Union. The station has three local points. 1. In a native hut at a considerable distance from the rest of the mission work, Miss Fleming teaches between twenty and forty heathen children every morning. As school comes at the very hour when they ought to be out digging their dinner, each gets a cup of rice every day. Miss Fleming also has a dispensary here, where she prescribes for the simpler diseases of the natives. They make a wry face over her doses, but come again for more. 2. In a much more pretentious wood and iron house, with two or three good out-houses in a spacious yard, is the girls' seminary (on a small scale as yet), presided over by Miss Gordon. It is ten minutes' walk from the native town, and about fifteen from the Central Mission Station, so as to be at a safe distance from the distractions and temptations of both. 3. The Central Station of the mission. Passing by a narrow path through the native town, we enter a beautiful little avenue or shaded path, at the end of which is the station. There is quite a group of buildings—two dwelling houses, the main one broad and low (African style), wood frame, iron roof and sides; the inevitable storehouse, a long, stout, iron building; the schoolhouse and chapel, corrugated iron with little bell-tower; plain seats and desk, mud floor; and the printing office, some one hundred and fifty yards from the rest of the buildings.

The dwellings are flanked on one side by what might be termed the orchard. Here are some fine orange trees in full fruit, limes, mangoes, etc. On the other side is the garden. The banana and plantain usually have the honor of a special plot allotted to them, one being the staple fruit, the other the staple vegetable. Peas, potatoes and yams are planted without order, and grow with little cultivation. It looks as if the whole garden were growing spontaneously in nature's rich profusion and confusion.

Beyond the station is a village, then a wood, a banana plantation, another village, and the crest of the hill crowned with a big rock, from which I saw the Congo many miles away winding through the mountains among the cataracts. This is a favorite walk with the missionaries.

The last morning of our stay at Palaballa—we were there four days—I went to this spot with some of our missionary friends of the *Arikuan*, who are resting here on their way up the river. It was a charming walk and talk, the last for a long time, most likely.

The path through the villages leads right through the midst of everything, in one place in three feet of a native house, almost under its little veranda. At several places the road leads by the grave of an African king, a huge mound covered as thick as it will hold with white man's crockery and glass-ware, broken vessels making up where the whole one's give out, pitchers, cups, mugs and plates, but especially jugs and bottles. These last give a sad significance to the monument, wholly unintended by the friends of the deceased monarch, for they too often tell the story of how he came to his death.

One of the most touching episodes in the history of this Palaballa Mission centres around the king who was reigning when the missionaries first came. He was their staunch friend, listened willingly to their preaching, was "almost persuaded," but would not give up the white man's drink, with which the traders were too ready to supply him, and he died unsaved, clinging to his bottle.

You would like, perhaps, in closing, a sketch of a day at
Tunduwa, a pretty fair sample of missionary life at this important station. We rise at six, and an hour or more is given to
private devotion. Breakfast comes at 7:30, tea and coffee, oat-
meal, with diluted condensed milk, cold chicken, ham, light-
bread and butter, and jam for finish. Family prayer together,
and then all hands go to work, the resident missionaries to
casting up accounts for carrier pay and rations, or to unloading
steamers and carrying goods up hill to their proper storerooms,
and this means bossing a gang of twenty Lundas. The visitor
may write or pack for the road, or help, or do nothing, as he
likes, maybe take a trip to Matadi to see how the railroad is
getting on, if he can find men to row. At twelve comes dinner,
soup, goat or fowl, and tinned meat of some kind, stew, rice,
African beans, maybe macaroni for a rarity; canned fruit, or
rice, cornstarch, or tapioca pudding. One hour's rest; no work
allowed; then a lunch of tea and biscuit, as they call our
crackers.

In the afternoon is lighter work, translation and the like.
Supper comes after dark; after supper, conversation or a game
of bagatelle. Missionaries out this way are "like other mortal
folk," joke one another, and tease the ladies, if they have the
good luck to have any around. They do not speak oratorically,
missionary address style, but are sober and business like, none
the less earnest for that. They are human, sometimes speak
too quick; sometimes say unkind things about other people
whose ways and ideas of work are not the same; sometimes lose
temper and quarrel, Paul and Barnabas-like, it is to be feared.

The climate has certainly an influence in this direction; not
on all, but on some naturally sweet-tempered men, making them
irritable and unreasonable. Especially under the influence of
African fever, one is not to be judged too closely for hasty acts
and words. Yet while the missionaries are very human, there is
one who is *very* God, working through them for the regeneration
of this dark land.

Diary, Sunday, June 15, 1890.—Led service at Underhill. Read
Moody's "Divine choice of instruments." Sheppard in bed—fever.
At dinner found my temperature 103; was sent to bed. Got to 105

by night. Clear of fever in the morning. Both up Tuesday morning I went by boat to Ango Ango and hired forty-three men from the Dutch house to bring up the bulk of my provisions and barter goods to Lukunga. Finished preparing loads; settled with Mr. Forfeitt; and off by 3 o'clock. Sheppard too sick to walk much. Started off in hammock.

THE TRAMP TO STANLEY POOL.

TUNDUWA TO LUKUNGA.

You will, no doubt, like to have some details of our 230-mile tramp from Tunduwa to Stanley Pool. We took the road Tuesday, June 17, the very day we got up from that attack of African fever, by the advice of our most judicious friends, who assured us that we would find the road good medicine, as, indeed, it proved. We had twenty-five men in all, and made quite an imposing caravan. Our bedding rolled up and put in big black valises, and our bedsteads, took three men. Two carried the tent; two took our pocket-book, which contained seventy-five dozen red bandana handkerchiefs and thirty-seven twelve-yard pieces of check domestic; four men carried the trunks; one carried the table, chairs and guns; one carried the "chop-box"— about three feet long, twelve inches wide and eight inches deep, containing corned beef, jam, hard bread and crackers, lard, butter, salt, tea, coffee and sugar, all sealed up in tins. Another carried the "canteen," which was a big bucket, with nice little kettle, sauce-pan, tea and sugar holders, bucket, two plates, a dish, two cups, two large and two small spoons, two knives and two forks, all fitting in under one cover, so that they could not be jostled while on the march.

But, the drawing-room cars, our Pullman palace coaches, were borne on a bamboo pole on the heads of two men. There were two canvas hammocks with pillows inside and a shawl spread across the pole—jump in and the men trot off as if they had no load at all. It was fine to walk as fast as I could for an hour, then call up the hammock men, climb in and rest, while they made even better time than if I were walking. In this way we travelled fast without getting tired. The caravan made a most interesting sight as they moved off, Indian file, up the hill. You could just see a line of black backs showing above the

5

grass, with a big bundle on top of each. One of our men carried a load of 102 pounds, and always got to camp among the first.

Our first day's journey took us over very familiar ground, by the route already described, from Tunduwa to Palaballa; the roughest road I ever saw, path ten inches wide, high grass on each side, and sharp-cornered flint rocks, fist size, filling the little ditch of a footway. The country is all broken here. One of the first Baptist missionaries said it was like going up and down a church steeple. The way takes us up and down hill till near the M'Pozo river. Then we drop down a hill like Blue mountain (near Anniston), very, very steep. We camped the first night at the river, as we had to go slowly; learned tenting in a very practical way, and made our supper on tea (Sheppard's make) and little crackers and jam, and breakfast the same. So when we went up the 1,500 feet pull on the other side of the river next morning we gave our hammock men a good job.

We were received most cordially at Palaballa, where we knew everybody, and had a cup of tea at once; and at dinner took the little boy's plan of eating fried chicken at Miss Gordon's, and smothered chicken and canned peaches at Mr. Hyde's. Mr. Clarke and the ladies of our *Afrikaan* party were gone to the Pool by the time we started, and there they take boat promptly for the interior, six hundred miles further up the river. A lonely place to work this would be but for the belief in the experience of Jesus' presence! I am praying daily for a strong hold on that blessed fact.

We rested till after dinner at Palaballa, and then took the road again. Our mode of travel each day after this was to start before sunrise, after a good breakfast on corned beef or bacon from the tins in the chop-box, tea and cabin bread, then march until ten or eleven, stop by some little river in good shade, dine on a chicken, bought *en route*, with the bacon left from breakfast, and tea and jam, or pawpaws and bananas, for desert. Sometimes boiled sweet potatoes helped out the dinner. The women bring the potatoes, chicken and other "chop" they have raised; sit right at the roadside, in some open place, and sell to the carriers and white men that pass. Some days the road is one unbroken string of carriers. So the women make a good thing of it.

We would rest after dinner until 2 o'clock, then march for two hours or more. Before sundown we stopped and camped, always by a stream of water. The *Capita*, or head man of the carriers, sweeps a place clean for the tent, and soon it is up, all the cords over the pegs, the water-proof floor in, the beds made and the mosquito nets spread. Meanwhile the men have made several fires, a boy has brought water, the chop-box and canteen are opened, the table and chairs untied and on their feet, an early supper, and then bed.

Our journey was a very pleasant one indeed. We got very fond of walking, besides it was inspiring to feel with every step that we were that much farther on our way towards the real work we had come to do. We would have had a very different trip six months later on. Then it would be both disagreeable and dangerous, very hot,—a kind of steaming heat from wet earth and grass,—big rains, drenching everything on short notice, and making great torrents of the little branches that cross the road every half mile. Now it is the dry season, the Congo winter, and everything is favorable for the road.

One day and a half brought us to the N'Seke river, a nice little stream, with elegant water and shade. I remember one tree in particular there by the river side, whose long arms stretched out behind our tent. Just think of limbs as large as a good-sized tree, and reaching out for forty feet, sometimes almost meeting across the big creeks!

A Belgian, or rather State officer, lately in charge of Stanley Falls Station, Captain Bodson by name, had camped by the N'Seke ahead of us. He was glad of an audience, and told me much of his place and the people there; his march to the Soudan boundary of the Free State by the Itimbiri, and especially of His Excellency Tippoo Tib. He had a boy and a chimpanzee, which this neighborly celebrity had given him.

It is funny to hear these State men's English (not English, but Kruboy), "Me look him"; "You sabby where dem dead men live?" The latter a question asked our Acras by Mr. Sjoholm, a Swedish missionary, meaning: "You know where men go

when they die?" Captain Bodson spoke the English he had
learned in order to talk with the coast men employed at his
station, and it was most amusing.

Eight fires under the green roof that night, with some eight
men at each fire, made a pretty sight. The sun was still high
in the heavens on the fourth day when we climbed another very
steep hill, and calling up the hammock men, straightening the
rug and buttoning up all trim, rode in style up to Mr. Ingham's
at Banza Manteka. That was Friday, so we could not wait
over Sunday, as we would have liked so much to do, but pushed
on (three hours late) next morning. I got a notion of this cele-
brated mission, however, before starting.

Mr. Ingham, now in charge (Mr. Richards is in England on
furlough), entertained us nicely. Such a good dinner the night
we got there! You will find encomiums upon Mrs. Ingham's
housekeeping in Stanley's "Free State." Mr. Ingham was a State
officer and has shot fifty elephants. He has kept this record
up lately by killing an enormous leopard, six feet from nose to
tail, and able to jump a six-foot fence with a grown hog in his
mouth. The morning after this monster was killed, the natives
flocked around, almost afraid to be glad. "He don't eat grass;
he eats meat every day," they said. Leopards seldom attack a
man, but I own to sundry tremors as I walked the two hundred
yards to my room that dark night.

The church here at Banza Manteka has between three hundred
and four hundred members, though nearly a thousand have
claimed conversion. The interest, though not at revival heat, con-
tinues. The iron church given by Dr. Gordon's church, Boston,
has its six hundred sittings pretty well filled, though the cold
weather causes much sickness and keeps many away. Some
twenty-eight villages belong to this community, some are miles
away, but the people come. It looks strange to see a handsome
galvanized iron church and a dirt floor inside. The men sit on
one side and the women on the other, like Methodist churches
at home. Mrs. Guinness says that the men make the women sit
by themselves, not because there is any social custom requiring
the separation of the sexes, but because the men don't like to be
troubled by the babies.

I saw the collection baskets in the church, and what do you think was their size? They were regular market baskets, and receive every Sunday a load of blue beads (the copper pennies of Congo land), and maybe a handkerchief or piece of cloth, but not often I fear. The ruling passion is trade. What they make they keep, and many of them are very "nigh"—I might say all. There is none of the thriftlessness and wastefulness characteristic of many negroes at home; still the Banza Manteka Christians can be liberal enough when they feel the necessity for giving. When the iron church was unloaded at Matadi in 1887, the natives volunteered to carry it up free of charge. It made two hundred and thirty-seven loads, and weighed five or six tons. They thus contributed in their own labor the equivalent of about $1000. So great was the desire to have a share in the work, that the women who could not carry, worked and earned the means to pay men to go for loads.

In the morning before we took up our march, I went through the villages and saw the improved houses the converted communities are building; inside you could see four-post beds, cupboards and tables, instead of the mats which formerly had to serve all purposes.

We spent Sunday on the road and had service with our men. I read Luke ii. 1–12, in the Ki-Kongo Testament, and we sang some Ki-Kongo hymns. It was fine to hear them sing, "We're marching to Zion," in Ki-Kongo. Then one of the men prayed in their language, and Sheppard and I in English.

Tuesday, June 25th, we reached Lukunga, called half-way to the Pool, 110 miles, in less than seven days actual travel.

LUKUNGA TO THE POOL.

Lukunga is the half-way station to the Pool, and in this neighborhood all the up-river institutions transfer their loads to other carriers from the Pool, who take them on. Our carriers were exchanged here. A lot came from the Pool and took the loads our first caravan had brought from Tunduwa.

Mr. Hoste (American Baptist Missionary Union), a capital missionary, has a good work here. He was a naval officer, and still shows the system, determination and the great secret of

succeeding in what he undertakes, which characterizes that
service. Stern and inflexible in carrying out his plans, making
things, and people too, give way, he is really gentle and loves
the natives to a passion. That is why he sticks here through
interruptions and frictions, and health that is never even fair, I
am told, and will neither go home nor die. But he does not
advise others to do the like, but to go to bed if they possibly can,
when even a little fever holds on a while. Mr. Hoste thinks
that the church at home ought to pay for his living, so he makes
no effort at self-support, but gives himself entirely to preaching
and looking after the boys he has gathered in a boarding-school.

I believe this concentration, and similar plans at Banza-
Manteka, have made these the only markedly successful mission
stations on the Congo. The ice was broken here only three
years ago, and now there are two hundred members from various
villages within a ten-mile radius. At night you can hear, besides
three separate prayer-meetings at the station, the singing of the
natives in all directions carrying on their own services, singing
in Ki-Kongo, "What can wash away my stain," "We're marching to Zion," etc.

Diary, Sunday, June 29.—A profitable, but not a pleasant day
until towards evening. Indeed, while Lukunga has been stimulating
to my spiritual endeavor, I have been in one steady fight (and many
bad falls) all the week spent here. Walked before breakfast by river,
and went across bridge and read *Rutherford's letters* and the *Christian*, of April 25th. At eleven, a meeting in the long, white mud
chapel. A stream of people had passed me at the bridge for some
time before. Mr. Hoste announced and raised a hymn, which the boys
heartily carried. As there are hardly a hundred hymns in Ki-Kongo,
all or most are quite familiar to the congregation. Mr. Hoste prayed
with much fervor. Another hymn. Prayer by Luwawa, native evangelist. Mr. Hoste read the promise in John xiv., that Jesus will manifest himself to us, and spoke on it about seventeen minutes. Luwawa
rose, one foot on bench and his body twisting nervously around. Began
slowly, but soon caught fire. Got his foot down and his hands in use
and tongue loose. Spoke like his life depended on it. Not ranting
style, nor very loud, but in a hot stream of emphatic words, and his
little eyes back under his forehead burnt like coals. His gestures
were not extravagant, but naturally animated.

Afternoon, a similar service, with about the same congregation. The low, rough benches pretty well filled. Mission boys with clean shirts and cloths from waist to knee; a few girls in plain dresses· Men, some stripped to the waist; some with clean cloth about shoulders and another about the loins. Women, bare shoulders; one large cloth to knees, or two aprons, one tied with string before the breast and other about waist. Strange congregation of believers met for the communion! Yet quiet, attentive, well behaved, though some eyes wandered and some slept (like Eutychus), in the warm room. The bread broken was the native bread, quanga. It is inspiring to see these fruits of work done in the past, and still more to know that it is going on steadily in many villages, where the converts testify daily and the question is on all minds.

It may interest you to know of my first efforts at preaching to the natives.

At Lutete, or N'Gombe's, I preached in English, and one of the missionaries interpreted; but it was very unsatisfactory, hard to "keep up steam." I like it much better to speak in "white man's *note*," though it was little I could say, and that in perfect innocence of grammar and of the language. Still I could tell for myself the story of Jesus, and they understood me. We were in touch. I did this with our carriers after we took the road; so soon as I could, held prayers with them, and told them in their own language who Jesus is, why he came to this earth, and how he died for sinners. It was the greatest pleasure to see how they listened to the "old, old story," which was all new to them.

We travelled from Lukunga to Leopoldville on the Pool, without special incident, reaching the end of our tramp, July 18.

As we approached Leopoldville we had convincing proof that important settlements were before us, in the large goods caravans which we overtook from time to time. They numbered from twenty to forty, or more, and I could see by the labels on the goods that the different caravans were bound for the different stations which are grouped at this base of upper-river navigation. Some of the carriers had boxes of provisions or tools, some bales of cheap cloth, or coils of brass wire, to be used as currency in trade with the natives; others bore kegs of powder for the State.

Leopoldville, or in native parlance, *Kintamo*, is at the western end of that curious lake-like expansion of the Congo, known as Stanley Pool. The roar of the first cataract of the Congo is in our ears at the station, while eastward the Pool stretches out twenty-four miles long and a few miles wide. Around the Pool we count six well-equipped white settlements; each of these the base of a chain of posts extending up the river into the heart of the continent. The communication between each base and its outposts is maintained by one or more capital steamboats, made in Europe in small pieces, weighing less than a hundred weight each, transported on the heads of the Congo natives to the Pool, and there rebuilt and launched. This is very wonderful to me; and to make it more so, I know of at least five new steamers on the way up, or already being put together. These three great trade companies, French, Dutch and Belgian, evidently have large faith in the commercial future of the Congo. And already, I am told, the two last have more than paid for their costly steamers by the sale of ivory.

The supply of ready ivory seems to be running short, yet this, it seems to me, is a decided advantage; for rubber is already taking its place, and a dozen other valuable products are waiting until the trader shall take a little time and pains to show the natives their value. We met numerous ivory caravans with loads amounting to at least five tons, counting all we saw. We met only a few caravans with rubber.

Three of the settlements at the Pool are Protestant Mission stations: the American Baptist Union Missionary Station at Leopoldville, adjoining the headquarters of the Free State, the mission station in charge of Dr. Sims, who is also surgeon at the State Post; the British Missionary Society Station at Kinshassa, a few miles up the south bank, and Bishop Taylor's "self-supporting" Methodist Mission at Kimpoko, near the eastern end of the Pool. Each of the Baptist missions has a fine little steamer, and these, though not the largest, are the best boats that ply the upper Congo. The American Baptist Missionary Union steamer is the *Henry Reed*, the British Missionary Society steamer is the *Peace*.

We were comfortably lodged at the American Baptist Missionary Union Station, and most kindly cared for. In fact, the way strangers' hearts have been opened, priceless advice and help freely given, events shaped so as to lead us plainly thus far, is more than I can realize. Truly, God hath been mindful of us.

You would like an account of a day (Sunday) spent with these kind brethren. At 6 A. M. my boy, Nkuka, came in with coffee—a very staid, important young gentleman, about ten years of age. His big, round head was shaved three weeks ago, and that makes him look still wiser. He is very black, very fat, very round. A cloth around his waist and falling to his knees, with a blue calico print shirt, makes his outfit. I don't suppose he ever owned a hat. This young man throws back my mosquito net, hands in my coffee, arranges for my bathing, etc., takes away the cup, and disappears until breakfast.[1] Mr. Blake, of the Guinness' Congo-Balolo Mission, and Dr. Howison, of Bishop Taylor's Mission, who broke his arm Saturday at house-building, and is here for treatment, slept at the end of the room. All move over to Dr. Sims' house for breakfast. Each man's boy stands behind his chair at table and waits on him. After breakfast we have prayers, and then there is a quiet time until nine o'clock service in the chapel. Dr. Sims led, doing all the speaking, as none of us could take part in the native language. It is nice to hear them sing, but Lukunga and Banza Manteka have spoiled me. Here there are hardly any believers, and I feel the want of a response. At the night service Scannel, whom we knew at Harley House, and who came out with us on the *Afrikaan*, spoke in English, and Dr. Sims interpreted.

We are now three hundred and thirty miles inland. The first hundred was on a lower river steamer. We stopped half-way at Boma, the capital. Fifty miles above Boma the rapids cut off navigation. There is Underhill, the English Baptist Station, and just above is Matadi, where is the beginning of the railroad to extend around the falls; but it is likely we will have to walk these two hundred and thirty miles for some time yet.

---

[1] This seems a universal custom in Central Africa. The natives send the brightest of their boys to the merchant, official, and mission stations to learn the ways and language of the envied foreigners.

We found it a long tramp, fourteen days of actual marching, and quite a while to wait half-way.

Stanley Pool is a widened stretch of the river at the head of the rapids, and the beginning of upper river navigation. Here we find people from most of the tribes on the upper river. In countenance and physique they are superior to the people we have seen. Their districts, too, are far more populous, according to what I can hear. It is among these we seek a field of labor. I leave to-day for Bolobo, five days' distance by steamer up the main branch, to confer with the veteran missionary explorer, Rev. George Grenfell, of the English Baptist Mission.

STEAMER HENRY REED.

CHAPTER IV.

BY STEAMER TO BOLOBO AND BACK, AND FROM LEOPOLD-VILLE AFOOT TO LUKUNGA, AND BACK TO THE POOL.

JULY 29 TO DECEMBER 3, 1890.

DIARY AND LETTERS.

ON THE HENRY REED.

Diary, July 29, 1890.—Mr. Billington, of the American Baptist Mission, consents to take me in the *Henry Reed* up the river to Bolobo, so that I may consult Mr. Grenfell. The charge is only the estimated cost of the food I use. Mr. Scannell and Miss Dalgarno, of the *Afrikaan* party, are also aboard.

It is exhilarating to feel how the little mission steamer defies the powerful current, and in a moment turns, advances, or retires when the way is dangerous, or dashes up stream at a good speed. This is a seventy-foot, flat bottom steel boat, a stern-wheeler, standing about twenty inches out of the water, and draws twenty-two under, when loaded. A light, flat, wooden roof, or awning extends from stem to stem, and is a necessity in this climate. . . . Passed Gallina Point. Crocodiles on the rocks, and many hippos in the Pool rear their horse heads to breathe, and eye us over. Had to waste a few bullets on them. Abundance of all game in these parts. Buffalo, hippo, elephant, and deer tracks cover the beach. Saw water birds, large and small, flocks of ducks and guinea fowl, feeding on the sand and wet grass. Many shots, but only two guineas to show.

When it was nearly dark we tied up at a long sandy beach, and the men were all sent for fire-wood for the engine, which is sawed into blocks eighteen inches long. Had supper in the cabin. All ravenously hungry. Fried quauga excellent: so are Miss Dalgarno's jam puddings. Sleep on top of the cabin; the awning about two and a half feet above us. Rather close quarters.

July 31.—At day, Mr. Billington calls the boys; and by the time we are dressed, we get a cup of coffee, and the boat is under way.

75

The wind makes big waves, so that we had to wait half a day for quiet water.

Leaving the expanse of "Stanley Pool," the width of which is not so apparent, owing to the great islands, we find the river narrow, about a mile wide and very deep, and high hills hem it in.

Saturday, August, 2.—We reach Bwemba Station (American Baptist). Some miles below, the hills receding leave a fertile lowland which the Bayansi occupy. They build their houses in a triple, or double row (with short breaks) for miles along the river, shading their long brown streets with the palm that gives the wine, *malafu.*

Anchored at a good sand beach with deep water, and see a new opening in the front, about six acres. Up the slope 150 yards, is an excellent frame house with avenue of pawpaws and plantains. Many fruit trees planted over the ground. All looks clean and trim, and all done in little more than twelve months by Messrs. Billington and Glenesk.

We stopped before reaching here at one of the first Bayansi villages. A trader threatened a native chief near there some time ago, and was shot dead on the spot. After a good deal of bad management, the State officials decided to visit the chief of the long row of towns that line the Congo just below here, to adjust the quarrel by a friendly "palaver." Mr. Billington was asked to advise the chief (Bonkanya) of the proposed visit. So he stopped at his town (Mobimo) an hour below here, and took me with him to Bonkanya's "palaver," shed, or council chamber. When he heard the message, the cool old chief replied : "Tell Bula Matadi (their name for all State officials), that if he brings 'Nganga Boko' (the missionary, Dr. Sims,) I will talk with him here, or I will go to your place if he likes; but if Bula Matadi tries to land here without 'Nganga Boko,' I will shoot him." No timid lower river people here! Bold, free, good as anybody, willing to welcome a friend, or one they can make something out of; but ready to fight, caring little for death. The men generally go armed with spear in hand, knife sheathed by the side, or a gun slung across their back, or all three. I am told women also go to war holding the husband's powder calabash.

Leaving Mobimo, we steamed along the beach, here rocky at the water's edge, crowds peering at us through the bush, or standing in the village streets. We passed a strange object floating. When near, saw it was the headless trunk of a man. Afterwards found he had been killed in the town next the station.

The men had a fine song and dance when we sighted the station, keeping time to the beat of the engine, and accentuating with hand and foot. A finale, which seems universal, is this: One makes a short, sharp "Ah!" in high pitch. The chorus rejoin, "Ah! ah!" in perfect concert and perfect unison, repeated once, twice, and all is still.

August 3.—Sunday, still at Bwemba. A better day than usual for me. Held a morning service; first for the station people, then a communion service. It was good for me to be there. After dinner Mr. Billington took me through the town adjoining. We passed the strip of land next the mission, and heard the voice of weeping, and saw women mourning. By the low window lay the emaciated corpse of a man, his body covered with cam wood. I think they were painting him.

A little further on we came on the old chief, Ebenda. He sat on a coarse reed mat under the tree, in the centre of his quarter, entertaining a few visiting braves. Drunk and silly Ebenda! The poor old man has been tall, finely-proportioned and powerful, now a shrivelled wreck. He points to a pile of seven skulls against his house; (memorandum on margin of *Journal*, "Dec. 22, skulls now gone,"), brandishes the spear that killed, and the knife that beheaded them. . . . All the afternoon a rapid triple-measured drum-beat in the town south of the mission, indicated a drinking and dancing frolic. . . . . Saw a woman who was sentenced by the king to be killed for lewdness and idleness, particularly that she wouldn't work. Her grave was half dug, her head was decorated by the women, and she waiting the end, when Mr. Billington interceded and had her spared by payment of 100 brass rods.

August 5.—Off up the river.

August 6.—Cut wood from a forest of copal. The gum was soon caked on the bark. The tree has a bark like beech, smooth and light colored.

9:30 A. M.—Anchored at Bolobo, after a beautiful sight of the villages and their tall palms on the shore as we came up. Met by Rev. George Grenfell, F. R. G. S., and Mr. Glenny. . . . I decide, finally, to stop here now. So good-bye to the last of our *Afrikaan* party, Miss Dalgarno and Mr. Scannell, who go on up the river.

August 7.—Much sense of the reality of my work, and of things divine for me. . . . . Copying map, lent me by Mr. Grenfell, of the Kwango, according to survey made by him in 1886. Aside from their utility, these maps are very interesting as finished scientific work of the highest order. . . . Mr. Grenfell discussed mission work, sketched the B. M. S. enterprise. Almost dissuades me from going to Kinkunji, as strongly as his modesty would permit, in favor of Musié.

At Bolobo there are mission-residences, store, cook-house, school, visitors' house, observatory, wood-work shop, photograph room, servants' house, machine shop, and charcoal kiln, and on the beach a wet dock and slip, in which to repair the *Peace*, and a wharf; altogether a splendid establishment.

To his sister, he writes: I write from Bolobo, a long way up the great river. From the veranda of the central house, which is Mr. Grenfell's, you would just now, if you were here, look on what seems a wide lake, about five miles wide, with a strip of green in the distance, as the edging of that blue sheet, "a piece of the sky fallen through from on high." When the sun sets, its wonderful good-night glories fall on that same sheet of glass; for we are looking directly west; and then it is not a bad sight. But though like a lake, if you saw one of the canoes shoot from behind the great tree on the right, and with only a few strokes now and then, glide pass at a railway speed, you would guess there was something of a current there. The canoes are beauties, very long and straight, and perfectly shaped, and if you are close enough to see, carved into long diamonds.

Monday, August 11.—Fever. Only well again Thursday. The fever Monday, 9 A. M. to dark. Tuesday, 5:30 P. M. to midnight.

Friday, August 15.—With Mr. Glenny at the towns north, for perhaps a mile and a half. Quite a procession gathered behind us. *En route* we passed a group of women dancing by the path, whether for joy or grief, I cannot say. It soon appeared our friends were leading us to some interesting spectacle. Unexpectedly I caught glimpses of what seemed a great idol profusely decorated with gaudy clothes, feathers and paint, sitting in state at the head of the street. Approaching we stood before the corpse of a man who died yesterday, and was propped up on a chair or throne of some kind. Around his head was a cluster of rooster feathers, his face was painted, smeared with several colors. The body to the waist covered with the red wood (palm oil being used to make it stick). The gay clothes that covered the chair enveloped the limbs and feet. Among the throng around him I counted six weeping women, who kept up the usual slow dance and wail. They had on nothing but fringed belts of grass, or green bark. . . . Another thing I often see is an old or sick person given up by friends to die. These poor creatures look like skeletons, and their faces show absolute hopelessness, or that reason has already gone. They lie beside logs in the ashes of a smouldering fire, or go creeping about among the bananas or plantains

A common sight in the towns of an afternoon is the women making kwanga. They fill their wooden trays (not quite full) of the soft, fibrous, white cassada roots, which have just come out of the soak-baskets in the river. A little roller, six inches long, and size of their arms, reduces these roots to a white paste, looking like butter in a piggin (only white). When quite to the required consistency they wrap this in plantain leaves, and it is ready for use. In little rolls, finger size, they keep it for home eating. In pound and two pound balls or rolls they sell it at market, steamer, or station, one ntaku for two pounds, or they dry it and make it into flour.

THE MANIOC PLANT.

August 17.—I passed a pleasant day. Spoke in the morning service to the station people and natives, James Showers (a Cameron man) interpreting for me in Kibangi. They come, but seem all untouched as yet. One Sunday at breakfast, word came that a man had been murdered near by. On going to the village we found the murdered man under a shed. They had dug into him with a spear, to find evidence of his being a witch.

August 19.—Mrs. Grenfell was called to the bed-side of an important old chief, Gobojacka, lately a hale old man, who, by undertaking a trading expedition against all advice, is in *articulo mortis*. He is not dead yet, but his son says that when sufficient "savelist," is got for fitting obsequies, his breath will be stopped by a hand on his throat. He has the cheek to ask the loan of 600 ntakus (brass rods, the currency here,) worth of "savelist" to be paid in ivory. A nephew has two wives standing guard over the dying man, to let him know the

moment he dies, so that he may seize his share of the spoils. Ten
widows will be left to mourn him.   Three women are selected as vic-
tims at the funeral.

.   .   .   .   .   .

Gobojacka, alias Goka, is dead at last; possibly by some dutiful kinsman sitting on his chest, says Glenny, who made a medical examination
the evening before.   We found his town all alive at dusk; the street
filled with women going through their mourning dances, eyes shut
and wet; professional grief on their faces; dancing slowly, or shuf-
fling rather, almost in the same tracks.

.   .   .   .   .   .

Went to Gobojacka's funeral, or rather some three hours of it, for it
lasts many days.   The town was full of people.   Every one of the
palaver sheds was full, and every spot of shade.   We watched the
dancers in the second street from the royal mansion.   Three rings,
women together, girls, men, all prancing up and down, clapping their
hands on the hollows of the bare bent elbow in a rapid 4-4 rhythm,
then each in turn prancing into the middle and executing a higher
flying prance than the rest. . . . . In a nook near the woods I saw a
party of grave and reverend seniors, one of them a "Nganga" (medicine man, wizard), who were consecrating the coffin, but would not let
us see what they were doing. . . . . .

A friendly old man called on Mr. Grenfell this afternoon, and while
talking, a pot of malafu was brought and set before him.   And the
bearer announced, "You are accused of witchcraft," and summoned to
drink the "inkassa" (ordeal poison).   The old man gave the pot a
kick that broke it, and sent the palm wine flying, so answering the
summons with defiance.

August 20.—Soon after breakfast the *Stanley* and *Ville de Verviers*
steamed up, and the Commissaire of Stanley Pool District, and the
Commandant, and five other State officials, with Dr. Sims, landed at
the B. M. S. Station.   They have settled the Mobimo palaver with
Boukanya, and put a post there, and came to do the same here.
They dined with Mr. Grenfell, making sixteen at table.   The dinner a
grand success, with plenty, and that excellently cooked and served.
But it was a dumb crowd, all foreigners, and missing their wine, no
doubt.   The two great dignitaries, and Dr. Sims and Mr. Billington,
made a visit to some towns down the river a little way, going in the
natty little *Ville de Verviers*.   But the chiefs didn't come to the
friendly conference summoned for the afternoon, only one or two of
them; so it is deferred.

August 21.—Commandant and Commissaire dined with us again. Mr. Grenfell intimated to the Commissaire, that a post, with only a few men, especially without a white officer, and the natives expected to feed them, will only start a row, and the poor men will be murdered sure. Besides the natives, once in conflict with the white power, will hardly draw the line at "Bula Matadi." They will say Mr. Grenfell sent for "Bula Matadi," and will kill him. They have said, "We killed one white man (the trader) at Chumbiri, and we can kill you all when we like." So they spear a goat now and then, and steal tools when they can.

It seems a shame that the State should get the mission station mixed up in their "palavers." Things are in a mess. Mr. Grenfell is very anxious, I see.

About 9:30, a few came at the summons of the Commissaire to "palaver," in front of the house. But the other eight or nine chiefs, in spite of the soldiers, who went to call them, refused to come. So the Commandant, little pleased, gathered those present around him and made them a short and sharp speech, through James Showers. He said he would wait till noon for the rest, and then go, to come again with two hundred men. Hardly had this conclave broken up when a line of thirty odd armed men filed through the station from the back. The advanced few and the rear few were armed with knife and spear, the body of them had rifles gaily ornamented with brass nails in fancy figures. Just behind the guns were armed musicians, first with a kind of flute; second, a queer signal gong, consisting of two bells of iron joined at their bases. The bells were shaped like a monopetalous flower, and made, when struck, a deep, rather sweet sound, not loud, but heard very far. Next came a brass bugle. Then the rear guard with spears. This company was followed by another and another from both directions, most of them just like this one in their make-up, until about three hundred men (and a few women among them) had assembled. Mats were produced, and the people seated in a semi-circle twenty-five yards across. The chiefs of the region, all except two, had come, and the ten present were called to a place on mats before the Commissaire, who occupied an arm chair in the centre of the semi-circle. Dr. Sims sat by him to interpret the Commissaire's French to James, who stood before the chief, and with expressive gestures, but quiet voice and manner conveyed the message to the chiefs. . Glenny shifted about from side to side with a black box under his arm. The people had little idea that he had photographed them from a half dozen points of view. After half an hour's

6

conference, the chiefs accepted each a State flag in token of amity (!), and received a douceur of twenty brass rods each. Lingenji, the chief who murdered a man a few days ago, sat well in the front, and said, as the flags were given, "Is that all you are going to give? You ought to give us five thousand rods to be divided among the ten of us."

It is not a poor picture, a company of these fellows, squatting on the ground, each with his spearpoint in air, above the elaborately dressed head and bare brown back, deepest solemnity on every face, especially the wrinkled, foxy, impenetrable countenances of the old men.

BOLOBO, *August* 19, 1891.

DEAR AUNT ELSIE: It seems very strange to be writing to you from "the heart of Africa," . . . but being here is quite a reality, and I have got quite used to black faces, or rather bodies bare down to the waist, and half way up the leg—faces not tattooed exactly, but cut in strange and fantastic patterns; scarified in such way as would scare-ify many folks at home. There is a big pun for you to give Jimso. . . . . . .

It seems as if the words and lives of the missionaries were having no effect on these poor people. But I notice that they come to the missionaries, especially to Mrs. Grenfell, with their troubles, and many came to the services. This, at Bolobo, is a splendidly equipped station . . . good, roomy, plain houses for the mission force, with space for visitors, and quite a village on either side the station, for the labor needed for the work. Mr. Grenfell, besides being a thorough mechanic, is a scientist as well. So he has one little house for his photographing and another for his observatory. . . . . .

I remember all of you at Vine Hill, often mentioning each by name at the mercy seat where we may meet, "though sundered far." . . . .

[A few weeks later, and having returned to Leopoldville, he writes to this same aunt.]

I am among good friends, who have done and are doing fine work. The Lord had opened their hearts to receive me as a co-worker, and they help me greatly by their advice, and in more substantial ways.

Sheppard is still away getting men for our trip of exploration. He is a treasure. . . The little mission steamer, *Pioneer*, lies at the beach here nearing completion. My fellow-travel-ler, Sully, and a very smart (bright, clever) Scotchman, Adam-son, are putting in the engines.

A Russian, who was captain of an English steamer, is sick in a room at the other end of the court. As I sit in Dr. Sims' office, I look across the fruit and palm trees right into his win-dow. He is a gentlemanly fellow. An English Testament on his table furnishes a handle I hope to use on him.

Mr. and Mrs. McKittrick, of the Bolobo Mission, are here. Mrs. McKittrick, who is quite bright, makes the evenings much pleasanter than they might be, by games of drafts and "word-making and work-taking." It wouldn't be gallant to say who is ahead just now. . . . . The Bateke think there is nobody like "Mundéle Ndom," the black white man, as they call Sheppard. I am very happy to think that you pray for him and me both. You know my greatest sin is in not trusting my Saviour as fully as I ought. Pray for me that I may. Five, ten, fifteen or twenty years, however much time for service he may lend me, it will not be long. "A little while and ye shall see me." How sweet indeed when we are all together there. "Help us to live as we shall wish we had lived when we come to die." You remember that was Uncle's favorite petition. I am now in better health, or feel so, than I was a year ago.

Your loving boy,   SAM.

Many interesting details of the stay at Bolobo and at Chumbiri and of the return trip to Leopoldville, including a description of a short trip up the Kassai, have to be omitted. He got back to Leopoldville on the 23d of September. On the 25th of Oc-tober Sheppard returned with twenty-five carriers, who, how-ever, refused to go with them to Kinkunji. It being impossible to move in that country without carriers, a trip back down the caravan route to hunt up carriers was necessary.

The *Diary*, October 28, says: "I set out for Nkonko, southwest of the Pool, with seven carriers, my boy, Nkuku and Makindu, an inter-preter, who also takes charge of the cuisine. Picturesque scenery to-day. Carriers coming towards us through the shaded glades. Reached Makoko very tired, but refreshed spiritually by talking to a Liberian and my carriers through Makindu about their souls."

A few days later he writes as follows to his McCormick Seminary class-mates:

NGOMBE, OR LUTETE, OR WATHEN STATION,
CATARACT REGION OF THE CONGO RIVER,
November 3, 1890.

To my dear friends of "The Fowler Hall Clan":

My last mail brought me a "feast of fat things" in the "clan" letters, and I want to show my appreciation by answering at this my first opportunity—not strictly so, for I haven't been busy every moment since, but rest is quite an essential, you know—in Africa, at any rate—and I have had enough work to require it.

I am preparing to make a trip East from Stanley Pool, to see an unexplored country, "with a view to settlement," as the churches say to the seniors, when asking them to make a visit.

My colleague, Mr. Sheppard, a very capable colored minister of our church, was away, getting men to carry our beds, tent food, clothes, and barter goods, when your letter reached me and I was packing the goods, so as to leave at once on his arrival. You mustn't think we carry all the food (or, as we say here, "chop") we expect to eat; only such things as tea, sugar, a little Chicago beef, in case we can't buy chickens and eggs, etc. The barter goods are great bales of cheap cloth and coils of brass wire (to be cut into thirteen-inch rods, called ntaku), with a few bells, beads, knives, etc. These constitute our pocket book. So it isn't so big a thing as it sounds, when we say seven men will carry our cash. The stuff to buy our men's chop must also be carried.

Well, Sheppard came to time with the twenty-five men, but they took a panic next morning and skipped. They had heard reports like those that frightened the Israelites on the edge of Canaan. So I packed up, and started down to this region, now well under white man's influence, to get some more men.

The first day I kept the caravan road, by which some sixty thousand seventy-pound loads are carried yearly on the heads of the natives of this region around the two hundred and thirty miles of cataracts, for the support of the missions, trade companies, and state posts on the upper Congo. Every ten minutes, I really believe, I met a little party of these carriers trotting nimbly through the pretty avenues in the upland woods, a line of shining black backs, surmounted by boxes or bales, and always in Indian file, though the State has had the various chiefs clear a road twenty feet wide all the way.

Though very familiar now, it seems to me like a dream, that this should be done in thirteen years after the discovery of the Congo.

The traders certainly see reason to believe there is money in it; but what does God mean by it?

In order to save the constant expense of tents for its agents, the State has put up, about every four hours' march along the road, a house for white men and a large shed for the carriers. I slept at one of these posts the first night, and left the caravan road early the next day to go to a king's place, who, I thought, might furnish me the men I wanted.

At 8 o'clock I reached a market, and stopped there until the people should come, that my men might buy "chop," and I might get news about my king.

The people began to pour into the open place in the thin woods about half past nine. Every road (and they were like spokes of a wheel) contributed a line of men, and especially women, the latter loaded with fowls, native bread (which is fine fried, called kwanga), mustard greens, green pepper, palm oil (there is no butter or lard here), sugar-cane, pine-apples, bananas, plantains (a larger banana, not sweet, but good to cook), tobacco, cloth made of grass, and great gourds of milk-colored palm wine. Such a hubbub as they all made! I never get tired of watching these markets. They had lots of things I haven't mentioned.

I slept that night in a clean, tidy house a little larger than half a railway coach taken off its wheels, and much the same shape, but made of grass, cane splits, and bamboo rods. It was the king's house. But he had no men for me. So I have made two days' march to this place, where I had the same experience with Makito, the greatest king on the lower Congo. But I may succeed with him yet.

I am entertained by the English Baptist missionaries, who have a magnificent station here, but have only a few converts.

. . . . I was much helped by the words of Christian cheer you
all sent me. I pray God's blessing on the great work you have
to do, each in his field.   Your brother,   S. N. LAPSLEY.

MANYANGA, *November* 10, 1890.

DEAR MAMMA: I am going to-day from Manyanga South to
Manyanga North, and am now in mid-stream in a canoe! The
canoe is part of an enormous tree trunk, nearly four feet through,
and though not very symmetrical, is a sound and steady craft.
I am sitting on a folding chair, placed on a mat facing down
stream (to the left side of the canoe therefore). Makindu, the
English-speaking mission boy, with my helmet, umbrella, and a
little tin tub full of cooking utensils and chop tins, is at my
right in the bow. Mwanga and my boy, Nkuku, are sitting to
the left, while the crew of three nimble boys from sixteen to
twenty years, are close together in the stern. They have each a
large red and white bandana handkerchief about their loins, and
a brass bracelet on left wrist. They make wild shouts and draw
in their breath, "psh psh," as they ply their very arduous task.
Such another river never was to be sure! It looks narrow (until
you get well into it), but the terrific rush of the currents and
counter currents, and the swirling eddies which burst just under
us amid stream (rare fun!) show that an inconceivable volume
of water is forcing itself down this narrow trough, only a mile
wide. I contrast with this the placid sweep and pretty dimples
seen coming down the Pool, where the Congo is a dozen times
wider. A vast crowd of carrier   wait us as we land, and leave
the boat free. About one h·   l loads of trade-cloth, great
iron-bound canvas bales, a   thick and three or four feet
long, are at the landing.

LATER.—I am now sitt·   , on the bank awaiting the canoe to
take me back. I have been to a great market, an hour's walk
away from the river among the hills, to see about men to carry
me to Kinkunji. I made an engagement with one old king to
come Wednesday, he promised five men, I may get more, I need
fifteen. Very fine people these, though less romantic-looking
than the Bangala, Balolo, or Babangi (or Bayansi, their neighbors call them). Back through the mid-day sun, not very hot

MANYANGA.—Photo. in " Le Congo Illustre."

to-day as there is a breeze, and the ground is not damp or
steaming. Had fun buying things of the native women. Bought
a pretty little pot and water-bottle of clay, mottled like castile
soap. Eight bananas for one brass rod (ntaku). I chopped all
eight in part payment of a debt to a creditor, who is very exor-
bitant and impudently insistent in this land—my appetite to wit.
The bananas are shorter than those at home, and ridiculously
fat; very toothsome withal. The salesladies were divided between fear and curiosity—they generally accepted my overtures
toward good fellowship, and waited on me with as many smiles
as the one who put on my first pair of kid gloves (kid or dog-
skin?) in Cincinnati, years ago. I must say I think their faces
pleasant when they are content with a band of beads, or white
buttons, tied around the forehead. Sometimes, however, they
make frights of themselves by smearing a black pigment over
the face. Their remaining attire is constructed less on principles of modesty than of measured economy; consisting, poor
things, of only two scanty aprons. They are nearly the worst
I have met in this regard. The canoe comes not. Thanks to
the bananas, I have a comfortable hour yet to talk to you.

Manyanga is at the head of a stretch of barely navigable
water, of which Isanghila is the lower end. Between here and
there are several rapids, navigated with extreme difficulty and
no small danger, by several large boats belonging to the State,
and rented by the great Belgian Company here. It is thrilling
to hear how the native boatmen dive down and fasten the rope
to a rock in some places; and then, those in the boat painfully
pull up hand-over-hand, and a new grip is taken, perhaps to
to the bank this time. The rope once snapped with Mr. Heyne,
my English host here, in the boat, and a day's hard work was
lost in fifteen minutes; for they stopped only on a little island,
glad not to go on to the cataracts below. Just a little way above
Manyanga, I believe, is the rapid where Frank Pocock, Stanley's last white man, on the first trip, was drowned. I can see
the white caps of the waves—they dart up like pale silver-flames,
at this distance.

Yesterday, Sunday, I took my man, Mwanga (a queer stick),
and my boys, Makiudu and Nkuka, and the inevitable bath-tub

loaded with my kitchen things, and climbed up the table-land to the nearest villages. In an hour I found a market, where one hundred and twenty-five women sat in a crescent with neat, conical baskets, full of the kwanga, cabbage and mustard greens, eggs and chickens they had raised, and a crowd was coming to buy these, and the slaughtered pig and goat and the malafee, which some of the men had for sale. Vanity Fair isn't the best place to preach, so I walked on to the town of Vunda. It is a large and old village, almost hidden in the plantations of bananas that flourish on its rich plateau. There are two or three smaller towns, sheltered on the hillside and adjacent valley, making in all, to my estimate, one hundred inhabited houses. I found many of them afraid that I was a State man, come to tie somebody up; but I managed to scatter the news that missionaries had come to teach them about God and heaven, and would like to visit them. So, my little census finished, I sat down under a delightful shade tree, read Joe Vance's sermon in the *Observer*, on Repentance, took a brief nap on the leaves, and awoke to eat fried quanga and part of a tin of salmon I was surprised to find in my chop-box, finishing with quanga, and jam, and tea. (Jam costs about fifteen cents a tin, only!) Makindu cooks what he knows how very well, so I revel in rich, crisp quanga. I came back by the market, found everybody bustling about to get away, women with baskets on their heads, men forming little knots to go off and drink malafee under a bush. But I managed to get a small and somewhat interested audience to listen to a summary of gospel truth. They took more kindly to my singing, "Sing them over again to me," and "Nothing but the blood of Jesus." "*Menga ma Jesus Kaka.*"

I thought when first I passed through this cataract region there were no people. But this time I have travelled for almost the whole way, off the caravan road, and find scores of villages hiding under trees, on hill tops (contrary to the Scripture), and some nestling in valleys. All of these people are accessible, curious, docile, anxious to work on wages, and are easily brought under influence. But they are laden with superstition, and worse, laden with sins, led away of divers lusts, willing to become "rice-Christians," eager, some, to learn English for the increase of money-making power, but like us, and all sinners, at enmity against God. I enjoyed speaking to them often. But speaking through an interpreter, who has a glib tongue, but heart untouched, is far from satisfactory. It is a strange, sad feeling that one has in speaking to people who show that the ideas suggested are all new and almost unmeaning. I am getting impatient to find my own flock, and have a longing, not unnatural, to be face to face with my life work. Yet the longer God protracts the preparation, the more my gain. I need it, you can't imagine how much, and after all, I may be often on the wing yet, like many another in this and other fields.

I am very happy. I enjoy something more of God's presence than for some time past. The home letters last week helped me up, and the *Missionary* did too. Tell Rob to be sure to let the *Missionary* have something from me against the Monthly Concert on Africa.

This is Mr. Patterson's gift pen and it is a great comfort. But even *it* won't write *without ink*, so I must give it up.

In constant remembrance of my dear mamma,

Your loving SAM.

P. S. The hymn you asked about, sung to "Jesus, the very thought of thee," is called *Bernard* in church books, and *Belmont* in Gospel Hymns.

WATHEN STATION, B. M. S.,
(LUTETE OR N'GOMBE, OTHERWISE),
November 26, 1890.

MY DEAR MAMMA: I am writing in Mr. Davies' room, in "the brick house" at N'Gombe, a very pleasant room indeed, plenty of rugs, furniture, curios from the far interior, artistically arranged all about: two small elephant tusks, for instance, on the writing table, which is pretty well littered, I regret to say, with the letters I have been writing all the afternoon. Mr. Davies, a tall, sober fellow, in pretty, light flannel suit of fancy colors, and a little native skull-cap, has just come behind me to invite me "to refresh myself" with a cup of tea and a slice of rich cake; I fancy, the production of Mr. Percy Comber's larder. That gentleman is nice himself, and has everything nice when he can. Poor fellow! he was married only last June, while I was at Tunduwa—I signed the book. Now he is awaiting Dr. Sims, who has been summoned post-haste from the Pool, to say whether Mrs. Comber can safely undertake the trip to the coast and to England. She has been sick over three weeks, and this seems her one chance for life. He is not strong himself. Still he is resting from packing and worry, affectionate fellow that he is, by amusing the house children with shocks from a small electric battery. You will infer that there is little worth having that can't be had at N'Gombe, except health; for the sake of which the missionaries, with the aid of friends at home, have been gathering comforts about them here for several years. Three large and well-built houses, plenty of smaller accommodations, stores, boys' houses and pleasant grounds; and barring the very sterile soil, the finest station in the country by far. I have been on several sides of it hunting for carriers, and am always struck with the view seen miles away of the three snowy roofs on top of the hill, all the rest of the station hidden by the grass and trees between.

I came here Wednesday (yesterday) with seven men and seven boys, secured in Manyanga (north) district, and registered at Lukunga Saturday. I enjoyed a good dinner at Mr. Bentley's table (just in time), and after a rest walked over to Makito's village, an hour away. Here I found his majesty within the royal enclosure, a square hedged with the quick-growing fence tree, and in his house entertaining some young men. A solitary gourd of malafu showed that business, not pleasure, was on hand. . . . .

This morning I passed through a town where I was yesterday. I had talked about buying a basket from a woman, and so I hunted it up, and found she had gone.

"Who will sell this basket then?"   (I expected she had made arrangements.)   A man stepped up.

"How many ntaku (brass rods)?"

"Twenty," he answered.

"Whoopee! Tuba!" (*i. e.*, "Say" again—a less price.)

'Ten, then!" he said, for a starter.

"I'll give you three."

Chorus from all around: "H-m-m-mm!"

I repeated, "Tuba!" (*i. e.*, say again.)

He said, "Kumi!" (10.) I said, "Ve!" (no.)
He said, "Nana!" (8.) I said, "Tami!" (5.)

And then I said to my boy, "Twala mbele" (i. e., bring a knife, which was worth five ntaku.) I take down the basket from the wall, handing him the knife, and start off.

He stopped me. "Ve! N'kento ka tendele ko¹ mbele." (No! the woman wants not knife.)

I to my boy, then: "Twala ntaku tami." (Give five ntaku.) The man said "seven." I hand him six and march off, knowing he is satisfied, but will never own it. Indeed, he came running after me with a better basket, for which he asked fifteen, as a "feeler," and went away happy with eight.

You asked about the seasons. From May to last of October, on the Lower Congo, and I think Kassai, it is dry, no rain at all, heavy dews, cloudy a great deal, and often at night feels very cold, like November. From last of October to Christmas is the lesser rain; needn't be surprised by rain any afternoon or night, some good, hard ones, with lightning. January is the short, dry season. February to May tremendous and sudden rains, filling the torrent beds that cut up this whole region, so that at short warning one may be separated from his men, tent, chop, etc., by an impassable river where he had crossed a dry ditch. . . . I was caught Thursday. At 3 p. m., a dark, blue cloud lined the horizon; a deep fringe of white hung over this like a white curtain for a great way around. Up to the meridian spread an innocent-looking gray cloud, and the sun shone behind. My men said, "Stop!" but the cloud didn't approach, and the wind was blowing towards, not from it. I went on a little, and then decided to take advice. "Twala nzo!" (i. e., Bring the house—tent.) "Malu! malu!" (i. c., Feet! feet!—quick.) The cords were in tangled knots. Before the poles were in their sockets the rain began. The fellows worked well; some under the canvas, some at the poles. Up it went, and we were fastening the guys in spite of the wind, when a big gust blew all over. I had on my Mackintosh, but they were shivering with the rain on their bare bodies. Some two hundred weight of water collected in the folds, while the capita, Zezela, and I tried to straighten

---

¹ Ka-ko, negation, like ne-pas, in French.

all out for another pull. The rest crouched under the tarpaulin ground-sheet, meant as a water-proof flooring. I'm afraid I shied a peg into the lot to make some of them come out and try again. But by getting the guys ready, the tent stood when we raised her this time, and there were plenty to drive the pegs and draw the cords taut. The travelling bed was in collapse. We quickly made another of brush, spread over the blankets (dry as a bone in the water-proof valise), and putting on a dry change I was comfortable in a jiffy. Those boys made a big fire in spite of " the present rain and the cold"—they sabby how. I had a cup of tea before I was dressed and took my quanga, tinned bacon and beef tea at my ease, turned in at dark and slept till *cuisinier* (they get this from the Frenchmen or Belgians), was jingling the chain-kettle for tea at daybreak. . . .

SUNDAY, *November* 29.—Have made four trips to Makito's, the last before day this morning, to catch him before he started on the case of gin presented by the philanthropists of the State. He was on a terrible spree yesterday. He and his fellows drank four large bottles of spirits before my face in a few minutes. It makes me shiver almost to see the poor wretches wriggle with delight as the fiery stuff burns their throats and stomachs. As Dr. Sims said yesterday, "sin is a long way ahead in this country," referring to the evil lives of white men, especially the State men.

I got nothing this morning by my trip but a good appetite and some more experience. So I'm off again.

Mrs. Comber, attended by Mr. Bentley, Mr. Comber and Dr. Sims, started for Lukunga yesterday. An hour after they left, came on one of the hardest rains I ever saw. I think they were prepared for it though. Mrs. Comber cried bitterly as the hammock men bore her away. Still she may get home to her mother all safe, but it is hard to give up a life's plans in a day and all the hopes of doing a useful, happy work with her husband here.[1]

I am much the better of this toilsome trip. I am not afraid of the road, knowing how to take care. . . . But good-bye now. "All joy and peace in believing," my wish for you, my darling mamma.   Your loving   SAM.

---

[1] Mrs. Comber died, and her husband followed her in a few months.

SHIP-YARD AT KINTAMO (LEOPOLDVILLE), WITH VIEW OF STANLEY POOL.

Photo. by Mr. ADAMSON.

CHAPTER V.

FROM LEOPOLDVILLE UP THE CONGO, KASSAI, AND DUMA-KWILU, IN CANOES, AND RETURN.

DECEMBER 11, 1890, TO FEBRUARY 1, 1891.

CONCLUDE TO GO BY WATER TO THE KWANGO.

RETURNING from Lukunga, Leopoldville was reached on the 3rd of December.

December 4.—The *Diary* says: Captain Dhanis, Commissaire of the new district of the Lunda and Kwango region, tells me of the dense population and hostile character of the natives in his district. . .

The Portuguese have abandoned their outpost, Kassange. . . . So I decide to use the men I have just brought from Manyanga in going by water to the Kwango. . . .

December 11.—Isabel's birthday. Sang, "O God of Bethel" at prayers. Soon afterwards we were off to select ten of my Manyangas for the trip, and have the canoe lashed alongside the *Reed*. Sheppard in fine trim. His little monkey, "Tippoo Tib," from Stanley Falls, is along.

We leave Leopoldville by the steamer *Henry Reed*, for Bwemba, through Mr. Billington's kindness, again. Mr. Raine, another missionary of the A. B. M. U., is fellow-passenger with Sheppard and myself.

December 15.—We camp above Kwa-mouth at the Misongo towns, in the Bayansi country.

December 16.—We buy a fine canoe for 2,000 ntaku,[1] and two good pieces of cloth. This gives us a fleet of two good canoes, having rented one from the Bateke King, Nguba, at Kinshassa. After reaching Bwemba I am sick there several days, but Sheppard looks up more men and collects paddles, kwanga, and mats, and other necessaries for the trip.

---

[1] About $10 worth.

[From Bwemba he sent back his *Diary*, from June to December
(175 pages), from which occasional quotations have been made in foregoing pages, and he writes the following letter home.]

Written at Bwemba, or Chumbiri, where two very kind Bap-
tists have entertained me three times, and twice taken tender
care of me in sickness,—Rev. C. B. Glenesk and Mr. A. Billington,—December 22:

My Dear Mamma: Just a line in addition to what the ending
of my *Diary*, just sent to Rob, will give you. We are going,
God willing, nearly down to the Kassai to-morrow. We have a
good crew and a lovely boat, and with awning it will be cool
enough in the river breezes.

My boy, eleven or twelve years old, is here to make bed, and
keep my things. We have tent, beds, chop-box, and cooking
tools, of course. I found one of my men had learned to cook
pretty well while with the State. Another is equal to washing
even a blanket, getting out *three-fourths of the dirt*. Sheppard
is a most handy fellow, and is now a thorough river-man. I
don't feel quite green myself now. His temper is bright and
even—really a man of unusual graces and strong points of character. So I am thankful to God for Sheppard.

Now that I am near the point I have been aiming at so long,
the junction of the Kwango with the Kassai, I am dissatisfied,
and wish we were able to strike further up the Kassai at once.
Though if other Protestants, or especially other Presbyterians,
could occupy the open fields (so promising!) higher up, I should
be glad to make the base for them, and let our own enlargement
be up the river system that joins the Kassai at Kwango mouth.
So you see I am in a strait betwixt two. God only can guide
me. I have none other to decide it for me. I have had some
good times of late and some progress in the knowledge of Christ
I trust, but many deadly chills, from which I seemed to rally
but slowly. Just as he rebuked my fever the other day, after
one night of it, so he has drawn me again to a closer seat by
Him. I often wish and hope that increasing spiritual life may
be the experience of you all at home, especially of the three
"littlest," whom I shall not see as little ones any more. I often
long for home, not regretting my work or call here at all, but
living in the dear scenes among you all, almost hearing your

voice sometimes. Every day, almost, something suggests a place where I used often to be, or a familiar name. Then I take a little trip there, and come back quite refreshed. I am *never home-sick*, not even when a little unwell. But I think now of two trips, one to you all in a few years, not more than four likely, from my reaching here; another to a lasting home, which I hope to reach, after a good deal of the good work I was sent here for. I shall take a Christmas trip, perhaps, in a few minutes, if I don't sleep too soundly, to see the Anniston Christmas. A merry, merry one may it be to the little folks, and the big folks too, and the young ladies from school! "Merry Christmas to all, and to all a good-night."

From your own   SAM.

December 23.—*Diary:* Being all ready for the start, I went with Sheppard to the chiefs of the men he had engaged, and we give "books," that is, little written contracts to each of the three chiefs of the five Bayansi boatmen he had hired, getting them at 190 rods [1] each, for a two-month's trip in the "river of the Babuma" (Kassai). A fathom of narrow red-blanket cloth binds the bargain. This gives us, with the ten Manyangas secured in the Cataract country, and Makwala, employed as an interpreter, and my boy, Nkuku, seventeen men in all, or nineteen souls in the two canoes. Sheppard divided the crew, making a Yansi boatman named Nkala, a magnificent specimen of a native and a beautiful waterman, captain of the smaller canoe, he having another Yansi and five Bakongo as his crew. We had the rest in the larger canoe. Both the canoes were loaded with great skill by Nkala, the load being carefully stowed amidships, a row of standards inserted on each side to keep all in. Paddlers were ranged fore and aft the cargo, a pretty thick row of bare black backs, most of them looking anything but at home with the new implements, the paddles; only the Yansis in the bow and stern being perfectly trained to the trade. We had three in the big canoe, two very strong fellows right astern, with big broad paddles, their blades painted blue by Sheppard. Their business was to steer and propel both

About 3 p. m. we pushed off from Bwemba, or Chumbiri [it is known by both names], with a cordial farewell from Messrs. Glencsk and Raine, who watched us out into the swift water. Then down we dropped fast. I soon had to knock away the little awning that Mr.

---

[1] About $3.80.

Glenesk had made to shelter me. It made the boat rock so that it was dangerous. At 4:45 we camped on a sheltered sandbank, had the tent up, and supper prepared by Nsenga, a handsome Manyanga boy, who is a good cook. Then we had prayers, Congo hymns, and good sleep, and I awoke quite recovered next morning.

December 24.—Off at 6:45 A. M. At 12:30 we stop to dine at Misongo again. "Tippoo Tib," Sheppard's monkey, affords unbounded amusement to the villagers, chasing and running from them by turns, finding shelter on Sheppard's shoulder, where he devotes himself to pretending to hunt for game in his beard and even in his eyes, with busy fingers and smacking lips. [Tippoo is a Stanley Falls monkey given to Sheppard by Mr. Vries, a fellow-passenger with us on the *Afrikaan.*] At 2:15 we are off again.

At 4 o'clock we are at Kwa-mouth, and find the steamer *Stanley* at anchor, with several big canoes and steel boats alongside, and having aboard plenty of Bangala, with the chicken comb down their foreheads, and other black soldiers and marines lounging about their cantonment, on the shore. The new Commissaire, Lenaire, is here *en route* to Chumbiri (Bwemba), and thence up to his capital at Equatorville. The *Stanley* is to go as far up the Kwango towards Kinkunji, as may be, and drop Mr. Hochstras, and let him go on in canoe. The *Stanley* is then to return to Musyé and ferry the "Expedition Vankerckoven" across the Kassai. It is now *en route* by land from Stanley Pool to Chumbiri, and is a little army of State troops sent to overawe and pacify the country.

We round the point into the Kassai, and camp in a lovely spot on the right bank (our left), with grand trees meeting overhead and covering a spacious open place made for camping. We dine on roasted ears of corn, kwanga, and chicken. Sheppard bought at the town near by, three chickens, some "goobers," and seventeen rolls of kwanga.

December 25.—Christmas day. At 6:40 we start and keep the right bank. We passed many points with rushing water; but between were frequent back currents made by this very strong water outside, which was a great help indeed. We each shot an eagle. We were often under overhanging trees; and the small canoe having some trouble under some low limbs, one fat Congo caught hold, and was left dangling in the limbs as the canoe floated back down. He and his partners then "struck" against their Yansi captain, Nkala. So at 11 o'clock we had to await them, and settle and quiet the rioters. We improved the time by stalking a guinea on a big tree in the wood near by, and scared off a lot of buffalo by the shot. We stopped there and ate, and then crossed the river, and felt how strong the midcurrent is, being swept far down.

You can imagine how it swirls around the corners (its course is like one of our crooked rail fences), when you think of the Kassai, Sankuru, Lulua, Loange, Kwilu, Kwango, and Mfini, all being rushed through between banks only three hundred yards apart. Besides, the banks are steep and lined with big boulders, and some of these have tumbled into the water and make whirlpools like a full-blown rose, fine to see,—at a safe distance.

But our canoes were made for the business (regular merchantmen), and our Yansis, at bow and stern, probably got their first ideas of the water when their mothers strapped them to their backs, and helped to paddle the canoe up this same river to Babuma, as they call Musyé. It is simply beautiful, the strength and grace and ease with which they carve the water in a delicate piece of steering, or bury their paddles in it to round a strong point. I can feel the boat spring forward when Mpururu and the "Bishop"[1] strike the water. Sometimes it is so bad that the three Yansis with us, and even the other two ahead, jump into the boiling water, and standing on rocks, I couldn't have guessed were there, put the boat through between the stones and past the bad water by main force.

But it will reässure you of the real safety of our canoe and goods, and surprise you perhaps, as it did me, to know that of these five professional boatmen, only one can swim at all. I say safety of our canoe and belongings, because if *I* didn't remember my swimming lessons in Big Mulberry Creek at home, *I* shouldn't be caught in such a place. I can't forget in canoeing or in hunting hippos that my life is not mine to risk needlessly.

Well, that exhilarating business has filled our Christmas day, heightened by the pleasure of getting the big guinea fowl.

Pulling along the left bank we heard a deep, mellow horn far up, and presently saw a fleet of six long Babuma canoes floating down, nobody paddling, only steering and floating; but gliding so fast! They were loaded down with piles of yellow pottery (unglazed) for Stanley Pool. We soon reached the village, a small Bamfunu town, not visible from the river. The people are like the Bateke. Fowls, eggs, and buffalo meat very cheap. We camp at another village in the edge of a plain, and had a fine Christmas dinner.

---

[1] Sheppard.

7

Here is our menu:—

1. Soup, ... Guinea.
2. Roast Guinea, Kwanga, and Worcestershire Sauce.
3. Roasting Ears of Corn.
4. Leg of Eagle and Buffalo Steak.
5. Papaws.
6. Roast Nguba=Mpinda=Goobers=Peanuts.

Then we had prayers with the Bakongo; then sleep, and a storm before day.

December 28.—At 6: 40 we are off.   By 9 A. M. we had shot an eagle, a duck, a wood-pigeon, and a hippo, who *would* rise and snort in forty yards of us.   Sheppard says it was my bullet hit it.   The monster sank, then an anxious minute, then big bubbles burst up.   "He's dead," Sheppard cried, "drowned"; and then explained how they often take a panic, and drown when shot in the head.   We spent some time on the sand bank waiting, and shooting, and then a yell and a dance struck up.   The hippo had risen, and was floating down.   We got into a canoe in a jiffy, but had a long, tough, patient pull before we could tow the great lump to the sand island.   Then all hands jumped out and rolled the "nguvo"[1] through the shallow water by the bank. Presently the *Stanley* came up to us, and we dined with Captain Matson and Mr. Hochstras, and the clever little Dutch engineer, while the steamer's Bangala helped our men cut up the "nguvo" and load it in the *Stanley's* canoes. . . .   Then our fleet was lashed alongside, and we pushed up the big river, making as much distance in the afternoon as we should have done all day, without the lift from the steamer.   I saw the little engineer's sketch-book full of pictures of many things interesting from every part of the Congo Valley.   After supper, the *Stanley* having tied up for the night, we paddled on by moonlight to a place where we could cure our meat.   A camping place was hard to find at night.   A big camp of Yansis that we came up on bade us look further, there was no room for "Mundele" (white man)! At last we found a fine harbor in a little creek, and landed about 10 P. M.   It looked as if not a match would light, but at last a fire was started, and the men rigged up frames of sticks, and covered them with meat to smoke, while every available vessel was filled with boiling meat.   Sheppard and I took the tongue.   We kept for our men about two hundred and fifty pounds, and left for the steamer's men near a ton.   Our men kept us busy squaring palavers between them. "Whose meat's this?"   "He's got my meat!" etc.

---

[1] Hippopotamus.

December 27.—We get off at 8 A. M., and see the *Stanley* just battling with the strong current away up river. We had had too much nguvo, and hence lazy paddling. We stopped to eat in a plain, where the hills stop, and the river gets out of the narrow gorge, crooked like a rail fence, into the open flat land where it widens immensely.

We see the first round houses to-day. Tippoo Tib keeps getting out of his basket, where he should sit with the chickens, and gets ducked in trying to escape to the bushes. In the afternoon a big red monkey was spied. Four shots were devoted to him. The last, a Martini-Henri bullet, brought him down. We found a good shady sheltered camping place for Sunday, and he was roasted for supper (lasted three days).

December 28.—Sunday, but an unhappy day for me, because misspent. Promised to fast; ate myself sick! Raining a little all day; the men glad of their mats, which they spread over hoops stuck in the ground, a little like a gypsy wagon top. The Kassai is a mile wide here.

[The copy of the diary sent home closes abruptly here, having by by some accident lost five or six pages out of it; but a letter written a few weeks later, and relating to this date, gives the following details of the occurrences for the next few days.]

On Sunday I began to think about getting sick; on Monday quite made up my mind, indeed I put on two coats and two or three blankets to sweat the fever out. When we went to sleep that night in a pretty little town half lost in plantain trees, children and chickens, it was gone, but it was anything but pleasant while it lasted.

Somehow whenever I am in the oven stage of a fever, I think of the dreadful fire to which these poor people are exposed, and then of the agony in which our Saviour said, "I thirst," and it does not seem much to bear. Next morning the Yansi "Capita" (Nkala) made a gypsy wagon arrangement out of mats, as a shelter above my bed in the canoe, and in that way I passed the towns that line the beach for miles, just there all called Musyé (or Mooshié). They nestle among the thick plantains planted in the rich low ground along the banks of the Kassai, with a gently rising green ridge behind.

In one of the largest of these we had the fortune to find her majesty, Queen Ngankabi, at home for callers. It is a nicely shaded group of ordinary houses, a row of skulls adorning the comb of the roof just in front. A group of people seemed undecided how to take the unusual spectacle of a white man in a canoe, and still more undecided what to do about our request for a guide to show us the best channel to the Kwango, and to introduce us there.

"Is Ngankabi at home?"

"Yes, that is Ngankabi," pointing.

"Good morning, Ngankabi," and I put out my hand, for I knew she must know how white people greet each other. So she came at once to where I lay, stepped into the canoe alongside, shook hands and then stood on the beach. She is a woman of fair height, not fat, nor very slender, with the small features and thin lips, characteristic of the Babuma. She wore only an ample cloth of closely woven grass, dyed black, much like camel's hair. She is quiet and dignified, and has the good manners that many royal persons on the Congo can show.[1]

We asked her for the guide. She said, "Wait for my son, he is coming, and will give you one, maybe." So we waited, but nothing came, and we soon withdrew and paddled along the bank, passing forty or fifty little clumps of houses, all hidden in banana (or plantains), you can't tell which, until you get near enough to distinguish the black stem of the banana.

At one little village we managed to get an entrance and stopped, but the people there, like all the rest, told us the next town above was "much better, much better." So we decided to try that fine town, make an early camp and buy kwanga, especially as I was still half in bed. I heard a great racket, plenty of little banjos and drums, and the air full of screams; but as it seemed to be only the women's ex-

---

[1] Here is Mr. Stanley's description of Gankabi as given in his book *The Congo and the Founding of the Free State*, Vol. I, p. 424.

"About an hour after we left camp we were met by two well-manned canoes, in the foremost of which there was a female paddling vigorously for a few strokes, and then in a peculiar style bringing her right arm akimbo to her waist. Ankoli recognized her, and cried out, 'there is Gankabi!'

"Naturally to meet such a celebrity, the Queen of Musyé, the friend of Gobila, and the principal person on the river, we halted very quickly; and without the slightest sign of timidity she steered her forty-five foot canoe alongside. This very action on her part denoted a person of character. She brought her paddle inboard, and with her right arm to her waist, she examined us keenly and attentively for some minutes without speaking.

"She probably was listening to Ankoli, who, like all other natives, begin at the beginning of a story and continue to the end. Her attentive survey of 'Bula Matadi' was with interest reciprocated. Excepting her hair and color she had othing negroid about her. Draw a figure with the Martha Washington type of face, color it with rich bronze, put short frizzy hair of a negro above, and one has a striking likeness of Queen Gankabi. If of full length, draw it to represent a figure of five feet seven inches, of sturdy, square shoulder, substantial form, with an ample grass cloth about her; bare bust, bare feet and bare head, with no ornaments about her except a heavy copper wristlet, and you have a life-like picture of Gankabi."

citement I didn't look out; but I saw that we didn't stop, and learned afterwards that they had offered to fight the best they knew how. The men brandished their spears. Those who had guns pointed them, and the women danced their little idols up and down, and chattered at us with all their might. Sheppard was a little amused and a great deal provoked at their folly. I don't think there was much danger of their shooting, unless we had actually tried to land.

The next big village was a little less wrought up, being calm enough in fact to reason with us, that as we were devils they thought it quite proper to keep us out. So we had to make for a strip of sand over a mile away, across the waters, paddling up and across the mouth of the Mfini, in water dyed black as ink in the swamps far to the east; then into the yellow Kassai water, skillfully avoiding the sand banks, where one can easily turn over if he tries. At last we landed, just at dark, on the only dry spot to be seen in that waste of water and low damp grass islands; specially guided there, don't you think? A big storm came that night, but Sheppard was equal to it. He ran here and there, always just in the nick of time, and saved the canoes from being swept down to Banana, and carried the long ropes into the men's shelters.' Then he swung on to the guy rope just as its peg gave way and the tent was getting ready to fly over land to Kiutamo.

Next morning I was up just in time to join in a fight between two of my boys. "Mundele is sick," they seemed to think; but the paddle came down on them very loud just as they fell to the ground. The very briefest fight I ever saw, I think.

"Kwanga out and in this hostile country, what shall we do ?"

"A hippo will bring them round." So we took four men. I forgot all about being sick. And after awhile we found a bay just full of hippos, fifty perhaps. A lively cannonading began. Quick as one let his head come well in sight within a hundred yards a bullet went that way. You ought to hear them roar, "vm-m," sometimes this side, sometimes beyond, until Sheppard got one right in the centre of the forehead and it was finished. Back to camp, on a large sand island, and a picked crew was detailed to go and watch for the hippo to rise. They went over and camped all night on the sand bank near where the dead hippo went down, and the other hippos made it lively for them. Think of a tremendous hog, tall as a man, too big to come in the front door, and with an enormous horse-head to match, coming snuffing and snorting in forty feet of you, and staying there for all you could do to scare him away. Several of the men cried like babies for sheer fright.

[We resume copying from the *Diary*.]

Neither camp-fire nor brandishing of torches nor shooting could keep them from coming on land and snuffing and snorting like a Mogul engine in forty feet of the distracted boys, Batula and Quininga, had hysterics and cried like babies. But at dawn, New Years, we heard a shout, which I think some of our crew had kept awake to hear, "Wiza Nlungu!" "Come (with the) canoe!" And the remaining canoe was off in a jiffy with all available hands.

But the game was not landed without difficulty. An old lady nguvo, presumably relict of deceased, would interfere in spite of all. At great risk of being spilled out of the canoe, or worse mishap, Nkala and his gang drew the big pile of meat to shallow water. Then the fun began. Axes and knives were busy, and tongues for two or three hours. We had our hands full keeping the young gentlemen from quarrelling over pieces of meat, as they were tossed over to the pile; though each man was pretty sure of getting half his weight in meat. Soon the Babuma scented the prey, and came as the eagles do to the carcass: the best friends we ever had! Some were allowed to carve, and they improved the occasion to abstract goodly chunks in an original way. Every few minutes a Babuma would have to go to his canoe. He walked very lame I noted, and presently another one, who caught his wink, would walk innocently to the spot, where his partner had stood by the canoe and to his great surprise, doubtless, discover a piece of meat, which had in fact been dragged there by the carver between his toes!

The Babuma had a lot given them, and they divided their spoils with great impartiality, and then readjusted the partition by a free fight, or game of grab. The prince, son of Ngankabi, looked on till they had finished, then he coolly stepped in and helped himself to the choicest share of what they had arranged so nicely. The rest of the day was taken up in buying kwanga in Musyé with part of the meat.

January 2.—Makwala, and Nkala, and crew are back this morning. We strike tent and are off, but have to stop when we had only turned the corner of the island; moor the canoes, cover the cargo with the tarpaulin tent floor, and pile in for two hours with the boys under the mat-shelters they had pitched on hooped switches. We stayed in them until the storm had ceased. We then went on without stopping until dusk, on the strength of plantains that Mpururu had roasted in his mat-house. We went by the side creeks among islands, to avoid the strong water in the main channel. But "*nota quæ sedes fue-*

rat," not "*palumbis*" but *nguris;*[1] and all of them smelt the blood of their dead kinsman, and the biggest bulls began to snort and move towards us, nose and ears out like enormous horses. But "they did not come nigh us," as it is written. We passed a few fishing hamlets on great sand islands, and at last came out into the main left, or western branch of the Kassai, a half a mile wide and very swift. On our left was an unknown expanse of sand, grass, water and mimosa, a shrub growing from six to fifteen feet high, soft stem and prickles, light green small leaves like touch-me-not, and large yellow butterfly flower. [See Botany if correct.] Beyond this was another channel, by the right bank; and on a dim horizon a long, low, wooded ridge.

It seems that these rivers all make, in the first place, a tongue of sand-bank in the middle, the deep water and the main channels being at the banks.

The night found us paddling uncertainly on, looking for high dry ground with some dry wood, until we were obliged to go across to an unknown village, in the edge of the grass plain, and take chances. Though timid, the people let us land and sold wood. The tent was pitched right in the opening before the beach, but it was nine o'clock before we got anything warm enough to eat. The wood was all soaked, and then only fire enough was made for tea and warmed salmon, a stray tin of which made its way with us through many vicissitudes and exposures, but (we were very thankful) it was still good. Mosquitoes that night. Small breakfast next morning.

January 3.—The Yansis said they didn't want to go any further. Were offered the privilege of stopping right there while we went on. But they decided not to risk being caught and tied as soon as we were gone, and so went to their work with a good will. The king offered us a goat as a token of good will, but we had no room for him. We passed slowly up under a sandy bank, averaging six feet high, topped with tall grass, and here and there a marsh thick set with a reed used for mats, a brilliant green. A light canoe propelled by a smiling couple (the head man who had offered us the goat, and his wife), skimmed past us as we toiled along. I should have said three rather than a couple, for she had her baby strapped to her back, but steered and helped paddle too with capital skill.

Their good report prepared a welcome for us at the town not far up, where we breathed the men, and bought some chop, goobers, kwanga, etc., and departed, leaving a crowd at the landing waving us goodbye.

---

[1] "Here are the homes of the hippos." (Free translation.)

Nguvo meat is free currency here. By the way, our partner of this morning got some nguvo meat for his kind offices.

Some seven towns were passed on the beach, and ten or more others are so buried in brilliant plantains that the houses can hardly be seen at the back.

We stopped and chopped at a town with round houses like hay-stacks, about fifteen feet in diameter at the base; and camped in another town early. Very nice to do so, as it was Saturday afternoon.

There are a few houses here, a little lagoon from the river furnishing clean water, and a safe harbor for the canoes. These are water folk, Babuma fishermen from Musyè, come to get fish, so their chief may have a good lot, ready dried, to take and sell at Stanley Pool, which is a hungry region, and a monied one, but a hundred and fifty miles away by water. Yet the canoes ply unceasingly between this region and that, forty to forty-five-foot canoes being used. We have two of that kind, and find a similar one lying among the little fishing smacks here. Nguvo still fetches plenty of chop, though getting mighty of odor. The head I kept for the uncommonly fine teeth, Sheppard's dash to me. Dogs, boys and women are contending for the pickings on it.

The children up to five years are naked except a harness of fancy colored beads, like pony harness. We notice cowries (small shells made in Birmingham) tied to the ends of babies' hair, some fifty on one little head. Some have heavy brass anklets.

We can see across this branch, and two miles up an opening, leading to the united Kassai, perhaps.

January 4.—Pleasant day. "Newness of life" in my lesson to-day. Our breakfast was fried eggs, and kwanga cooked with fragments of tinned bacon, and boiled sweet potatoes, and tea with brown sugar.

Had palaver with Nkuka, who stole some potatoes, and wanted to fight honest Baba, the deaf and dumb boy who pointed him out, and then when committed to tent for trial, packed up his traps and made off for a near village; the other boys followed, and bye and bye he turned up in disgrace, for I had taken his book (contract) and with-hold it and prospect of pay till he proves a better boy.

Have just finished Farrar's *Life of St. Paul*, Vol. I. Very stimulating to mind and heart, though I can't agree with him always. Read also Daniel, Hosea and Joel to-day. The boys gathered to hear us sing "My faith looks up to thee," to "God save the Queen" (America), and some other hymns.

A Nganga, or medicine man, has been busy all day in a house fifteen feet from our tent. Profane eyes are not granted a peep; but we heard a banjo going incessantly, and the sound of incantations. The Nganga would jabber a few words, and the patient repeated them as rapidly, then a shake of the rattle, then another sentence also repeated by the patient, then a rattle, etc. After a long time the patient comes out with mystic lines in red and yellow ochre drawn down his chest, and around his shoulders, or a row of colored dots down his breast and back.

These are migratory fishermen of means, Babuma from Musyè; hence their shabby houses here, but they have plenty of stuff and chop, such as kwanga, corn-meal made into little black rolls of dough by mixture with bird seed, and it is good fried, and they have plenty of potatoes and goobers. The Bamfunu live half a mile back, I think, in the well-fixed, cosy towns among the plantains.

Service after early supper; "Flee from the wrath to come;" Makwala interpreting. I asked them "Do you know how to keep from the awful fire of wrath?" Their "No," was sad to hear, and they felt it so, I thought. And sad it is that we can hardly make it intelligible, the whole idea of spiritual religion being so new to them.

January 5.—Brisk trade before starting. Coasted along sand-bank on left bank, passing a wooding camp of Stanley's, with a good chop town near, but back from the river.

What is that? Makwala's canoe stopped, he talking English with a great lean fellow on the bank, who says his name is "Isaac Abraham," and is a man left by the steamer, and is pretty far gone with hunger and mosquito bites, for the natives stripped him of course. We took him in and gave him chop.

We got into a shallow channel, and had to back out; but found the back road rather difficult, not deep enough for big canoes, going over a corn-field, as Sheppard puts it. But came out into the reunited stream, and find on the same bank a very nice Babuma town back a hundred yards from the bank, and having a deep pond full of grass before it. A canal cut from the river turns this into a fine harbor. We crossed this in our canoes. Stopped and dined and bought chickens, and a punt pole, made of a long palm-leaf midrib with a spur spliced to the end, the better to push the canoe along in water shallow enough. We also bought a fish-basket to serve as a coop for chickens and "Tippoo Tib."

Saw a hopper filled with ashes of grass, whose soda-salts (instead of the usual potash or lye, as in our best ashes,) were being leached out, the liquor to be evaporated and then furnish the native salt. It is a gray stuff, very queer to taste.

Large, round houses eighteen feet in diameter. Cordial welcome. Crossing the river we entered Wissman Pool, an enlargement of the Kassai, somewhat like Stanley Pool, on half scale. We thought it wise to call a palaver with our men, and let them into our plans, that they might be reässured, by knowing that we had a definite aim and destination on this unknown river, and that we are not going to get them into any scrape. Then we sent Makwala and Nkala ahead with canoe and men, to find a camp for night. We caught them at dusk pulling reluctantly out from a desirable town. Young spokesman on land will not look at dash of cloth, nor hear of our camping there. We were Ndoke (devils) as at Musyé, and if we slept in the town we might carry off some of them by night.

In no very cheerful mind we put out into the dark water again, for we were running the risk of catching on sand-banks and being capsized by the strong current. But we were guided safely to a white streak visible for some hundred yards, and are comfortably housed and fed again; camped on a large sand-bank high and dry, in the Pool, off the town which repulsed us.

This town lies at the base of a long ridge which extends at right angles back from the river, and is a conspicuous landmark for many miles (both up and down), on account of a remarkable row of borassus, straight, erect, and distinct, like a file of soldiers, and a quarter of a mile long, I suppose.

The borassus is a palm, which grows to a good height, generally on lonely, grassy ridges. Straight, smooth stem, with strange bulge from half way up to the crest, like a bottle upside down. Crowned by a cluster of fronds, each like a palmetto fan before it is fastened together, and much like a modern windmill.

January 6.—We didn't start on acccount of a threat of storm, which was soon made good. A white line rose from the northern horizon and soon ascended drawing a white cloud curtain after it, and as this mounted higher it was followed by another, black-blue and awful to see. A gray rain-cloud climbed up after these two. In five minutes the three were mingled in a driving mass of low storm-cloud, and the wind rose and drove us into the tent, which was secured against the worst. After the storm, too much wind held on for us to try to go. So we hunted hippos. We were interrupted by "Sail ho," and the *Stanley* came down. The captain took our foundling from us, and showed us a map of his Kwango trip. Said he had passed a little creek on the right going up, of which he had some doubts now, was afraid it might be the real Kwango, the road for Kinkunji. If so, he has put Mr. Hochstras down in the wrong river, for he passed this stream. But he has left him in a land of fabulous plenty, on a plain by the river, the other branch. He and the little Dutch engineer (the only Dutchman in State employ) are very kind and hearty. "Kassai," the native dog, was left as company for Mr. Hochstras.

January 7.—Up a big river, with a line of small towns on each bank, much more numerous on the north bank. A narrow line of sand islands in the midst of the mile and a half of water. We threaded our way among these and came out where the stream is one again for a little while, and crossed the southern half to the south bank. A troop of nguvos blustered mightily, had to get a bullet among them to quiet the big bow-necked bull that led them towards us.

It was 3 p. m. before we found a good place for chop. That was in a little town of round houses. We bought some eggs, and chopped quickly. Saw a little house full of wooden idols, with heads rudely carved, dressed in bits of cloth painted red (handkerchiefs). They couldn't be induced to sell them. We moved on a little and camped a few hundred yards away at the upper end of the towns, beginning where we chopped. They were very much pleased to have us, but I noticed an axe in one town, which I knew no steamer sold, unless some hands stole it and let the natives have it.

January 8. Start off early in a little channel along the left bank. The country in from the bank is lower than the present level of the river, and holes are cut through to let in the water, and fish too; the little channel had a row of sticks almost across, and to these are tied baskets for fish, from which a fisherman in his canoe was taking up the nightly catch, when we passed this morning. And yesterday evening the women were splashing the water out of the little pools they had made to keep the surplus fish, to get ready for supper, or sell to us, just as a farmer's wife would go to her coop for chickens, put up for like purposes.

This is the beginning of the special region of the Kassai fish-trap, of which I have read. We meet them at every nice piece of woods, and at the river side, revealing the presence of people, even when their towns are hid by the forest. A lot of stout sticks, from four to six feet long, are stuck firmly in the bottom, where there are some three feet of water at the bank. They form a square or cylinder with the door in front. This is closed by a neat falling door of straight reeds or sticks which is suspended, to drop by a trigger, which the fish springs when he takes the bait. We find some down early in the morning, and the fish inside waiting the rounds of the fisherman.

There is another town half a mile up at the mouth of a little channel, in the edge of a dense low-lying forest. A large canoe lay at the beach loaded with pots of malafu, or massanga (sugar-cane cider), almost ready to start for Kintamo, we heard. I can hardly believe it, unless it was an expedition from Musyé, of Babuma middlemen.

We came into a stretch of quite still water, not even a back current. What next? We pass some woods and reach a low plain which comes to a point, where another stream, yellow with sand and very swift, joins the Kassai, entering it through a maze of sand islands; this must be the Kwango.

An hour and a half brings us to a large village[1] (on a clay bank six feet above high water perhaps), where a crowd of people gathered to see us. They were a little timid, but not ill-disposed, afraid to invite us ashore, yet not at all desirous that we should leave. So we landed quietly and stood about, as unconcerned as could be. They crowded around us in a few minutes, but if we happened to look straight at any fellow, he would dodge behind somebody like a flash. Finally Sheppard, born trader, started buying wood and fish, and the ice was broken. Women crowded around with enough wood to build a small shanty, and fish for two meals, fresh, sweet and large, for a trifle.

The little black monkey, "Tippoo Tib," was the object of unbounded amazement and delighted admiration. Every wise wink, and every time he stuffed another goober into the little pocket in his jaw (for storing chop when his little stomach is already stuffed), called down shouts and screams of laughter.

We chopped under a circle of small trees planted as an arbor. We had sun-perch, corn-bread, bananas and tea. We called for our coats, but the wall of people around us kept the wind off, so we didn't need them. We prepared a dash for the king, but they persisted in denying that they had one, though Makwala asked in Kiteke several times, and they quite understood.

We withdrew to an island opposite, camped, and went for hippo. We soon found a drove, but though we wounded several, we got none, though I got fever from wading too much. We returned to camp and found plenty of people had come to see us.

January 9.—During the night the tent wanted to go away in a storm, which would have been bad for me, as I was already sick, but it was kept safe by "Mundele Ndombe," as they call Sheppard (ndombe means black, and mundele means "man with clothes," but it is the usual word for white men, as none but white men wear clothes). Shep-

---

[1] Boleke.

pard during the storm was here, there and everywhere, fastening the ropes and keeping things safe.

As we were finishing breakfast, two notable canoes crossed the swift stream to us. One had in it eight men, one handsome young fellow with a brass bound paddle in the prow. The other had a crew of women, headed by one with a pleasant face, wearing a large waist cloth of checked stuff, the only nice cloth in town perhaps. They brought wood and kwanga. There was the usual chaffering (in signs counting on fingers), during which we had occasion to bring out our goods to sun! Stretched the sixty-yard piece of save-list (coarse flannel) to its full length, and sunned even the brass wire, to the great admiration of our visitors, who seemed to think that it would stimulate trade to have us for neighbors. We gave a present to the notable woman, whose name is Antinobe (Greek), of some cloth and salt, and received a handful of kwanga in token of appreciation.

My fever coming on, I turned in between the blankets and ordered tea. The fever went pretty high, but was down to normal before midnight, thank God!

Sheppard went after the hippo we wounded yesterday, but came back empty handed. A great crowd had come from the town opposite. Antinobe's father, who seems to be king, turned up and accepted his dash, coming into the tent where I was lying, to acknowledge it. Sheppard says there were three or four hundred here, and such a hubbub! At sundown Sheppard could hardly get them away; so our prayer for their confidence is answered.

Boleke is a town of three parts. Near the northwest angle of the Kwango delta is the residence of the queen. Next, south of this, is a most compact town of round houses, two hundred yards long, and some fifty deep, there being three rows of houses parallel with the left arm of the Kwango. These houses are like great hay-ricks, large enough for many people (packed Congo style), and are as close together as tents in a cantonment, with only room enough for comfortable passage between them, and enough plantains and other small trees to make the place habitably cool; and then there is another collection of houses a little further up stream.

On the slope of the clay bank are drawn up at night a line of light canoes, so numerous that they make a kind of gridiron, and it's a pretty sight when they come back at evening, coming round the top of the island, where we camped, and shooting across the stream in twos and threes, like birds on the wing, lighting exactly; all loaded with fish from many a shallow and pool in the delta. For these people are, first and foremost, fishermen, and seem a pure and simple race, as fisherfolk should be. Perhaps the Master will have his Peter and James and John from them before long.

They have the pleasant small features of the Babuma, and like them are part or connections of the great Bateke race. Makwala's Kiteke carries us very well through. There are plenty of children, and the people seem healthy. [The awful rotten sores of the Bayansi are not found: a people of good morals.]

January 10.—Departed after an exciting chase of chickens which had been turned loose to graze. Our course up the Kwango is nearly due south. Some ten canoe loads of people had come to trade, or to look. Telling them we were going up their river to find a place to build a house and live, we left them on our island and started.

One of the elders of the town waylaid us at an opening in the grass, two hundred yards up, and begged us to return and accept a dash he had for us, which is only one of many efforts to induce us to stay. We promised to come back. Antinobe's father was at the third, the upper town, and endeavored to persuade us to build on a place he would give. "No need to go up river," he said.

We hugged the bank on the right (our left as we went up stream), going under overhanging limbs, to which the high water raised us uncomfortably near. Under one great limb, the current swept us into the lower branches, and out in strong water and nearly turned us over. It only scraped off four or five boys, who took to the water or to the tree, and we left the Absaloms to catch us by land. But on their way to where we stopped for them, three or four natives demanded pay for passage, and whether for fun or experiment, they grabbed Mampuya, who yelled for me. But he forgot my name, so he called Mr. Clark's, "Misitu Colicky! Misitu Colicky!"; and that was his nickname for a good while. A rescue party went ashore, and the natives left quickly.

We camped in a town an hour and a half up. It is a large and roomy rural town, its houses not jumbled together, but divided by plantain clumps, and garden patches. There is one little arbor and square, shaded by lime trees, and two iron-wood trees, where we have pitched tent at dark this Saturday night, with groups of pacific villagers around us. They show no peculiarities of dress or marking, and have the small, sometimes skimpy get up of the Boleke folk.

Sheppard struck up trade at the beach, and so we got in. The beach is quite unique in having some nine little pits in the hard clay, evidently used as mortars for crushing the oil from the pulp of the palmnut, and the discarded kernels, inside the red brown pulp, have formed an artificial beach.

January 11.—Sunday. I read Amos and Zephaniah, and worked out a list of kings and prophets with their eras, as best I could. The people say there is another big town near, to whose king this belongs.

They say elephants come and ruin their madioca gardens, which are a quarter of a mile away. At night we heard a man yelling to frighten the "nyau"[1] away. If Mr. Nyau heard his caterwauling, I wonder if he ever comes back.

The villagers developed sad hankerings after our property. We left sundry articles of clothing and knives with them as keepsakes. During the evening they kept lying around and trying to slip the boys' cloths off them from behind. Sheppard watched them to catch one of them with the cloth in hand, but they were too sly for that. They actually pulled at his five-shooter as he lay snoring at the fire (eyes open), but he didn't like to let that out of his grip. The name of the people is "Bankin Kima" (the local name of the clan).

January 12.—At noon we stopped at a town, where the few people insisted on shrinking in, trying to hide behind their shrugged shoulders and elbows (hands clasped behind neck). We asked, "Nsu?" (meat). Response was, "We" (no). Asked again, "Bakaba?" (kwanga). They answered likewise, "We" (no). But we sat down quietly and ordered chop, and by the time the boys had it ready, their confidence had so grown that they brought quantities of plantains and plenty of eggs and fowls.

There was also a great deal of nsafu, a fruit of the shape and size of a small egg, only slenderer, purplish in color. When put in the coals five minutes, or boiled, the pulp becomes soft like butter, with a savory flavor, rich and acid, as nice salad. A sack of seeds is left. There was a beautiful, low, branching tree called "pome," making a dense, cool shade, and a fine place for palavers at midday.

Pulling out we paddled under an island strip near the same bank, the left, which is lined with a deep fringe of wood. Thus sheltered lies a town, or succession of them, our chopping place being one of the furthest down stream. At the landing places under the trees, groups of interested spectators watched us pull slowly by. [Stopped here again January 24th.] These are the same people here as at Boleke, indeed it is not five miles away.

---

[1] Elephant, pronounced "Neyou."

Our men got in a good humor and started a song, transcribed here:

Air: *To be sung with enthusiasm.*

M fu mu ma tu - za Ngu di n ga nga hm!   M

BARYTONE AND BASS (*impressively.*)   hm rm hm hm

fu mn ma tu - za ngn di nga nga hm.

hmmm   hm

Before sundown we encountered another stream coming in on the left bank, and camped on the first or westerly of the islands in the mouth. The mouth forms a true delta, and has three arms, two of them one hundred and fifty yards wide, the other smaller.

It can hardly be twenty miles from the Kassai. The land lies low, not a hill in sight, but fine forests bound the horizon, and the angle between the two rivers that here meet is heavily wooded. This is the home of the water fowl, big and little, and there were some fifty hippos lying on a sand-bank in mid-channel. Before night closed with rain, I got a wild duck: a long shot for me and my sixteen bore. There is a small town on either side below the junction.

Four men came from the nearest town, with a goat to sell, an old "Daddie" being the principal salesman, with three other assistants. "⸺ ' ' knives," Sheppard offered. "No! ten" (counted on fingers). "Tau. 'u, we usually give thirty" (that is, Sheppard pointed down the river, pointed at the goat and shook his fists three times). "Sixty" (six shakes of "Daddie's" doubled-fists). Sheppard takes a bit of flannel, four yards, measures it by the length of his outstretched arms twice. "That is, two fathoms, and see how regally it wears;" wrapping it about his own waist. Daddie's partner points at the cloth, and then at the bundle of brass rods and shows ten fingers, that is, "ten ntaku to boot." Sheppard recommends that the old gentleman convey his live stock back across the river, and wait for a more unsophisticated customer. He puts his finger to one eye and gives that feature a pull more expressive than pretty, and waves to the other side; but don't let them go for all that. So, after awhile, we got the goat at about one-third Kintamo price, as they wouldn't drop to one-fourth. But not so fast. Daddie's second says, "You said a knife, too." Sheppard assumes lofty disdain and indignation, saying to one of our boys, "Moyanene, tie this goat tight! gentlemen, let me show you to your canoe"; and all part in high good humor.

January 13.—And they see us off most kindly this morning. We cross the mouths of the Duma. Running the gauntlet of the fifty hippos aforesaid, we were very nearly swept down by the current on one that wanted to fight. We were kept safe though, and caught the pass at the very point of the island and didn't have to shoot. But you can imagine my valorous attitude, standing guard in the big canoe as it glided past the point, with my Cape rifle cocked, and Sheppard with his pistol.

We enter the Duma, or Kwilu. Clear black water, loth to mix with the yellow Kwango, as cream and strawberry juice hold apart, with a wavy line of division. Another song, and the canoe sped into the deep bay the Duma forms just above its mouth on the western side. We went through one of the channels between the four little islands in the mouth, into the main channel, three hundred yards wide, which we crossed to a good town on the right bank. It sits among the trees a hundred and fifty yards back, a swampy piece of high grass in front. Through this the people have cut a canal, so the canoes can pass up to the town. Our big canoe couldn't go up the canal, the bends being too short. Some men at the beach, on a dry point below, pointed a gun at us to induce us to seek chop higher up.

So we pushed off, and are away again between banks everywhere low and swampy. With difficulty we found a dry spot hidden in bushes, under which we thrust the canoes and chopped. [How good our chop did taste those days.] There is a row of villages behind the strip of forest on the river, the land being quite high enough, a quarter of a mile back.

On our way up we are attacked by Mrs. Nguvo, whose calf was doubtless hidden near our bank somewhere. Sixty yards off she popped up, snorted and was gone; but we could see a faint ripple moving toward us, and she parted it at fifty yards. Snorted, and did the same at forty, thirty yards, and the same instant, crack! a bullet struck a little short and bounced to her head. She rose again pretty soon, but two hundred yards off.

There was a lovely plain between the woods on the south bank, like a field of ripe grain. We are going east—east—whereas the Kwango

8

comes from the southwest. We find room for the tent in a dense
wood on the hill-side. An elephant-path to the water showed it to us.
Close quarters! An elephant came round and blew his horn, which
the frightened Manyangas answered with interest, and he went his
way. Big rain. A small Congo rolled through the tent, and moist-
ened things somewhat.

January 14.—Dense forest on each side. Apparently flooded
throughout. There is a grassy plain behind it higher up. I am
already tired of being shut in between walls of green; the river is so
much narrower than the Congo or Kassai that the trees make a
greater difference, quite shut out the view. But the dark green is
often relieved by the rich clothing of vines of a lighter shade, which
climb thirty or forty feet from the water, and sometimes break into
hanging columns.

We ran into a little bay where lay a new canoe, the fresh chips all
around. The people presently found us out, and came timidly at first,
but finally crowded around us with a fair amount of chop. But
kwanga is running low.

This is the first village which is actually on the bank of the Duma.
We pass noble forests of great trees of varied colors, bark and style of
growth, with lofty and wide-spreading branches, and but little undergrowth to spoil the open view beneath. It is a "veritable parc
Anglais," [1] as the Belgians would say.

Little canals every few minutes are piercing the forest, and probably
affording passage for canoes at high water. Some are left open, some
are closed with fish-proof fence of sticks, with only space enough left
for the insertion of traps. Sometimes there is a little shelf by this
aperture, which I don't understand.

These Kassai fish-traps would indicate that there are people here
that are kin to those on the middle Kassai. Saw a new style of fish-
basket at the town we passed at noon. It is a cone with the base
drawn up inside, but there are no angles except at the apex, and all is
gracefully curved.

The current of this river was slight yesterday, but it seems stronger
the further we go, and rushes under low hanging limbs so hard that
it is dangerous to heavy laden canoes;—necessary to keep the head
out until the stern has cleared the tree. The small canoe neglected to
do this to-day (indeed Nkala always turns in out of the strong water as
soon as the head has passed the limb), so the current got the canoe
broadside and turned it square, at right angles to its course, the paddlers lost control of it, and into the bushes it swept. They tipped her,

_____

[1] A real English park.

and quantities of water poured in. The boys took to the tree, and so lightened her. Nkala and his fellow Yansi held her steady and baled for dear life, and presently they followed us up again.

We find a camping place in the edge of the forest on the left bank, where elephants had broken down the trees for us, somewhat. There was a fresh print of a tusk in the bark of a tree eight feet up, and mud which he rubbed off against the trunk. Loud horns, answering each other from left bank to the right, at sundown, probably giving warning that a white man (rare visitor) was on the river.

January 15.—Hardly any progress, and nearly out of chop. We waited long on promises of kwanga which didn't materialize. As we toiled along I called to Nzczela to start a song. "How can we sing when kwanga is finished?" They have plantains, but are lost with any bread but kwanga.

In the afternoon we ran into an inlet on the left bank, landed and opened negotiations with a handful of natives. "Bikaba! Bikaba!" (kwanga) we pleaded, and showed cloth, knives and brass rods. You could see their eyes sparkle at the sight of the spear-pointed case knives. So I made signs to the effect that only kwanga would fetch knives. So we got some kwanga and corn. Nkala, the Yansi captain, and Makwala, who had an eye for trade, were gladdened by the sight of a fine tusk of ivory, two and a half feet long and thirty pounds weight.

Before chop was ready two strangers came up. Evidently they were Bakongo! And this slim one Makwala says is his "brother," actually his "brother," his blood first cousin, and is from Ngombe Makito, on the caravan road from Lukunga to Stanley Pool. [This boy is with us to-day, April 13th.] They had come up on the *Peace*, and seventeen of them had deserted on the Kassai somewhere. "Plenty chicot (cat o' nine tails) and small chop," was their excuse for deserting. All but these were lost trying to find their road to Kiutamo. They saw some of them speared by native tribes on the way.

"Where's the rest?"

"Don't know."

"All right, go get your stuff, if you have any, don't tell anybody, but when we start jump in and come along with us."

These natives are lean and ill-favored, too grasping and treacherous to trade, and besides, they have little to sell. They name one price for their ivory, and they claim another when that is brought out to them. Their game seemed to be, to chaffer until plenty of goods were brought out on exhibition, then raise a row and make a general grab amid the confusion. Sheppard had seen this game played before, and got our men and goods safely into the canoe, keeping the villagers quiet by a little firmness. There was one gun among them, the rest had bows and arrows. The gent with the gun promptly retired at the start, and left his partners to help themselves through the difficulty. The two Congos got aboard and came with us, in spite of howl and claim of five pieces of cloth.

The villagers had seen our rifle, revolver and double-barrel.

We went and camped on the grassy bank opposite, and divided the goat bought a few days ago. The two capitas, Nkala and Nzezela, were commissioned to prepare it. Parted it between the three messes, aggregating nineteen men, in solemn conclave. The head and skin, and most of the intestines, were included in the distribution.

I saw a new type to-day, a man of large size, with marked Indian profile, with his hair rolled into a thick queue, nine inches long.

January 16.—Set out in low spirits, kwanga finished and four men sick. But our Provider had prepared two towns for us, where, after the people had time to decide that we were not dangerous, we got plenty of kwanga and corn for the present need. The men brought bows and arrows, no spears nor guns, but sold bows for three ntaku (brass rods), six cents. Very strong bows, I could hardly bend them; hard redwood that glistens like mahogany. The arrows, light, twenty inches to two feet six inches long. Some had sharpened wooden heads (poisoned?), some iron, beaten rather thin. Six inches from the point is a joint in the shaft. The part with the head fits into a socket in the other part, and is secured in it by a string wrapped around. The obvious design is that the head may remain in the wound when the shaft is pulled out. Don't see any poison on the heads.

The other town very friendly and eager for trade. They begged us to stop all night, but hadn't any chop to sell.

At 3: 30 P. M., we passed a deserted camp of booths, perhaps left by a big Yansi trading expedition we met at the junction of the Kwango and Duma (a long way for them to come!).

We had passed, when Sheppard thought he heard somebody in it, and so went back and called. A wretched object, almost a skeleton, crawled out of one booth, too far gone to care whether saved or not. He was another souvenir of the *Peace* fugitives. We prevailed on him to get aboard, and gave him some chop, in which he took more interest, poor fellow. Friday, to-day, so that shall be his name, by Sheppard's suggestion. He had a scrap of raw elephant hide, not quite sucked dry, in his piece of basket. Deformed by a crooked hand, a stammerer, and hardly strong in his wits. We were very happy in having picked him up, barely in time too. Camp late, in thick bush, but dry. Dark before all straight. Last bit of candle went to-night, except a morsel saved against accident.

January 17.—Fine day's progress. Some exceedingly strong water, but Sheppard, who is pilot now (we are tired of the Yansis putting us into the bushes), skillfully used the current so as to make it throw us across more quickly. Passed two gents who were peeping at us from the forks of trees. Chopped in a lofty, open forest, "veritable parc Anglais" again.

Nkala brought us a new fruit, size, shape and skin of a muscadine, but red, and has a stone. Tastes sweet, but leaves a flavor of turpentine in the mouth. From cut bark exudes a gum much like pine rosin, but less pungent and more aromatic. The Bayansi call it ntsumbele (the correct spelling of the name of their town, which we call Chumbiri).

Begin to pass a chain of wooded islands. Camp in wood, on north bank, opposite island No. 4. A loud noise startled us, and I heard cook exclaim "Nyau!" (elephant: au is sounded like ou in out). Sheppard went to see about him, and presently we heard the crack of his rifle, and I hurried through the tangle of brush and broken trees to share the hunt. Heard Sheppard say in a queer voice (meant for me to hear and not the elephant), "Don't come; they are right here!" Lo, and behold, he and Nkala were safe up a tree! an example which I followed quite promptly. He had had a close shot, and had put the Martini-Henri bullet into the elephant's ear. But when the brute seemed unconcerned about it, he did not try another until he had made sure his retreat. And the elephants went a little way off for awhile.

The natives came after the shot, to see who and what it could be. Brought their bows, but had no mischievous designs; rather good-looking fellows as they came through the woods with their bows in their hands. We soon made friends, and they went away and came back with some chop. They say "There is a good white man up the river not far, who buys plenty chickens, and has made a big house." We heard the nyau before day, breaking down a tree in the woods not far from the tent. The woods here look as if a cyclone has been throwing the trees about, big trees six or eight inches through.

January 18.—Sunday, a mixed day for us. Sheppard had to buy chop, for the men were out, there being a steady stream of natives with kwanga, goobers, etc. I had a good time apart in the forenoon, but spoilt the afternoon by eating too big a dinner, as I have done in other places besides Congo.

I chatted with Makwala, Nkuka, Nshimi and Ntino about the soul and spirits and sorcery. They believe that the spirit (moyo) leaves the body at death and lives in the woods; Nkuya they call it then, or if a bad or mischievous one, Ndoki (devil). They say the Nganga, or medicine man, usually comes from a distant town. His principal function is healing the sick. Bats are his familiars. He claims to have a special posse of ten bats, which nobody but himself can see. These he puts in the sick man's house, after putting green peppers on all objects in the room except the patient. "Bats," he says, "don't like pepper," and they light on the sick man, and leave a scratch on his arm, which shows that they have exercised their healing powers on him, and then they go to the ceiling. The Nganga then goes outside and joins the men who are drinking palm wine (malafu) to the patient's health, an essential part in the curative process. Then he addresses the bats, and the men all hear the bats answer the Nganga; it sounds as if many men and women were answering from the roof of the sick man's house. Makwala and the other boys say they have heard this sound. And they have seen the Nganga work another wonder. "Put boxes, cloth and anything you want to, inside a house. Let all the men go out except the Nganga. Presently all the goods will be found in the Nganga's quarters, another house, though you watch between the houses and can see nobody pass from one to another. When you pay the Nganga a ransom, you can get the goods back."

In the evening I spoke about the fall, and the devil's history and present ways. "You think the Ndoki (devil) busies himself mainly to make you sick, hurt your trade, etc. He is wiser than that. He goes about to make you do wrong, sure that if he can do that, he will have you altogether in his hands after awhile."

January 19.—At 10:35 A. M. we reach a plain on the right bank, where Mr. Hochstras, whom we met on the *Stanley*, was standing by the water-side to meet us. It was pleasant to see the blue flag, with the lone gold star, waving over a goodly little station, the first on this fine big river. There is a fair-sized house of hewn sticks, walled and thatched with grass, and quite a cantonment of booths, all in an open square, cleared out of the grassy plain; and the whole done in about fourteen days. He has about thirty good soldiers to do the work, and I see the preparations for another house for Captain Dhanis, when he comes.

But think of it! He has sent Cameron, his sergeant, a capable Lagos man, in a canoe with six men and plenty of ammunition and chop, to go up *this river* to Kingunji, for canoes. Cameron has been gone seven days. I try to show him that this is not the Kwango, but the Duma. He stands to it that this is the Kwango, because it is the larger one of the two branches. I reply that, though wide, the

Kwango has plenty of sand-bank, which it would be hard for the *Peace* even to pass; whereas the Duma is deep all the way, and could float any steamer on the Upper Congo. Also this point, where we are now, is nearly E. S. E. of the junction, by my compass.

He says he misses the hills about Kingunji, and well he may. This country is as flat as a pancake, and the black water is good proof that there is plenty of flat, swampy country up stream from here. By the way, this must be a long river, too, for the same reason. I tell him this would be Captain Dhanis' best road to Nuala Yanvós.

I had a cup of tea in his pleasant living-room, which he has made quite homelike, and has nice table, side-board, desk and shelf, rough enough, but neatly covered with cheerful cloth. Fancy hats, photos, a row of pine-apples, etc., on the wall, make it look quite natty.

The station is in the edge of a three-hundred-acre grass plain, and surrounded by a numerous and friendly population, who bring the greatest abundance of country produce for sale, and at ridiculously low prices.

In the afternoon Mr. Hochstras and I went out for guineas, only to come back poorer by four cartridges. These are a smaller kind than the gray ones that grow tame at home They are wild everywhere here. [This is "Lower Guinea."] They are, perhaps, properly called partridges, and are much like prairie chickens out West. They are brown, with bright red feet and gills The gray are called "nkilele," the brown, "ngumbi."

We had a lively discussion after chop, on the Kwango question. I had misplaced, that is, put my maps in the wrong box. and left them at Kintamo; so I could only cite the natives at the town below the junction. They said, "You'll come to two rivers, one on the right hand, Nyali Mbe (red); the other, on the left, Nyali Mpiri (black); which I found, and these same names Mr. Grenfell learnt from the natives five years ago.

Mr. Hochstras replied, "I asked Matson to let me go up that water and look if he live Kwango, and he say no, this live Kwango; that another pool like Wissmann Pool."

We had a big storm at night Grand cannonading ten miles off at first, then we heard the artillery train rolling quickly towards us, finally halted and roared at three hundred yards distance.

January 20.—Reveille on the Duma! Faraji, the Zanzibari table boy, sounds it very well.

Yard full of chickens and goats, like a farm-yard!

The soldiers have been making a fence of tall sticks all round. The people raised a row when the Zanzibari soldiers ejected an intruder from the enclosure.

Many styles in dress of head and person, and varied types of features, in the immense crowd who come to sell chop, bows and arrows, blankets, goats, and fowls.

We bought two goats for eleven handkerchiefs (twelve handkerchiefs cost in England, in one piece, 1s. 5½d = 35c., and are worth twenty ntaku at native prices at Manyanga). Sheppard was seated on a mat in the centre of a ring of these traders, chaffering, bantering, joking them, and working them down in their sliding scale of prices. He soon had a pile of good things around him, especially some neat calabashes and some strips of buffalo hide.

By the way, yesterday we found a rare curiosity, a box or basket of small sticks, with a stick running through three pairs of loops, the under one of each pair being put through the upper, and the stick passing through the under one haspwise. I have been trying to make a picture of it for you, but I can't do it.

Sheppard is taken with violent nausea from an overdose of quinine, a bad habit he has of taking two weeks supply at once, to save trouble. In the afternoon, fever rose to 104, but went down at night and didn't come back.

After lunch I went with Fuani, the Zanzibari head-man, Nkala, Makwala and Nkuka, to see the nearest town up the river. Two men of the towns were waiting to serve as guides and to introduce us. We found that the towns lie parallel with the river, behind the trees that line the bank, and that a main path runs back of all the towns, with little paths leading off to each town as we came opposite it, just as at Chumbiri and Bolobo. The guides belonged to the farthest towns, so we took the trunk line through to their home. Their town has five clumps of houses, each framed of midrib of the borassus palm, roofed with leaves of same, which also, neatly woven in on the bias, close out the weather on the sides and back. The front, under wide eaves, is made of something like cane splits, the yellow alternating with the others, burnt brown or black, or else a yellow, a red, and a black.

We cross a pond, or full branch, of dark water, colored like tea, from a swamp through which it makes its way. That's where the Duma gets clear black water, like Dismal Swamp water! We returned through the row of villages near the river, and found five neat little clumps of houses, built like the first lot, but sprucer and in fresher colors. They look very cosy amid their gardens.

Among the trees that shaded them were a good many dark green orange trees, and under one of these was a group of native men carousing on their native wine (sugar-cane, I think). "Every prospect pleases, and only man is vile." I estimate there were forty-eight houses here, and from two hundred to two hundred and fifty souls.

In one house I found a fully equipped loom for weaving grass cloth, that is, from the inner bark of the mpusu palm, I understand. Three stout sticks form a frame, one is fastened to the roof, and one is supported midway between the top one and the third, which rests on the ground. Simple but complete, with the comb-like arrangement and shuttles. I don't know enough of it to be more precise.

Found Sheppard still hot, and put him to bed. I slew a ngumbi (guinea), very red gills and feet, brown back, and grey breast spotted with red. Delicious chop.

January 21.—We conclude to turn back. Wish we could go on, but a State canoe has already gone farther than I could hope to go, and I can see Cameron at Kintamo. My men are discouraged, and one is sick, and not much time is left on their contracts, so they need no persuading to get ready for the down trip. They cordially agree to decorate each canoe with a flag of bandanas. Three little goats, bought at one-fourth of Kintamo prices, made figure-heads for our little flotilla.

Good-bye to our friends at the river-side, leaving a fine blue flag with Mr. Hochstras as a keepsake. He is the same young man we saw near Ngombe, on our first trip from Lukunga to Stanley Pool. A very pleasant and bright fellow.

Down stream like a steamer! Men singing all the songs they know. Mpururu, whose doings made us christen him St. Nick, used to whistle the following, as they sang—

Heavy slur notes sliding into one another.

The drift of the words is somewhat obscure, but sung slowly by several mournful voices it has quite a weird effect.

A fine chance for compass and map! We camp at a grass bank, where we chopped the goat, of which occurrence our crews retain lively recollections, and seem to think it a happy precedent, as shown by their reviving one of their early songs. "Sumba nkombo na sabalanga" (buy us goat for paddling). Opposite is the tough town where we picked up the two stray Congo men.

We passed Camp Friday this afternoon. "Fulliday," as the boys call him, is another sort of fellow now. Very grateful, and usually busy at drudgery the others like to dodge.

January 22.—Leisurely start. We stop at a town to make certain that Makwala is correct in saying that the whole river, as we've seen it, speaks Kiteke. I think it must be nearly true.

At 12:30 we land on the easternmost of the islands in the junction of the Kwango and Duma, being attracted by a shoal of hippos towards the upper end. A snow-drift of white birds sat near and nearly scared away our game, by flying with a roar of wings as we drew near. But the hippos stayed near, and one or two arose every minute. Sheppard popped one as quick as a flash before he could hide again under water, a lovely shot. The men had him on the beach in half an hour after we landed, and cut a few beefsteaks out of him to eat over night.

January 23.—I should have had a good day's work, but failed to "Seek him early," and so idled away most of the day.

Sheppard bossed the carving, and gave each gang a part to jerk (dry) over a slow fire.

I got some doves, which made a fine "mwamba (palm-oil) chop."

Moyarene had a row with Mpururu; the latter trying to hold Moyarene from behind, got cut in the forehead with a knife, and swore he would spear the boy. We told him that we would tie him up for Bula' Matadi, if he repeated or attempted to carry out the threat; and ordered Nzezela, the boy's capita, to whip him, which was done; and then we had peace.

To-day walked out with three cartridges, and came back with three doves, one duck, and one cartridge.

Sheppard and I crossed the right arm of the Kwango delta at its head, and visited the town in the angle of the rivers. We found a long but sparse string of rather neglected looking huts named "Mbe."

The people, back from the right bank of the Duma, here are called Balilaxa (x equals the German ch).

January 24.—Most of the meat is pretty well dried, and so we load up and are off at 8 o'clock. The canoes have all the load they want to carry, the gunwales being within six inches or less of the water. We stop at the upper end of the town, where we chopped on the 8th of January. The town is a mile long, in groups, of course. We went ashore, near the top or upper end, and walked through six groups, each averaging eight large houses, which are round and generally built in circles with a yard enclosed and kept clean as a pin. Orange and nsafu trees make a delightful shade, and there are plenty of chickens and goats, and, in one town, a good many new-made pots drying in the sun, preparatory to baking. The people are pleasant and well-behaved.

In the woods, between this and the next group, we came upon a circular space under a great tree, which the boys recognized with glee as a Zandu, or market-place; indeed, there were lots of fresh pine-apple rinds lately emptied on the spot. That is why we could get but little chop, as every one had bought and sold all that they had or wanted that morning. The markets are held once in four days, just as on the Lower Congo. Above and below the houses which we visited we saw four other similar groups, making altogether a population of four or five hundred. Makwala says that there are one hundred fighting men.

We see plenty of pine-apples in the bush by our path, between the groups. Several pretty streams fall into the river above and below the villages. They say their name is "Mbe," and that they have no king; which means that they are afraid that we have, or may have later, some bad palaver for him. A large Babuma trade-canoe lies on the inner side of the island, and near by is a camp of booths with a red flag over it.

Our whole crew is eager to get on to Boleke, where there is plenty of fish and kwanga, and everything is so cheap and the people are so friendly. We hear rumors here of troubles below, whether near Boleke or Musyé I can't learn. We dropped down to Boleke by 2 o'clock, the men all singing and flags waving, and land on the island where we camped before. Nobody comes to see us, though there are plenty of them on the beach looking across at us, and shouting when I killed a duck. We arranged the camp for a stay of several days, using the great rope left by the *Stanley* in the bushes on the Duma, as a chain fence, hanging it on our fancy paddles driven down as posts ; thus making a very nice looking fence around our camp; the Congos' mat-house being on one side of the yard, and the Yansis' on the other, and the tent in between. The yard was swept clean, and there were bunches of bananas hanging from a paddle stuck up in the yard. After awhile, a canoe with one man and one woman stopped by to say that there had been a fight between the town on the north bank, just opposite the Kwango mouth, and some State people in a small steamer, and that two white men (another report says one) were left there dead, and the steamer was gone away for help; and the quarrel was because the steamer took the people's wood without buying it.

Could it be Captain Dhanis going to relieve Mr. Hochstras and take him to Kingunji?

We assured them that we were not Bula Matadi,[1] that we would not hurt them, and that we had nguvo to sell, and we made the ambassadors a small present of the meat.

I can see the pillars of smoke now going up from the burning town in question.

Now the canoes begin to stream across and a great crowd surround our camp, showing much fondness for Sheppard, but rather afraid of the other "mundele." Before the crowd came there were a great many of them swimming in the deep swift stream.

January 25.—Sunday. There was a crowd here from midday on. They brought things to sell, though we told them yesterday that we wouldn't buy to-day. The Yansis needed watching, as they were trying to sell the nguvo entrusted to them. A crowd collected, especially near the hippo drying frames. They would come to me or to Sheppard with hands on the middle part of their persons, which was made to appear very much emaciated, and they would say, "mfumu! mfumu! nzala! mfumu! nzala!" with great patience; so we had some meat sliced up and divided among them.

At the afternoon service there were a hundred and three people altogether, and they watched and listened with fear, curiosity and pleasure, all mixed in varying proportions. Our friend Antinobe, with her quiet face, her little boy and her same check cloth, is always on hand, and is made happy by various small presents, which she returns in some measure with kwanga. We asked her to get her father, who had offered to give us land before, to come to-morrow, Monday, to see us, and then we would go with him and see the town. "All right."

January 26.—A good many are on hand this morning, though more have gone up the river, four or six women in each canoe, on their way to market, I suppose, from the baskets of salables they all have.

The men with fish-baskets and other appliances in light canoes skimmed away to their fishing grounds at sun-up.

About 9 o'clock we went over to see the old gentleman about the land. He had been here early, but didn't talk business, only admired my double-barrel and the duck it had brought us (my sixth), but soon went away to his fish-traps, Antinobe said. It was she received us in town, and when we said we were starting to the upper town where he lived, she hastily stopped us and went herself to fetch him. A roll of matting was shown us and we sat down to wait. Another mat was

---

[1] Not State officers or soldiers.

spread in front of us, likewise in open air. An old man whom we see about very often came and sat on it. He is a crafty-looking old fellow, and reminds me of Mfunu Matuba at Manyanga. He made Makwala sit by him and we waited. Crowds of villagers thronged about us. We managed to get a little fellow once in a while to come and shake hands. There are plenty of little ones here, and they look very well and fairly happy. But the crowd thinned down to a score of children and a few men, and still we waited After an hour there was a stir among them and the people began to gather. Antinobe came up with a dripping paddle in her hand, and then by another way, and with some dignity, her father appeared. He is a man of good presence and would naturally command respect. Seated by his colleague he waited in silence for us to begin the conference.

We told Makwala to say that we had come back according to his invitation, to see the land they had offered us, that we wanted to pay for it if we found it good, and would go back to Kintamo, get our stuff, and come and live here.

He replied, "We should be glad for you to settle, and if you build, all right, but we can't sell you the land. We are not the kings, and we can't help you, if the king should be angry."

I replied, "Then tell them, Makwala, another town up the river Bampwono) wants us to stay with them, but we like this place, if you can be as good as those people."

"All right, go to them" (Makwala answered for the two elders). Or if you want to stay here ask the king of this country."

"Where is he?"

"He is at his town."

"What is his town?"

"Kimbuta. [I think this town apochryphal.] It is far away. Don't ask us for land."

The old man got up and walked away, ending the palaver abruptly, much to the satisfaction of the old women, who had stood behind him and grunted at him their distrust of each proposition as soon as we made it.

A flat disappointment to us.

We came back floored, and had some difficulty in grasping the promise of guidance, but we did that. In the afternoon, we decided that we would select a site on the right bank, in sight of the town, and hold it temporarily, till the people thought better of us; come and sit down before the town, so to speak, and wait for their timidity to wear off, and then build nearer.

As we were starting, a young man whom we liked, the one who came to see us on the former visit, came to Makwala and hinted that the people feared trouble from our men. I took this chance to explain that our business was not to trade, but to teach the will of their King and ours, the God who made us both; that we teach that God forbids men to kill, steal, and commit adultery; and that our teaching is the best pledge that we will be good neighbors; that we should have some men to feed and so furnish trade for them.

He asked if Kintamo, our country, had plenty of women. Makwala answered that there were plenty. He said, then, that we should bring wives for our men, as they didn't want their families disturbed. He then suggested that we go to see their queen, Ngabile, who is "Mama-nene," the great mother.

While they were speaking a canoe landed near us, and we learned that it was the daughter of Ngabile coming to see us. She approached our fence rather shyly, carrying her little boy on her left arm. She was dignified and quieter in manner than the other women. She was shy, but had none of that boisterous timidity that runs and screams whenever we turn around. She had a great brass ring about her neck, a single cloth from her waist to her knees. The boy wears not a thread but that upon which his bead-necklace is strung. Sheppard bought the peanuts she brought. We gave the young prince a fathom of our best cloth, and to his mother a knife. She promised to come back to-morrow with her mother.

The crowd of young men stayed late talking with Makwala. They managed to understand his "Kiteke," as spoken at Kintamo, very well.

"If Mundele comes back," they said, "let him bring people that speak your language, not those men's," with significant gesture toward the Bayansi, who were always in a row, and often with the natives.

"Who are these Mundele," they go on, "do they come out of the water?" They count us odd fish, no doubt, but better that than ndoki, devils who spirit away sleeping people at night.

We go to bed thankful and hopeful.

January 27.—We are all day waiting. Not many people came, and the two we wanted didn't come. We went over to see the land opposite the town for a temporary site.

January 28.—Made the final survey of the temporary site, and at last, about 10 A. M., we broke up camp, our men nothing loth to go. The people kept away, and don't seem sorry that we are gone. This is not surprising though, as there was a fight between the white men and their neighbors so lately.

We dropped sadly down stream, and stopped to eat at our old sand-bank in Wissman Pool, after which we kept on till dark; and camped on a narrow strip of high grass bank, very near our camp of January 2nd. We had very primitive arrangements for supper, as it was dark before it was made. Hippos and buffalos disturbed some of us all night, assisted by the natives, who came up stealthily in their canoes, smelling around, to find who we were and what was our business. The whole river-side is astir. Something awful seems to have occurred between the natives and Bula Matadi. We heard from some who hailed us as we passed, that Ngankabi's son has been seized and carried to Kintamo.

January 29.—We are up and off at 3:40 A. M., by moonlight. We passed Musyé at 6:30. We see plenty of people with canoes camping on sand-banks above, as if refugeeing from Musyé. We see nothing wrong, however, at Musyé, but pass on down in mid-stream. We go slowly through the flats below Musyé. We were caught a quarter of a mile from shore in naughty wind and water, and the light had a weird yellow look, but we reached good shelter below in time to miss the storm. We got into the narrow swift part before evening, and it was pleasant to watch the banks slipping by, but hard to find a sleeping place, the banks were so steep down to the water's edge, with great boulders sometimes jutting out into the river. At last we rounded a point, and spied a little nook, where we camped, and slept on a fine sand beach.

January 30.—Off before day, but delayed somewhat by the wind and waves. We were at Kwa-mouth by 10:30, where we had a cup of coffee with the good brothers of the Catholic Mission of "Berg Ste. Marie." We get here the news of the trouble between the "Van Kerckoven expedition" and the people of Musyé district. They have burnt the town opposite Musyé, and brought down a great lot of canoes which are here at Kwa-mouth now. Chumbiri is burnt, and the whole country profoundly excited.

One of the fathers says, "We haven't any more meat and can't get good fish." And I notice that he does not take any of the meat, though it is good.

One of them remarked, "If we had a steamer we would go up to Luluaburg at once. We found the natives at Ngete very much attached to you (Mr. Clark is probably referred to), and so our Father Superior at once decided not to locate there." Perhaps they would like for us to let the Kassai alone, but they did not say so, and indeed made us very much at home.

It was pleasant to meet civilization and hospitality again, not to mention sugar. Didn't we pelt them with questions about the little world we had left five short weeks ago! "Where is the *Reed*, the *Peace*, the *Pioneer*, and what steamers are expected down?"

While we rested at the mission, Makwala had bought us kwanga, and by 1:30 all was ready, and we are off, crossing just ahead of a wind storm; and by the time we had reached the French, or right bank of the Congo, the current had swept us away down below the mouth of the Kwa, or Kassai.

The *Ville de Bruxelles* comes in sight. She is a magnificent steamer, with two decks, swift and strong. She belongs to Bula Matadi. I crossed and went aboard to tell them of Mr. Hochstras' being in the wrong river, but found they already knew it. Slept aboard till the moon rose, first reading the latest dailies from Brussels, telling of Parnell's fall and Baring Brothers' failure, and the other doings in the great outside world.

Recrossed at 1 o'clock and got a cup of tea and some kwanga, and finished my sleep in my own tent.

January 30.—We passed the strong water off Gauchu's Point in high feather, our flags flying, men singing, and an old ivory trader from Chumbiri to guide us down. The old fellow had on his big cap of wildcat skin, having his little daughter to bear him company. The poor little girl's mother is dead. We picked him up yesterday and find that he is head-man of Yela Gela's town, and is the man who struck the head off the corpse I saw floating down from Chumbiri in August.

We rested on the great sand-banks below the towns at Gauchu's.

"Sail ho!"

"What steamer?"

"Hand the glass!"

"The *Henry Reed!*"

We are soon aboard, and spend Sunday at Kimpoko, and on Monday morning we are at Kintamo.

February 1.—I am back at the Pool in the best of health, thanks to our Father's care, and am fatter in flesh by a good deal, but by no means fairer, "for that the sun hath looked upon me."

CHAPTER VI.

LETTERS.

To Lukunga and Back.

THE purpose of the next trip, that by steamer up the Congo, Kassai and Lulua to Luebo, and the preparations for it, can be seen from the following interesting extracts from letters written in the interval, February 6th to March 17th, between the journeys.

Nearly to Mfume (six hours out), West of Kintamo,[*]
En Route to Lukunga, *February* 8, 1891.

My Dear Mamma : My supper is almost ready, but I will delay it (let it cool), while I sketch my company and surroundings. I know you would like to see the boys, ten in all, who have brought my tent and traps thus far from the Pool.

The tent is ready, bed up, and mosquito net spread, to provide against the "nyum-i-nyums," as my Congo boys call that pest. The table is very neat, with a clean Turkish towel for cloth, and snowy rice, crisp-fried kwanga, and fish and tea, defended by a line of pickles, pulverized ginger and marmalade. I can forget that the table is only my wooden clothes-box, made at Kintamo, if I minded it at all.

The boys are standing or sitting or moving leisurely about a fire, on either side of me. Half of them are bare to the waist and not bad looking to my accustomed eye, with rich brown skins, kept clean and smooth by baths at almost every river crossed. The rest have shirts of their own making or nice cloths, and are not bad either. Nzezela I see is mending a rent in his waist cloth. He is my head boy, made such because he secured the rest for me, and helps manage them.

---

[*] Leopoldville.

129

The light is fading on the hills that encircle this one on which we are camping. On most of them are little plantain-shaded villages, with rich madioca gardens on hill-sides near, making this the principal source of food-supply of the big settlement at this end of the Pool.

Supper and prayers finished, I taught them a new hymn, a very free translation of "Saviour, like a shepherd lead us," made by Mr. Banks, in his old days when he was in the Bakongo's country. It embodies a great deal of useful and saving truth in a pleasing hymn; it took. Afterwards I described, half in words, half in signs, the separation of the sheep and the goats, and asked them where I should see them that day. It was encouraging to see them silent, and thoughtful I hoped. They usually say very promptly that they expect to go to heaven. I then offered a short prayer in Kikongo. I began in English, then a Kikongo petition, which they might share, came up, and then another, until I covered most of our needs to-night. It wasn't correct Kikongo, but my lingo, which they understand perfectly.

Papa asked how I went about studying the language. I haven't sat down to this language many times. I read some of a little grammar, enough to learn how their words agree at the front end, instead of the latter end, as Indo-European tongues do. For instance, "Bantu bambodi" means good men, from muntu, man, and mboti, good. "Kinkuti kiame," my coat; "binkuti biame," my coats. The rest has been picked up by asking questions: "What do you call this?" ("nkia beno tuba yaya?"). The hymns and the talk of white men were instructive, because nearer my reach than the colloquialisms of my boys in their common talk. But when my boys address me they usually employ familiar words, so the one or two new ones are noticed, hunted down and added to my stock, the increasing dimensions of which is a matter of increasing amusement to them. They have just called from the camp to ask me a question, and on my replying in good grammar, they patted me on the back very patronizingly.

I intend to write a full letter on the Congo for some Northern periodical. I desire to draw the attention of Northern Methodists—the church, not an irregular skirmishing society like

Bishop Taylor's, and especially the Presbyterians, Dutch Reformed and United Presbyterians; will write also directly to the boards of the latter bodies, that we may by all means secure some adequate reinforcements on the untouched Kassai.

I am going down now to make a contract with Mr. Todd, by which we may divide the expenses of transport *pro rata* with the Congo Bolobo Mission, and have them guarantee to forward loads to Kinshassa for a fixed period. Then I have arranged with Major Parminter, director of the great "Societe Anonyme Belge," for storage and transportation to the Kassai.

Sheppard and I shall probably leave then, to see the whole upper Kassai. We shall stop up there, sending a final report back, and orders for needed goods to accompany the reinforcements, and fix us up finally.

I wrote by last mail recommending Boleko at the mouth of the Kwango, on the condition that further exploration does not show something better. A choice, I wrote, between a good and a better. Kingunji I have given up as a base long ago. It might be as accessible as Stanley Pool, as soon as the caravan road is finished thither, but the railway and the river are facts that demand that the country be evangelized along the rivers, as they are being opened for commercial and political purposes.

Sheppard and I shall go by the *Stanley* in sixteen days, if I am back in time, and the charge is not too high; otherwise by the *Florida*, named in honor of General Sanford, who founded the Sanford Trade Company, from which the "Societe Anonyme Belge" has sprung.

The road is the pleasantest of all occupations out here to me. Plenty of air, exercise, appetite! Leisure, care-free, to think of business—knots often untangle themselves—and to walk with my distant friends. Often the thought of my mamma rises to the surface, as if in the midst of a conversation with you, the other part being under the surface of consciousness, as so often it seems in dreams. I can't tell you what I think of then; it don't seem right to put it on paper; besides, I can't. Oh, I forgot to say that the pick of my boys, Senza, the pleasantest and most satisfactory servant I have found, seems to be trying to find out the meaning of this strange story I have been telling him for three months. He isn't conscious of the desire, but he comes now and sits with me and waits for me to talk about God and the way to him through his Son. Senza's is the finest face I have seen here, in appearance a combination of two young Caucasians I know of; can you believe that of a Congo boy?

LEOPOLDVILLE, CONGO INDEPENDENT STATE,
March 10, 1891.

DEAR PAPA: Mail time (the mid-month mail) is only a week off to-day; so I want to make sure of a word to you this time. Important and lengthy letters to Dr. Houston and Messrs. Whyte, Ridsdale & Co., shut out the wind-up even of the home letters, already begun for last mail. You may imagine how diligently I studied the catalogues and consulted Dr. Sims and Mr. Glenesk (who is here awaiting Mrs. Glenesk's arrival), when you know that I had a $400 order to get off, besides a string of hints in regard to the expected reinforcements, the outfits and other arrangements of these gentlemen.

Well, I know much more about business than I did to-day twelve months back, when we took the London and Northwestern from Liverpool to London. "Hitherto hath the Lord helped us," I am very sure, and it gives me good hope that he means for us to do good out here. I am awaiting only the steamer which shall take us up the great river, which we have come to regard quite as our home, though we go like Abraham, "Not knowing whither we go," but possessed with a desire for a full occupation of the whole valley, and trusting to Him to show the strategic point for us to begin the attack. We found that seeing with our eyes the very spot has a magical effect in clearing away the haze that embarrasses all calculations based on the best descriptions by another.

I have been over to Brazzaville and arranged with Mr. A. Greshoff, of the Dutch house, a £45 bill of cloth bought for the other Kassai trip. The bill was £60, on which I get 25 per cent. reduction, and that leaves them an enormous profit, I believe. My boys paddled me back to Kinshassa, where I slept at the mission (B. M. S.), and in the morning went up to the Belgian house, a twenty-minute walk up the south bank, passed the abandoned Dutch house, now held by the "Societe Anti-esclavagiste," the new State post, and the deserted town of King Nchulu, where the new Leopoldville is to be ere long.

At the Belgian house I found Major Parminter, about to start for the French side of the river for lunch. He tarried to say, in answer to my inquiries, that he would store loads for us at Kinshassa and forward to any point on the Kassai, main branch, or Sankuru, at 10 francs to Kwa-mouth or short of there, 15 to the Kwango or between Kwa-mouth and there, 20 to Sankuru or intermediate points, 20 to Luebo (or Lusambo) or intermediate points. White passengers to Kwa-mouth 120 francs, to the Kwango 180 francs, Sankuru 300 francs, Luebo 350 francs.

It seems to have been ordered by Providence that we should come at the very instant the Kassai is being opened. The "Societe Anonyme Belge" have completed and equipped their line of stations up the Congo to the Falls, and intend this year, within six months, to open four new stations on the Kassai, besides the one they have at Luebo. To their two 500-load steamers, they are adding two 1,000-load steamers and two more small ones. One of the big boats is coming up now; the rest are almost finished at Kinshassa to-day.

Major Parminter, who is director of the S. A. B. in this country, amenable to the administration in Brussels, will not promise to carry any of my loads to the exclusion of his own loads, yet he showed me that since rubber is the staple of the Kassai trade, and is cheaper to the bulk than cloth, there will, of necessity, be less cargo on up-trips than down; so I need not doubt the feasibility of carrying on our limited transport through the S. A. B.; there is always passenger room, and down-trips are half rates.

The Major is the most delightfully cultivated man I have met here, or anywhere perhaps; an English gentleman and soldier who has moved in courts on the Continent. Slender, small hands and feet, delicately dressed in tasteful light flannels, with snowy linen (a rarity); a very pleasant face, regular features, clear open grey eyes, thin mustache and beard. It is interesting to see his autocracy display itself when the attachés come in from time to time with a question, and it kept me wide awake

even to tell him my experiences and observations up the Kwango
and Duma; much more in talking business. I found it convenient to be in a hurry to get back to the mission after the
preliminary interview the afternoon before, so as to take my
bearings before the final agreement. When I left him finally, I
wrote him a formal note embodying what I wanted to know,
and got from him a written statement covering the whole ground.*

I have been to Lukunga and arranged that Mr. Todd, of the
Congo Balobo Mission, shall do all our transport at about £1 a
load; and I got back here in seventeen days, in time to close up
letters for the mail. I lost some of my Manyangas; home-ties
too strong when they actually saw their town. But going by, I
got two, Nzezela and Nlandu, and have now as many men as we
can afford to keep up country, engaged for a year. At Manyanga, I didn't find my good friend Mr. Heyn; gone home very
ill, though convalescent now.

This will give you some idea of my business arrangements;
very strange it would have seemed if I had dreamed it fifteen
months ago. I think we shall suffer from delays, etc., until we
do our own transport with a Presbyterian Mission steamer.

We have a fair lot of chop, another sort, better off than when
we went up before; and then we lived like dukes and counts in
the new, fresh country, though rather hungry for sugar in some
form, which we provide this time. We take sufficient ammunition and plenty of guns, a fairly ample set of tools for a beginning, and plenty coming some day. Bedding and clothing in all
abundance, am thankful to say. Not at all "flush" in barter goods,
but shall get on, I am confident. We made calculations without
allowing for the cheaper rates up the river, among the still unsophisticated bushmen, an advantage which we are sure to
have, and of which the arch-trader, Sheppard, will not be slow
to avail himself (I let him do most of the buying).

Oh, I meant to tell you of a good providence that came to me
in meeting Major Parminter again at his station at Manyanga.
I had made a big account there the other time. A pile of cloth
and trinkets had been consumed in alluring the Manyangas to
enlist for Kingunji, amounting to something over £4 per invoice

---

* See the wisdom and value of this at beginning of next chapter.

price. Well, Mr. Heyn had no authority to accept a check, so I promised to pay in cloth when it came. It came while I was at Lukunga, but as I was about to pay, the Major appeared and said a check would do. So the account was made as per invoice, doubled to cover expenses, and I drew a check for £8 8s., with a glad heart at not having to pay £11

LEOPOLDVILLE, *March* 15, 1891.

MY DEAR ROB:

. . . .

We are now on the eve of the most momentous departure we have yet taken. On Tuesday morning, day after to-morrow, we are to start for the Kassai. We take passage in the *Florida* to Luebo, with a pretty clean-cut outfit, not even taking our famous canoe. There we intend to buy the needed craft to float back, down to the point which we shall have chosen on the way up, presumably near and below the junction of the Sankuru and the Kassai, in the nearest edge of the great Bakuba race. I am disposed to think that the large town in the fork of the Loange and the Kassai will meet our requirements. Why go so far? Why not stop at the mouth of the Kwango for instance? The only reason is that, from all we can see, the finest and the future dominant Kassai tribes are the allied Bakuba, Bashilange and Balubas, living in and near the ellipse, and enclosed by the Kassai, Sankuru, Lubi, and Zambezi divide.

I am in excellent strength and spirits, thank God! And I trust I know more of Him than before, and that the things of His kingdom are much more real and present to me than they were at home.

. . . . ,

CHAPTER VII.

DIARY FROM MARCH 14 TO APRIL 21, 1891.

To Luebo on the Steamer Florida.

THE *Stanley*, in which we had engaged to go, did not come; why, nobody knew. I was spending my waiting time on my first "balance-sheet," a sad tangle, which cost many days and nights to untangle, when Sheppard came suddenly back from a Kinshassa visit, to say that the *Florida*, our only other resource, would leave Monday morning at six o'clock. And that was Friday evening.

Saturday Morning, March 14.—I went to Kinshassa, to the "S. A. B." Station, where the *Florida* lay. Mr. Clotens, the manager, sent for the captain of the *Florida*, and we proposed that they should take for us forty loads, with our canoe towed along-side.

"Impossible," said the captain to Mr. Clotens, "we would never get up the Kassai with the poor pressure our lame boiler can make, and you won't let me stop for adequate repairs."

So they had it up and down! Mr. Clotens insisting that Major Parminter's promise must be redeemed, and the captain saying that with even twenty loads, besides the four hundred (fourteen tons), already aboard, he would not risk the prospect of ever reaching Luebo. But Mr. Clotens, inspired by the Major's letter, which I happened to lay open before him, promised to take Sheppard and me and eight boys and twenty loads, each load being seventy pounds.

"Small allowance," said I, when I went back to talk it over with Sheppard. "And no canoe," said Sheppard; "but this is the only chance perhaps before August, unless we canoe it again." So we concluded that we would make a grave mistake in not accepting. Accordingly, I went back to the "S. A. B." and tied the bargain, and learned that we might have another day.

Monday, March 16.—I was up at 1 A. M., trying in vain to get my correspondence off. No headway. Too tired. Early in the morning was at work, opening, selecting and repacking our provision boxes, packing three good assorted cases for the trip, and packing the rest to follow us. While Sheppard, with the little boys, finished the job, I

136

took the large ones to the State office to be registered as workmen for one year.

"But you haven't license to employ them, and I can't give it; it must come from Boma," objected the Commissaire. So I went back to Dr. Sims, who pulled us through as usual. He persuaded his patient, the obliging young acting Commissaire, Caiton, to let him employ the men, which he did, and gave them to me. So I got my five big boys bound for one year, for twenty-five francs ($5.00).

Sheppard got things ready to go by three. I stayed to close up the business, while he canoed our stuff to the *Florida*, and got back by 7 P. M. Then there was the final bustle and confusion and the discovery oft-repeated, "There is another thing left out, and none in these trunks."

But Mr. Ellery undertook to put things up for us, and send them according to instructions, as his mission is employed to transport for us anyway. But his main reason was sympathy and goodness.

9 P. M.—Moon not far from down. "Where is Nzezela?" "Sleeping at 'Bula Matadi's.'" (The quarters occupied by State employees.) We had to leave him, and tramp through the dew and uncertain light of the setting moon, six or eight miles to the steamer, and were asleep by 1 o'clock.

March 17.—I was up by 5:30 A. M., because I fancied we were on the point of starting, being roused by the angry voice of the captain at my door, scolding the engineer for not rousing his fireman in time to be off at six.

We had coffee in a little bamboo hexagonal pagoda, its roof hung with cheerful red cloth, Sheppard on Mr. Clotens' left, I on his right, and the ranks filled with engineers, clerks, etc., around the big table. After which, we were off at last; I carrying Mr. Clotens' receipt for a £60 check for our passage to Luebo, with men and loads included; the most momentous departure since that from New York, Wednesday, February 26, last year.

I found myself singing the last four lines of a hymn I heard in England—

> " Wherever He may guide me, no want shall turn me back;
> My Shepherd is beside me, and nothing can I lack.
> His wisdom ever waketh, His eyes are never dim;
> He knows the way He taketh, and I will walk with Him."

We start with a fair day, and are installed in the 7 x 9 dining-room of the *Florida*, and are not sorry, after the fatigues of last night, to have leisure to enjoy our beds, which are spread on the benches on either side of the weather-beaten mahogany table.

At Kimpoko we stopped to take on a State officer, going to Lulua-burg with twenty soldiers. Sheppard and I had time to go up and say good-bye to the friends at Bishop Taylor's mission, who bade us, I thought, a most affectionate God-speed. They seemed to feel badly that we came out only last year, and are already off for the very district they came for four years ago. But I can't accept the credit, until we have stayed and settled up yonder.

The State officer is a well-disposed young fellow, who has picked up some "small Engleesh," as he calls it, from his black men, and is will-ing to be pleased and to please. The Captain is a Belgian too, of uncommonly simple and pleasing politeness, and is very desirous that we should be comfortable and satisfied, and we are.

The dinner included delicious soup, chicken fried with balls of rice, savory gravy and macaroni. Not bad, was it? Yesterday's exploits had left us ravenously hungry.

The engineer rooms next back of us, with his door opening to the engine. He is an interesting man, with large, strong frame, large regu-lar features to match, dark eyes, hair and mustache getting pretty grey. He was sick to-day, and took two tabloids from my medicine chest, to his great improvement. He contrasts strongly with the two Belgians. They are small, pale and light. The Captain's eyes are typical Teu-tonic blue, a full-blooded Fleming no doubt, though his French is good, I am sure.

The *Florida* travelled well, stopping at dusk. Then the crew, the soldiers, and my boys were marshalled on the sand under the wooded hill, and were given tools and orders, and left to bring in a full tale of firewood. We supped and chatted awhile, Sheppard and I solacing ourselves with tea, and the others with spirits, taking but a small amount, however, of necessity, for their superiors give them small allowance, and they economize with all care, as running short would be a calamity to men who have used strong drink, as we use tea and coffee, since they were babies.

An early bed and good sleep.

March 18.—We stopped at 2 : 15 at Lisa, the first State post out of the Pool. The young officer, whose name is Simar, wanted provisions for his men, having started without warning, on an order sent from the Commissaire at Leopoldville, by this same vessel. "And we need eggs and chickens and goat too, non-getable at Stanley Pool."

There are here at Lisa three houses and a shed for soldiers, and good wood behind, and a large town a quarter of an hour down the river by canoe; that is, it used to be there. But the great Vankerckoven expedition has been there, and Sheppard, who went down in a canoe, didn't find anybody at the old place, if he found the place at all. He did find very rough water on the way, with a wind driving the canoe back, and waves dashing right over it, almost pitching them all out. And such a rain! I don't remember seeing any like it, in Africa yet, so hard and long, equal to Alabama rains. Everybody on the steamer except we, who had good rooms, was drenched. Sheppard came in after we had finished dinner, wet and cold, but he didn't suffer from it. Only we lost half a day, about.

March 19.—We were stuck hard aground by yesterday's wind and waves, the paddle spinning round and round, and the whole available force was put in the water to push her off, but it was long before she cleared.

The young Belgian shows a *naïf* curiosity about our ways of worship. He stayed a long time after breakfast to see prayers. I postponed and postponed so that he shouldn't think we forced it on him, and guessing that he would wait for it. He did wait, but of course knows only a few words of English, and less about religion as a real thing, though familiar with the most elaborate of its forms.

About 10 o'clock, noticing that he was "poorly," I felt his hand and "fed" him the thermometer under the tongue, and found that his temperature was 104. I tucked him in in a jiffy, and rigged up a temporary room for him, and he was better by night, with the fever all gone.

March 20.—Getting along very slowly, reaching Kwa-mouth after dinner at 2 P. M., instead of 10 A. M. We have only a small amount of wood, and can't venture into a strong river like the Kassai, which is so bad for wood too, and so we must stop and wood at the mouth. We turned that way, and saw a black cloud behind the hilly bank. Lightnings licked out red tongues, like a mad snake. up and down the black sheet, but we got over, and around the rocky point too. The winds and current were then too strong for us: keeping us ten minutes in one spot waiting. Then the waves began to pitch the boat from side to side and up and down, and I fully expected her to go down, and to have to swim out. But after a fearful passage we were dashed against the sandy beach. a little way above a long line of rocks, and got back to our wooding place after all, about three-quarters of an hour before dark.

Just then we saw a steamer coming out of the Kassai, and it crossed and ran in, stopping a mile and a half above us. I ran up with my new boy, Mpiata. I found that the steamer was the *S anley*, and that she had barricades put up all round, six-foot high, made out of big sticks and planks. Captain Matson and the little Dutchman, the engineer, were very cordial, and merry to have gotten out of the Kwango without bullet holes in them. They had a big palaver just above the junction of the Duma (or Kwilu) and Kwango. They were attacked furiously and persistently for days on the way. The natives were well-armed, and their bullets went through thick plank, and the captain and engineer each had narrow escapes from flying bullets I also learned that Mr. Hochstras, whom I left up on the Duma two months ago, was killed by a hippo in an hour of Kingunji, and after all danger seemed passed!

I returned to the *Florida* in the same canoe from which the hippo threw Mr. Hochstras. "A thousand shall fall at thy side and ten thousand at thy right hand, but it shall not come nigh thee." All these perils might have been ours if we had been directed in a slightly different course.

I was late getting up, and was hurried out by the news of the arrival of one of the Belgian Catholic missionaries with a canoe, to be towed up to Musyé for provisions.

The fire-bars or grate of the boiler need repair already, and hence we are delayed till 7 o'clock. Then we try the Kassai again, only to be swung around and swept down three times. Then up a little way, around another point, and then another, with same experiences. At noon we are not around the first big bend! We simply can't steam up the middle, not having enough steam and having too much load. With five hours steaming we have made only a half-hour's progress, constantly struggling with a desperate mill-tail affair, that shoots down between a wall of boulders and a reef of sand and big black angular rocks. Just think of it, the whole Kassai pressed into a current about 150 yards across! Sheppard was at the wheel and just edging through the last of the bad part—pop! and a noise of a dragging chain, the rudder chain had broken and there were the rocks awaiting us. I ran for a piece of wire I knew about; and Sheppard ran back and took charge of the rod connecting and controlling the rudders themselves, and put her into the sand-bank ten yards below the rocks.

"And the fire-bars are no good," came up from the engineer, Mr. Sirex.

"What's to be done?" says the captain.

"We'll never make it, let's go back to Kinshassa." But the captain would not agree to go back.

These two well-disposed men can't understand each other: the least cause of this being that Mr. Sirex, the engineer, a Dane, speaks no French, but tolerably fair English, and the captain speaks only French. So as interpreter I had a chance to mediate between them, with the key to the position in my hands. No matter what was said, nothing offensive got from one to the other, except when the captain tried English, or misunderstood the engineer and anticipated me.

"Let the engine cool, and I will repair it the best I can; then I'll say what we can do." The captain agreed to this, but at dinner announced that he would go till he broke down, then send to Kinshassa by canoe. A difficult piece of interpreting was when the captain wanted to say that the doctor at Kinshassa had forbidden Mr. Sirex cognac, for they had had a row about Mr. Sirex taking too much gin and cognac, and getting sick. Coming through me the captain's views on this subject reached their destination in quite a dilute form, a tincture of the original, as one might say. We didn't get away that day, or all the next, which was Sunday.

March 22.—Sunday; not a prayerful day. Found some profit in *Bacon's Essays*, a mine of shrewd knowledge of men and things. Many capital suggestions of ways one should treat "superiors, inferiors and equals." Remarkable how highly he prizes a policy which develops the wealth and spirit of a nation, the policy which has made the English people!

Le Pere at last gave up the steamer, and started with his canoe to Musyé, Sunday morning about nine, after his prayers from the little black book with a cross on the boards. At meals he offers his own grace, and he makes curious little motions with his finger on his breast and forehead: and we offer ours—as unsatisfactory in his eyes, doubtless.

March 23.—We are off at last, with the boiler in shape, the engineer and his West Coast men having been hard at work all Sunday with bellows, hammers, anvil and drill, straightening and staying the wrought-iron bars and replacing the spoilt cast-iron ones, which will not bear the straightening. So we got past that bad place and some others, and reached by 12 o'clock a fenced town, where Sheppard and I had gotten plenty of provisions when we were here before. But the "portcullis" was closed, and we soon saw the women and children with their stuff on their heads hurrying down the bank and away, preparing for the attack they thought we had come for. So we left them, but were presently stopped by a threatening cloud, and we tied up. Found plenty of good wood and lots of buffalo tracks, but no buffalo, though Sheppard hunted them diligently. Kwanga only for supper. Mr Sirex sighed. Mr. Simar remarked on it; the captain took it as possibly a reflection on him.

March 24.—Sheppard is off early after game in a canoe. The captain got tired waiting at the hippo sand-island, and whistled: so Sheppard came off with only four ducks, just as he was about to get plenty; two of the four were given as a present by a man to whom Sheppard had given some hippo meat when we were here before. "Found after many days." So everybody in the cabin is happy with a good dinner, and good progress the rest of the day, until we eased into the place where we had stopped with the *Stanley*, December 26th. The big anchor went ashore, borne on the bare shoulders of four Bangala, lithe, muscular fellows, as almost all of them are. Sheppard goes to a village near by, but got no kwanga, and saw plenty of guns. I have been giving medicine to the sick wife of one of the Bangalas.

March 25.—A fruitful day. "Giving all diligence." We had a big rain, which continued up to 11 o'clock. We saw another big drove of hippos in a shallow channel between the sand-islands, some of them switching their dumpy little tails, just to make Sheppard mad. We stopped directly after noon for wood, and the Captain, Sheppard and I went with a good crew to get a hippo. Too many "mundele" however. Several were struck, but none happened to get a fatal wound. We paddled about among the sand-islands rather aimlessly all the afternoon, though the captain got four brown ducks with two cartridges. So we went back without the meat for the men, though there was plenty for us. Such a pitiable lot of fellows: not a square meal for a week almost, and hardly a crumb for two days, and plenty of hard work all the while.

All three of our fellow-travellers are in a row about chop. "No jam, no biscuit, no sugar," on one side. On the other, "That Bula Matadi man (Simar) he chop all jam, all small bisque. One box jam one day!"

To Mr. Sirex, who don't understand French, the young Bula Matadi replies, "Compagnie Belge mehr riche as l'etat. Compagnie get mingi, mingi (Kikongo for much). L'etat no get, Bula Matadi give good chop, compagnie no give." [1]

March 26.—Storm at 3 A. M. There was a lively pitching of the

---

[1] Mr. Simar gives us in this one sentence a sample of the prevalent mixture of tongues. Here are French, German, Kikongo, Kru-boy, and English, all together. He means to say that while Mr. Sirex's employers, the "S. A. B.," are richer than the State and get "much, much" chop, they give poorly to their employees. While, on the other hand, the State, which has but little, provides liberally.

steamer at her moorings. Poor Mr. Simar had to take refuge in our cabin. The wind was followed by rain, but we steamed well past Musyé in spite of the hungry men aboard, who cried out, "Mundelo tala!" (white man look). "Dwata diampwina" (a village big). "Mavata miamingi!" (villages plenty). "Lumba madia!" (buy chop). But the captain remembered the death of a predecessor on the *Florida*, and kept out of a town which had just had a big palaver with white men. He seemed too cautious for us. For at this very moment there is a white man in Musyé, the priest from Kwa-mouth, who has won Queen Gankabo by procuring from Vankerckoven the release of her two sons, taken by the expedition in January. The old lady went down herself with twenty or twenty-five canoes and came back a happy woman, and the sworn friend of the Belgian missionaries.

But we didn't stop. We passed a whole string of other towns too, some seven or eight of them on the grassy bank, with the fine cluster of plantain-shaded villages named Bosaji, fifteen minutes from the river-side. At the last or next one to it, where there appeared small prospect of buying anything to eat, the captain did halt, being now pretty sure that his wood would last to a wooding place above.

The men were so hungry they couldn't be got away, whistle as he might, and they had to send back a canoe for five missing men, after we were under way again. We passed the town where we spent Sunday, January 4th, and stopped at the very spot where on January 5th, we picked up a man from the *Stanley*. Great palaver to get exhausted men to go through the waist-deep water for wood half a mile away.

March 26.—I am awakened by the chicot, administered under the auspices of the captain and Mundelo Bula Matadi to a soldier who wouldn't cut wood. Chicot is a strip of hippo hide slit, and the ends twisted for thongs, leaving a handle. It is thick, stiff and hard, and the thongs are like a flexible half-inch augur. It makes a terrible mark where it strikes, at first a white streak, then a long welt. The culprit, if he happens to deserve the name, seldom shrieks, but writhes and gasps piteously after the tenth or fifteenth blow. Neither of these white men is so cruel as careless, and don't learn enough English to half understand an interpreter, and go off before they know why, thinking that chicot is the only means of controlling the African; but with these desperately hungry fellows it don't do any good.

March 27.—We are here all day, getting wood, the fellows managing to shirk cutting it. Two soldiers stole off to the village, and the people caught and tied them, but the Wangata (from Mr. Banks' town at Equator), went to the rescue, and they were released at once.

Sheppard takes a notion to have a small dysentery, and by the morning of the 28th, he had a very high fever on top of it, which gave him much nausea, and cut off his rations.

March 28.—We are off again, stopping at the very place applied for first as our station. Sheppard has a high fever, headache and nausea.

The captain is in extremities for something to eat for his men, and for wood. "I shall go mad, I shall get sick," he says, as he paces up and down the bridge or little porch in front of his cabin aloft. We turned into one village where the people seemed quiet, and just as the parley for chop seemed ready to begin, bump! we struck a rock and the sounding-man called out "One fathom, Matadi," and the captain pulled for the place I showed him, and got a little chop and wood.

March 29.—It is Sunday, but we travel all the same. We pass Kwango-mouth in the morning. Across a waste of sand and water, two miles away, a great waving cottonwood tree, with a forest a little behind, marks our old favorite town, Boleko. Several streams bring the Kwango water into the Kassai, which here is more narrow and deep than usual, with two wooded islands opposite the Kwango delta, and villages behind these islands. The water of the Kassai is very red, as if just washed off of a hill of red or pink soapstone clay.

This immediate section is very much excited against "Bula Matadi."

We enter a noble avenue three-eighths of a mile wide, between two walls of solid green. There soon begins a series of islands lying along the mid-stream, their luxuriance of verdure showing finely the brown of the river, which widens to more stately proportions in their honor, not a gorgeous but a serious beauty, much to my taste.

By noon we reached some villages, and the captain waved handkerchiefs of long bandana from the bridge, and thus invited them to come and bring chop in exchange for the handkerchiefs. He points to a place up stream where we halt for the rest of the day. Before long, plenty of wood was found, and a brisk trade in chickens and eggs and kwanga and nguvo opened up; bandanas, beads, little bells and brass rods being given in exchange. Sheppard began to eat again to-day, but is still rather feeble. Here was my treatment for him. Ipecac to begin with, then Dover's powders, quinine and a calomel-jalap tabloid every few hours, and they produced visible results, under God's favor, and on a fresh constitution.

Yesterday was it? Lately anyhow, I had a long discussion with Mr. Simar, who develops more sense, great courtesy and considerable cultivation. The day we passed Musyé without stopping to feed our

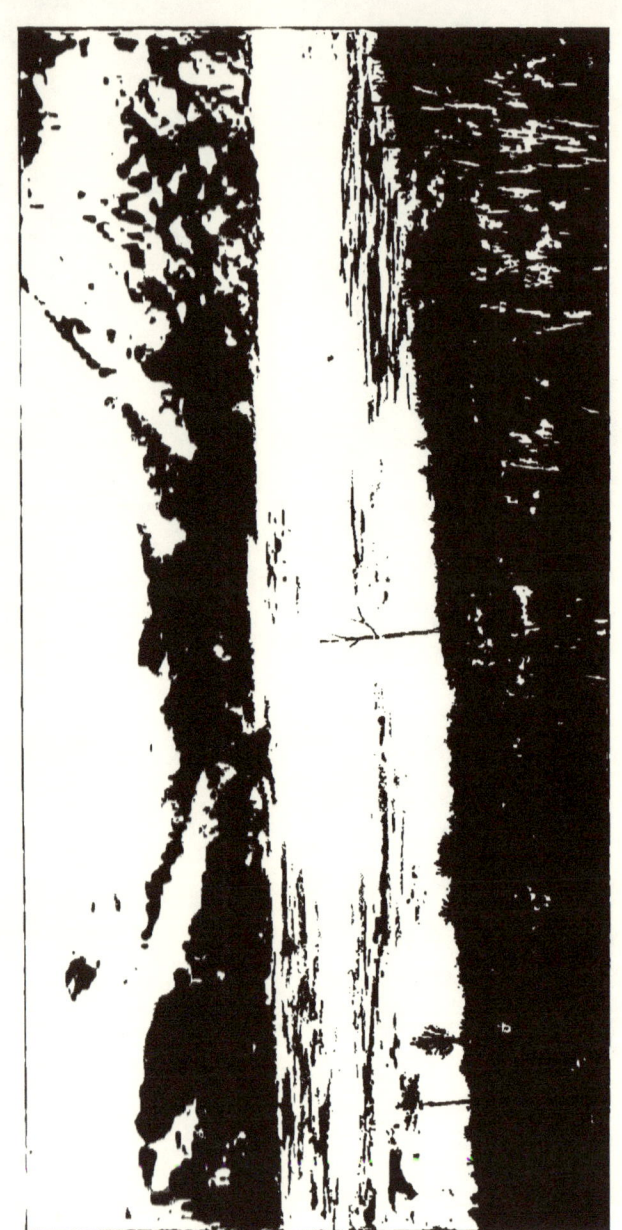

THE RAPIDS OF KASONGHA.—Photo. in "Le Congo Illustré."

hungry men, I opened our box in the hold and took out two tins of beef, meant for Sheppard and myself, and gave them something to eat. Mr. Simar looked on, and said politely that God would reward me, "S'il y un a" (if there be one). Well, that afternoon, I found him pensive, full of presentiments of bad news from his people, of whom he is very fond. I said I often had the same, but it was a help to know that they and I are in safe hands, God's. "S'il y un a," he said again. I looked at him. "Est ce que vous l'avez vu" (have you seen him), he said, in response to my look. I soon saw that he knew the familiar arguments against religion very well, and I guessed he knew the opposite ones.

So I said, that if he couldn't convince himself, I couldn't convince him. If he wanted an argument he couldn't get it with me. If he had difficulties in holding to his mother's faith, I might help him, for I had the same; but the most probable solution of the problems he raised was that of Christianity, that I had in my own experience convincing proof of the truth of Scripture, and moreover I saw no reason to reject historical facts attested by proper documents.

He asked for the original draft of the returns of taxes, taken at the time of our Lord's birth, signed and counter-signed by proper officials; he wanted to see the "documents." I replied that the original documents for Scripture could be found in public libraries and museums to-day, the four chief ones being at London, Paris, St. Petersburg and Rome. He was much interested in this aspect of the question, in the recent discovery of the Codex Aleph in the Convent of Mt. Sinai, etc. But dinner broke us off for the time.

March 30.—We left an eager crowd of villagers on the beach, with half their wares unbought, and got off at 5:25 A. M. Five or ten minutes brought us to the famous pass called "Swinburne rapids," after the first captain of the *Florida*, a fine young Englishman (he died near Lukunga), who stuck on a rock here; and many another captain has "seen mpasi" (difficulty) here, for there seems to be only one safe passage, and that *is* only three feet above the stony bottom at low water, and it is very swift.

Thus nearly are the upper Kassai people to being cut off from Christianity and civilization, for nobody knows how long!

I went up to the bridge to see the captain make the pass. There are three small wooded islands abreast, four channels therefore, all full of rocks. Macaulay, a Sierra Leone man, was the pilot at the wheel. He and the captain had a bet of one hundred utaku as to whether the sounding-pole would find bottom.

10

The man with the sounding-pole calls out "No Sunday" (no sounding), and again and again repeated "No Sunday, No Sunday;" but presently he called out "Two fallom (fathom), two fallom, Matadi!" really only six or eight feet, and seven times in twenty minutes the sounding-pole showed reefs of rock uncomfortably near the surface; but at last the passage is safely made.

Now the green wall of trees and vines is broken by landing places cleared under the tall shade, with canoes drawn upon the beach, or starting out to the steamer, with something to sell. Plenty of people crowd into the openings and call and beckon us to stop. Behind them are their houses among the plantains, a picture not at all bad, which we enjoyed all the forenoon. Plenty of villages, especially on the left bank.

On the right bank, about a mile above the rapids, is a fine open square under tall trees well-known as a great market. No market-day to-day, however.

The people here must be the same kind that we saw on the lower Kwango, but better kept, larger and fatter, though without the fine features one could find at Musyé or Boleke. Their hair is arranged in a fashion new and only met once or twice on the Kwango. There is a tiny cone of hair at the very apex of the cranium, then radiating from that are little plaits sticking down all around the head, *bangs* with a vengeance! The men carry a handful of spears. On the heads of some of the spears were small blades; other heads were only a point of iron. These spears are for hunting big game. The men are large, muscular fellows, as fine an average as it is usual to see anywhere.

Toward the afternoon the country changes altogether, the lofty forest is behind us, and we are in an open, rolling prairie country. There are boundless grassy slopes dotted with little mounds of green, and crossed by belts of wood coming down to the river-side, where they join a strip of bush like an old fence row, which lines both banks a little way. The river is still about half a mile wide. There are no islands, not even a sand-bank or rock, at this high water. Still I think this fair open prospect would hardly tire me as soon as those sombre walls of green. But the villages are small, few and far between, and look a little lonesome in the edge of the grass, with only plantains for shade. The wood is damp and hard to find for strangers, and most steamers are comparative strangers here, as no one steamer usually has business here more than once a year. Just as our poor captain was getting in a fidget, he spied a patch of trees with a lot of good dry ones in the edge, and so we camped there, anchoring by a clay bank seven feet above the water, thick-set with stiff grass. Below us was a small village, whither our men went and got some kwanga, but no eggs. They found the people busy carving up a big crocadile that they killed to-day.

March 31.—The wood proved not the best. The steamer moved slowly and the captain fumed and fussed.

A black cloud that we had seen for fifteen minutes, began to give strong wind, and the water was very strong too; and a little above and out from the line of rocks the two became too much for the big boat and slow engine, and drove us broadside right into the bushes, a fearful crash of breaking branches, rushing water and smashing wood-work. The anchors held just then, and we waited for a calm, with only a battered cabin to grieve for; the captain's eyrie having gone into a big tree, to its cost. We cut loose from it, and our wood being low and seeing some a little way up, we went towards it; but missed the mark, and came in broadside again.

"Ces gouvernailles!" (those rudders), said the captain, "who can steer without a rudder?"

"I can't see whether the rudders are wrong or not until you take out the cargo from the after-hold, and let the stern up," said Mr. Sirex. So it was done, and Mr. Sirex pronounced the rudders in good condition; but having got the cargo forward, he stuck to keep it there, and succeeded. The stern was lightened, and the paddles, instead of having to lift several hundred-weight of water as each one strikes in turn, only dip in far enough to make the stroke and lightly rise from the water without waste of steam-power.

April 1.—We made a fine start to-day. The wheel spins round and the boat goes better at fifty pounds of steam than at seventy pounds before, making thirty-two revolutions a minute, against twenty-four before. We come to sand-islands again this morning, and a pleasant strip of wood along the right bank. Somewhere behind those woods are the fine people that Kund and Tappenbeck found between the Kassai and Lukonye. I would like to see them! The country presents a very different aspect from that of the Lower Kassai, or of the section just this side of the Kwango. We camp by a small forest, but were disappointed in our expectation of finding dry wood, as there was none except an immense tree of very hard wood, a task to cut, even if the axes were good, and hard to split too. The men chopped awhile, and then stopped.

At 1:30 A. M. there was a big storm. I heard the wind and waves slapping the sides of the boat. The captain began to call to his men to come from the beach and save the steamer. Then Mr. Simar was driven up to take refuge with us; and then by flashes of lightning I could see that the stern was slowly slipping in shore and pitching up and down with the waves. Mr. Simar cried out, "Nous partirans, l'encre ne tient pas!" (We are moving away. The anchor doesn't hold.) The stern-anchor was really dragging. The captain kept shouting, and finally, going out, I found that he had three Wangatta, and they were preparing to cut the limbs towards which we had slipped. Mr. Sirex came too with caution, and presently the limbs were out of the way. The wind soon made way for the rain; a better alternative by far.

We had peach pie to-day. It beats hard-tack.

April 2.—I was wakened by the crack of Sheppard's rifle and a shout, but he didn't get the nguvo. Then a worse racket began. The head-man of the soldiers was getting fifty "chicot," *i. e.*, fifty blows with that instrument. Then Mr. Simar and the captain came, without a word from me, and began to defend their action. It seems that the men had all stopped work; and eight Wangatta, on the captain's approach, had taken to the bush; so the head-man gets the "chicot." We wait here all day while the captain goes up and down in a canoe for wood. Mr. Simar is sick, and I put him in my bed. Fever!

When Sheppard was sick, I was breaking an egg for him, when my boy, Mpiata, saw something in it which made him stop me, saying, in his Kru-boy English, "Small boy for this egg." He followed the analogy of his language, which has a single word, "mwana," to indicate a small boy or a small chicken.

This afternoon three canoes from some neighboring village came with things to sell. They are good looking and of fair size, seeming to have plenty to eat at home. The women's short hair was worked into little twists or rolls from the point of the head to the forehead. They had mostly little rolls of kwanga, eight inches long and not quite as large as your wrist, wrapped in leaves and tied with grass, which they were selling four for one ntaku, *i. e.*, two for a cent. It appears that bread gets or remains dear as we go inward, while meat gets very cheap. We can get a good chicken for two or three ntaku, while they cost twenty at Stanley Pool. The small boys run their canoes along-side the steamer, and those whose arms are long enough trade across the gunwale, and there is a lively waving of hands and reaching of them across with ntaku, or cowries, or beads, or handkerchiefs; the vendors as eagerly shouting and handing out the kwanga, or chickens, or whatever they have to sell.

I noticed to-day that the spears have larger blades and longer handles than I am used to.

April 3.—There are a good many people here this morning, but the villages are hidden by bushes or islands. The river to-day widens again, there appearing one main (?) channel, a quarter of a mile wide, and others lost amid the maze of sand and grass islands in a bed two miles across. Now the grassy slope gives away for occasional forests, and then, pleasing change, there are steep little grass-covered ridges near the water hiding the country behind, and ending in a twenty-foot bluff overhanging the rushing, rocky stream.

At 9 o'clock I went to the bridge and took a look at Mount Pogge, a distant blue knoll, visible between nearer ridges of pale green. Then near noon we came to a still wider reach. There were islands of some size and clothed with forest trees, instead of the tiresome mimosa scrub. There were feathery *elaïs* palms near the water and the great wind-mill borassus on the grassy ridges.

These are the Basongo Mino, the "Saw-tooth cannibals" so called, but seem as decently disposed folk as you would care to see. We came to a village, and were landing for chop and wood, when the people watching us, waved us *by* (not *down* as they would at one of our flag stations at home). So the captain obediently turned around, and spent two hours hunting for a landing below, only to return to fifty yards below the village, whose citizens erst so fearful, now came eagerly to trade. At the same time a big canoe with seventeen men and women pushed bravely between the *Florida* and the beach, and opened a brisk trade. They had for sale kwanga and handsome little gourds, figured with pointed knife and the top cut out in notches so as to fit tightly on again. There was one handsome horn, or tusk, like mother of pearl, and there were little aprons woven of the inner bark of the palm, ornamented with little balls, like those on a baby's cro-cheted sacque. Two of these, each ten inches by eight, constitute a lady's attire here. I also saw a purse of antelope skin, with two pockets to carry any small object, except money, of which you know there is none here. One gent was desirous to sell his dog (to be eaten of course). The currency we paid them was brass rods, cowries, beads and handkerchiefs. The cowries are little shells made in Birmingham, England, and are like those we children in Selma used to play with, calling them pigs, only these are smaller.

I saw several women who had lumps under each temple. I observed that the old grey-headed man, who was probably a chief, had two of these lumps on his forehead. I observed that their arrows had on them heads of iron, jointed near the head, so that when the wounded man tries to pull the arrow out, the head stays in the wound. I see a new kind of hair dressing. The men's hair is put in two or more large rows from back to front and extending over the forehead a little.

I see Mr. Simar to-day dressing the wounds of his men, even the one who received them under chicot by his orders; a transaction he regrets very much.

April 4.—When I awoke this morning we were exactly opposite Mount Pogge, which is about three hundred and fifty feet high. Two long slopes on opposite sides lead, not abruptly, up to a grassy cone. There is a peaked ridge parallel with the river. The side towards the river is the steeper, and is alone clothed with forest trees.

We camp on the left bank, at the point where Lieut. Kund crossed the Kassai. A big "K" cut with an axe in the baobab tree here at the landing marks the point of crossing. We had a nguvo hunt in the little lagoon, and find her ladyship and the little lord nguvo in the grass forty-five yards from the canoe passage, but we couldn't induce her to come out into sight, unless we had shot into her dining-room, and then she might have come out in too big a hurry, and being little I might have got "trompled on," as our old African at home "Uncle Josh" used to say; so we don't provoke her. The captain says there is plenty of wood, which the people have cut and bundled for us, and we help ourselves, and the people don't raise a row, but sell us provisions as usual. Three of us go to bed sick, for lack of exercise probably, and want of some variety in our food.

April 5.—Sunday. The captain doesn't start until he has chicoted some five of his Wangata. They yell like everything, and so I hope they aren't hurt so badly, only receiving some fifteen cuts each.

Four canoes pursue us with chop; they are little slender black canoes, looking like fancy horse troughs, twelve to twenty-five feet long, with two to five paddlers, and the paddles larger than usual, and shaped like spades on cards. They do "scoot," keeping up with the "dikumbi" (steamer) very easily. Finally poor dikumbi "hit the grit" literally, and stopped perforce. Then the captain, making a virtue of necessity, gave his men leave to buy chop, and they proceeded to take it, jumping into the water, spilling the owners out of their canoes, grabbing chickens and the like. The people got away as quick as they could, yet were not so much frightened as to prevent their selling what chop they had left. At 3 P. M. we camped at Mpendi: so Mr. White, B. M. S., names the town.

It was a rare picture. I was reading and looked up to see, just beyond a bank clothed with soft and varied foliage, a neat comfortable cottage on a little shelf of clear ground, with a cluster of banana trees on each side and branches of forest trees meeting overhead. On landing we found there were ten houses, for the shelf extends a little way in between the high bank or hill mentioned and a little yellow creek. "Peculiar houses," says Mr. White, "first of the kind *we* have seen. Doorway some four feet above the ground, and is a hole eighteen inches square reached by a trestle of sticks." The houses are higher than any I have seen on the Congo, and more in the proportions of our own houses. Mr. White says they have a "squarish look," which results from their not being so squatty, like all other Congo houses are. These are nine or ten feet to the comb of the roof; the house is about eight feet by ten, and the roof is of borassus palm leaf. The sides are weatherboarded with reed or bamboo or palm midrib, but very close and compact.. On the whole they are most like our notions of house-building I have seen, though for some time I have noticed the same in Kassai houses.

Canoes came over in spite of a big rain. The men wore the best native cloth I have yet seen. It is thick as jeans, and with patterns like percale, though not so closely woven probably. It is made of mpusu, the inner bark of one kind of palm. Around one man's waist I saw a cord for all the world like that which we wear on dressing-gowns, tassel and all. One woman has only a curtain of grass before and behind, fastened on a waist-string of grass rope; this is the only such dress I have seen. The usual attire just here for the ladies is the little apron with balls in front and a cloth like a small fringed towel behind, secured by a girdle.

Where did these people, whose utter simplicity shows that they have seen very few white men, learn designs in work and weaving which I had thought peculiar to us? The velvet cloth of the Bakuba, the little balls on the women's aprons and a lunch-basket with a hasp, bought on the Kwilu, all show more skill than we credited them with.

There is another town back from the river. Sheppard was there during a rain and stopped under the eaves of a house. The people sold us plenty of fowls, one goat and a good deal of wood. I noticed one high bank to-day, flecked here and there with a pretty carpet of a wide-leafed fern or other similar herb. The foliage is very prettily varied. It is often lighter than on the Congo, and besides curtains of vines with festoons and streamers, there will be in every hundred-yard-piece of forest canvas, one or two trees, furnishing a variety of another color, such as pink spring-time leaves, or red September ones, or a sprink-

ling of red berries, or as yesterday a tree having leaves of green with
crimson fringes; so it seemed at any rate, and the look of it is the main
thing to our tired eyes.

We are wandering through a maze of low islands, some of them
wooded, and some only sand and grass. Some of them are about two
and a half feet under water, and their existence is only ascertained by
hearing the cry "Two fathoms," and then ting! ting! ting! ting! (these
four bells tell the engineer to slow up), then we hear the cry "Four
feet" followed by one ting! which means stop, but that we have already
done with a bump-crau-aunch!—we are on a sand-bank, ting! ting!
ting! "Quenda mai!" (go into the water) the captain cries to his
Wangata. Splash, splash. All overboard. Then five minutes of
grunting and pushing, many of them concentrating all their energies
on the former, and we are off again.

Mr. Simar is very ill to-day, and seems to have hæmaturic fever.
Kind Mr. Sirex is greatly exercised; will come to the window and
talk to me as I sit on the opposite couch from the patient, and express
his anxiety, and exhort Mr. Simar to sweat and let it all come out;
and so I have to carry him off. By and by the fever goes down, and
Mr. Simar is at supper.

We stop at a place where there is much wet grass and myriads of
mosquitoes, even before dark, and the men can hardly work. There
was a tornado in the night.

April 6.—No wood to start with, and the usual talk about chicot
and other unpleasant palaver, which melts into better feeling as we
get well away at 9 o'clock, and have a good morning, steaming without
touching a bank anywhere—first day we can claim that in a long
while. The river is narrowing, with a forest on both sides and the
land rising. We stop at a town with the same kind of people as at
Mpende (if this is not the real Mpende), and the houses are not so
high as the other Mpende; with roofs and walls of leaves, one edge
in and one out, a shaggy coated house.

The women have the tribe mark. Hardly any of the men have it.
Many of them are of lighter complexion than usual, the hair is worn
bushy, but without the elaborate dressing I met a little below. They
have copper rings on wrists and neck, which are usually heavy, and
not quite meeting about the wrist, and made of native copper. I saw
a lovely shopping-bag of cloth, decorated all over with tufts of colored
thread; and I also see more of that thick "percale" cloth, noticed a day
or two ago. We buy chickens and eggs (the latter all bad). We get
also a goat and a good deal of Indian corn meal in leaf packets a foot

high and four inches in diameter. They are very welcome to us who haven't seen any bread but hard-tack for ever so long. The village is in three parts, each of which lies along the bank, and is ornamented with plantains, and sheltered behind by a forest which is on rising ground. Indeed, the scanty place for these forty houses has been lately cut out of the virgin forest, taking only space enough for two rows with a twenty-foot street between. I bought a bugle here, not very large or fine, for four ntaku.

April 7.—The left bank to-day shows a decided hill all the way,

fifty to a hundred feet high, and is clothed in dense forest to the water's edge, where it ends in lovely drapery of thick vines in varied and fantastic shapes and patterns. Here and there are patches on the hill-side of grass or gardens, and here and there a village, with the elais palm plumes, notable as we scan the slanting floor of tree tops from mid-stream. The Kassai seems half a mile wide on an average to-day—a lovely stretch of scenery.

Mr. Simar shows very bad symptoms again. Though not very ill, the hæmaturia symptoms are quite marked. We made a long run to-day, without many sand-bank incidents. We saw lots of hippos as usual, but not very near. Sheppard and I each struck one, but we did'nt get them. The sun was going down and the forest near which we steamed was all swampy near the

THE MALAFU GATHERER.

river, with no camping place in sight; but, turning a corner, we saw one of the prettiest of sights: a bend in the stream with a high hill for bank, and clothed on this side in richest forest verdure to the summit, a hundred and fifty feet sheer above, the foliage soft and pleasantly diversified with all shades of green, and here and there a spark of scarlet. On the other side of the angle is a red clay cliff, and it is equally adorned with patches of green and crested with tall trees.

Curious enough, on one of the tallest of these trees, a palm, apart and set off against the sky, hung a malafu gatherer, thirty feet from the ground, and on the edge of the cliff, like a spider or monkey for all the world. He was supported by a stout bark hoop around his waist and around the tree, with his feet pressed against the tree, and his back against the hoop. He was arranging the gourds inserted in the base of a frond to insure a good catch to-night of the juice of which the malafu or palm wine is made. The steamer ran into a little black creek under the cliff, which is here wooded again; but I can see through the opening in the leaves a group of natives with torches, on the top of the cliff.

I put Mr. Simar in my bed to-night, and arranged a good place with my mosquito bar and blankets on his camp-bed outside. There was a storm during the night, and I had to re-adjust more than once to get right under the waterproof spread to help the poor old roof.

April 8.—Climbed to the top of the cliff, and found a nice town on a level plateau; two compact rows of houses with an eighty-foot space between them, this space partly occupied by a royal divula [enclosure], which is a house and little yard not much finer than the others, which are plain, fair, leaf-roofed and bark-lined, with walls made of palm midribs. There are twenty houses in each row. The people are pleasant looking; Sheppard thinks they are like the Bayansi, only not so well fixed up. A little hair braiding, but not much attention to this; all of them wear a single waist cloth of native "percale"; their bodies are profusely ornamented in fancy figures. As usual in this part of the country, many wear rows of small bracelets on the same wrist. I saw the king with his sceptre of buffalo tail. I found him very affable, and he sold me a very nice little tusk for one bell. There was a brisk trade in red-wood, not ground off or made into rolls. There was a good deal of other ivory which they would not sell. They are said to resemble the Bakete people.

We pulled out of our creek at full speed astern, and had a close shave. as we were about to run the stern into the bank and break the wheel; but the captain gave the signal and Mr. Sirex reversed at full speed and so saved us. The captain is nervous about snags now, having struck on one last night and hung up awhile. We spent two hours wandering among the shallows, touching sand-banks, drawing off and coming at them again like a quarrelsome ram. We passed two nice leaf-roofed towns, with twenty houses in each, set gable to gable so close as to touch. From one of them on the mainland, canoes with goats, fowls and ivory came among the sand-banks to us; but they were

A LOGGING HIPPO.

so silly they would not come close enough to sell. but stopped six feet
off, so we left them. But one was spurred by this to paddle hard and
catch up and hand his ivory, a tusk two feet long, into the steamer,
receiving for it two strings of beads.

On the left bank the water is a very red yellow, from the Loangé
river, which is not very far up now. We are approaching the region
where it may be our privilege to work.

While at dinner, Macaulay, the pilot, called us to see a troop of hipppos
on an island near. We went for them in a canoe, and got in thirty
yards before they ran. We gave a big whitish one several bullets,
but he went after the big black one and the middle-sized one, and the
wee small black one, like a tornado to the water, all of them switching
their tails and snorting and splashing the water far and wide. We
had some more shots at them as they lay out from the beach with their
heads up, looking to see what had scared them so. But we had to
leave them there, as we had no more cartridges with us. We camped
by a wooded slope, in order to get "nkuni" [firewood]. Since three
o'clock we have been near the left bank, in water distinctly pink; one
would think that it had blood or at least paint in it. It comes
from the Loangé or Timbwé or Tenda river, which enters not
many miles above here, coming in from the south. The rudder is
out of fix.

April 9.—I awoke late and found we had not gone yet. Mr. Sirex
examines the rudder and pronounces the left rudder in a bad state,
and we had to wait to repair it, but were off about ten o'clock. But we
have bad wood, rotten and wet, and hence poor steam all day, and
plenty of contention in consequence as to who killed "cock robin."
Still he died, *i. e.*, we made only two hours all day.

We went by the south or left bank, which rises from the water's
edge a hundred feet, clothed in lovely woods of tall trees. Here and there
is a clearing and a little village nestling in its nook on the hillside. The
houses are Swiss looking, and a good many on this bank; almost a
heavy population on the other. We came at sundown to the source of
this red water, the Loangé itself, entering by a single mouth sixty to
a hundred yards wide, swift, and blood red almost. The brown Kassai
water shrinks from mingling, while clouds of red seem slowly to pene-
trate and force itself among the brown. The Kassai just here is very
narrow, not two hundred yards wide, and a high wooded point faces
the mouth of the Loangé. All the banks are densely forested.

Up the Loangé, on the left bank among the trees, is a small town.
Up the Kassai, on the right bank, is a fair Bakuba town, the first of

them as far as I can be sure; but the mark is the same, beside the eye
or cheek bone. They are pleasant spoken and looking, and brought
us a pile of dry wood. In a few minutes, in every opening between the
jumbled houses, streamed men and women bearing sticks to the
captain. There were some fifty houses, without any order, having only,
by chance as it were, a space in the centre for trade or palaver. The
houses face any way and every way, and are new in style. The roofs
are of oil-palm leaves, looking like a head of straight hair combed
right down. The sides are boarded or battened outside with ribs of
same; but the corner posts and the end rafters are prolonged and stick
up a great way as in an Indian wigwam; and either a grass wall-court
or a covered entry is in front of each. There seem to be some hundred
grown people here, all busy carrying on a lively selling of kwanga
cider.

At this Bakuba town there was a great row about some hungry
steamer men stealing goats from the town's people. I ran out and found
everybody stirred up, and the captain coming in with a drove of can-
didates for the chicot. As my men had been given some of the stolen
property to hold, I went into the matter too, and helped as interpreter
to see that the prisoners got a hearing, but they were convicted and
flogged. I was wakened the next morning by hearing a louder racket,
and went out just as some of Mr. Simar's men were led up amid great
hubbub to get chicot for stealing or losing a number of axes. Mr.
Simar had taken chloral at my hand last night and was still asleep.
The captain lashed one fellow right and left and ordered him to lie
down for a good dose, when I stepped up saying .

"S'il vous plait, cet homme ci est a M. Simar, et il dors." [If you
please, this is Mr. Simar's man, and he is asleep.]

He, in towering rage; "Pourquoi m'arrêtez vous?" [Why do you stop
me?]

I replied, "Et ils font leur defense que vous n'avez pas encore en-
tendu." [They are making their defence which you have not yet heard.]
He rushed in to arouse Mr. Simar, but failed to awake him. But the
whipping was suspended, and all axes turned up at once but one, as
soon as looked for. Meanwhile, Mr. Simar awoke, full of smiles and
acknowledgments for the good sleep; "but had dreamed about palavers and chicots." I reported what I had done in his name and in
his behalf; and the captain coming up while I was speaking, I fool-
ishly thought myself bound to repeat what I had said to Mr. Simar.
The captain having lost all control of his temper, asked me to consider
myself as only a passenger on the steamer. Then Mr. Simar pitched

in, and a painful scene followed.[1] I think, however, the captain will
see and think better of it before the trip ends. There is a necessity
of punishing the goat thieves promptly and severely, otherwise we
would be in danger of rows with the natives.

We passed in good view of Ngung (?), the largest single village on
the Kassai: a compact village of two or three thousand inhabitants
on the hillside, south bank, one mile above the Loangé mouth. The
houses are so packed together that the whole space occupied does not
seem to be more than thirty acres, perhaps less. There are other
clearings on the wooded hillside for gardens, and I thought I saw one
good "new ground" with fine corn on it. The plantations seem to
be all up stream from the towns, so that the loaded canoes may have
the advantage of down stream in bringing home the harvest.

The same morning a few hours up from Ngung we reached other
"twin cities," almost facing each other across the river. That on the
south or left bank is Basili, a large village; Mr. White says it belongs
to the Bazolele, but they seem to me to be Bakuba. The town has
some hundred and fifty or two hundred houses, low and old, and
huddled together. The people are good looking and well behaved.
(But give them a chance and they are arrant thieves!) Immediately
on the landing of the steamer they began to run up, men and women,
with arms full of big sticks of wood, and chaffer with the captain for
a good price. This being quickly settled, the wood came pouring in
faster than the captain could hand out the big blue cylinder beads.
They had it piled up ready for instant use on the steamer's arrival.

Meanwhile, we spied some rare beauties in the way of cloth. On a
strong ground are worked, in a raised velvety nap like plush, symmetrical and tasteful patterns, colored black and straw color; and I got
a mat, six feet long and four feet wide, worked in red and yellow half
diamonds and lozenges. These are specialties of the Upper Kassai
people.

We went on past a number of pretty nestling towns, and Sheppard
and I selected a pretty ridge and point, at the bend between Basili
and these towns, as our possible station.

In the afternoon I heard a shout, "There is a soldier!" and sure

---

[1] Writing to the "Mother Confessor," to whom he generally confides things,
he thus reflects on himself for this affair:

"And I have not been diligent and vigilant enough to keep the peace, and
have even got into the row myself, though I haven't done any "railing," I am glad
to say. But it was a very lazy, self-indulgent pastor that could'nt keep his flock
pro tem. from getting into such a mess."

enough, in blue blouse and red cap, a state soldier paddled out to us from a little riverside town. We took the canoe alongside to where we camped, and sent him back with a dash for his "father and mother" in the town, and a message that if they would bring him up and the other six, his fellow-captives, we would give a good dash. It seems the people saw the seven runaways from the "Ville de Verviers," in January, and took them in, fed and cared for them in a sort of honorable confinement; each man being adopted into a family. Our messenger showed where his "mother" had just trimmed his hair neatly. Before he got out of sight, his "father" and another native caught up, received the message from us and promised to return that night. In the morning early, we got them, all seven, and their hosts departed proudly with a gorgeous dash, viz., seven handkerchiefs, seven ntaku, seven big blue beads, sixty or eighty cents, say a dollar's worth, for two months for seven men. If we could keep ours at twice that rate it would be cheap living.

We passed Sankuru mouth from nine to eleven A. M. There is a wide delta full of long islands, some sand and grass, some low bush and some forest. I could see the ridges between which the Sankuru flows. It is estimated that the Sankuru runs 15,000 cubic feet per second, the Kassai above 45,000. The Sankuru is clear deep water, the Kassai a brownish yellow. The Kassai is to-day a compact, narrow stream with a swift current. It is about eight hundred and twenty yards wide, twenty-two feet deep, and the current is about four feet per second, and the height above the sea about thirteen hundred feet. The Sankuru is about five hundred yards wide, fifteen feet deep, with a current three feet per second.

There is plenty of wood aboard to-day; so things are pleasanter. There are no villages in sight this morning, only big woods, but a few canoes are plying every now and then. At 10:45 we passed a village on the east or right bank. There are high wooded slopes rising right from the water's edge, with red clay banks cropping out here and there. The men are getting hungry and chop running low.

April 14.—My twenty-fifth birth-day. "How wonderfully God has led me through the past twelve months."

We passed several villages without stopping; at which I expended much needless indignation. At dinner time we stopped for wood by a flat wood with plenty of dead trees and a new town on the beach, a quarter of a mile down. There are larger towns inland. The captain, Mr. Simar and Sheppard went in a canoe for chop. Are these people Bakuba? There is no velvet cloth, but plenty of looms for plain cloth, and an abundance of everything. A "hearty town" as Sheppard describes it. The captain got a fine carved cup—a figure of a man with the cup within. Sheppard got a funnel and a large cup elegantly carved in black wood. They got a fair amount of chop, no kwanga, but plenty of corn meal and plantains, and especially of fish. There are many people here, but as they live behind the riverside wall of thick bush, the steamers and explorers failed to see them.

April 15.—More wood. We push ahead. The river not very wide. Here and there a cluster of green islets and a big bush island with clay banks peeping out. The wooded hillsides have a rich variety of foliage, from an etherially brilliant light green to bronze green. At 11:30 we passed the mouth of the river Langalla, and also this morning passed a small one called Lakedi, both on the right or east bank. I think that the headquarters of a great king are inland, up the Langalla. We made a good, long day's progress, but late in the afternoon came very near being wrecked in a very simple piece of water. There is a strong point where two down currents meet from above and rush around it with tremendous force. This forms great swirls in the line of the current below, and a strong back current on either side of the united current below the point. We came up near the bank and steered across the strong water. When the bow got into the down current the stern was still in the up current, and of course the steamer got a sharp turn-around; and this performance was repeated several times, and the boat was wheeled around like a floating stick and went full speed toward the bank. By a special providence the steamer was turned in time, so that, though much frightened, no damage resulted.

April 16.—We were delayed by the hanging of the anchor. Sheppard joined the divers, who ascertained that it was fast in a limb fifteen feet down. He went down the chain, not hand over hand, but hand under hand. He and Macaulay afterwards hauled it out with a windlass, the steamer pulling a little also. At noon we stopped again for wood, and lost about two hours by a repetition of the morning's frolic with the anchor. We stopped for night at a little islet which harbors a dozen canoes and has two little fisherman sheds on the bank. We went up a steep hill by a well-worn path, getting wider as the land becomes more practicable, until we found the road, a fine rustic avenue with the bushes lately cut away some three yards on each side; though if it had been twenty yards the natives would have still walked in the single file path in the middle. Presently we arc on a grassy plateau, and soon the sound of brisk trading is heard. Here we are in sight of town, and find it walled! The wall is a rectangle, and is made of the same material as the walls of the houses; it is several hundred yards each way, though I couldn't get a chance to measure it. Groups of men and women came from the town up to where we were.

They wanted to sell us chop, and greatly desired my little mirrors, saying by signs, "Come in, and I can please you, I am sure," like a good merchant. I crawled in through a small hole at the ground, which was the only gate. Sheppard followed me, but could hardly make it. Inside all were busy trading, for every soul had left the steamer except the captain, engineer, Mr. Sinar, and two or three boys. My merchant hurried me from the yard in which I first found myself by a good wide gate into a large rectangular plaza, with a few trees in it, and a grand shed fifty feet by thirty in the middle.

Sheppard and I are agreed that we would like much to preach under that shed.

There were larger crowds grouped around various parties from the steamer, buying chop in quantities for their respective messes. Nice looking people. Cleanly, head shaved, except a chignon at the apex, and this topped by a natty little cap, fastened on with ivory or fancy brass hairpins, lady fashion. Picturesque effect, erect, graceful, easy carriage, clean, dark body, yellow cloth hanging from the waist, and the topknot dressed fancifully, or covered with a little grass cap.

I was led into another yard, for all open on this plaza, and found some of my own boys buying there. My guide took me into another small door yard, his home. His wife and her little boy (who was dressed like Adam) sat in this gate. A crowd of girls and women began to enjoy the lookingglass; and so I asked for cloth in exchange for it, and a fine one was finally produced. The women have specially fine features, small noses, very thin lips, and are very light colored. They are frank, given to laughing, and have pleasant, soft voices. My friend's wife was a pretty little woman. Another partner now insisted he could beat the proposed bargain, and seized my arm and conducted me in triumph into and across the public square, through a yard, across an alley—all fenced off some way—into a second yard, and finally into one inside of that. He turned me round, and behold under a shed by his house sat the chief, Makima, a pleasant fellow, with his chignon and ample red waist-cloth. A group of women and children were near him, and one, his wife (or favorite one), sat by him under the shed. There were the same pleasant smiling faces, and

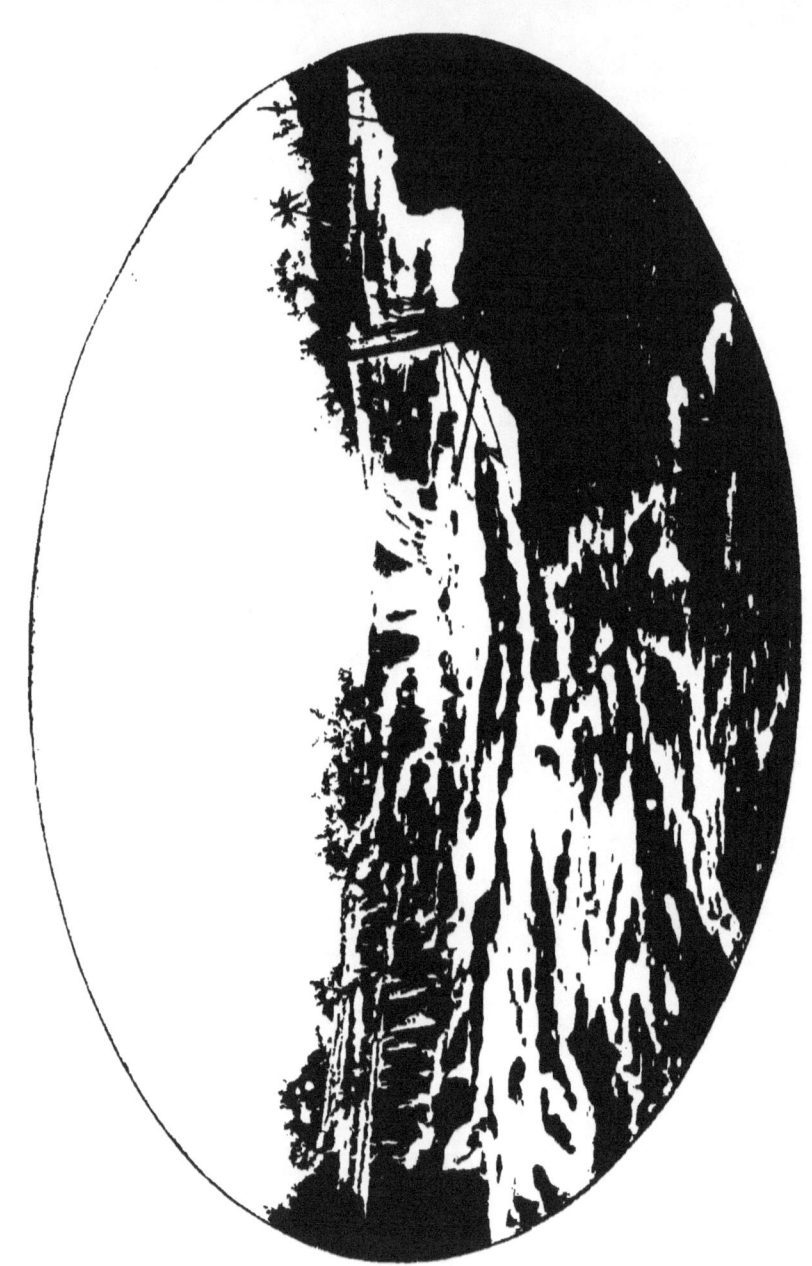

FALLS OF LUMBOULA, NEAR LUEBO.—Photo. in " Le Congo Illustre."

intensely interested voices, eager to tell me something, but not quite intelligible to me, you may be sure. But I took the seat offered me, dashed the king and his wife (her first), and then asked for the cloth, which not coming, I went away to make the best of the fading light elsewhere. Sheppard got two exceedingly fine pipes, the stems large and two feet long, the mouth-piece the drum-stick of a big rooster, I think; the bowls and stems are finely carved. The bowl of one is a fine head, the ears, eyes, mouth, and hair very finely done.

Mr. Sirex's messenger got my piece of cloth. I am a poor trader!

April 17.—We enter the Lulua about ten this morning, leaving the Kassai on our right, flowing between a row of green islands and issuing from between two far blue ridges.

Maybe we will know those hills some day!

We see again the invariable reluctant mingling of waters: the deep clear brown and the muddy yellow. The muddy, hill country water is from the west, as always in the Kassai, from Kwa-mouth here. The Lulua seems very small, but deep and swift. More signs of natives, canoes, and new bits of villages on the bank; for these people are not river traders, and are only now moving to the bank, to meet the steamers, I think. I see fishing huts on the bank and fish-traps, especially a little fence of sticks in the shallow water or little creeks, to profit by the falling water, now that the high water is beginning to abate. There are many islands in the Lulua, and most of the way we are steaming in a narrow channel, fifty yards wide. There is beautiful foliage on both sides, and it is wooded all the way as far as we have gone. We stop at ten o'clock for wood, and camp early for the same reason.

April 18.—The men are all glad and dressed in their best. At nine o'clock we passed a ferry, where a great trade road crosses the Lulua, and I can see the open road under the high trees, and three stout canoes on one side. The *Florida* once camped here, so Macaulay says.

Mr. Simar is again sick.

At noon we rounded Luebo point, and came in sight of a group of plantains, and, shaded by these, a double row of small houses of mud with thatched roofs. Then we saw the ample thatches of five or six large adobe houses, tastefully disposed on a fair table-land in the right angle made by our little Lulua, and a large creek on our right, the Luebo.

The grounds are well kept and are graced with rows of palms, still mall, like great ferns, with fronds eight feet long. A heavy palisades

11

of sharpened posts ten feet high completes the square begun by the two streams.

All of us are on the bridge but Mr. Sirex, who must stand by the engine. There are two sharp whistles, and the station is astir. Soldiers and workmen and a crowd of other humbler blacks are rushing about. Finally all gather at the point between the rivers. Our boatmen have got the drum which Mr. Simar sat on at the table, and are having a breakdown (dance) under us now. Now our glad hosts prospective are shouting welcome to those they know, and station boys are pointing out to each other faces or objects they recognize on board.

Now we are ashore, meeting the two agents for the company and the agent for the State, and the commissaire du district du Kassai, who may be able to help us greatly in our plans, by giving at once his sanction to our application for land.

Good chop in the "Salle-a manger" of the station!

Everybody is deep in their letters, the first for many months. Every little while comes an exclamation from one of the rooms at the side, where somebody had fallen on a bit of startling news. "Le Prince Baudouin est mort!"[1] "De Prinz Baudouin ist gestorben!"[2] We are invited to stay a little while as guests of the chief of the "factory" (trading post), and can board as long as we choose. We have a quiet afternoon while they are unloading the steamer's cargo. Before supper we are summoned to share a bottle of brandy on the veranda before the dining-room. Naturally we let the rest enjoy our share.

There is plenty of fresh meat here. At our evening meal we had soup, liver, sheephead, chops, stew, and some simple pudding. There were Irish potatoes, grown here, and other vegetables with the mutton—not goat. Mr. Engrens has a great herd of goats and sheep. We brought our own boys, chairs, cups, forks, knives and spoons. The house and service and all is such as is usual on the Congo, only the house is higher and more stable-looking than any clay house I know; and they speak to the boys in an unknown tongue, Baluba or Portuguese. There are many boys here from the Portuguese on the coast, particularly from St. Paul de Loanda and Malange.

The influence of the Portuguese and Belgians is nearly balanced, but even here plenty of coast English (Kru-boy) is spoken by Portuguese slave boys. The whole region has been for generations a

---

[1] Prince Baudouin is dead.   [2] The same in German.

centre for slave trade. I believe the great trans-continental slave route is below this, but there is an open road to the coast by Malange; (Dr. Summers came to Luluaburg that way), and the Portuguese of course know how to use it. The State forbids slave-holding, but has a provision whereby persons may ransom slaves, who then come under the control, "guardianship," of the ransomer for seven years; then the slave is finally at liberty. These liberés (freed men) must be registered as such before the commissaire du district, I believe. When the State overpowers a big slave trader, they get great numbers of slaves, who pass into the seven years' guardianship at once. At Equatorville (from the Mobangi and Lolongo rivers), at Lusambo (from the vicinity) and here, there are many liberés. The Compagnie has many here; and children are offered (for sale the dealers find it) at one, two and three dozen bandannas a head.

There is a great Bakete village two hours from here across the river on the north bank, and a smaller but fair one nearer. There is also a Portuguese trade post, or small branch, here on the north bank. By what title it is owned I don't know. One of the chiefs of it went to Stanley Pool last year with a flotilla of canoes carrying ivory and slaves. He got into trouble on the latter score, and has not got back. I saw his camp on a sand-bank last July.

Two big fat riding bulls rove at liberty about the place, and at Luluaburg, seventy-five miles up the river, they have buttermilk every day. Chickens at three, six and nine cents each, and goats are plenty.

The rage with the white men newly arrived at this El Dorado is to get some of the rare knives and battle-axes. You ought to see them—perhaps you will some day—and the mpusu palm cloth with velvet figures, and that with the soft satin feel about it, and the mats, and the fancy baskets. But to us the interest is, that it is the centre of influence from which the lines of trade radiate, where the State must make its capital for this district, instead of Luluaburg, I think; the point of contact, the point of attack, on the people of a vast region.

A letter under date of April 21st adds the following:

We are advised to locate across on the north side of the Lulua, half way between Luebo Station and the Bakete town of Bena Kasenga. The latter being about forty minutes walk from the ferry at the station.

I am pretty sure of getting this place. You may safely think of me as here, busy and happy. A heart full of love to you and all the dear ones. I am hungry to write to each. But so busy! Never mind. Settled soon, please God!

CHAPTER VIII.

LUEBO.

AFTER receiving the foregoing account of the trip up the river, there was long wearisome waiting; but after many months there came the diary, narrating the life at Luebo, which follows:

April 23, 1891.—We've had a house-raising to-day. The town of Bena Kasenga is in a very good humor with us, but is not inclined to trade or work for our ntaku. They want cowries. However, Sheppard managed before very long to persuade them to sell him a very nice house, ten feet eight inches square on the inside, and nine feet six inches high to the comb. It cost sixty ntaku, worth about one dollar and twenty cents, and forty cents worth of cloth. This paid for the moving to our clearing, three-quarters of a mile away, and raising it, or putting it up again. It was a great haul for four men to carry, one side at a time, resting against their backs, but they came running and singing. The roof was double, or more than double, weight, but it came at last, trotting along almost folded up, but showing four pairs of bare legs. Trenches were dug for the walls. The master mechanic from Bena Kasenga dug them with a little hoe he had in his belt, walking backward so as to keep the right line in his eye.[1]

The walls, one by one, were lifted and stood in their places, and shaken back and forth, to make the ends of the frame sticks settle into their holes. Then posts were planted inside at the corners, and the walls made solid by being tied with withs to the posts and to each other.

"But how are they going to put on the roof?" we asked each other. They simply put it on by main force, as they had often done before, and it rests there and needs no tying.

Sheppard is sleeping in the house now; we have divided the candles and keep each his house (tho' mine is the tent, which I hope to give up to-morrow night, as Sheppard has engaged a house for me).

---

[1] These houses consist of thick mats, tied to a frame-work of poles.

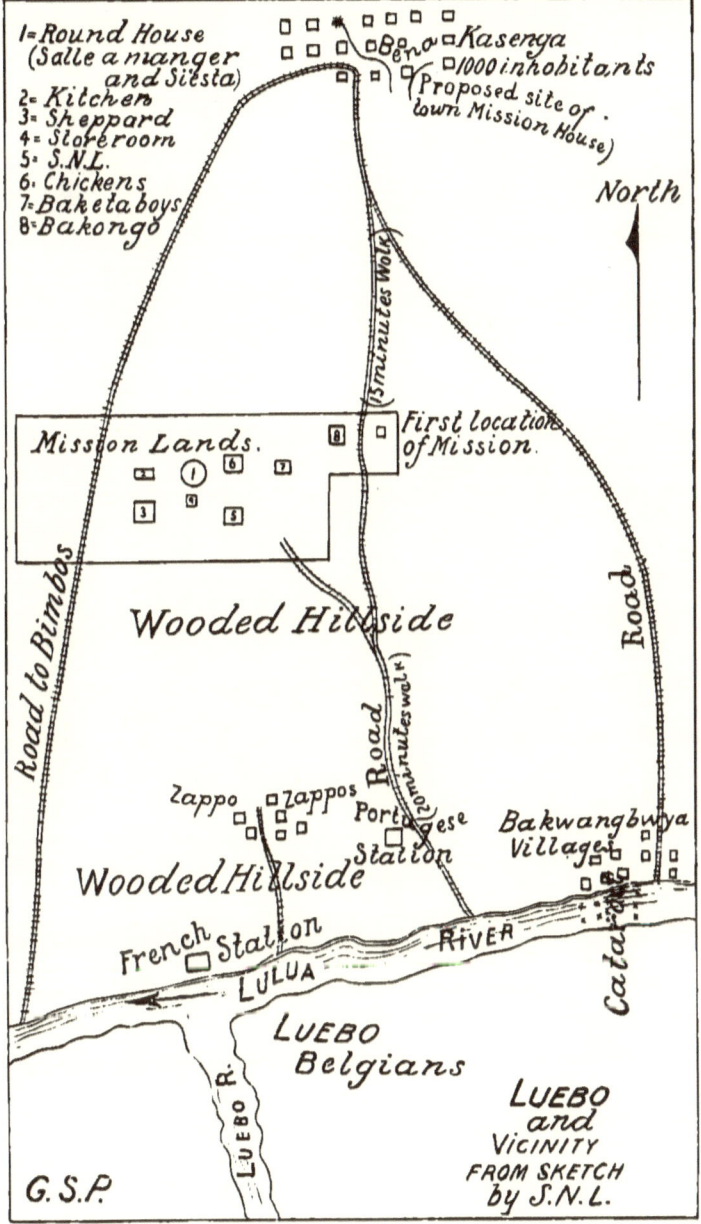

1= Round House
(Salle a manger
and Siesta)
2= Kitchen
3= Sheppard
4= Storeroom
5= S.N.L.
6. Chickens
7. Baketa boys
8. Bakongo

Bena □ Kasenga
□ 1000 inhabitants
(Proposed site of
town Mission House)

North

(5 minutes Walk)

Mission Lands.

First location of Mission

Road to Bimbos

Wooded Hillside

Road

(10 minutes walk)

Zappo □ Zappo's

Road

Portuguese Station

Bakwangbwya Village

Wooded Hillside

French Station

River

Cataract

LULUA

LUEBO R.

LUEBO Belgians

LUEBO and VICINITY FROM SKETCH by S.N.L.

G.S.P.

The *Florida* that brought us here went away yesterday morning. I felt indeed cut loose at last—some sadness, some solicitude, much joy and satisfaction.

M. Le Commissaire is very pleasant to me, and speaks of coming over to see us, before he leaves for Luluaburg. Mr. Engeringh's housekeeper was sick yesterday and he called me in to see her.

April 24.—Went over right after breakfast to see our friends at the Belgian station. I stepped across a black snake, the first snake I have found in Africa. Mr. Stache, the impetuous little "Germanish" Catholic, second in command at the Luebo station—Mr. E. is first— left yesterday for Wissman Cataracts on the Kassai, to buy ivory. He went on foot, not even taking his riding bullock, the roads are so narrow and overgrown. M. Le Commissaire is better; seemed pleased when I gave him part of the contents of an ergot bottle in our medicine chest, for his hæmaturia .

From where we sat on Mr. Engeringh's veranda this morning we heard a noise in the bushes across the little Luebo river, not a hundred yards from where we sat, and out came an antelope into the stream, and with her were two dogs. They swam together, hardly getting an inch closer or farther apart for two hundred yards. Away they went out of sight around Luebo point and into the Lulua, where the canoe caught up and took them all in. So we stayed and chopped venison. While I was writing, M. Le Commissaire came with the law about house tax, and the blanks to be filled by me. We went back home, being paddled across the Lulua in the big dug-out, by ten Accra boat-men and Logos head-men. We got five Bakete, whom we found "standing there idle," to carry our five loads up to our clearing, a twenty minute's walk, at what amounted to about two cents each. I bought an axe blade; really a good-sized chisel, native make, with two handles of wood hardened in the fire—one to use the blade as an adze, the other to use as a hatchet or small axe; the direction of the socket making the difference. Before long, Lisa, a woman, came along with a hoe to sell. I got it for three handkerchiefs—about eight cents. We bought some palm oil and rigged up lamps: simply letting a plaited rag lie in the open cup of oil, one end out.

The boys worked well to-day. By our return at 2 P. M., they had cleared a good space around where they are to put up their house. Sheppard went to town and got a mortar, for beating up mandioca into flour. He also exchanged five little bells for two hundred cowries.

April 25.—Midnight, a great commotion. Sheppard was moving about very rapidly, and even dancing, and addressing the people in

impassioned tones. On inquiry, I learned that a column of driver
ants had entered his house and taken possession. They even came
under his blankets and covered him: hence his animation. They
happened to be marching by and smelt the palm oil inside. We made
various reconnoissances with torches and candles, found many columns
pouring across the open space near his chimbrie, and many large
bodies deployed as skirmishers. One line had reached my tent door
just as I got up. A fire stopped them. I looked around and met
another body of them making for the back of the tent, where there
was a greasy spot black with them. . . . S. slept in the moonlight till day.

Got up my chimbrie by dinner-time. Not so large as S.'s, but there
is a door in mine down to the ground, besides the window through
which the former owner entered. Sheppard's has only a long window to climb in through. We planted a row of pine-apples in front
of each house. A party of Bakuba came by and bargained with us
for beads, and left with us twenty cowries to keep the bargain open
till Monday.

Sunday, April 26.—Quiet day. Stayed at home until 3 p. m.; went
into the town and walked through it. Five or six good double streets;
houses well built of stick, frame, palm leaves, and splits like cane,
polished neatly outside. A party followed us through the town, and
everywhere the people had ready greeting for "mukelenge."

"Mukelenge! eh! moyo, mm malengela!"

I reply, "Mmmm Malengela!"

This is the usual greeting and reply.

"Malengela" means good. Moyo is "salaam," well being, health, etc.

Rain caught me, and I took refuge under one of the many sheds
here and there in the centre of the village street. A fellow refugee
under the shed had a corn-stalk "beechee," which proved to have
more music in it than its looks promised. Before the shower was over
I had worked out on it a pretty fair accompaniment to "Blessed be
the fountain of blood," which song had been in my mind all day.
Many people were preparing or eating their early supper, as I could
see as I passed along. One young couple were chopping cozily together
as I looked in on them. Another good soul said to me: "Lamba
bidia," the precise words in which Nkuka's mother, Lolo, at Kintamo,
would tell me she was cooking chop. This shows the similarity of the
languages.

Every corner and cranny in the town has its inkissi or image, and
generally the rudest you could fancy in construction. The features

are portrayed by three cuts in a stick. Two strokes make the mouth, as many each eye, and the finish is planting it before the house or at the cross-road. But it is enough to keep them from believing the gospel; and we shall have a hard fight of it, no doubt, for even our boys still believe in the power of *nkissi*. One of these *nkissi* posts was sprouting. Was it a good or a bad omen for the Bakete augurs?

Busy folks. Very few were without something to do. But the principal business outside of bread-making, the great palaver of the women, is the manufacture of plain grass cloth. But it is not made of grass at all, but of the inner strips of the leaves of a small, dark palm; like the Elais palm, but not so large, and with prickles on the edges of the leaves. This cloth palm is grown all through the town, and there is a large patch of it besides, just beyond the town. I saw the manufacture in all its stages—boys stripping off the outside of the leaf blade, and leaving the delicate pale green ribbons within, and tying them in hanks like yarn. Men were separating it; threading the loom with the warp (is it?); and then came the clack of the simple but complete weaving machine, the simple, silent passage of the long polished stick which does duty as shuttle, and thus the usual every-day waist or loin cloth is finished. But the women pound a few choice pieces in a mortar with flour of maize or manioc till it is soft and satiny to the feel. These are dyed and worn on swell occasions.

April 27.—Our Congo boys in making their house went to the bush and cut a great lot of palm midribs, and got a man to bring in a bundle of rattan. The midribs were split and tied to the slender stick rafters by the split rattans; a flexible and very tough string.

Sheppard makes a shed in front of his house; begins to-day, employing some of the town people—two or three big boys. It is an important fact that these people like to work, and know how to *hire out*. Some Congo tribes won't do it for love or money. Two clever little urchins planted around my house pine-apple plants they had got in the bush. We bought some copper battle-axes; all very fine workmanship. I bought many hundred cowries for beads. Sheppard bought some with cloth. I got a native mandolin for two cents' worth of brass wire. It has a gourd for resonance; has a staff and three strings.

April 28.—Sheppard's house, and that of the boys, progresses well; ready for the thatch. I buy, with a double handful of beads, a goat, and a gem of a knife, one blade of native copper, eight inches long by two and a half inches wide, well made, and the black handle inlaid with strips of brass, hatched in regularly, and strangely tasteful.

A small trading party of some eight or ten Bashilange, from Ka-lemba, the great chief at Luluaburg, who has many thousand people in his town, passed this morning *en route* home. They had rubber and chop, some fowls and a parrot, but wouldn't sell anything. They had true tattooing with ink, especially the women, on brow and around the mouth, in most elaborate and faultlessly regular curves that did not deface them, and they had pretty and very interesting faces; the most prepossessing Africans I have seen, having European features and some of them having light complexions, mixed, as the Bakete are, with others of darker color.

WHITE ANTS.

Very hot to-day; sweltering and wilting. Last night and night before had palaver with "Nsilili"—the white ants. After the ground is swept and cleared of these rascals, their enemies, great, black, high-steppers, large as small wasps, come out of the ground, as by magic, and march around defiantly. They come from far, and go back with their nippers loaded with the white ants. The white ants infest the fresh, damp earth of my house. They crawled up the bed-post, and chopped a hole in my mattress before morning big as my hand, almost. I have made a big fire around my bed-post to-night, and feel quite secure until morning. Never fear, it will not hurt the post. I can cut another and plant in its place if it does. The bed-stead is a frame of small sticks lashed tightly on two side sticks with vines. These rest on four forks planted in the earthen floor, and sup-port an elegant horse-hair mattress, steamer rug, double blanket, and Austrian rug, in which I am luxuriously comfortable. My palm oil lamp is splendid, gives a blaze as big and strong as a student's lamp, without chimney of course, and makes plenty of good light when not in a draught.

The boys sitting near our rough tea-table out doors, after supper, have been telling yarns about how leopards do small boys when they catch them alone. "You hear a queer squeak about fifty yards away; the next thing the leopard's claws are in the boy's eyes, gets him down, licks him over and swallows him!" so says Mpiata, my boy.

Next the boas come into discussion. When attacked by a boa, a Bakongo knows how to thrust out his left hand, with fist doubled up as if to strike, perhaps. Then the boa thereupon swallows the man's arm. Then the Congo man, no wise scared, rips up the defenceless snake with the knife in the free hand. ("Give the Nyoka one hand, and when he swallows it do him *so* with the other." An appropriate gesture completes the little drama!)

Baba and Mpiata paid me an evening call. Baba, you will remember, is our deaf mute, who is so deft with fingers and quick with all the senses that he does enjoy. No bigger than a boy of eleven, though chunky and strong and shrewd enough for his sixteen years, he is a little irritable, and quite original and independent in his notions and ways. He expresses himself by saddest cries, is uncommonly intelligent; knows all about his own country, people and productions, all he could learn without instruction from books. He loves to confer with us, especially with Sheppard. His sign language is full and most expressive. It is equal to indicating anything he knows, is very natural and funny; and he is so shrewd in the observation of characteristics; *e. g.*, white man is indicated by pinching his nose—those "sharp-nosed people." Baba is the son of a chief down below Stanley Pool.

April 29.—The boys' house progresses. Two young women, belles from Mr. Engeringh's station, come over and make known their desire of marrying our two big boys, Ngoma and Mampuya. The matter is under consideration. I went over to Mr. Engeringh's for some more of our goods in store there. M. Le Commissaire not so well—slight fever again.

April 30.—I haven't slept well some nights; try a Dover's powder. Plenty of rain yesterday and to-day. Feverish at night. Sheppard buys two hens and two roosters.

May 1.—Good rest last night. I make a frame for a little hip-roofed veranda to my chimbric. Sheppard's veranda is a great success in all but looks.

A party of Zappo Zappos came by this morning with chickens and goats. We stopped them, but they asked double price for everything. They are fine looking folks to see, but have been given to chopping people and dogs. We let them go on. They came back in the afternoon with a gun. That was what they were after, and was why they would not trade with us.

The "young ladies" mentioned above are on hand to-day again. I found them installed and preparing supper in the tent which the boys occupy till their house is finished. So I escorted them, accompanied by their disconcerted bridegrooms, to M. Le Commissaire, who will see that the "ladies" remain on their side of the river until they are sent for. Our senior goat has not turned up to-night.

May 2.—Rain to-day. Sheppard's parrots thriving, but not advancing in command of the vulgar tongue, like Barnaby's "Grip." Driver ants discovered at dawn by S. and his cupid of a boy, Susu (re-named Sukie). They had made out three bands, like the Chaldeans, and crossed our demesne on a foray into the wood on the east of us. S. spied one brigade climbing the trees and making other ants and grasshoppers "june." (Do you remember your slang?) Two sisters from the town came by and helped expel the drivers. We found the columns condensed to two heavy lines, mostly making for home again, loaded with little grasshoppers, crickets, and such small game, by the thousand—a first rate entomological collection. Sprinkled manioc flour across their road. They don't like it, I think, because it clogs their legs. They began to thin out, especially when the two women from town threw among them bunches of a certain leaf from the woods.

I went to town and succeeded in getting six eggs for ten cowries, the proper price, but the nsolos (chickens) were held at ten times their value, as if by general pre-concert. One handsome mpuma (chief), with a little cap on his top-knot, adorned with soft, brown hawk's feathers, barely tinged red by nkula (cam-wood powdered), took me through the long street to his private seat, at the top of the street. It was a circle of houses, twelve in number, enclosing a court thirty yards in diameter, with a small shed in the centre for work, such as weaving, crushing Indian corn, manioc roots, etc. He had a cock caught and brought to where we sat—I on his stool, he on his goat skin, two or three wives standing around. One wife (the favorite I judged) brought me manioc flour, which I bought. The nsolo was at an impossible price, but we parted good friends without trading. He has a lovely knife in his belt, elaborately wrought, with handle of hard wood, like ebony, inlaid with alternate rows of yellow brass and native copper.

May 3.—Our first communion—wine and cakes of manioc flour were the elements. The boys witnessed it. We called attention to the fact that we showed forth the Lord's death and coming.

May 4 *and* 5. Roofing to my veranda goes on; so does the boys' house, and the clearing of the bush on the east side of the path. We get plenty, *plenty* of chickens. The embargo is up, it seems. We have a goodly number of pullets and quite an avalanche of roosters, from the Bakuba, I think—certainly from some town back—with combs all cut close, as if prepared to fight.

Night of the 5th.—At prayers I paraphrased the ridicule of an idolater in Isaiah xl., but as gently as I could, with the turn it takes in Isaiah, from the negative to positive. It was suggested by the exploits of wizards, which the boys related as common in their country. Very clever juggling, I must believe.

Coming back, heard the goat tramping about. Something up! Light! Nsalafu (drivers) again. By the time we could get our men to the scene, with dry grass to burn in the drivers' road, the army had reached a point within eight feet of Sheppard's house. Baffled there, they tried every point on our line, now away up in my corner, now by Sheppard's, now in the centre. The manioc flour did a little good, but not much, though they passed but one line of it, it is true. Where the column turned back on itself once, I watched it, a foot wide, almost solid, shoulder to shoulder, close as they could get, and marching quickly as they do, I guess they must pass at the rate of a million in about four minutes, perhaps. Though not the largest kind of ants, one of them would be big for Alabama, and they bite and destroy and clean up any animal matter, like grease or oil, as the locusts wipe up the grass. This morning there was not a trace of their ravages, except where a blazing tuft caught a pile of them feasting.

May 6.—House-finishing drags along. Hot. Marriage palaver still hangs on. Monday I went to M. Le Commissaire and he declined to let the women come at all. Siku, his interpreter, was by to-day on a message to the king of Bena Kasenga to come over to see the Commissaire.

Siku was servant to Major Wissman; then entered the employ of Dr. Summers, interpreting the Doctor's sermons to the Baluba; was with the poor Doctor when he died near Luluaburg, just starting for Luebo, the steamer, and home. The carriers wanted to bury Dr. S. on the road, but Siku made them take him back to Luluaburg, where his body lies, "far from his kindred and their graves." "But there still is a blessed sleep."

May 7.—Busy on accounts. Corrected balance sheet. Sheppard begins an addition to his house, rather an extension. We employ two active young fellows from the town for one month at one-half a piece of handkerchief each, about forty cents, perhaps, counting invoice price and subsequent expenses. One of them, Chinyama, came into service in this wise: He and the other, his chum, finished my shed roof yesterday. Just at eventide, a man came along with a dog; too much for Chinyama! Must have that dog, but it cost six handkerchiefs. "Would I lend them to him?" "No, but I would advance them to him on his taking a written contract to work a month."

Done; and his chum quickly followed suit. Good beginning. At Bolobo and Chumbiri, among the three score or so of workmen, not one comes from the Bayansi of the neighborhood, I believe; certainly very few, except house boys. A better region, this, to open a new work. We shall not import labor, unless we need skilled mechanics

A big man in Bena Kasenga died yesterday. Sheppard found the Ngangas (medicine men), a whole string of them, advancing on their patient in columns, and each squeezing into his mouth the juice of leaves which they carried, then, all together, they rubbed it down from the throat into the stomach, and nearly crushed the sick man to death out of hand. So I'm not surprised to hear of his death, from the boys who were in the town goat-hunting.

May 8.—Great preparation for the funeral in the town and much wailing and lamentation, which is executed strictly according to prescribed form. A good case of handsome matting, stained shiny black by the resinous smoke of the tropical woods, was prepared, and the interment took place this afternoon. They told us it would be to-morrow. Perhaps they feared that if we knew the time and attended, the ghost of the departed would suffer in some way from the presence of the inexplicable white man.

Made a map of our site here, and a formal application to occupy it, and went over to see the Commissaire and present it, but only showed the map, as he is coming over to-morrow to see us and the Bakete. He sends the application, with his approval, to the Governor General for final ratification.

May 9.—The Commissaire and Mr. Engeringh came by and sat a few minutes with us. He seemed pleased with our progress Indeed, it does look as if somebody had been working about here and lived here too. At the town he told the people they must sell to us at fair prices; "and after awhile," said he, "when they have a good house for a school, you must send your children, to learn to read and write and work at useful trades." We had some coffee made and offered the two gentlemen, and had the usual pleasantries about the "Congo table" and bill of fare; but they preferred the fresh palm wine they had brought from the village, and it was very nice indeed; sweet and fresh as new cider. M. Le Commissaire left, saying, "If I can help you in any way, write me to Luluaburg."

I suppose my Congo name will stick to me, as many others have kept theirs for good. Our boys call Sheppard "Ngela," "the hunter," and me "Tomba Njila," which euphonious designation is from *Tomba*, to find, and *Njila*, the road, hence, "path-finder."

In the village the other day I came up behind a man who seemed boring a hole in one little stick with another like it. They were little dry sticks, size of my finger and a foot long. The one he held still on the ground with his toes, and he turned the other between his two hands, rubbing them back and forth. A little plate, shaped like a fig-leaf, with the stem for a handle, caught the dust this made. Presently, as I watched, I saw that the upright stick was grinding out a brown dust, as if scorched, then smoke, and at last, when the man blew on it and held a piece of tow to it, it blazed. I had seen fire made with two sticks for the first time.

Two young ladies, daughters of a man who lives at Mr. Engeringh's, came over and expressed a desire to marry two of our boys. They belong to a tribe of exiles who came from across the Sankuru, and are named by the other natives from their chief, "Zappo Zappo," perhaps because his people had the first guns, as Tippo Tippo (or Tib) got his name from the sound of his rifles as he attacked the backwoods people for slaves. The Zappo Zaps have been cannibals very lately, without doubt; the Bakete say they eat dogs and people (equivalent in native mind. The Bakongo say the same of the Bangala). But the Zappo Zaps are the finest people about—magnificent men and handsome women, and carry themselves quite as an aristocracy. Chiquaqua and Vwila have pretty faces and figures and dress nicely in African style—plain white or pretty print draped about them in a graceful way, leaving bare only the ankles, shoulders and arms.

Sunday, May 10.—Not a good day, and I had hoped that I was through with unimproved Sundays.

The two little Zappo Zaps again. They say their papa will come to-morrow to "give them away." (No, not that by any means, but I don't like to say sell them, though that is about it.)

May 11.—Early over to catch the Commissaire e'er he left Luebo, and give him the formal application to hold this ground for good. We could hardly get permission to take Sankuru mouth, or rather Basile in the present unsettled state of things, and Luebo is a site worth holding for Protestant Christianity.

I forgot, yesterday before breakfast Ngoma's sweetheart and another woman, claiming to be the proprietress or mamma of Ngoma's and Mampuya's both, made their appearance. These are different from the Zappo Zaps. After chop they came around, and Ngoma's bride-elect was finally betrothed, and told to come to-day to stay. But the mamma, it seems, likes Mampuya too, as well as her daughter does, and arranged that the latter should go away with the party of Bula

Matadis and leave Mampuya to her. But she was told that she might return Mampuya's cloth, that had been given her for the daughter, and leave with the said daughter. So to-day Ngoma's girl comes, and and the two little Z. Z.'s, the senior of whom is to console Mampuya, and the younger is courting my boy, Mpiata, and won't take "no." But the papa could not come. He had to make one of those fine copper battle-axes for Bula Matadi's collection of curios. So the Z. Z.'s must go home and wait.

After supper. "Go call Ngoma, and let us dress him up for his wedding." In comes Ngoma, quite sheepish, and in his every-day clothes, and behind him his Madia (pronounced much like "my dear"), her cloth stretched to cover her blushing face.

"Shame on you, Ngoma! Where is your wedding garment? Here, take these and go across to my room and put them on."

Presently the bridegroom stands by his lady dressed in a new cloth and Sheppard's shirt (lower extremity outside, not within, the nether garment), and Sheppard's coat, and a handkerchief about his neck.

"Where is Mampuya?"

"In his house"—mad like Achilles.

"That won't do. Fetch Mampuya." Done.

Sheppard, standing before the couple, asks the sealing questions, which, after passing through the medium of several interpreters, is answered as it ought to be.

"Take her hand Ngoma! Not with that one, with your right hand," and Sheppard made a simple prayer in English for the happiness and holiness of the union thus formed, which may God grant.

Yesterday Siku came over to say "good-bye" before going back to-day to Luluaburg with his master, M. Le Commissaire. I used him to question the people sitting under my little veranda about God, as they know him.

"Oh, yes, Ngambi, same as Fidi mukulu (God in heaven!) He made people and ground and trees. Yes, he is a good man, very good man." But as it is the devil who can do mischief, they are more careful to manage him with charms, etc., than to have anything to do with God, whom they apparently consider an easy going person, that don't care what people do—"and all the nations that forget God."

But what a find, all at once, and so soon! To-day I got both nouns and verbs from a party trading and chatting in my room. I used the words as soon as I caught them, in what I guessed was their meaning, and they seemed to understand at once. So down went my prize in my little book.

May 12.—Woman palaver still vigorously agitated. Went early to see Mr. Engeringh, to find out how he "wived" his men.

"Oh, I tell the Zappo Zaps to bring me a woman."

"And you pay — ?"

"Two pieces of handkerchief."

"And that finishes it ?"

"Quite. A man three pieces, or four if he is plenty large. If there is as much to eat on a man as on three goats, he brings the price of three goats, that is, three handkerchiefs."

"But they don't eat people near here ?"

"The Zappo Zaps chop people, or have done so; but they buy to sell to tribes East."

"The Bakubas, east of us, are not cannibals ?"

"Perhaps—certainly not. But they buy for the profit on selling to the Sankuru tribes; and as the point of view of the final purchaser determines the price, and the consumers are cannibals, the price of a man is generally determined by the amount of meat on him."

"But," said I, "to return to the women ?"

"Oh, I keep them on the State plan, by which they are mine for seven years, and then free. While under my control, I give them to those of my men whose terms are long, and who are glad enough to accept; and I require them to be faithful to their man."   . .

He made himself very pleasant, asked many naive questions about my religion and sect. Strange that a singularly shrewd, clear-headed and hard-headed man, and honest withal, should know so little about the Reformed faith and practice, having been baptized in the Dutch Reformed Church! I thought I perceived more respect for my religion this time. Returned to find Chiquaqua, Vwila and their mamma, awaiting my return. Well! mamma and girls are seated on goat skins on our left. Mampuya and Mpiata, with Ngoma to help explain, on our right, in the shade of Sheppard's house at two o'clock.

"Well, mamma, these four young people like each other and want to marry. Now, we, 'God's white men,' like people who marry to live together forever afterwards. We don't want to rent your daughters twelve moons like some folks here"—no objection, though we got this translated with some difficulty—Little Vwila (a minx, not a whit abashed) and Ngoma explained most of the hard words, and I did most of the talking.

I went on : "So the girls are ready to go to Congo land, when their husbands' moons are finished here ?"

"Congo! nash !" (no), said the mamma, taken aback.

So, as we couldn't get past that knot, the conference broke up, and they all went home, the brides intendant much put out, but not giving up. "We're going to 'Tala' (*i. e.*, 'papa') about it," said Vwila.

May 13.—House progresses. I go guinea hunting with a boy from the town. "Path-finder" (and bad finder) went to right of the town road toward Bakumbuya town. Made circuit and came into the town by a road new to me, but in the same open common, and the same dozen boys were playing shinny with a ball of rubber (not hard to find here). Thirsty, I begged a drink of malafu from a vender who was coming in from his trees with calabashes swung to the pole across his shoulder.

"Show me first thy penny!" or rather "nashi mibela!" (no cowries) was the startling remark; but my little guide put in, "Never mind, come to my trees, I'll give you some right from the palm." So I hunted towards his trees, where I played with a bevy of little girls who had been catching grasshoppers to fry for supper and eat with the soft kwanga or mfundi. Went on in the circuit through the west madioca fields, and came in on the opposite side of our clearing from that on which our hunt began.

Surprised to find the brides prospective still here, and proposing to stay. The boys all denied their presence, but a candle revealed them and explained the drum and other preparations for a Congo wedding. They were sent under escort to the Portuguese place, and the bridegrooms got "chicot"; that is, I cut two good switches and wore one out on each. The whole lot lost their chop rations for the day. I made it my palaver.

May 14.—Catching little Vwila at the ferry, I took her over to explain to her father. Found him seated by his forge, an axe, native style, almost finished in his hand. She had him under her small thumb, evidently

Presently we arranged for a conference in Zappo Zap's house. Present, mamma again, a small sister (acquaintance of mine) all smiles, Ngosolo, one of my Congo boys, and Vwila. Vwila took it from her father and rehashed it to Ngosolo, who in turn served it up to me. I understand almost as many of their words as Ngosolo, but natives can talk without many words. Anyhow, I understood that I could get absolute control of the two young ladies as their father (!) by the payment of a good dash. Six pieces of handkerchief would have done it, but I preferred to pay full double price and tie it tight. So I promised to send the bridegrooms to-morrow with four pieces of handkerchief for each girl, and then I made the "mamma" happy with a looking-glass, and departed.

Returned at dusk. "Where is Mampuya gone?" "To town."

"Come on, Mpiata." I got these two gentlemen in a little moonlit glade and said: "You've made palaver for wives six days, and no good result. I've bought the two girls you want. They are my children by law for seven years. If you want to stop with me on a long contract, I will give you Vwila and Chiquaqua for wives."

"All right," said they, especially Mampuya, who is hit hard.

"How about one hundred moons, Mampuya?"

"All right—a hundred," said this Jacob.

Chop finished, the grooms are dressed. Mampuya in a fine new fathom of cloth and Sheppard's coat and cap—a most killing combination with his super sober phiz. Mpiata in some striped breeches he got somewhere, a shirt, neck cloth of my large handkerchief and a little red and white jacket of mine. Very swell.

"Spread the rubber carpet under Sheppard's shed! Every boy hold a long new candle! Mampuya, your bride will come and stand there."

When I started up a new wedding march "Luiza a kundi a Jesus" (Come we that love the Lord) to the tune "We are Marching to Zion" Sheppard went and led the ladies in. Meanwhile Mampuya held on to the rafters with one hand; and Mpiata's hands, sad to say, were in his pockets. The ladies take their places, pretty as need be, but a little sheepish. Sheppard offered a very brief prayer. I made a concise translation of Mark x., 6-9, and put the questions. They joined hands, Sheppard helping Mampuya through his ordeal, and I Mpiata. Another very brief prayer, and I told them they were joined for life. Finis—"no Sapi"! (wait! and I made each of the brides a small dash. Then the party wanted to go; their chop was waiting.

"Allez! Good night," cried Ngoma, and they left. But we were very happy in securing these pleasant additions to our party, and by the contract getting control of four hopeful lives to shape for at least three years, God willing. The two little ex-cannibals, who still speak sometimes of chopping *me* (!) are thus introduced within the pale of civilization and Christianity.

May 17.—Fulfil my engagement to go with Mr. Engeringh to Bena Kibash. Canoe awaited me, and so did chop. Three eggs, so fresh I could almost see through them, were sent out and came back, three in one little frying-pan for me, and three in another pan for him; a bit of mutton, fried banana, and coffee, and we rigged up our bulls for

12

the trip. They carried us at a good rate through the forest. The path has just been widened, making it pleasanter to travel and giving a stronger sense of the grandeur of these giant trees. They are not so large in girth, or don't seem so, but so tall. In two hours to Bena Kibash, where the sheep and goats of the station are kept. It is a Baluba town of, say, three hundred souls, the first of the tribe I have seen. The houses are built in rows, but are of wretched character, and the people are huddled in front of their huts, lean and idle, as if the whole town did nothing but smoke the Indian hemp (diamba they call it), which I fear is the case. Back to dinner with Mr. E. Suffer from sun and riding too much.

May 18.—Sickish. In the woods all day.

May 19.—Walk in the town. Found a sick woman and gave some needed physic.

Bakongo are clearing up and burning off our land preparatory to putting in corn, perhaps. Sheppard's house, under the hands of Bakete boys, progresses.

May 20.—Sick all the middle of the day, short, sharp fever.

May 21.—Better. Mpiata's heart having moved him to make a table of wood, I marked off and started the sawing of the stick into boards. Almost finished by night, four boards three feet by four inches. Mr. Engeringh came over in the afternoon to see us, bringing a leg of an antelope his dogs chased into the Luebo and Lulua to-day, also some papaws, most refreshing, and some bananas and plantains, and made a kind offer of fruit whenever we should send for it, and also of trees in plenty. Agreed to take each week half of a goat he should kill, and be charged half the price. We bought a ram sheep and two nanny-goats to-day.

Madia (Mrs. Ngoma), whose name is correctly pronounced "my dear," and Chiquaqua (Mrs. Mampuya), are ailing now several days, and give the community some concern, but especially Sheppard and me, who are bound to see to their various dosings.

May 22.—Palaver of sick girls. A puzzling business for us. Planing the boards the boys have sawed.

May 23 —Go over to the town with a piece of spangled cloth saved from the lot I had of the Dutch house for Kwango trip, to see how much it will fetch on this market. Went into Zappo Zap's quarter, a little half square of some six houses, with a shed and a group of low shady "cloth palms" in front; a tiny little quarter, not fifty feet across, but busy as a bee-hive. A dozen of the Zaps sitting Turkish fashion in the shade—all hard at it; the women weaving the smooth, stout mats only the Zaps can make (our houses are furnished with them); the men engaged in the various stages of cloth making, from "Daddie" Chitunga, the head of this group or family, who was stripping the silky ribbon from the palm blades, to the one who wove the thread into strong cloth on the primitive loom. They haven't any land, so their industry and skill in handicraft, and shrewdness as traders, was to fill the gap. Got a bid of 7,000 cowries. Not enough.

Sunday, May 24.—Quiet, profitable day after breakfast, and a still hour. Service with the Bakongo. Spoke about the passion of Jesus. Transcribed seven Kongo hymns, which have stuck in my memory; the only singing we have for the boys; as I am not up to writing Kongo hymns. Wait awhile, till we sing the gospel in the dialects of the Upper Kassai! Dinner interrupts the exercises, not unpleasantly. Finished, and then a little more touching up of the hymns; then a nap in the hammock, under a fine shade, behind our houses. Mpinta wakes me up presently with some freshly parched goobers.

I go on with Guthrie on Ezekiel xxxvi. A pine-apple, present from a little boy from Bena Kasenga, is chopped with my two "daughters" in Chiquaqua's room.

Visit to the town, to find my patient nearly well.

May 25.—Visit Mr. Engeringh and get fifty-seven pounds cowries for the fine cloth—six yards. Mr. Stache is back from Wissman Falls. His ivory is on show, several thousand dollars' worth in that lot of tusks, spread out before the store door, say twenty-five tusks, big and little. Some worth one hundred dollars each. The Company will clear about half of this. Of course they don't do so well everywhere.

Find some Bakuba have been to see me with a pig, for beads. After dark they came to feed the pig and bring the flower of their town, doubtless, a really beautiful woman, with pretty small mouth, not badly formed nose, and eyes like a gazelle, a modest and womanly and charming expression withal. A candle was brought to see the pig eat his supper, and she, Mashamba, saw for the first time, I suppose, a white hand. She got her husband to hold it for her to examine. Then, bolder, she felt it curiously, up to the elbow, indeed. Every little while she would edge up to examine the wonder again.

May 26.—Board making for our chop table, a small affair; but hard wood is no trifle to plane. Bakubas spent some hours here. Couldn't agree about the pet pig, but I gave the pretty princess a dash of cloth and beads. She came back after starting to make sure her eyes hadn't deceived her about those hands; (anything but white outside the sleeve).

Half of a goat from Mr. Engeringh—a permanent arrangement—one a week, we pay half.

May 27.—Messrs. Engeringh and Stache come up and sit awhile, and take us bathing in their big boat. Very pleasant; no crocodiles. Mrs. Ngoma still quite sick. I am up many times in the night to give something to ease her. Vwila, Mpiata's wife, is growing on us; such a pleasant, cheerful and energetic temper. So fond of her sweetheart in her pretty way, and good to everybody, while as mischievous as a kitten. I like her immensely, and pray that I may see her a fine woman and useful Christian, among these poor people.

May 28.—Messrs. Engeringh and Stache came over to invite us to keep the birthday of the former with them. They were in very lively spirits and cut many queer antics, to account for which each accused the other of having enjoyed their morning's wine too much. But when a shot at a target was proposed they held their guns as steady as we did, and the vicinity of the red spot on our fig tree was warmed up pretty well.

Marched over to town and called on Kwete, the chief "mukelenge," or king. His highness was away at Bena Kapunga. Back home, a masquerader waylaid us in the edge of the town, enveloped in a costume made to imitate a bare body adorned with long fringes. The nose was the beak of a queer bird which carries an immense false beak growing on top of the real one. A hawk passed over head at the instant and Mr. E. brought him down like a rock, with the right hand barrel of my shot-gun. The natives rushed on the prize and fought manfully for it, making short work of the palm frond fence, within which it fell. I dined with the gentlemen of the company, and went in the boat to a bath at the island below the rapids. At table, a discussion, in which they held that it was impossible to discover a grammatical system in the languages of the natives; that those like the State and company agents, who use such native words as they pick up, without any care or special study, were better understood by the natives than the missionaries. In an after dinner walk with Mr. Stache, who is an educated man from the Jesuit school, I convinced him that there was more known of the principles common to Bantu tongues than he had thought.

May 30.—Went to Bena Mana to see the town and make friends with the kings. One of them, Mbuya is away. The other, Kwete, received me with courtesy and gave me palm wine (very bad), and goobers, and at parting two big roosters. In return for which I gave him twice the value in cloth, beads, cowries and ntaku. The town is two-thirds the size of Bena Kasenga, with newer houses, but no appearance of thrift and nothing nice to show. The people had no pride in their personal appearance. But Kwete had (wonder) a fine brown ox, which was driven by me accidentally that I might see it, just as I left: the only ox among the Bakete.

Chinyama had got weak in the knees crossing the last bog, with me on his back, so I had to sit in clothes wet to the knees, until they dried, pending the palavers. Killed two of the great birds with the double beaks, which you may see if I don't get tired keeping them, also a parrot, my first chance at one, though thousands fly over my head in a week, I suppose, chirping, whistling and squawking. This was a long shot with heaviest shot—managed to break a wing.

May 31.—A quiet Sunday. Sheppard puny. I had a fever at night from excesssive heat of sun, to which I was a little too much exposed yesterday.

June 1.—Pretty well again. To see Mr. Engeringh. Got a good lot of beads, plain, small, white, fine for trade, in exchange for a piece, twelve yards of elegant cloth for "Madame" Stache—I would add, poor girl; but she is happy, and don't know that she wasn't married just as her husband would have married a wife in Belgium. When he was sick she would expose herself to a similar attack saying, as if it were a matter of course, "If you die I will die too." So she got a nice dress. Chop, and then a bath at the island.

June 2.—Kwete, of Mana, spent last night here, sleeping in the addition to Sheppard's house. Brought two of his wives, one son and a little daughter, "Mayowa" Kwete by name, just as we say Kate Lapsley. The daughters of another chief (Shamba), are named Bula Shamba, Mbomfa Shamba, Mweshi Shamba, etc. Kwete brings a fine little female goat for dash. But how to adjust the return present? When smaller trading was dispatched I gave myself to my visitor, at ten o'clock, and he chaffered and begged and objected and was hurt and "trampled on" as to his feelings, unless I should give such and such, until it was three o'clock; when he decided he had squeezed all he could out of me, and retired in good order like Jacob, with the loaded women in front, himself and his son bringing up the rear. Sheppard still sick.

June 3.—Called on Senor Saturnino, the Portuguese trader, whose place lies on the way to the Lulua, an old trader who has seen thirty-five years in Africa. Was politely received, and found him poring

over a thick book, which might have been a Bible, but turned
out to be the dictionary instead. I noticed a nice coverlet on his
travelling bed, and he gave me a canvas deck chair, but his other outfit seemed to be small. He left a good place at Mwang Angoma, on a
branch of the Sankuru five days away, two hundred kilometres, he
said. Found him about to go to see Mr. Engeringh, and we went
together. After a chat we went to bathe, and were persuaded to return
to supper. During supper Mr. Engeringh pushed the subject of
taxes, which had been under discussion, and suggested that Senor
Saturnino could hardly afford to keep this place, which his agent
Carvalho had made and abandoned. At such a distance from
Mwang Angoma he could hardly get the taxes off of it. So Senor S.
proposed to sell to me for £100, cente livres (a hundred pounds),
he said. We understood him to say cinq livres (£5), to which I
agreed, very much obliged to Mr. Engeringh. We further spoke of
Carvalho, who hasn't sent any word to his chief since his departure
eleven months ago. He took ivory, rubber and checks to the value of
$16,000 to buy a small steamer, with which Senor S. hoped to enlarge
his trade greatly. It seems a little as if Senor S. has lost the earn-
ings of his thirty-five years' exile.[1]

June 6.—Sheppard, with Susu and Baba, and a good Bakete boy,
Mayoyo, accompanies M. Stache, on a trip to Wissman Falls of the
Kassai, three days west, where the latter makes trade. They will
return by the mouth of the Lulua, to see what sort of a country for
trading that is.

June 7.—Quiet Sunday; first regular Sunday-school; began with
Noah, questioning on Adam and Eve, Cain and Abel, of whom I
have recently taught them. They seem to take interest, but have very
hazy notions. Finished at night.

June 8.—Boys clearing behind the house, giving a sense of room as
well as more air. First school; after a service dismiss Ngoma, Mampuya
and Chinyama to work, and I instruct the rest on the anatomical construction of B-a-ba. I use charcoal on one of my new planks as a
board, and impress the shape of the new characters on their minds by
copying them with sharp sticks on the dirt floor of the house. "This
is the name of a boy you know well (Baba), see how much better is
this way of indicating him than trying to draw a picture of him."
They began to take an interest in this concrete style of teaching.

Sunday before last, as Sheppard and I were sitting before my chim-

---

[1] *Later*—Carvalho is coming with a little steamer of his own when the French
house has finished it.

bric in the forenoon, some Zappo Zaps came by with a beautiful child, a little girl, and the Congos and Vwila at once beset me to stop them. They were going to sell the child in Bena Kasenga. The little thing wasn't afraid of my white (?) face, like most of the children, but came when I called her and stood by me, not afraid even when I put my arm around her. Very reluctantly I let her go on, to find a Bakete home—not seeing how I could rear a little girl in this awful hot-bed of corruption, without a lady to take care of her. Besides, when seven or eight years old, she would be considered my wife by all these people, and my statements, seeming to them false, could only make the matter worse. After the bath, Senor Saturnino and I went with Mr. Engeringh to supper, and staid the night. It was then that we found that Senor S. had meant a hundred pounds, not five. To be exact, he wanted £111 and some shillings and pence, to make a round five hundred thousand milreis Portuguese.

We had some pleasant talk, in which Mr. E. showed what seemed to me a strange aversion to religion—strange, because I had thought a man so unacquainted with its very outside should have been indifferent to it; and at the same time he showed a stranger sentimentalism in matters of morals. He harangued against war, for instance, and capital punishment. By what right does society take away life, when not one man on the condemning tribunal can tell what life is! But what a sophism, and what a stretch of the claims of his agnosticism! His objection against our God is, that he has not given a sign of his existence which Sieur Engeringh should not be able to doubt. However, in the matter of capital punishment, he believes it right for him to kill a mutinous soldier, who endangers the lives of a whole trading party; which I don't deny him, though I would hesitate to do the like. I had one or two things that I thought would lead to a proper and frank talk on these matters, but I couldn't get in a word. Mr. E. is one of the shrewdest men I have met, and shows marvelous ingenuity and justice in managing his place.

June 9.—Spent quietly at home; called on Kwete in the afternoon, late. Last night learned the antecedents of my girls, which didn't surprise, but pained me, and put me much to prayer.

June 10.—Mr. E.'s men, who were sent to take a man of Bena Kalamba, who had robbed some Bakubas on their way to sell ivory to Mr. Engeringh, had a warm reception, and one man was wounded by a poisoned arrow in the elbow, only a prick, but it was like a snake bite, swollen and painful by afternoon. We went to see Kwete about it, and so prevented a panic at Bena Kasenga, which is only one hour from the naughty Kalamba people.

Thursday, June 11.—No sleep last night from 11 to—say 4:30—small fever. So lay down until near noon. At 7:30 the dull, heavy foggy morning grew darker, like twilight, and we had a very nice little rain, the first since the new moon in May; right in the dry season too. Put the boys to planting corn in our new ground. This is the dampest climate I know—a good many days in the wet season, and every day thus far in the dry season, has opened with a heavy fog, through which one couldn't see objects at one hundred yards,—a Scotch mist rather; and there is a peculiar quality in the atmosphere that condenses the moisture of our breath, making us breathe out smoke as in winter time. The sun makes a dull blur through the gray curtain. At 9 A. M. the curtain rises, but falls and shuts out the stars again about 9 P. M. In the early morning, the dew drops from the leaves in the woods around us like rain—a dismal sound to hear in the gloom just before day. However, we don't get sick, and every day the boys put the woods further from us, with axe and hatchet. Mr. Saturnino is making a fine turnpike, fifteen feet wide (without the stones), from his place to Bena Kasenga—Mr. Engeringh pays the rations of the men working—in order to attract the Bakuba to Luebo with their ivory. Word from Sheppard and M. Stache—arrived and well. Go over with note for S. to go by Mr. E.'s men to-morrow

June 12.—Slept at Mr. E.'s and came back much better. Villagers of Bena Kalamba send to ask if Mukelenge Mai (the king by the water) will accept five goats and call the palaver finished. I make a big row about a few ntaku left in an open box and missing on yesterday. Call palaver of the Congos, and finally convict Mampuya, who confesses, takes his dressing with great philosophy, and gives up the chicken he had bought with them. Yesterday bought nine hoes; had one already. They are very queer to our notions; instead of an eye in which the handles goes, they have a strong point, which is inserted into a socket in the handle. The handle itself is a stout stick two and a half feet long, with a great knob at the end, into which the hoe is inserted by the blacksmith. J.'s birthday to-day. God bless him!

June 13.—The table nearly finished. Bath, chop, and sleep at Mr. Engeringh. The three of us (Senor S. was there) saw a rare show after supper; the Kio Ko dance by the young women of the rubber caravan from Luluaburg. They are Bashilange, belonging to the great Kalamba. Eight or ten of these girls formed a circle, facing inward, so as to exhibit the gay addition they had made to their ordinary costume,—a bright colored cloth passed through the belt behind making a waterfall (do you call it ?)—quite Parisian at any rate, whatever it was. Then the eldest led off in a striking tune, to which the rest responded in unison. In time with this music the circle moved round, not stepping, but advancing sideways, on heel and toe alternately. The bare feet marked the lively time with a thud. The song was responsive, solo and unison chorus of fine strong treble voices. It ended in a refrain in thirds and octaves, thus:

At the beginning of each measure the dancers bowed to the ground, their arms hanging down. But to get an idea of the dance you must conceive of the fine, clear high voices and the effect of unison and measure. Slept at Mr. E.'s again; a bad plan; demoralizes my people.

June 14.—On way from the river, found Mampuya trying to get his wife to go back from her people, who have moved to Senor Saturnino's village, and with whom she was stopping while convalescing. I cut the knot by calling Kasongo, her father, and telling him if she didn't report before sundown, I should make bad palaver with him. She came.

At service—Abraham's call, departure from his people, journey and sojourn of faith. Evening, offering of Isaac. Afternoon, a Zanzibari came to see our people. "Standeley" (S. S. Stanley) come Sankuru, Mukelenge Mai (Mr. E.) get book (letter) from Bula Matadi Malange (the Commissaire at Luluaburg); all soldier go Malange to-morrow." Went to see Mr. E.; he had a note from M. le Commissaire, to the effect that the Stanley had gone to Lusembo, not bringing letters to any-body but to M. le Marinel, at Lusembo. M. le Marinel is evidently a favorite with the powers that be, and is probably doing a good deal of solid work for the State in his corner. Well, did any of my loads come to Sankuru mouth for me, and, not finding me, go back to Kintamo?

June 15.—Mrs. Mampuya didn't want to go to get water with the rest. All right, I took a small rattan and started to see the young lady; but Vwila thrust her own water pot into Chiquaqua's hands and headed me off, saying that Chiquaqua was good now, got the latter's pot and joined the others. Some Baketes brought me to-day sticks for hoe handles. These are as big as my arm in the sleeve, two and a half feet long, with a fork at the end. With a tiny adze they worked the sticks down to size, and worked the end where the fork was into a knob, which don't split because of the stout grain of the incipient fork.

June 16.—Saw Kasongo working the hoe handles—quite a part of his trade, for if the hole is burnt (gimlets are unknown) at the wrong angle, the tool won't work well. Kasongo has made a nice little village in the bush, by Senor Saturnino.

June 17.—Gave the women "books" to work, but they took it so hard after the first half day, that I decided that I must go more quietly, though not disposed to leave them to the temptations of idleness, nor without the discipline of steady work; but they have never had the smallest experience of it. Senor Saturnino went away to-day for Monsangoma; says he will be back in fifteen days.[1] Rubber is passing in large quantities to Mr. Engeringh almost every day. Yesterday a party of his people came by with red-wood (cam-wood), which is in rough, dark, brown sticks or chunks. He uses it in trade with the Bakuba from Lukenge's, who give him just twice as much value in ivory as the cam-wood costs. The rubber is caught from an incision in the tree or vine, stewed until viscid, cut into strips, which are rolled into balls two inches in diameter. Then the balls are stuck together in rows of five, or double rows of ten, and these stuck together in blocks of one hundred. The rubber from the tree is yellow, from the vine pink (not cooked), black or muddy grey (cooked). The former is better and rarer, and brings the higher price. Mr. E. has got in several tons since the *Florida* left. Most of the rubber is from the Bashilange, either direct from Kalamba and smaller traders, or from the Angolese traders resident at Luluaburg, who buy, bring and sell it to Mr. E. The ivory used to come from the Bakuba; they would bring it only to the edge of the territory of their vassals, the Bakete at Kapunga; but Mr. E. has opened another district, Wissmann Falls (Mr. Stache's beat at present), so that the Bakuba of Lukenge must come all the way or lose their trade—they have competitors, in short.

June 18.—A strike by Ngoma and two smaller boys under his influence. Suddenly took notion of renewing an old palaver which I had settled three times before, and at the sound of the work-bell presented themselves, made their demand, and as I told them to take their tools and quick, they marched off the place. Put Ngosolo and Chinyama to squaring a stick for boards, dimensions of a cross-tie. Strikers showed up at dark very meek. I put my house in order, went to Mr. Engeringh and left them to think over it.

June 19.—Papa and mamma's wedding day? I'm not certain.

---

[1] September 21 not returned yet.

Palaver with Congos. Sentence the strikers to lose half their next week's rations, a month's pay each, and as to the demand, I gave the cloth as a dash to the three who didn't strike, and gave the malcontents nothing. Ordered Ngoma to give his pupils their allowance of birch; he got up and left. "Well, you may go or stay: if you stop at Mr. Engeringh's I will have him arrest you." In a few minutes he decided to stay and take what was coming to him. "Wait a minute though," so all three went and reinforced their cloth with another and thicker cloth under it, which, I suspecting, having indeed heard of the like device in another country far from Luebo, quietly requested each in turn to undress, and the palaver ended in a few tears. In ten minutes my men were working like beavers, and in the best of humors. Palavers again! Vwila (et tu!) had a pout at Mpiata, and went to her father's.

June 20.—Sent to Kasongo to say that if he wanted his daughters back he might have them for the eight pieces of handkerchief I gave, and two big goats (a small forfeit in native ideas, for relinquishment of contract formally agreed upon and ratified by a bonus received, especially such a large bonus). The girls came back somewhat tamed, with lowlier notions of their independence. Big dance at Bena Kasenga in afternoon. Some fifty women in their best, *i. e.*, a new waist-cloth, or one freshly colored with red-wood powder, and the body anointed with the same put on with palm oil. Perhaps five hundred other women, also in holiday attire, followed in the procession, which moved with a swinging cadence through one street after another, stopping at the squares, to give special exhibitions. These dances are all, more or less, lascivious in intention and effect, as are the songs to which they keep time. A pitiable sight was the little baby girls in the crowd, all innocent-looking, many bright-eyed and pretty, imitating the immodest gestures of their big sisters and even their mothers—immodest? often frantically obscene. Poor children, who have never known what a pure mind is, all example and tradition corrupt, and, add the influence of a climate never cold—what chance for them, without an aid entirely superhuman?

June 21.—Joseph and the Lord's prayer this morning. I go to Mr. E.'s, and stay to supper, and had the straightest talk on religion we have had yet. I paddled the canoe over in the moonlight, with Mpiata and Vwila for cargo.

June 22.—We go to Bena Kibash on the bulls. When I come back, find Nlandu and Ngosolo have finished seven boards, seven feet long, four inches by three-quarters.

June 23.—Ngoma and his partner, getting tired perhaps of working on the big saw, took their stick down to the trestles for the hand-saw, and spoilt a fine stick of hard, solid grain.   The big scaffold, six feet high, is for the cross-cut saw, which I am trying in the capacity of a rip-saw.   It is hard on the boy who is on top to stoop at every stroke for half a day at a time.

June 24.—The scaffold saw works—the two boys with the hand-saw are learning too—they have a stick of soft wood. Visited Bena Kasenga; found a poor little girl with a swelling all around and through the knee joints. Promised to come to-morrow and get medicine. A crocodile seen in the Lulua. We must take more care how far we go into the river to bathe.

June 25.—Doctored my little patient at Bena Kasenga, a lady-like sweet little girl; but fear I can't help her much.

June 26.—Tried to find a shorter road from the river to Bena Kasenga. Found a road through the great madioca fields, but it was much longer. Met a parrot and shot it. There are thousands passing over head, flying like the wind, and whistling all the way. Also in Bena Kasenga was over persuaded to shoot a hawk sailing over head; was much complimented by the admiring villagers, when the bird doubled up and dropped. Then the small boys and the big ones made a scramble for the feathers to wear in their hair. Mr. E. sent me yesterday some papaws, which I enjoyed immensely; not so juicy as a cantaloupe, more mellow, not at all tough, big as two fists.

June 27.—Saturday. Expect Mr. Engeringh to-morrow, so we have big cleaning up, clear a chamber in the thick bush, sweep the leaves from the floor, ready for a mat carpet which matches nicely with the high-pitched leaf roof.

June 28.—Mr E. comes at eleven. We had finished service early. Still on Joseph. All hands on the dinner, which consisted of, first, soup, of chicken, tomatoes, and goobers boiled and mashed. Very fine! Second, fish, broiled, Mpiata caught yesterday in his basket. Third, chicken, minced and fried, with rice balls. Fourth, scrambled eggs. Fifth, smothered chicken; was it? no, should have been baked chicken; but we had chopped enough meat, so that number was omitted. Sixth, pudding, of my manufacture, very small, round, heavy and hard, omitted by request after trial. Seventh, tea, as bad as before. In Bena Kasenga saw women go through the Baketo dance. It was very creditable to the musical ability of the Baketo, but a disgusting and saddening exhibition of their degradation. My little patient came and led me away to give me a dash, which I shall return to-morrow. Mr. E. got word to-day of slaves, seen by his men at Lukenge, sold by Mr. Saturnino to Lukenge, and kept by that king to be killed on the next occasion of state, as when a wife dies; then a slave must go with her to Nzambi, as the people here express it. What can be done?

June 29.—Some Zappo Zaps from Luluaburg came by with a group of slaves. I wanted to get a little boy and girl, but could secure only the girl, a poor little creature, perhaps six years old, very timid, light as a mulatto, not a bad face. I think I shall call her Mary Adams, and ask Mrs. A. G. Adams, of Nashville, to support her, as I am authorized to do. Paid value of half a dollar; no, six bits for this little girl! two dozen red bandannas.

On Saturday, the first break in our family. The mother, or wife of the owner of Madia, Ngoma's wife, came and said she wanted Madia to go with her to Malange (Luluaburg). We had no written contract, and the native law, which makes the adjustments of a formal palaver binding, didn't hold here, because the people who have any business at Malange know how to complain to the State, and nothing but paper will satisfy Bula Matadi, least of all, native law, which the State plumes itself on having replaced. So I asked Madia if she wanted to go, and when she said yes, I dismissed her at once with a small present. She was married the same day to a Hanssa or Accra man in Mr. E.'s service, but was sent away shortly to Malange. Last Sunday somebody entered my house and took a considerable quantity of beads. I fear the Bakongo know more about the affair than they have told. I have lost cowries also. I left both unguarded by lock and key, thinking it sufficient to know how many I had. I fear it was a fatal temptation to the Congos. I feel very badly about it.

July 1.—An Accra opened the box of Mr. E.'s boy, and took out five handkerchiefs which had been entrusted to the boy by Mpiata. Many cross-examinations, but little light on the question. It seemed quite simple that he should have given part of what he received to Bunga to keep. But the dates don't tally, though the numbers do—always five.

July 2.—Prosecution of Mpiata breaks down, to general satisfaction.

July 3.—A party of Zappo Zappos (though under another name) come to sell rubber to Mr. Engeringh. They are men of Panya Matemba's town above Lusembo on the Sankuru. Also a party of Bakuba from Bena Siam near the mouth of the Lulua. They have slender, well-made canoes, in which they stand and paddle with long, broad-bladed paddles. They made Mr. E. a dash, a huge fish, and received a dash in return.

July 4.—Survey the right bank of the Lulua for a good beach. Find that there is plenty of water and apparently no rocks from one hundred yards below the present landing for a distance of a quarter of a mile. At night Chiquaqua left her husband and returned to the Zappo Zaps.

July 5.—Moses, morning and night. A quiet but not profitable Sunday. I shall not go after Chiquaqua again: Vwila hangs on; seems to care for her man in good earnest.

July 6.—Go to Mr. E.'s in the morning with soap and candles to go to Sheppard with his caravan; find him sick, but busy buying rubber. A summary process. One Accra grabs the basket of the nearest Zappo Zap or Bashilange, as the case may be, empties its contents into a larger one, ready for the purpose, and suspends it on the scale. Mr. E. adjusts, reads, and says one fathom (funk-a-dime), two fathoms (ma-funka mabida makolo) strong cloth, the latter if the vendor has brought a big basket full. He steps inside the store to the counter, seizes a piece of cloth, measures the length from one finger tip to the other of his outstretched arms. Bakan cuts it off, thrusts it into the hand of the buyer, and thrusts him out of the way. "Next." So several hundred-weight were tossed across the counter to join the big pile behind, while I stood by fifteen minutes perhaps. Find myself hotter than I should be, by dinner time. Service and school, and a little lounging, and study of Zappo Zap's variety of the Bantu speech under Vwila, writing in my hammock. Friend from the town made a headache medicine for me—some leaves crushed, rolled up in a conical shape within another leaf, from which I squeezed the juice, drop by drop, into my aching eyes, and to my surprise, for it amused me greatly, I had no more headache. Went to see how Mr. E. is, with four eggs, my usual dash. On Tuesday, Wednesday and Thursday, boys were sawing boards; and on Wednesday, I fastened my things up in good shape and spent the night with Mr. E. Thursday morning, find Chiquaqua back. Call the Congos together and administer a general lecture, also a dash to the whole band, except Chiquaqua, who naturally wasn't much surprised. Saturday, find Mr. E. sick at bath time.

Sunday, July 12.—Service. Subject: "They could not enter in because of unbelief." Imitate the children who dared to cross the border and enjoyed the land; not the fathers who feared and died without the light. Evening—The lost sheep. Went to dine with Mr.

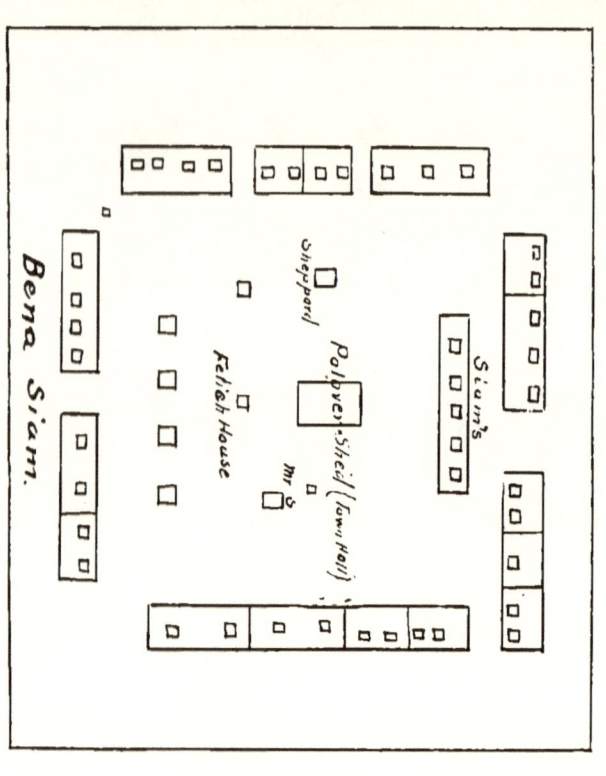

Bena Siam.

E. who is sick in bed. Hear that Sheppard and Mr. Stache are at Bena Siam, a Bakuba town on the Lulua near the Kassai.

July 13.—Udju (Lagos man) comes to ask me to go and see Mr. E., who is very sick. Find he has had hematuria. Spent most of the day with him, until with the abatement of the fever the flow of blood ceased. Quinine, Dover's Powders, and cathartic compound (calomel, jalap, colocynth, gamboge) did the work. Udju called me out to kill a big snake. "Stick no fit, get gun." "I don't see any snake." "There in the bush, like a handkerchief." I saw a wide ribbon, green with brown spots, and presently he was out on the grass, headless and writhing—a bad one; sleeps in the day and bites at night; size of your wrist, three feet long. At home, found that Mampuya had stolen my salt, almost all.

July 14.—Tie Mampuya's hands behind him, and order him to stay in the bush at the bottom of the clearing as a punishment. I tried (on intimation that Vwila's mother was well disposed) to get a written permit for Vwila to stop permanently with Mpiata. The disaffected Zappo Zaps, led by Chiquaqua, forced the poor girl to refuse, and she took leave of us very silent and sorrowful.

July 15.—Vwila could not stand it longer, broke loose from her people, came up the road at dusk, smiling all over her little face, blushing at the same time—black people do blush, you know. Their word for shame means an emotion felt on the face.

July 17.—Went to chop with Mr. E.; returned to find my runaway boy, Mampuya. Mpiata found him in Bena Kasenga, hid. With the three Congos he led his captive home, then turned him loose, saying to him, "Mundele says you have seen enough *mpisi* (trouble) for the salt you have stolen. You see he can tie you or flog you as he likes, but he says you are free now, if you would run away, go." I found him in his right mind. Another little boy, Shamba, son of a chief in Bena Kasenga, asked to stay with me.

July 18.—Mr. E. and I suddenly took the notion of visiting Sheppard and Mr. Stache, who have reached Bena Siam. Two fine little Bakuba canoes, cutters, carried Mr. E.'s outfit, two of our little round dug-outs from Luebo, served for Mr. E., myself and my things; the big canoe carried the cowries for Mr. Stache. We dropped down stream quick enough, passing the clearing under the big trees, on the right bank where the Bakwambuya come to make malafu. Ten canoes tied up at the bank. Every little while we passed ferries, indicated by landings opposite each other. These ferries are on the trade routes between the line of Bakete towns, four or five, that lie inland

from the right bank, below Luebo, and the Bakete, who live in the
angle of the Kassai and Lulua.   Camp on a sand-bank and reach
landing of Bena Siam

July 19.—Find it a walk of upwards of an hour to the town, forest
and then plain.   Surprise the two white men, who are vegetating in the
town, growing quite wild, we found, living much like the natives,
though hardly so well.   Took them to task, for they can, with same
expense and no trouble, have a chimbric kept clean, a comfortable table
of slats, a variety of meats and vegetables, food more temptingly
cooked.   They had no tea, had thrown it away, perhaps it was a bad
tin.   But they were famously in with these Bakuba   Fine race of big
men, modest, pleasant-looking women   Very proud, don't take insults.
The most artistic race I know, even the commonest utensils have an
attractive shape, spears and knives are good.   There is a special
variety of the famous Kassai cloth made here; call it plush in distinc-
tion from the well-known velvet.   The town is built in the usual
Bakuba style, a series of rectangular walled enclosures, formed a large
square or rectangle and enclosing an ample court.   What I call "wall"
is the same close fence of palm leaves and splints, on stout stick frame,
which makes the walls of houses.   Ivory is coming in.   The company
will put a station here at once, build a house for a white man to live
in and talk the palaver of ivory—*i. e.*, chaffer for the price   This
must be done with closed doors—both the buyers and the sellers are
interested in keeping the final price a dead secret.   Far from water,
must buy water needed for cooking, etc.   We arrived hungry and took
the dinner which had been prepared for our hosts, finished it, and later
helped them discuss a second.   The drink is malafu.   Sheppard and I
drink it not without misgivings, as to whether it is safe policy; but
when the water is dangerous to drink habitually, without boiling first,
and there is another healthy, refreshing drink, furnished by nature,
at the simple expense of taking it from the tree, the burden of proof
falls on the prohibition side   The effect of the malafu is laxative; the
immediate precursor of African fever is constipation usually—ergo?
The exigencies of pastoral work here may prove that it is necessary
to prohibit.   We shall see.   The malafu is like cider, ferments as it
gets old.   That of Bena Siam is the best by far that I have tasted—
more acid, more saccharine, and with a pleasant milky body to it.
Susu and Baba much grown.   They were radiant as they ran to greet
me.   At supper we still had some capacity   To soup, bouille, greens,
were added roast chicken and Saratoga chips (madioca answers finely)—
then Mr. Stache's madioca flour pancakes.   Mr. E. requested that the

cook make one hundred. He didn't fall far short. After supper the
town clerk (or Siam's prime minister) stood in the court and addressed
the people, who could all hear from their houses. Sheppard, catching
his drift, put up one of his friends, who answered the clerk from the
other side and corrected some of the unfavorable remarks the said
clerk had thrown out. S.'s man urged the ivory people to bring their
tusks and sell without fear. Monday I leave Sheppard, and we return home. Arrived Tuesday evening, July 22. Bena Siam is the
first town of the Bakuba on the right bank—an hour's more paddling
will bring us to the Kassai, and not much more to the landing of
Bena Makina, described page 160. Saw a party from there; fine men,
almost giants. They are Bakuba. Makimo is "Mwana Lukenge";
that is, he is the son or brother of the late Lukenge, the Pharaoh of
the Bakuba. Now his two brothers are both become Lukenge, so
the dynasty has divided. The principal town of Lukenge is two days
from Bena Siam.

July 31.—Month goes out in palavers. Mampuya tells that Ngoma
has taken soap. Sustained by Mpiata. Ngoma says yes, but Mampuya took the beads to the value of two months' pay. "And how
many cowries did you take?" He says, "Not me one, all took." "All"
denied. "No chop until you own up." They begin to get hungry.
The women, seeing a storm coming and flush times at an end, with-
draw to Kasenga on French leave. Mampuya goes to the bush again.
The Congos finally own "we took, but not much," and have the de-
duction made on their accounts. A road has occupied us seven days—
the boys have opened the narrow trail which has served as path to the
river and made a good road, to be better when the ground is leveled and
smoothed with hoes. Timbers for a boys' house, 30 feet long, ground
smoothed for it opposite my house. The other day I went over to Mr. E.'s
to see a king of the Makioko—Maila—from Maimonene (great water),
situated on the west bank of the Kassai, midway or just below the series
of the Wissman cataracts. The old man has a negro face, an affable
manner, far from dull. He lives a little way from the sub-station S. A. B.,
operated by Mr. Stache. Says the white man would get tired buying the
quantities of ivory that will come now that the market is open. He is
of the race that lord it over the region of the headwaters of Kassai, and
the branches of the Kwango, "the Arabs of this region," Mr. E. calls
them; "the terrible Makioko" (according to Commisaire Lienart).
They have been the middle-men between traders here and on the coast.
Maila, our friend from Maimonene, has seen the "river of salt," the
Atlantic, at St. Paul de Loando. He had on two caps, a velvet cape,

and several other European garments, but a skirt of red blanket. The Kiokos have and sell European cloth, gunpowder, guns, and good salt—*i. e.*, sodium chloride (Question: from Europe or found in Africa; probably both); not the potash-magnesia stuff that is leached out of grass ashes all over the Africa I know. True, every trader through whose hands it has passed has taken some out and filled up with sand (so Mr. E. says), making a gray coarse powder; but the sand sinks in water and leaves a good brine. That's how Mr. E.'s cook uses it.

The biggest news of the month is the capture of Kalamba's town of 10,000 inhabitants at Luluaburg—the great Kalamba, who has been to Kintamo with the Wissman expedition, who is carried by eight men, too good for the ground—who has imposed a new religion on his people, the Bashilange, commanding them to give up malafu and to cut down all the palm trees, to smoke diamba (Indian hemp) in all leisure moments, and during the whole of every other night with the variation of lascivious dances; whose people threw pepper into the eyes of the men of M. Braconnier, the predecessor of Commissaire Leinart. Kalamba wanted to crush the Zappo Zaps. There was a palaver, then a bold decision of M. Lienart, a warning and defiance, then a sudden attack on Monday morning (13th instant), penetrating the palisaded cidadel of Kalamba, which was burnt after the capture of plenty of cattle and goats. The effect will be to assure in a great measure the safety and ascendency of the white man in all this upper country. Kalamba's people came from the S. E. in great numbers, and settled on top of the Baluba. Their villages line the road to Malange—eleven on the way. They made the rubber trade, buying from the bushmen, who make the rubber, and selling to Makioko, or Mr. Saturnino, or Mr. Engeringh. A federation of great chiefs joined to make a big town near where Luluaburg now is, and made one of their number king—Kalamba, to-wit. Their power quite shaded the "flag with the golden star," until M. Lienart decided to put it to the touch—brave his fate, to win or lose it all. He has declared himself King of the Bashilange, ex-officio as Commissaire du district du Kassai. I think it right to give thanks for this Providence.

August 7.—Road-making. Access of comfort in the acquisition of chickens from Mr. E., at a dollar a dozen, counting the original cost and all subsequent expenses on the four pieces of handkerchief given for each dozen. Sheppard and Mr. Stache bought seven hundred at Bena Siam, and when the present installment reached here Mr. E. called me in. Lisa, the gentle-mannered friend of Sheppard and me, is keeping my little girl, bought, or rather ransomed, June 29th. She

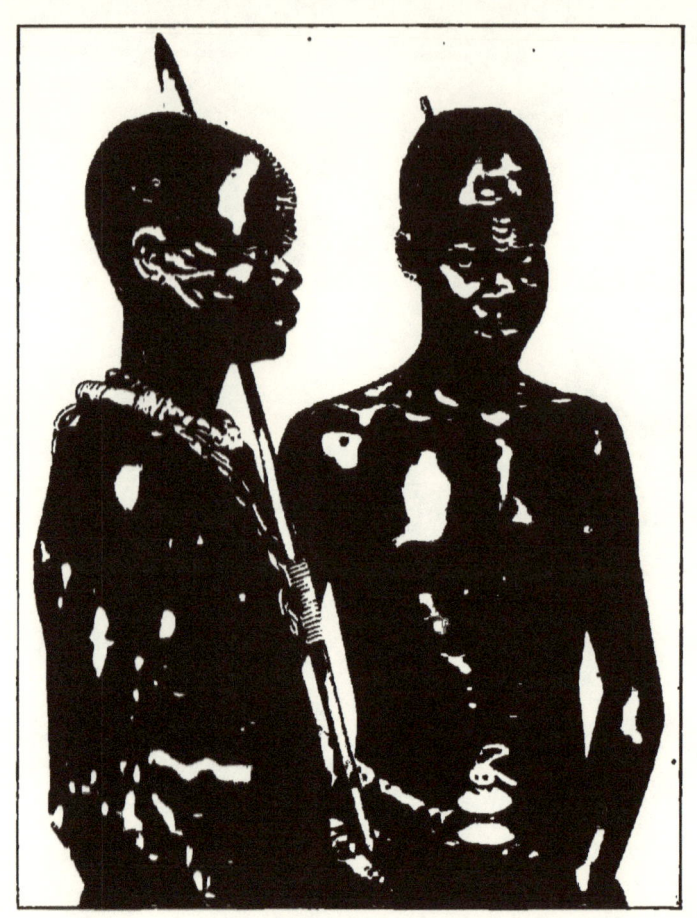

BANGALA —Photo. in " Le Congo Illustré."

was a pitiable object. Chop and kindness have quite transformed her. Lisa told me lately the Bakwambuya are the same or kindred people with the Bamoyo, who wear only two small pieces of cloth, which are suspended from a string about their waists! Why? "Nsambi (God) tuma (told) bantu (their men) bakala-kala-kala (of long ago)"; and that is why each of Lisa's teeth is filed to a point. Tradition is traced to Nzambi—as the heathen said, and the Jews said.—Deut. iv. 19. My patient of May 19th gave me a little bunch of fish—she has wanted to acknowledge the service, but only yesterday was able to buy the present. But I shall not remain in her debt! The most genuine case of disinterested gratitude I have met. She isn't strong yet.

August 15—Saturday.—Road finished yesterday. Sheppard back to-day from Bena Siam.

August 17.—We go with Mr. E. to capture a big slave-raider at Bena Kampunga, an inland town of Bakete, three hours distant—a great slave and ivory market. Albes, who escorted Cameron from Katanga to Bihe, camped here once for trade.

Bakuba come to-day *en masse;* there must be ivory here with them.

We expected to find a crowd of Bangala from Kwango. Slavers run away. Bakete and Bakuba begin to rifle the camp. We stopped them—took three pieces of ivory, seventeen slaves, and, as we couldn't get near the leaders of the party, we returned with our plunder, leaving three men to lie in wait for the responsible heads of the slavers. The three westcoastmen overtook us as we approached Luebo, bringing a man who proved to be a king of the Makioko, not Bangala. A nice-looking young woman among the prisoners cried all the way, and rejected all offers of food, saying she knew the white men had caught them all to chop them. The captured chief, when he saw our prisoners, at once claimed the young woman as his daughter, and little Gatula as his granddaughter. He was sent back to say to his friends that they could get their property and go away in peace, as it was the west-coast raiders we were after, but they mustn't come back.

The town of Kampunga being decidedly opposed to having their slave market broken up, took the Kiokos from the messengers, and sent word that any white man or white man's servant would lose his head if he came within their reach. The Kioko sent word that they would leave their slaves and property, and send more slaves and ivory as indemnity for intruding into Bula Matadi's land and white man's ivory market, if we would call the palaver finished. At this point we reported to the Commissaire and asked instructions. I asked for permission to take the slaves for the mission as "liberés." (Denied later.)

August 21-24.—I was sick, our place so hot; I took refuge at Mr. E.'s. Mr. Stache arrives Monday, 24th. I return the 25th. Tuesday, Sheppard and I found a better site, more pleasant and cool, and, we think, healthful.

August 28.—Having bought a house from Bena Kasenga to serve us as store, we hired a gang of Bakete, and our two houses, with the new one, were taken down and moved over to the new place, a side at a time, much as Samson moved the gates of Gaza, only half a dozen men instead of one. Queer to see the whole roof trotting along, on a dozen brown legs that show below—cross between a terrapin and a "thousand-legs."

September 1.—Congos moved over the addition S. had made to his house, put a partition in and ends, which gives them a spacious house with two rooms. A space of two and one-half acres is almost cut out, and a good road to the big road I made from Mr. Saturnino's to the old place. Part of the plot we chose has lately been in madioc, and took little work; other half in woods, but not heavy timber. Good soil, gentle slope, just on the brow of the great hill that rises from the Lulua. Immediately behind us is a great field of madioc, perhaps fifty acres in one field, though only about twenty just in sight. This we shall get from the Bakete, as we need more room. And the rest, between the field and the river, a gentle slope for a great distance, is only lightly wooded, so that I hope to see good pastures for cattle before long. Plenty of work, grubbing up the stumps, making our place habitable.

September 4-6.—Sheppard almost sick again, worse than I had been, yet not very bad, thank God. We are glad to do so well, really good health for Africans. I never felt such vigor.

September 7.—Mr. E. the other day sent a picture magazine to Bena Kasenga as a summons to all Bakete to be at home next morning. "Bia Kiaiabwabo (Mr. Engeringh) kulua (is coming) ambo (talk) bwalo (palaver) na (with) Bakete."

He told them he would buy the ivory of Bakuba at Kasenga. They promised to build him a house—are on their heads that they are going to get the fun and profit of a big ivory market. Road from the river to Bena Kasenga finished. The Bakete have gone to work covering with palm leaves the sides and top of the frame Mr. E.s men put up. Traders brought news that M. Leinart, the Commissaire, is at war again with Kalamba. Zappo Zap, the young king of the people, who was named after his father, is helping the State. The post at Makado, half-way, has been taken by the Bashi-lange, the two Baluba soldiers captured, and the Zanzibari forced to run away, turned up at Luebo Sunday. A rumor says that the Kioko are going to attack Luebo. Not likely. Mr. E. has not recalled Mr. Stache for all that. There is little likelihood that anybody can capture a white post: but it is bad for a mission to be identified with operations which, after all, only aim at making the people willing to accept foreign rule. It is doubtful whether missionaries get more immediate good than harm from "State protection." But without the present secular occupation, the missionaries would have been obliged to conquer a foothold, inch by inch, as on the lower Congo. The State makes this interior field accessible.

Mr. Lienart heard of a tusk of ivory being offered to Kalamba, and accepted as tribute. He seized it, on the ground that none but himself could levy tribute since the late palaver. The Bashilange said that was a little too much, and that though they had run away the other time, they shouldn't yield so easily again. Several have been killed on both sides, and the road to Luluaburg is impassable. Mr. L. has not had a steamer with supplies since last fall. He lives on loans from Luebo: got a few bales of handkerchiefs three weeks ago.

Ngoma is our head man now. Mampuya is back, but his woman never again, I believe. Vwila is doing very well. Another woman (bought by Sheppard while away), named Kafinga, is a strong Moluba. These ladies will plant our goobers and corn at once, as the rain began five days ago with the new moon. The boys enjoy the new place—dance often at night to the big drum I bought lately.

Mr. Lienart took and burnt Kalamba's town; Kalamba fled, leaving great flocks and fields. War ends!

(And here ends the diary so far as it has reached us.)

CHAPTER IX.

LETTERS.

THE rest of his story is told in the following letters, received subsequent to the last date in the diary:

TO HIS BROTHER JAMES.

LUEBO, *May 3*, 1891.—Our first communion Sunday, the second Sunday in our station, is just finished. Sheppard and I have just said "Good-night" after prayer by the supper-table out doors, and a talk and song. Two of the boys are rolling about on the floor to find the softest spot, or the one that will best fit the peculiar curves of their respective backs.

Our first choice of station, not necessarily the final one, is a little glade in the forest on the north bank of the Lulua river, twenty minutes' walk from the ferry of the Belgian trade station, on the south bank, and fifteen minutes from Bena Kasenga, a Bakete town of 1,000 or more. We reached here on April 22d.

On the 23d we got up our house, ten feet square, bought from the natives, and brought by them on their heads with great enthusiasm. A few days later a second "chimbrie" was ranged in line with that first one, and now the boys have nearly finished one for their own occupation, so that, with the tiny kitchen, we have a town of four houses already.

We have had the grass and scrub cleared away, and planted rows of pine-apples and plantains in proper places about us. Some impression has been made on the woods also, so that presently we shall have some two acres to begin gardening on. I haven't been able to keep my hands off these buildings, and indeed I made the frame of the little veranda to my house myself, because my boys don't "sabby" a hip-roof, like those in front and rear of our old Vine-Hill home.

The natives are passing all through the day, and usually stop for a chat and look, principally the latter; though, for the matter of that, I think we could talk with Kaffirs or Nyam-Nyams fairly well, what with the similarity of the Bantu languages in the common words, and with the universally current sign language. I have picked up some ten or a dozen words of Kikete (Ki means language, so Kikete is the language of the Ba-kete, the prefix Ba- signifying people), but not enough to do any good. I know "nsolo" is chicken, "bungi" is plenty, "kakesi" is little, "malengela" is good, "bi," "bosh," or nosh," all mean no, or not. But my little Kikongo helps no little. Sheppard has little Kikongo, and less Kikete, but he is powerful on signs.

The people bring us manioc (first cousin of sago or tapioca), in the dry root, and in flour. We have already collected a little flock of chickens, besides the one or two we "chop" every day. But it is hard work to buy the hens, as the natives love eggs, too.

Often the traders from the bush pass with baskets of rubber, or tusks of ivory, for Mr. Engeringh, of the Belgian house, to buy.

The rubber is in small balls, made of thin narrow strips rolled up. They catch the juice from vines, stew it, cut it into these strips, roll them up, and it is ready to go to Europe. Mr. Engeringh sent over ten tons by the *Florida*, on which we came here, and he has 30,000 pounds in store now. He also sent some tusks of ivory, some of them beauties, weighing close on to a hundred weight.

We had a delightful service this morning, but in the afternoon had "palavers" with the two big boys, Mampuya and Ngoma, who "have pretty girls on their minds," and tried to mis-use a passport Sheppard gave them yesterday, so as to get them wives from among the "young ladies" in Mr. Engeringh's quarters. So they made the acquaintance of that which drives foolishness from young people's minds, and they will wait until we get them married in due course. Then Luamba must get mad with Baba, because the latter youth, my clever cook (who is deaf and dumb), cleared him out of the cook-house, according to orders. I found Baba staggering from a blow on the brow, made by a stick. When Luamba came in from a brief retirement in the woods, whither he had fled from justice, he was dressed also; and now we have great peace and satisfaction—a clear, pure atmosphere, as after a storm.

We are out of the world now, if it is possible to be so in the heart of Africa. I am not lonely—plenty of work—plenty of company, and more of heavenly companionship than I used to enjoy.

Still, my mind goes back in the quiet nights with great fondness, and a sort of sad delight, to the scenes and people which made me, and still are a part of me; and the sadness is in being cut off from them so effectually. I remember vividly the day you told me in the garden that you felt called of God to preach, and that we were to go to the University; then that Sunday in the Mathematical recitation room, when you organized the Y. M. C. A., and many other scenes that followed. . . . I am often with you at Hampden-Sidney, and in memory visit Hartsell and Somerville and Fairview, and am always wishing now I could get another shot at those people. I could take better aim now, it always seems. But my game is here.

I hope immediately to begin cramming my note-book and my head with words and idioms I can pick up constantly, even from the children, who love to come and pull up grass for a few cowries (little shells), and from people I meet every hour, and then before long begin to give them ideas of our Saviour's life and death and of his interest in their souls. Perhaps in six months I can stand up and speak in the town before a formal concourse of people.

I caught yesterday an instance of the alliterative concord which is the key to all Bantu idioms. A woman was helping us sprinkle manioc flour across the line of march of a foraging army of ferocious "Driver" ants. (This clogs their legs, it seems, and makes them turn and clear out.) She used the expression "Dina diame"—*Dina* is name. In Kikongo and Kibangi name is *Zina*. In Kimbundi it is *Zhina*. "Ame" means "my" here as in Kikongo. To say "my name" she said "dina diame," the "di" being required to be prefixed to the "ame" to accord with the first syllable in the leading word "dina." The same rule obtains in Kikongo, and now I am accustomed to sticking on the prefixes. I do it quickly and without thought in my rough Kikongo talk with my Bakongo boys.

I want to see another station at the mouth of the Sankuru river when our reinforcements come, and our supplies; and from Sankuru mouth would work up that river, placing our next post one hundred miles up, and possibly move them inland toward the capital of the great Bakuba king, Lukenga, some of whose people I have seen trading here.

Well, it is getting late in the night and lonesome. The owls are claiming more attention than is comfortable and cheerful. Visions and footfalls of leopards take possession of the imagination after 10 o'clock. So I must say good-night to you and my little partner and namesake, and his little sister. I would like mightily to kiss them good-night.

P. S., November 14.—A steamer has come at last, and this will soon start to you. Indeed, four steamers have come, and two more commercial establishments are planted at Luebo.

We came just in time for the "boom." We have now a house of two rooms and a hall-way, built of round poles, and covered, roof and sides, with mats of palm leaves. On the roof the mats are three deep. The floor is the earth, but levelled and covered with mats. We are expecting Mr. and Mrs. Adamson in a few months, two perhaps. Then school and building in earnest will begin.

With much love and prayer, Your brother, S. N. L.

In a little note enclosed with above, under same date, November 14th, he says:

I am very well . . and very happy, except when I let things make me careless about seeking God's help and comfort in prayer. I like the black folks very much. They are not stuck up, though they are ready to stand up for themselves, and they like much better to keep on good terms. They are very funny and lively, and make good company. They keep pretty clean, especially those that live by the water-side, who have skins like velvet, soft and smooth. They all believe in sweeping their yards and houses in the town (and no African but lives in town). If any fellow is lazy about it, they call a town meeting, and make him pay the price of five chickens or a goat, and the rest have a feast at his expense, which makes them all careful.

To his Brother Robert.

Luebo, *September* 30, 1891.

Dear Rob: The coming of the *Florida* with our mails has opened a new epoch in our Luebo life, and stimulated even me to a little more diligence in getting ready for the coming oppotunity for sending off letters. Your time to profit by this has come around, if I can collect my thoughts sufficiently. But the little group near me in the "pavilion," where I write at the cleared dinner-table, seem bent on distracting my mind from the undertaking. These boys are trying to squabble like women over the work in their laps. Ngosolo is making Sheppard a shirt, but is more intent on convincing the "Mokete" Chinyama that he is kyanana (nothing), because of a hat he owes to Ngosolo, &c. The Bakete bend over the rattan they are splitting into strings to use in making Madame Kafinga's house. Little Ntumba is rocking herself on a section of a tree I used for a seat while my camp-stool was in the hospital.

Sheppard and the men are busy enough putting up the sticks for Sheppard's house. But the principal cause of my wool-gathering is the Kasongo palaver, which I described to papa, and which is yet unsettled.

The five months at Luebo have been a period of experience rather than of progress in divine things, leaving me wiser, perhaps stronger, but sadder certainly, as I look back and ask if I have grown in grace.

The isolation from Christian influences, even of all books except my Bible and English hymn book, and the constant contact of godless influences, has certainly lowered my level of Christian life, chilled me, and kept me always in a series of internal apologetics. Only when I could assume the aggressive, and show Mr. Engeringh that our faith is not "a cunningly devised fable," and that our experience has resources of happiness he cannot understand, and when I saw how transparent and inconsistent are the sophisms by which he has blinded himself, could I *feel* what I always knew, that my feet are on a rock. My devotions have been as a whole unsatisfactory, and I am still without a *system*, which brings uniform, steady efficiency in prayer; and I have known many fruitless days. It is to my shame that I must say this, and humiliating when I see that we have still been kept safe, and have got on, though slowly.

After a long period of aimless floundering, I have got started on the Bakete language, with some three or four hundred words, and an idea of the structure, which is worth much more. But the words most needed, such as "life," "spirit," etc., come hard, and Luebo is a bad place to get a language, because five or six other tribes, Bashilange, Baluba, Zappo-Zapp, Bamoyo, (Bakwam buya) Biombo, and Bakuba, all trade at Bena Kasenga and with the S. A. B., at Luebo, and many of the slaves that come from the southwest are bought by the Bakete. So how do I know when a word is really Bakete, or only part of the hash spoken in trade at this great market?

I think that decided good has been done to the Bakongo who are with us, especially in the daily meetings. One of them, Ngosolo, responded to an invitation to lead in prayer, intended for some of Dr. Sims' boys, who had come in to our evening prayer at Kintamo. I have since thought I saw evidence of grace in him, though his character is very imperfect. His prayers have probably instructed the rest, more than my broken talk.

Recently I asked Sheppard to take charge of the Congo's daily meetings, and gave him full swing. I was surprised to come in one day, and find he had made them all try to lead in prayer. Two of the new ones developed some gifts of expressing their desires, and show their interest in the service, and an improved demeanor in all other matters. But I intend to transcribe for you one of Ngosolo's prayers. They are edifying, and often strikingly fresh and appropriate.

Sheppard and I had to laugh when he told me of the discussion between the two big boys, wise Ngoma, and hair-brained Mampuya, as to which should have the privilege of leading next day.

November 12.—Now I must wind up for the mail. The diary, a stupendous volume, will reach you with this I trust. I hope you can read it. If any steps described therein don't meet your approval, wait a bit; perhaps under the guidance of God's Spirit I may turn back and retrace them, or may see such good ends reached as may prove their wisdom.

The two most perilous are keeping women on our place, and not enforcing total abstinence. I am thus far of opinion that the opposite in either case would be wrong. The burden of proof lies with the other view.

The thing that I am most ashamed of, as I review the six months at Luebo, is the small spiritual progress made, and the amount of unimproved time allowed to slip by. I humbly hope that He that is able is enabling me to improve in both of late. One simple plan has helped me, viz.: make out on Sunday a schedule of subjects for devotion for morning, noon and night during the coming week, leaving space between the lines thus inscribed for the record of what work was accomplished during the day corresponding to each topic. It has helped me.

I haven't seen the *Christian's Secret*, etc., which you were going to send me. I should prize something quiet and straightforward on that line. I sometimes find an artice in *The Christian* of London, that helps me.

With warmest love and sympathy,   S. N. LAPSLEY.

Your suggested scheme for evangelizing is not impracticable at all, but it is not possible till one knows how to speak better than I do, or any one else of the white colony here. I am anxious for the day to come, but must do the next best thing meanwhile, somewhat still-hunt fashion, hand picking. I am sure some impression has been made, but how much?

LETTER TO HIS SISTER ISABEL.

LUEBO, *October* 4, 1891.

" Your summer in Alabama is past, but our spring is just on. We have had four months of dry, cold weather, with barren-looking hill-sides, rusty, leafless trees overhanging the dusty road, and almost hiding the more faithful ones that keep their green. 'Dry,' I said; yes, from ten o'clock till sundown, and dead hot out in the open exposed places. But when the dew begins to fall it is a very rain. By the last watch before day— the hour I used to wake often—I could hear the uncanny sound of the water dropping, dropping when there had been no rain; and a dense mist fell then or about sunrise, so you could'nt see fifty yards; and it was cold enough for more than my two good blankets. But a few weeks ago the rains began nicely,—not too much, but a good drencher every evening,—until the ground was ready for the seed. Then the women of the town, Bena Kasenga, held their annual meeting, to assign to each group of friends their patch to plant of the great fields north, east, south, and west of the town. Now the roads are walled with a mass of first green like our woods at home in April. . . . . .

The weather too is very pleasant, especially here where the big manioc fields behind give the breezes room to play. The hunters are glad of the rain. They can follow the trail of their game. Some are at it all day; and more than that, you can hear all through the night, any moment, the long calls exactly like a horn far away in the forested hill across the river, whether it is to drive the game, or to keep in call of the rest of the party I cannot say. . . .

[Speaking of the possibilities of good in the way of woman's work, he says:]

"Any good woman can do so many things we men cannot, even if we knew how, and essential things too. You should see the ladies at Lukunga. They don't preach at all, but they teach, or rather direct the teaching; instruct, lead or point darkened and slow ones. They do as much as Mr. Hoste, I do believe; and they are very happy too."

LETTER TO MRS. KAY.

AMERICAN PRESBYTERIAN CONGO MISSION,
LUEBO, *October* 24, 1891.

MY DEAR AUNTIE: God has kept me safe and happy since I wrote you last, and has enabled me to see the work begun at

Luebo.   To-morrow I hope to speak to the people.   I have now enough "Bokete," as the natives (the Bakete) call their language.

A Christian soldier from Zanzibar, a pupil of Bishop Stare, and who also knew Bishop Hannington and Mr. Mackay, has lent me his Kiswahili Testament, and owing to the similarity of these Bantu languages, it may help me in the little translation I intend to make for use to-morrow.

We are on very good terms with the Bakete of Bena Kasenga, though some of them think that old Shamba (the chief) went too far when he gave me Shamba Mwana (Shamba-son) to be my personal boy.   This little gentleman is ten and a half years old, I should say, and is coal-black, with a fine strong face, not like a negro, very much.   His blackness is more conspicuous because he wears only a single garment, which covers the middle third of his figure.   He is not afraid of anything or anybody; is frank, self-respecting in his manner, sunny tempered, always laughing, but inclined to rule whoever is next him.   We like him very much, and the town wakes up when Shamba Mwana is seen following me across the common just before we get to Bena Kasenga.   You will be a bit surprised to learn that I have become something of a doctor.   How, I don't know, unless by having first to take a good deal of physic from others, and then learning to dose myself and Sheppard   On the steamer up, I had four patients (a dozen counting the black folks), who sang my praises on my arrival here, and helped to make us welcome neighbors.   The pretty box of medicine ($25 worth) had some share, it may be.   I began to take a little medicine to the town, and now I have many cases a day, and they have all got well, though three or four were bad ones.   I discharged a light case of dysentery to-day.   I use mostly only a few things I know well, such as calomel and jalap and Dover's powders, with carbolic acid for washes and ointments, and iodoform.

Shamba Mwana says they have a song in my honor like this:

Mutomba Njila watuambiku bwanga,
(*Translation*):· Mutomba Njila (that's me) gives us medicine.

Watumenekesa moyo.
Makes us see health (life).

It is always a good means of interesting them in the "Balm of Gilead."

But now I must leave you to get ready for to-morrow. I got your message inclosed in Tillie's note, and it made me glad.

May God bless my dearest auntie.

LETTER TO MRS. R. A. L.

LUEBO, *October* 25, 1891.
SUNDAY NIGHT.

MY DEAR SISTER GENIE: The promise of a good day was poor, when Mr. Clotens, of the *Société Anonyme Belge,* came in on us, at the end of a rather lazy breakfast hour. And he staid until nearly 10 : 30. So my Sunday meditation began late. The station boys and women came in for prayers, as I came back from seeing Mr. Clotens off. We had a pleasant little service, and I settled to seek a fresh store of grace, with which to begin next week on a higher spiritual level.

Little Ntumba came in and sat down in front of an array of "*Children's Friends*" with pictures, and went to sleep on the mat. Early dinner was brought on and dispatched—not very plentiful to-day—and yet I had not got much help, and felt much discouraged.

But God was pleased to answer my prayer, by giving me "purpose in prayer," through the use of a pencil; and a few petitions and promises took definite hold of my heart, I trust, as they lay written before me on my little desk, when I sat alone in the intense solitude of tropical noon, when all others were gone away. Then I made a little sketch of what I might say in town to-day, largely a translation of Paul on Mar's Hill, with the clause about the Saviour enlarged till it balanced all the rest of the discourse.

About 3 P. M. I found a quiet corner with a group of women I know very well. The houses made a screen from the noise of the street, and the subject came up naturally.

My patient, lounging opposite, reported herself as nearly well. "That's God's doing," I said, and asked what she knew about Ninliule.

Bomba, nursing her poor little baby (which I think will die), and another woman opposite, began to listen and repeat everything, to be sure they heard rightly. Milembo, a great friend of Sheppard's, comes up between two of the little houses, and I asked her again. She answered right along and explained fully, when I stopped to breathe.

She said the Bakete knew God made and preserved us, and everything, and gives us everything.

"Yet," said I, "you don't clap your hands softly three times, so," (then I imitated their manner) "and say, 'Wolah'! as you would if *I* gave you only a present of a little salt."

"The Bakete would sing to him, if they only knew how," said she. And so I went on explaining who Jesus is, and they listened earnestly, with some doubt about his coming again in the clouds. But the usual complaint was, "we have not heard this: you white people know, but we don't."

I think I shall have more satisfactory progress each time. The first difficulty is to be understood. If I had more of the Spirit's power I should be more able to compel them to hear and take it in.

I had a few cases of sickness, as always now, before I turned back to supper. I have had good success, and am thankful to see that it helps one to get influence and a hearing. The thing that has left the happiest impression, as I look back on the day, was a sermon by one of the English leaders of R.'s holiness friends, Canon Moule, of Cambridge, on the New Testament Christian, as shown in the Epistle to the Ephesians. What he is, chap. iv. to the end; how he is able to be it—the first three chapters.

October 26.—A busy day—morning—superintending Mpiata plane planks for a door to the new store room, and mending my pocket rule, when two women came, and one said: "My little daughter is very sick; you must come." She would not be put off. I got there at eleven o'clock, and found the child in spasms, from a rising in the head. I came back for mustard plasters and hot water appliances, and was thankful to see the child come to very quickly, and made the family kill a chicken to make it broth. Wonderful! They live so poorly and are so stingy. I am very glad and thankful; it will help me greatly at the town. I have three cases now. One is his highness, Kweto himself.

Afternoon: Made the door, put in the posts, arranged the hinges, all ready to swing the door in the morning. Went at sundown to see Chickwakwa, our old protege, who is sick. They were surprised to see me at Kasongo's, after his naughty behaviour a few weeks ago. Maybe they will learn by it that our Master is a peace-maker. I am urged to demand a goat of the Bakete, the usual fee for treating a bad case of sickness. The gratis healing is another surprise to them.

LETTER TO HIS MOTHER.

To his mother he writes about this time.

. . . Shamba Mwana, the heir and pride of old Chief Shamba, brought matters to a head to-day at 2 P. M. His lively disposition and absolute lack of discipline, little bushman that he is, have gradually got the better of his early reverence for me. Yesterday he needed a boxing before he would bail the canoe (with his hand). To-day I saw him tickling dumb Baba during prayer. He knows better, as well as R. A. L., Jr., does. So I took him down the road and wore out a switch on him, probably his first experience of the kind. He packed his little stock pretty soon after, (a mat and two cloths I had given him) and struck for town ———. I looked up about 5:30 to see Shamba Mwana leaning a little sheepishly against the door post, but in an angelic state of mind, and "so thankful and willing to please."

TRIP TO LULUABURG.

To a younger brother he writes this account of the trip to Luluaburg, or Malange:

LUEBO, *November* 19, 1891.

DEAR RUTHERFORD.—I decided yesterday to go to Luluaburg, and, if possible, engage workmen there for our buildings and clearing. So this morning, the boys and I mended my travelling bed, and in the afternoon we counted thirty-five dozen ban-

14

dannas, and got out two long pieces of brass wire, and four
hundred brass rods thirteen inches long, cut from the wire. This
is the currency with which to pay our way. We filled a box
with provisions, and I had Vwila and little Shamba Mwana
pack a covered basket with some changes of raiment for me, and
then at evening we crossed the river, to get a good start to-morrow; and I am now writing at the Belgian Station, the guest of
Mr. Engeringh.

Two Bakete volunteered to go with us, and the whole party
are all agog to be off for "Malange," as the natives call Luluaburg. At dusk we heard a terrible hullaballoo at the landing,
other side of the river; and when the cries became articulate,
Shamba Mwana began to giggle. "It's Shamba Mboyo's mother.
She don't want him to go with us to Malange."

MWANTUMBA'S, November 20.

Left Luebo about 8 o'clock, which was a late start. But it
rained until a good while after daybreak, and everybody slept.
It is the rainy season now, and here this season is greedy. Not
content with a storm every other evening or night, and a burst
of rain like a water-spout, it holds on and on, till long after day,
and the clouds don't disperse until nearly noon. Then the sun
bursts out and makes up for lost time. It seems literally to
smile one. But we took the road with a rush, travelling just
four hours to this place, I only stopping once to sit down astrad-
dle Ngoma's load for fifty-nine seconds.

There is along with us a crowd of women going back to Malange. They came down to Luebo with the Zanzibari soldiers,
who went away on the steamer, and they have been waiting at
Luebo, until there should be a party going to Malange, so they
could travel without danger of being caught by the Makioko on
the way, and sold as slaves. They led the way, a string of seven
or more of them, and they brushed the water off the grass, which
was convenient; and here they find tomatoes and go for water,
and cook the dinner for my boys, which is more so.

After the big bush which fringes the Lulua river was passed,
we walked on a high level plateau, covered with grass like
broomsedge, but richer looking, dotted with clumps of thick

trees, sprinkled with low scrub trees, much like apple trees. There ought to be game on the plain, but I haven't seen any yet.

The boys haven't walked for a long time. So to-day's tramp did them up pretty thoroughly. I have therefore asked the old chief for a house, had it swept, the rubber rug laid down, the camp bed put up, blankets nicely spread on it, mosquito net hung, a table improvised and spread for dinner, and the boys put to work to make that a success. The Baluba of the town seem a little surprised, not at seeing a white man, but at such a tame one, with well-behaved men too.

LULUABURG, *November* 27.

The road has not been favorable to letter-writing; yet it was not an unpleasant trip by any means. To resume my story. I woke up at four o'clock next morning (the 21st), had my coffee and oat-meal prepared while the bed was being packed and the little things stowed away in various pockets and bags. Then, when it was just plain daylight, I called to the Malange ladies to "light out" and show the way; and the caravan, eighteen besides myself, filed away through the grass, which was bending with heavy dew, and almost meeting across the narrow path. The young people got up steam, by singing snatches of their songs, cracking jokes on each other, repeating the funny things that were said the day before, and trotting briskly under their light loads.

We marched steadily for five hours, threading our way most of the time through a great forest. I hardly stopped walking once; was almost careful not to sit down and rest, as I find that I hold out better that way. Reached Kakamba's town about 10:30, to find the town deserted and partly burned—fear of the State soldiers. We "chopped," and, as it was Saturday, and I wished to do double that day, and so earn the Sunday's rest, we pushed on   I was taken aback to find, when I had made four hours from Kakamba's, that it was three hours' march still to Mokano's, the nearest place where I could get a roof over my head against the storm which threatened. We got in by 8 o'clock, and the people of my caravan were so well trained that in a little while the house was found, and swept, bed made, and

chop spread before the camp-stool, from which I hadn't wished
or needed to move. The carriers and the women, too, were
given brass rods with which to buy chop, to eat, drink and be
merry; and we went to sleep very gladly.

PREACHING AT MOKANO.

Sunday (the 22d) we awoke, not very tired, and none the worse
for the big march of twelve hours, except that I felt as if I had
been beaten with rods from my waist down.

I had the pleasure of explaining very simply the story of the
gospel to the two chiefs and about a hundred of their people,
and of finding them very curious to know about the future des-
tiny of the souls of men. They must be in the habit of talking
and guessing about these things, as they sit together the moonlight nights.

But there are two sad things about the people on both sides
the Lulua, far, far above Luebo, the region of which Luluaburg
is the capital. They all, who are old enough, smoke the Indian
hemp—*diamba*, they call it—and its effect is like that of opium.
They are all lean and dreamy-looking; that is, most of the crowd
that gather around to look at me are; and the children look
poor and scrawny. The other sad thing is, that the only mission
that they are apt to have here is the Catholic Belgian mission
at Luluaburg.

The *diamba* pipes are queer affairs—simply a great gourd,
big as a bucket, with a hole at the stem for the mouth of the
smoker, and another at the side, in which is inserted a large
bowl for the leaves of *diamba*. Everywhere in the villages the
diamba is growing, and grows, like most bad things, in the rain
and the drought.

THE JOURNEY RESUMED.

Another early start on Monday, and by noon we halted in
good shape at Ndumba's, a big town which had war with the
State some months ago. One of Ndumba's men drew a bow,
whether at a venture or no, I can't say, but with a poisoned arrow in it, which found its way straight to the knee of M. Lienart, the Commissaire. So the Ndumbaites got off more easily

than they might, if the Commissiare hadn't had such good reason for wanting to get back home. They must have got over all
that now, for they swarmed around me, seemingly greatly pleased
at being allowed to look as much as they liked at this new kind
of white man. They said it seemed funny, and I told Ngoyo,
the woman who got me water, to say that my King, whom they
know as *Nzambi* (God), likes black people as well as us, and I
couldn't properly be bad to them, even if I wanted to.

One of Ndumba's women gave me her house, and moved into
one beside it, though unfinished. She also "dashed" me a
dried fish as I was eating my supper.

The next day, Tuesday, was the only bad one of the six. We
pushed on from day-break until two o'clock, over the hills—bad
ones and woody—and far, very far away, to Kalamba's. My
left knee isn't well yet from the wrenches it got then. About
ten o'clock we passed the thicket of bananas which marks the
deserted town of Chinyama, where Dr. Summers died on his way
back to England and health. It makes me sad every time I
think of him, that so brave and good a man should have been
taken away with his work only begun, and not able to go on
without him. The people loved him very much, and talk about
him as if it had been yesterday that he died.

At Kakamba's I saw six or seven head of cattle; and I was offered quantities of young bees, roasted with a little oil, and what
is more, I ate quantities of the same, and found them very nice

On Wednesday we passed village after village surrounded by
gardens, but mostly deserted and partly burnt in the war. The
people have gone to the bush. The ruins remain of nice little
houses which the chiefs had made for themselves after the model
of the clay-walled houses of the white men. We took a good
rest at Kakamba's at noon, and marched into Luluaburg in the
evening, in good time. The country near Luluaburg is hilly,
much like that around our Vine-Hill home; only the hills, though
gently sloping, are higher and there aren't enough trees to shut
off the prospect. The woods line the creases down the hillsides
and fill the bottoms of the valley, and their dark green makes a
pleasant set-off to the bright green of the grassy mounds and
ridges, especially where the light has begun to get soft and

mellow in the sunny afternoon. Have you begun to like that
kind of pretty thing? But I expect that you are not just beginning now, but that you know a pleasant view when you see it.

AT LULUABURG AT LAST.

Well, before reaching Malange (Luluaburg) we came in sight
of the fields of corn and manioc and goobers, belonging to the
Zappo Zappos; here a big patch of twenty acres, then another
of fifty, and another of one hundred and fifty. We walk a long
while through the corn, until we sight a long village of conical-
shaped grass houses, covering a ridge for more than half a mile.
That is the village of the Zaps, and the tall cone half-way up,
with a flag floating aloft on a very high pole, is the house of
King Zappo Zappo himself. We climb that ridge and at the
top get a view of a large group of grass roofs with trees peeping
through between, on a fine plateau a mile away, and the girls
all cry, " Malange! Mukelunge! Malange!" They call me and
all white men "mukelunge," which means king. Down the
slope to the little brook at the bottom of the valley, where everybody freshens up, puts on or adjusts anew the new cloth got at
Luebo, and all climb the last hill in a body behind me. The
approach to the station has the same effect as the cornfields had
on me, of making me feel, a moment, that I was in Alabama
instead of Africa. There is an avenue graded up to the top of
the hill, lined with trees and about as wide as Ninth street (Anniston). On either side are houses enclosed in a fenced yard.
One side, I have since learned, belongs to the interpreter Jose;
the other to Seeku, whom I knew at Luebo, long ago with M.
Lienart. At the top of the street is an opening of the same
width, which admits into a large enclosure, where there is a
circle of brick houses thatch-roofed, facing on a yard full of
pretty trees a few years old, with flowers here and there.

Lieut. Rom led me to the Prince de Croy, a young Belgian
officer mentioned in a former letter, and who is now Commissaire
of the Kassai district; and I received a welcome and quarters.

LULUABURG, *December* 10.

I stopped at the station several days, from Wednesday until
Wednesday following, looking around, asking people questions,

and looking for workmen, for slaves to ransom, and for a bull and cow to buy. Not much luck at first. But as I determined on Friday to go to Zappo Zappo's, and try my hand there, whom should I meet on the way but the young Prince Zappo, himself. He was coming out of Seeku's place, and he came up with Seeku and a party of his people, and asked to be presented to the new white man. Zappo is a very handsome young fellow about twenty-three years old. He wore a cloak from the waist to the knees, and another thrown over his shoulders, and a folded handkerchief, tied about his head in a rakish style.

"Is that cloth you have in that bundle? Let's see it." And he led the way back into Seeku's, where we sat down and Seeku (of whom I wrote R. as Dr. Summer's boy, and also interpreter for the Commissaire) made the palaver for us.

Zappo offered some slaves for the strong blue cloth I showed him, and suggested that I make him a present and arrange it as a matter of friendship rather than of business. I agreed and gave him eighteen yards of the blue cloth, and some twenty yards of brass wire, not cut up into rods, seeing he was a king.

Next day I went over to see him, about half an hour's walk. He received me in his front porch, and had his present brought— a good looking boy of nineteen years, a girl about sixteen, and a boy of eleven. These young folks were not sorry of the change, only asking if they were to be sold again.

I said; "No, you are my children now," and I gave them cloth and plenty of chop. So they are immensely pleased.

Sunday, I was very tired, my lame knee making a small walk a fatigue. Monday, I ventured to go to see the great chief Kalamba, who since the State drove him from his village, lives five hours away. But I only got as far as his former capital, of which only the traces remain. The gardens are already grown up in grass, though it is not six months since four thousand people occupied the broad plateau.

Tuesday I had to lie on the shelf, for my lame knee to recover from Monday's trip.

Wednesday evening I got on the road again, to visit Mr. Saturnino, the Portuguese trader I knew at Luebo. The guide lost the way and cost me five hour's marching, but my knee regained strength, and I landed at a village of Angolais, from whom I engaged eleven workmen, and the wives of five of them, and my host agreed to go with me to Luebo and to settle there, if he found it good to be there.

Saturday morning I was welcomed at Mr. Saturnino's, and fed and treated as if I were a prince, or three princes.

When I left him Monday morning he gave me four pigs to take to Luebo, as the start for a drove. The fellows he ordered to carry the pigs to the town where I had left my new employes, did'nt enjoy their task, as the pigs were somewhat restless and inclined to make remarks. So two of them pitched their pigs, baskets and all, into the bushes, and made off. Ngoma found one of them. To-night I am fixing to sleep at the town of the Zappo Zappos, with my big caravan, seventeen men, four women, one baby, three pigs and two dozen chickens.

These Zappo Zappos are part of a tribe of cannibal marauders from far East of this. Their chief fell out with his bigger chief, Mpanyu Matomba, on the Sankuru, and emigrated to this place five years ago, with some eight hundred people. Their houses, like themselves, are both tall and big, and square, with the corners rounded. They make on me the impression of being peculiar, not like others. Their mode of living has been to hunt a town weaker than themselves, surprise it at daybreak, catch all the people and kill those too strong to make slaves of; then sell the slaves for guns or anything that is current, goods, goats, ivory or rubber.

LULUA RIVER, STEAMER FLORIDA, *January* 6, 1892.

I finished my visit to Luluaburg, December 10th, and said good bye to my friends there. They were very kind to me. The Comte d'Ursel is a big square young Belgian, with a very kind heart and level head, but he has been allowed to wreck his health by fast living in the army, all because he was a Count, poor boy. He helps steer the official course of his cousin, the Prince de Croy, who wants to distinguish himself by great improvements in the Station. He seemed to be really glad to have me there, and walked and talked with me often in the mornings, and gave me good bargains for a bull and cow, and asked me back to see him.

I made the trip home quietly, not to hurry my little folks and live stock, a miscellaneous caravan, much like Father Jacob's in miniature; but still I reached Luebo in six days, limped thirty miles the last day, and dragged into Mr. Engeringh's, down the avenue between rows of tall bananas, through the silent Station, and up to the big front door, where my friends sat on the veranda in the twilight.

The next morning we ferried the caravan across.

I found Sheppard had improved the place greatly, cleaning and clearing up the ground and planting us a banana avenue up to the front door, Mr. Engeringh giving the banana trees.

I have had another fever, which I charge to a great hole in the back of my undershirt, which made me susceptible to a sudden change from hot to cold. Thankful to be quite well again by the second day of the new year.

New Year's afternoon we heard a whistle which we recognized as that of the *Florida.* Such a shout as was raised!

The need of supplies for our Station, and the state of my health, determined me to go down on the *Florida* to Stanley Pool, a journey which the state of our transport arrangements has long suggested as desirable.

Letter to His Father.

STEAMER "FLORIDA," KASSAI RIVER,
BETWEEN LULUA AND SANKURU, *January 8, 1892.*

DEAR PAPA : To-day finds me well on the way, and on a very pleasant way. The prospect of meeting old friends and conferring with old advisers, with more intelligent inquiries to make of their experience than when I saw them last ; of receiving the new contingent to our mission, with whom we shall be more closely allied than if we were kin almost, if God will ; of making up at the Pool the first full, satisfactory equipment for our business that we have known—all this is enough to make me feel light and hopeful. We are a very congenial party, too, as far as that is possible, outside of the household of faith. Mr. Engeringh,

always sturdy, plain, genial, and wide awake, and so kind at the
bottom; Engineer Van Kouteren, a level-headed Fleming, with a
twinkle in his eye—(Mr. Sirex is dead!); the captain, well-disposed as ever, and very pleasant, now that things go well:
plenty of chop aboard, too. We have three dishes of meat,
each with some nice accompaniment—the courses driven "tan-
dem," European style, not abreast, as we do it. Coffee at 4:30
in the morning, when the engineer stamps back and forth between his boiler and his cabin over the noisy sheet-iron deck;
then Shamba Mwana and Mr. Engeringh's Tumba (boy, very
small and black) enter cabin, light candle, and put two steaming
cups on the table between our berths. Dress and wash, and
steamer gets off; then we sit down to coffee and a bite, not before I have had a quiet time by myself. Then I go up on the
bridge, get medicines out of the captain's cupboard, and come
down to my seat on a box among the Lagos boat hands forward.
They hang their sore legs overboard for the rushing water to
wash them for treatment, and come up and present them in
turn for medicine. There were nearly twenty sores this morning, some twice the size of a silver dollar. I find a solid satisfaction in easing somewhat their pains—something accomplished!

I have five Congo men on their way to home and pay. Some,
perhaps all, will go back with me "when they have seen mamma,"
as they always say; and we shall have a nucleus of trusty fellows, whom we can make do anything or go anywhere, for I
picked them up fresh, and we have trained them. Mpiata is
my major-domo, permanently, I hope; his contract binds him
until I go to Mputu (white man's land). He can speak very
fair and very funny English, wash, cook, boss workmen, or hold
a hand himself—is a gilt-edge river-man. Little Mrs. Vwila,
his wife, is also aboard, going to see the Congo land, and report
to the Kassai folk, and to be servant to Mrs. Adamson for the
time. Shamba Mwana, my table-boy, is also taking his travels,
eyes wide open, but not surprised at anything, not he! nor
afraid of anything or anybody. His mother's people, headed
by Uncle Musangu, raised a terrible row about his father's letting him go to "Malange" with me in November, and made his

2 Vmia. 4 Ngasena. 6 Mpiata.
1 Nianoc. 3 Shamba-Mwasa. 5 Natsu. 7 Lyamba.

NATIVE SERVANTS.

Nos. 1, 4, 5, 6 and 7 are Bakongo, hired at Leopoldville, March, '91, to go to Luebo. No. 3 is the son of a Bakete Chief at Bena Kassengo, volunteered as S. N. L.'s personal servant, and was with him when he died. No. 2, a Zappu Zap girl, bought for four pieces of handkerchief as a wife for Mpiata, No. 6.

Photo. by Mr. Adamson—Jan. 1892.

little life extremely bitter when he came back, even though I attended daily on his sister Bula's little Siangu (pronounced Shangoo) every day till the awful sore on her heel took her away. Since the death of the little girl the mother's folks were unexpectedly mollified, and Monday what was my thankful surprise when Shamba and Musangu came together to the mission and sat down on the veranda. A pause. "Shamba Mwana wants to go with you to the country down river." "Good!" I say. "I am his father, and Musangu here (the uncle, tough old case) is his mother (!), and we agree, only we count on your bringing us back a nice dash of cloth and beads." So the ice is broken at Bena Kasenga. The most popular boy in Kasenga, known, too, all over the Bakete country, child of two "royal" houses, has gone to Mputu (its all Mputu down country in the Bakete mind).

Yesterday we passed out of the little Lulua into the Kassai, which isn't at all little. The river Kassai rolls to the junction in six streams, divided by five beautiful wooded islands. Behind the sloping forest hides the almost unknown country of the Tukongo on the left bank; our Bakuba friends are on the right. The first station in their land has just been founded by M. Stache ("S. A. B.") just below the mouth of the Lulua. They occupy the left bank, from there down to the Loange river, I hear. Stopped 10 A. M. at Bena Makima, which I saw last April. The chief is the son of Lukenge, but was not ashamed to keep us waiting until three o'clock for four promised goats, of which only one turned up, after all. Dropped down to Bena Dibivé, a Bakuba town a quarter of an hour inland (there are no towns on the river, only fishing camps). Saw a woman whom we knew very well away up at Luebo. It seems then that even these Bakuba trade at Luebo. It is far. Yesterday overheard a small palaver between Mr. and Mrs. Mpiata, in the course of which she reminded him, "You didn't give me any marriage-cloth— you have no legal rights" (by black folks' law, i. e.), which was settled by my prompting the young man to make the significant present, and her acceptance removed one little matrimonial difficulty. The acceptance of a present, after full understanding of terms of agreement, is binding with all Bantu tribes.

From the Lulua mouth down to the Sankuru, almost, there are a good many beautiful islands—some, clumps of dark green trees rising out of the brown water, some, meadows of rich grass and lines of something like alder. The latter are ornamented with an affair which looks very much like swing-frames on pic-nic grounds; two tall posts with cross-bars—gymnastic poles, perhaps! But a native will inform you that a heavy beam, with sharp point downward, is usually hung at the top, which is thrown down when a passing hippo runs against the string below.

January 9.—We turned loose to-day. No delays for chickens or goats; indeed, all the important villages are out of sight inland. Only a fishing camp, or, perhaps, a landing, with canoes moored, half-hidden under the trees. They often shoot out, these slender canoes, propelled by two big Bakubas, who wave fine fish, just caught, and offer a bargain. From the first Bakuba town, Bena Siam, on the Lulua, near the mouth, we see these beautiful canoes, twenty feet long, very slender, and perfectly symmetrical—the paddle, seven feet long, very heavy, but likewise perfectly made. It is amazing how the watermen make these little crafts plow the Kassai—it looks as if they ought to go to the bottom every stroke; you can hardly see the boat among its waves—but it goes!

Reached, at five P. M., a new town in sight of the Sankuru, or of the ridge on the Bassongo Mino side.

January 14.—We are in the Congo, an hour or two out of the Pool, and four hours from Kinshassa, where the *Florida* is to unload her burden—very gladly, if the badly shaken old craft feels anything like her officers. We have been shaken up very badly by the big waves which the stiff breeze from the ocean raises every day.

Unfortunately, too, Captian Carlier felt called on to find fault with Engineer Van Kouteren, and that somewhat stubborn gentleman payed him back, I guess it from his pouting. At any rate we average thirty pounds of steam instead of sixty. But the good old river stood by us and bore us down whizzing. We can see this evening the ridge which closes in the Pool on the east. Left Kwa-mouth this morning. Between us and it saw a strange sight near sundown; a flotilla of great trade canoes, when the breeze up river fell at evening, pulled out of shelter which had concealed them, and moved down stream, a line of eighteen, Babuma from Musye-way, is my guess, with sugar-cane, beer, pots, and fish for the big towns on the Pool.

To-day a poor soldier from near Lagos on the west coast, sent down from Lusambo with consumption, died aboard. His countrymen, though strangers to him, helped me make his last experiences of this world a little more tolerable than he found it with the expedition—he didn't feel that he died friendless. Oojoo finished smooth and square with shovel, the grave the other Lagos men had hollowed in the plain with big knives and their hands. I spoke and prayed with the living, and they made a neat mound over the dead. I told the sick man last night a few words to tell to God as he lay awake, and this morning he was dying.

Well, I wanted to give you an idea of the Kassai, seen as a whole, for we have come like the wind, and seen with older eyes. I should have given each day's story when it happened, but Mr. Engeringh and I took a fancy to learn to work the wheel, and get something of a pilot's knowledge of the steamer's route among the sand-banks. This plan worked nicely for awhile, but the wind gave me a fever the third day, so I had to nurse myself awhile, and didn't risk the exposure again.

At the Sankuru mouth, Saturday, we called in to speak with M. Cadenas, a pleasant, frank little man in charge of the station there, Beua Bende, named after a neighboring village. He told me that the people inland (the awful Bassonge Mino, saw-toothed cannibals) were friendly and peaceably disposed towards the white man. The Sankuru is dark brown and has plenty of water, though not nearly equal to the Kassai.

On the way again, we passed a pretty stretch of river, banks lightly wooded and rising in pleasant slope to perhaps a fifty-foot ridge, a quarter of a mile back. Sometimes the ridge was covered with palms as thick as they could stand. Not far below Sankuru we began to pass neat little towns, one after another; we were almost never out of sight of one, all snugly nestled at the foot of the slope near the water's edge. I estimate that we passed four thousand people's homes that morning; more—for

Ngung at the mouth of the Loango has half that many,—say six thousand along the river bank from Sankuru to Loango. Basili, near Ngung, is gone; Mr. Clotens burnt it up.

Sunday the steamer went ahead as usual, and the goat buying was resumed in earnest. We have passed out of the region of Bakuba temple marks, fine velvet cloth and mats, and tall houses of palm leaves. Now we have timid people, who make *percale* cloth, and live in houses whose great wide roofs come nearly down to the ground, and are entered by a loop-hole hidden up under the eaves. Roofs and sides are made of forest leaves, fastened one edge in, other out, giving them a strange appearance. Indeed, the houses from Loange to Mt. Pogge and past, all have doors away up by the roof, and a platform, or series of them, to climb up by. Many of the towns are on the grass islands which divide the stream into a dozen channels, all big enough for rivers, and the mainland recedes into the hazy distance.

Mr. Engeringh did the chop buying. Once the people all ran away and left us their chickens and other worldly goods. Mr. Engeringh, not a whit put out, had the chickens caught, calculated what the people would value them at, stretched out the payment, cloth, like a long flag on a house top, and came away. Then the people, who had been watching it all, decided this was the man for them, and came back; hunted up chickens we had never dreamed about, and in half an hour from landing we had bought forty-six chickens and left the natives exultant— and so were we. A few such raids quickly raised our stock to twenty goats, several pigs, and fifty chickens, with which we were content. Monday afternoon I steered around Mount Pogge, a nice green mound high as George's Point, at Vine Hill. It is on the right bank. We had plenty of wind and big waves.

Below Mount Pogge we reached another stretch, and different, reaching nearly to the "Swinburne Rocks." This section is characterized by a rich prairie, sloping gently to a ridge, which is usually surmounted here and there by a picket line of lonely wind-mill palms. As we were floating out of this region Tuesday morning, we heard "Sail ho!" and soon drew up alongside the little " *Ville de Verviers*," *en route* for Lusambo, with Captain Dhanis on board. Here and there in this part we see a strip of woods lining a little water course down to the river. Hardly any people. But inland, are my old friends on the Duma, which is only a few days' march away; and to the right are the people spoken of so highly by the German travellers Kune and Tappenbeck. Tuesday afternoon put us through the wooded section, with forested banks, openings under the big trees, lined with people on land and canoes in the water. Another striking element of the scenery here is the dark green masses of leaves and vines that rise to a hundred feet height sheer out of the water without a fringe of sand. Between these islands the channels are beset with dangerous rocks. A straight course would take a steamer to destruction, as Mr. Swinburne found out, long ago.

Camped in the lower end of this reach, just above the mouth of the Kwango, on Wednesday. Thursday, Kwa-mouth! Friday, Kinshassa, at 11:30 A. M. Chopped at the Belgian house, where there are between twenty-five or forty-five white men to feed, over half of them belonging to the expedition of the Katanga Syndicate. This is a union of the S. A. B. and the Katanga Company, and has taken two of the smaller steamers of the S. A. B., " *Roi des Belges*" and " *August Beernant*."

LETTER TO HIS MOTHER.

LEOPOLDVILLE, *January* 16, 1892.

Reached the Kinshassa S. A. B. station at eleven yesterday. It is a big affair now, a regular ship-building yard. Dined with M. Butaka, who kindly sent me down to Kintamo (Leopoldville) in his boat with six Bangala oarsmen. I stopped to speak to Mr. Gordon, the sensible colored man from Jamaica, in charge of the English Baptist Mission at Kinshassa, and reached Kintamo without accident. Mr. Camp left the big workshed he is roofing to say his welcome.

"The doctor is up at his house; don't know you're here," he said. Dr. Sims seemed pleased to see me, and then Mr. Adamson and Mrs. Adamson!!! You don't know how satisfying it is to see a white lady after so many months of savagery. Adamson has done himself a good turn, and us too. His wife is pleasant looking, gentle and tidy, and reminds me of my Glen Addie friends, Miss Mary T. and her sisters. Mr. and Mrs. Adamson keep well. Mrs. Adamson keeps house for us four. Dr. Sims and I making up the number, and she makes other good things besides chop and tea. She has just fixed up the doctor with a new mosquito bar; and an official inspection of my quarters was made on pretense of showing me the pretty little Gleichman baby. I hadn't a pillow case on the little pillow from home. You see Shamba Mwana, the young bushman, is forgetful, and I only discovered it when he was gone off to sleep in some nook or corner of the *Florida.* So I was reminded of my carelessness, by Mrs. Adamson's coming to me with a pillow case, asking leave to put it on the pillow.

LETTERS TO HIS FATHER.

Since reaching here I have opened my ledger, under Dr. Sims's instruction in book-keeping, and incorporated therein all the scattered accounts of the mission up to date. The last back accounts were entered to-day.

I have purchased also of the English Mission S. A. B. and the French house nearly £80 worth of goods suitable for the Kassai; enough I hope to last until we receive the large invoice ordered last November from Whyte and Company.

I am writing out by bits the grammar of the up-country talk as far as I have mastered it. Mr. Adamson improves the waiting time by making the molds for a brick press, by means of which Luebo is to be built of burnt and pressed brick. Remember, Mr. A. has already put through one big job on the Congo, the remounting of the steamer *Pioneer.* His father was a large contractor; built some of the famous Liverpool docks. Mrs. A. is making clothes for the bachelor contingent here, and chop for her man, Dr. S., and me. I am well and in excellent spirits. I believe the "A. P. C. M." is going to do good, and to get started at it before very long, if God wills.

Where are the others to take the new fields that we could begin to open to-morrow ?

P. S.—Found unfinished and brought to date, February 19, 1892. Mr. Clotens left Luebo five days after we did; came by way of Lusambo; reached here 13th February. The Comte d'Ursel, whom I left sick, died, poor fellow, at Luluaburg, January 5th. Mr. Luff, Mr. McKittrick, Mr. Comber, and Mr. Bröholm, all friends of mine, have been taken in the last three months. We should be humbly thankful that I am kept well. I have not yet been dangerously sick.

TUNDUWA, March 12, 1892.

DEAR PAPA : The above address will no doubt startle you. A week before I left the Pool I had no idea of coming; but shortly after the date of my last to you, under this same cover, I got an answer from the Governor-General to my application for the land at Luebo. He said that the ground in question was already given away, and that I must find another place, near Luebo, if I liked. As the "Commissaire de district" had seen my ground and assured me officially that it was unclaimed, there must be some mistake or some trickery. . . . . In any case, I judged it worth the time and expense to come down and finish the business in person.

On the way down I found more disturbing news. Dr. Guinness left a letter for me at Lukunga, saying that the present transport arrangement will not be convenient for the C. B. M. much longer. . . . . . I believe that if Mr. McKittrick had been spared, this arrangement, suggested by him, would have stood. . . . . However, I feel that when I have looked around and got at the business the transport can be arranged.

. . . .

I have been amazed at the progress made by the railway people here at Matadi. . . . . The trains carry to the Mpozo, and the construction is going ahead beyond. . . . . We hope four years will put it through to Stanley Pool.

I am writing in the same house we occupied nearly two years ago. My open door is a frame enclosing a picture, which, to

15

me, is always striking—the monster hill that shuts Devil's cauldron on the up-river side, carpeted with grass, pale green, varied with wrinkles and dotted with trees, small by the distance, but distinctly seen through the clear atmosphere. At the foot sweeps the Congo, hardly five hundred yards wide, but rolling down like—no other river on the globe, certainly, and looking more majestic here than in the cataracts, or where it stretches for miles in width. At the top, the loveliest thing in this or any other country, the blue sky, "serene and far"—there's some poetry for mamma. I haven't time for a line to her by this mail.

To-morrow or next day I go to Boma, D. V., for the palaver with the Governor. Mr. Grenfell and Mr. Bentley think I shall get through all right.

Your loving son,   SAM.

P. S.—BOMA, March 17, 1892, 10 P. M. Back from dining with the Governor. He was very obliging—only heard my case at four P. M., put it through, and handed me the letter when we came to dinner. Thanked God and took courage. I go back to Matadi to-morrow.

LETTER TO MR. WHYTE.

The above was his last letter home; what follows was to his very kind friend, Mr. Robert Whyte, of London:

BOMA, *March* 17.

DEAR MR. WHYTE.—I am awaiting at this moment an answer from the Governor-General, appointing me an audience with him.

Boma has become a busy place since I came by here two years ago. A big Elder-Dempster boat, which discharged here a few days ago, passed down this morning from Matadi. Hatton and Cookson's Liverpool boat came in this morning; three smaller steamers, which go, however, to sea, have come or gone these two days. As I write, the Antwerp boat is unloading at the hotel pier. A truck, which holds two hundred boxes of gin, has rolled by several times fully loaded. There are some fairly good shops, too, by which I have made myself pretty comfortable, and made up for the scantiness of the outfit with which, in my ignorance, I came to Africa; for you must know that most of what I brought in the way of clothing is long since finished.

(Resumed March 19, Underhill, B. M. S.)

But you had rather hear about Luebo, where we have our first station. I need not—yes, I had best say that it is on the Lulua river (the third affluent of the Kassai, on the eastern bank), and at the head of navigation of the Kassai, in effect, because the Wissman Falls are not far above the confluence of the Lulua and the great river. So our post is the meeting point between the Upper Kassai people and the white people's commerce and the white people's religion, now. Whether due to the presence of the white traders or of immemorial usage, there is a concourse of native traders from widely different and widely separate tribes at Luebo.

We used to live in a little glade on the wooded plateau through which the big trade road passes. In the same day I have seen caravans of Bakuba from the east, bringing ornamental mats, painted in several colors, and the coveted tusks of ivory, and the delicately formed and featured Bashilange from the southwest, followed by slaves laden with baskets of the little rubber balls, which are the forms this staple starts with on its long journey to markets and consumers.

I know not how many droves of hungry slaves have been marched past the door of my hut (it was). Most of these were sold for goats, which were driven by with at least as much consideration as the human cattle were. A more pleasing occurrence, frequent in our little home in the woods, was the passing of the hunters from the town of Bena Kasenga, not far away. Every man and boy is arrayed, or disarrayed, in the scantiest garb consistent with decency, and carries the strung bow over the shoulder, a spare bow-string wound about his brow, and a scrip of skin or basket work, containing arrows and the two dried sticks with which he makes fire, if he wants a warm lunch. (I have seen the fire rubbed out of these sticks.) In addition, some lead hunting dogs by the leash, each dog with a wooden bell strapped under his body, that his master may follow him in the chase; and some carry great nets rolled up, into which the game is to be driven.

In the town, men and women divide the work (unequally), the women finding the bread, of which cassava and millet are the main bases. They also flock to the river for fish, etc., in season. Where there is clay the women make the earthenware. The men divide among them the trade of cloth or mat-making, making the palm wine, hunting, and each man builds the house that shelters himself and family. They are very genial and good humored, as you know, and lying, stealing, and impurity are considered disgraceful, but are universal, almost. They have an idea of God, the creator and preserver of all things, and a tradition that a closer acquaintance with him once existed. But they have no intention to submit themselves to him, and no idea that they need a Saviour. Will you think of our work for these, when you remember the dark places of the earth!

.　　.　　.　　.　　.　　.　　.　　.

I had begun to get hold on grammar and vocabulary when I was called here. Hymn-making and translation will soon begin, I trust. Kindly remember me to Mr. Black and Mr. Ellis, and any other friends who remember me, and accept this letter as an judication that I have not forgotten your kindness to me when I was in London.

Sincerely yours,

SAMUEL N. LAPSLEY.

CHAPTER X.

THE END.

AFTER the cheery letters from Tunduwa and Boma, just copied, the transition to the last scenes is sadly abrupt. These letters reached here the second week in May, having come from Africa in the same steamer with Rev. W. Holman Bentley, who, the day after his arrival in London, wrote the following, which was forwarded, and reached us on the 17th of May:

BAPTIST MISSIONARY SOCIETY, 19 FURNIVAL ST., HOLBORN,

LONDON, E. C., *May* 3, 1892.

Robert Whyte, Esq., London:

DEAR SIR: I have just returned to England after my second five years on the Congo, having arrived yesterday only, and hasten to discharge what is to me a most painful duty.

Our brother Lapsley, of the Southern States Presbyterian Mission to the Congo, has been called away to the higher service in heaven, after a few days of fever at our mission station at Underhill, near to Matadi, at the head of the navigable portion of the lower river. He died on the 26th of March. Knowing that you are the agent for his mission in London, I address myself to you, and beg you kindly to inform the directors of the Mission of their sad loss.

As you are aware, his colleagues are far away in the interior, and are not likely to hear the news for some weeks. We therefore assume the duty of acquainting the home officials. Allow me to supply such details as I am able to furnish.

At our station of Wathen, 144 miles from Matadi, and 80 miles southwest of Stanley Pool, we three times had the pleasure of a visit from Mr. Lapsley, and learned to respect and esteem him highly.

While waiting at Underhill for our steamer for the journey home we were surprised to see Mr. Lapsley arrive. He explained to us that he had several matters to arrange with the Governor of the Congo State.

.   .   .   .

Mr. Lapsley very wisely determined to settle the matter at once, and personally. . . . Everything was arranged with the Governor in the most satisfactory manner. . . . The next day Mr. Lapsley returned to Underhill.

Before this trip to Mboma he had been very well, feeling all the better for the long journey down country; but on returning from Mboma he said that he had felt the sun very much. During the night he had a slight fever, and a degree or so of increased temperature during the next day warned him that all was not quite right, and the usual treatment was adopted, with a fitting dose of quinine. During the day he told me of his satisfaction at his success at Mboma, and we hoped that the fever would soon pass off, and he start back to Luebo to carry out his many plans, and push on the work.

He had once or twice suffered from hematuric fever, and was all the more careful during this little fever that was then upon him.

During the night his temperature rose again, and hematuria developed. At six o'clock the next morning I started on my homeward journey, and just shook hands with him. Mr. Grenfell, of our mission, was at Underhill, as well as my colleagues, Messrs. Graham, Pinnock, and Fuller, so that he was well cared for. Mr. Grenfell's experience dates over some seventeen or eighteen years.

Mr. Pettersen, the senior missionary of the Swedish mission, was also there. I was delayed a week at Banana, and, just before starting, received a letter conveying the distressing news. I copy the following from Mr. Grenfell's letter, which is all I know of the sequel:

"The hematuria lasted for thirty-six hours only, but the fever was persistent, and at noon on Saturday (the seventh day after hematuria appeared), March 26th, he passed away.

The news of his death came as a great shock to me, as it will to all his friends in America. It is a terrible loss to his mission;

for, apart from the courtesy, shrewdness, and tact which distinguished him as specially fit for the delicate and difficult task of starting a mission in such a country, he had acquired most valuable experience and information, as well as a fair knowledge of the native languages. Of course the language of his district is quite unknown to me, but he was conversing very freely with the native boy who accompanied him, and we discussed together many grammatical points, which would be common to us. . . . .

The field is great and wide, and great are the opportunities *now;* what they will be when the Catholic mission and the new Jesuits get to work, who can tell? I earnestly hope that the Presbyterians of the Southern States will support earnestly and vigorously this mission to the Kassai, and be in no way discouraged by this terrible loss.

Believe me to be, yours respectfully,

W. HOLMAN BENTLEY.

This was followed in a few days by a letter from the Rev. R. H. C. Graham, dated Underhill, March 29, 1892, containing the following, in addition to what had been told by Mr. Bentley:

. . . "The usual treatment was adopted, and the Rev. K. J. Pettersen, of the Swedish Missionary Society (who happened to be here at the time), kindly took charge of the case. . . . When it became evident what the issue would be, Mr. Lapsley gave a few directions about his things; told where his will was to be found; spoke of the prospects of his mission when he should be gone, trusting that God would more than fill his place; and, commending his native lads to our care, he said he was 'going home,' and sent 'good-bye' to all his friends. Soon he became unconscious, and remained so until he went 'to be with Jesus,' at ten minutes past two, Saturday afternoon, March 26th.

"We laid our brother's body to rest, on Sunday morning, in our little cemetery among the trees down by the river-side, where sleep quite a number of our brethren 'until he come.'"

The Rev. T. A. Leger and W. A. Hall, of the A. B. M. U. and Rev. A. Young, of the C. B. M., came over from Matadi to

attend the funeral.   Rev. K. J. Petterson, of S. M. S. and Rev.
G. and Mrs. Grenfell, Rev. J. J. and Mrs. Pinnock, and Mr. J.
A. A. Fuller of this society, being also present at the service,
which I conducted.

A great many native carriers who were here came to the
service, and I had an opportunity of speaking to them and also
to our workmen and school children of the Saviour in whom
our dear brother had trusted, and in whose service he had given
up his life for the sake of Africa.

I shall enclose herewith a copy of the will made by your son
at Stanley Pool on his way down from the river Kassai.

Again assuring you of our united sympathy, and prayers for
you and yours in this bereavement, I am, dear sir,

R. H. C. GRAHAM.

The following is a copy of the will:

WILL.

"The year one thousand eight hundred and ninety-two, the
twenty-fourth day of the month of February, I, the undersigned,
Lapsley, Samuel Norvell, Missionary at Luebo, give and bequeath to my father, Judge James W. Lapsley, of Anniston,
Alabama, United States of America, my English Bible and my
watch, and I further give and bequeath to the American Presbyterian Congo Mission all other property and effects of which I
may be possessed within the Congo Independent State, and I
hereby name and appoint Sheppard, William, and Adamson,
George, executors of this my will.

"(Signed,)   SAMUEL NORVELL LAPSLEY."

"Nous, soussignés, Aaron Sims, Bachelier en Médecine, et
Georges Frank, sous Commissaire de District, résidents à Leopoldville, déclarons que le présent testament a été fait devant
nous par Monsieur Samuel Norvell Lapsley, le vingt quatre
Février mil huit cent novante et deux.

"(Signed)   AARON SIMS.

"GEORGES FRANK, *Sous Commissaire de District*."

We certify that the above is a true copy of Rev. S. N. Laps-
ley's will.   R. H. C. Graham.
George Grenfell.
J. W. Pinnock.

The execution of the will, together with numerous allusions
in his letters, show that this early termination of his labors was
not unlooked for by him. Upon his medical examination at
home, before his acceptance as a missionary by the committee,
he was reported to be in perfect health; but his friend, the
doctor, warned him fully of the dangerous African climate. He
simply replied: "That will not deter me." The reader may
recall the following from one of his letters on a preceding page.
"I think often of two trips, one to you all . . . another to a
lasting home which I hope to reach after a good deal of the
work I was sent here for. . . . However much time for service
he may lend me, it will not be long. 'A little while, and ye shall
see me.'" How brief this "little while" would be, none of us
realized or appreciated until the shock came, and found us,
though constantly fearing, yet all unprepared.

And we had little idea how full was the appreciation of his
work and character, and how wide-spread the grief over his
death, until the mails brought us from all parts of our church
and country, and from other lands and churches, letters and
papers, telling how heavy the blow was felt to be. Many were
from strangers to him and us, but all breathe the same thought
and spirit, of which the following brief extracts are examples:

EXTRACTS FROM LETTERS.

*Rev. K. J. Pettersen, of the Swedish mission near Matadi, wrote,
under date, September* 12, 1892: "It so happened I was here arranging to start building a station for our society, near Matadi,
when your son took ill. He seemed to me to be in low health
generally, although he said he felt well, and had had very little
illness. He said he had had several hematuric fevers; but,
apart from that, he had good health. Yet he dreaded another
such fever, and said several times he wished that fever would
leave him alone.

"He went down to Boma and returned. Not feeling very well, he staid in bed, but made very light of his ailment. . . . .

"On Sunday morning there was a repetition of hematuria. I got him to bed at once, and applied the usual remedies. . . . . Having had a good deal of experience in the sick-room, as well as a hospital training, I was asked to take charge of the case, which I did willingly; and, except one night and a few hours of daytime, I spent all my time attending to Mr. Lapsley.

"He kept very quiet all the time. He did not once mention death until the last day, although I could find that he was fearing the worst all the time, having been made to believe that he could go through only a certain number of attacks of that fever.

"I had good hopes of his recovery until the early morning of the last day, when I found that the temperature did not fall as low as usual. Instead, it gradually rose, but I still hoped I could check the fever. We tried all we could think of. I had not mentioned my fear to him, but when I told him we wished to try a cold bath, he said, 'Yes, and if that doesn't succeed, you will find my will in my bag, and other valuables are on the table. Other instructions I have left with Mr. Whyte.'

"We tried the cold bath, and brought the temperature down a good deal. However, it rose again, feeling which, he said: 'It is no use. Bless my father and mother. Please tell them I go home to be with Jesus, where I wish to meet them. I am sorry for my poor mission, but they will find a better man. Say good-bye to all my relations and friends.' After that delirium set in, and he soon quietly passed away."

From Dr. Sims, whose great kindness and generous hospitality the foregoing pages abundantly attest, we have a letter, dated Leopoldville, September 1, 1892, from which we copy the following words : "I dearly loved your son, and regard him as a real martyr. I warned him to go home, but he wished to complete a definite work before that. Too much goodness for his strength !"

Mr. Matthew Addy, of Cincinnati, wrote : "Not often have I felt more sad than in reading the notice of the death of your son. To cheerfully leave the home he had, with all its fond associations, to willingly spend his life in one of the darkest regions of heathenism—this was too much. . . . Christ sent for him to come home."

From Mr. L. A. B., of South Carolina : "Thousands of Christian hearts through our church mourn with you to-day."

From Rev. N. Bachman, of Tennessee : "He permitted his workman to lay a few foundation stones, then called him to a brighter field; . . . but the work will go on."

From Prof. Blake, of Greenwood, S. C.: "May the heroic example of your son stimulate others to rush forward to fill up the gap."

From Miss E. J. B., of Virginia : "We only knew him by his work. . . . . From the beginning we have traced his career with eager interest."

From Rev. W. H. Clagett, of St. Louis : "His gentleness, consecration, affability, everything about him, drew me to him in a peculiar manner.'

From Rev. R. M. Du Bose : "For days, under the stunning effect of the blow, I could go no further than to say, 'The Lord God omnipotent reigneth.'"

Col. Reginald H. Dawson writes : "It was a glorious death. The soldier who falls in the battle front fighting for his country is praised of all men ; but the noble life spent in the service of God . . . exercises a power for good that cannot be measured. Your boy is blessed. Many a noble sainted martyr has had to struggle through long years of weary waiting and wasting labor before he has been judged fit to wear the crown, but this noble boy has in a brief space been called by his Lord to his kingdom."

From Mr. M. W. P., of Virginia : "I loved your boy as I never loved any one out of my own household. . . . I was saying to my little N., 'how strange that Sam was taken just now,' and she repeated the lines, 'Shall God's appointment seem less good, than what thyself had planned.'"

Col. John C. Graham writes from Carlsbad, Germany: "I was greatly shocked and grieved. . . . Such splendid physique, good health and good habits! I expected him to go through all the hardships. . . . I had studied his character and found in it the rarest qualities we so much love."

Rev. P. Gowan, of Mississippi, writes: "We have all been bereaved; as a church we have sustained a common sorrow."

From Rev. M. H. Houston, D. D.: "The attractions of the world above are becoming brighter to us year by year, and we soon shall be there. Yet there is a consummation better even than the departure to be with Christ. It is the dawn of that day when, over all this regenerated earth, there shall be no more curse, no more sorrow nor crying, for the royal Saviour shall make all things new. Your gifted and attractive son, by his devotion to the Saviour, by his zeal and self-sacrifice, has done an important part in hastening the arrival of that glad day, for the 'gospel of the kingdom shall be preached in all the world for a witness unto all nations; and then shall the end come.'"

From Rev. T. W. Hooper, D. D., of Virginia: ". . . . Sam has been translated from the jungles of the Congo to the Paradise of God. . . . The God of missions will take care of his own cause."

From Judge Jonathan Haralson: "It seems but yesterday when the little fellow, our neighbor, was running around, barefooted, genial, bright, and happy. How little did we think then of the wilds those feet would one day tread, and of the moral heroism that would fill his soul!"

From Rev. T. M. Lowry, of Georgia: "In his letters and diary I noticed a maturity of thought, a wise forethought in planning, a whole-hearted consecration and fearless courage, which we do not often find in one so young."

Senator Morgan writes from Washington: "The sad news distresses us as much as if dear Sam was a member of our family. His life was very precious to us, as his memory will always be."

Rev. A. L. Phillips, writing from the General Assembly at Hot Springs, says : ". . . O, sir, my heart cries out for Sam, but my faith whispers to it, 'Peace, be still!' . . . When Dr. Houston yesterday announced the death, the whole Assembly was moved, and many wept."

From Rev. W. J. Sinnott : "All day yesterday the loss we have sustained was present with me as a heavy weight on my spirits. . . . A church of nearly 200,000 members mourns with you. . . . May it not be a trumpet call to the church to renewed consecration, because 'we know not the day nor the hour wherein the Son of man cometh ?'"

Rev. Dr. Stillman writes : "It has completely unnerved me. I loved him tenderly. I admired his simplicity, purity, and nobleness of character, his lovely traits, his entire consecration to Christ, and his heroic, even sublime, devotion to his great work."

From Rev. H. M. White, D. D., of Virginia : "Never have I felt so deep an interest in any one man not related by blood to me, and never have I been so grieved. I have been reading the lives of missionaries for forty years, but no one of them ever got such a hold on my heart as he did. I have eagerly read every line published by or about him that has come to me. Macaulay's lines over the tomb of Henry Martyn have been in my ears off and on all this day as appropriate to him :

> . . . . 'For that dear name,
> Thro' every form of danger, death, and shame,
> Onward he journeyed to a happier shore,
> Where danger, death, and shame are known no more.'

I can think of no one whose course so much resembles that of our dear Lord as did his. Not Carey's or Martyn's, for they went among a people with some civilization and under the British flag, and in companionship, at times, with British officers. Your noble boy penetrated to the centre of the "Dark Continent," and settled down there for life to save others, and others he saved—himself he could not save. What a record! It will move the hearts of God's people—the old to prayer and praise, and the young to gird themselves with fresh zeal and devotion for a century to come. For years the poor Africans will be asking about him, even as Sir Robert Porter says he was asked by the Persians about 'the religion and the Book of the man of God, Henry Martyn.' His memory will be embalmed in the church long after you and I have passed away and been forgotten. His life will be a fragrant incense from her altars for many, many years. I never saw your son, and learned but to-day that you probably lived in Anniston, Ala., and so I write for my own sake."

His venerated preceptor, Rev. Dr. J. A. Waddell, of Virginia, writing of his bearing the banner of our church into the depths of Africa, says: "The cheerfulness he manifested in all his sacrifices, privations, dangers, and sufferings, is now a permanent impression of memory, and an assurance that he was right in regarding the Congo as the shortest route to heaven."

Mr. E. T. Witherby writes: "Yesterday, in one of John McNeill's sermons, I found the following, which I venture to think finds a deep response in your soul:

> 'I have a son, a third sweet son,
> His age I cannot tell,
> For they reckon not by years or months
> Where he has gone to dwell.
> I cannot tell what form is his,
> What looks he weareth now,
> Nor what a shining seraph crown
> Adorns his holy brow.'

His name is enshrined with Livingston and Hannington and Mackay. I cannot see their names without seeing his And those grand words of the Litany, "The noble army of martyrs praise thee," have a new meaning as I think of the new name enrolled therein."

Rev. N. E. Clemenson writes from Utah Territory: "His consecrated and consistent life was a constant inspiration to me, while his earnest, loving words were of priceless value in my hours of sickness and discouragement. He was my dearest, truest companion in the seminary."

Mr. Robert Whyte, of London, writes to Dr. Houston: "In the few days he was in London, in March, 1890, I learned to know him pretty well. His guileless nature seemed to open itself to any one whom he trusted and who wished to know him; and I shall always cherish the memory of the young and earnest missionary. I may add the hope that Mr. Lapsley's wise, and in the providence of God, timely arrangements as to securing the site at Luebo, will be felt by you to be an indication that your church should earnestly go forward in the prosecution of the mission to which Mr. Lapsley has given his life. You will see (from Mr. Bentley's letter) that such is the hope of our Baptist friends. The tidings of his death may be blessed to the calling of other workers of like spirit, and our dear friend's noblest monument may be the winning to Christ, through the efforts of your church, of the people for whom he has given his life."

From Dr. Hampden C. Du Bose, Soochow, China: "Life is not to be measured by length of years. The Lord asks his people to be consecrated. Your son taught the Southern Church that lesson, and it was felt throughout "thirteen States.""

But of the many tributes and testimonies received, none is more touching than the following:

LUEBO, CONGO INDEPENDENT STATE,
W. C. AFRICA, *May* 26, 1892.

DEAR MRS. LAPSLEY: I know that you have wondered why I have not written, or why I was not the first to break to you the sad news; but, as you may know, we were a thousand miles apart. And at this point of the interior we get a steamer once, or per chance twice, a year.

About the first of January your darling son was sick with a fever. In three days he was feeling much better. A steamer—the "*Florida*"—came in just then. Mr. Lapsley and I both thought that a change for a month or so would be beneficial to him, as he also had some business with the governor about our land. And he thought to accomplish this, and to look after the transport at the same time. So he secured a passage, and left, January 6, 1892, for Stanley Pool.

Dear Mrs. Lapsley, that Wednesday morning, February 26, 1890, at the foot of W. 10th Street, New York, just a few moments before the "*Adriatic*" left for England, you placed your arms around your boy, and gave him his last kisses and God-speed till you should meet again, and turning to me, remarked "Sheppard, take care of Sam." We went at once into Mr. Lapsley's cabin, and prayed that the good Master would comfort you and protect us. We held daily communion with God. We spent a month in England, being together always. On board the steamer "*African*" we held daily private prayer, and would often mention and ask special blessings upon our parents, whom we were leaving. We entered Africa, and proceeded as we procured information. We have never been separated for any length of time since we left America. I can place my hand on my heart and look straight up to God and say conscientiously I have kept the charge you gave me. I have loved and cared for him as if he were my own brother. The last words of one of his sisters at the depot in Anniston was, "Sheppard, take care of Sam." It has not only been a duty of mine, but a pleasure. I have nursed and cared for him in all his sickness. And he has done the same for me. When I have been sick his eyes knew no sleep. By my side he would sit and give medicines. On our canoe trip up the Kassai he was quite sick with hematuric fever. It was the rainy season, and we were unduly exposed. So we camped for three days on a beautiful island near the Kwango. There was nothing that we could get that was nourishing for him. And he remarked, "Oh! I wish my dear mother was here. She would know just what to do for me!" Shortly after this trip we came to Luebo, and here we have labored as best we could in promoting the Lord's kingdom. Every day we would have prayer, and lecture with our people. Not only has he been zealous to tell the natives of Christ, but the French traders also. Many nights, when all was wrapt in sleep, he would be walking up and down the walk, communing with God.

Yesterday, May the 25th, when the steamer blew, I at once ordered the people to sweep the walks and fix everything in order, so that the station would present a nice appearance. I hurried to the river, and crossed in a canoe to meet him and bring him home. I entered the steamer and asked for Mr. Lapsley. The captain informed me that he had not come, and at the same time handed me a handful of mail; so I hurried and opened a letter to get some news, and oh, how sad the news! I was struck dumb. The letter read thus: "Your friend and brother has joined the faithful of all ages." He who left me a few months ago, and said, "Good-bye, Sheppard; God bless you; I will return by the next steamer," dead? Oh! is it possible? He, my comrade and co-worker, from whom I have not been separated these two years, now dead? I at once returned to the mission and broke the news to Mr. and Mrs. Adamson. They were struck to the heart. It was sad. Oh! more than sad. And the men, women, and children weeping for him they loved. And to-day (the 26th) they have been crowding in and asking is the news true? The greatest weepers were the chief's family, whose son was Mr. Lapsley's personal boy.

My dear Mrs. Lapsley, what am I to do? My friend and brother has gone to be with Christ, and I shall see him no more. No more kneeling together in prayer! No more planning together future work! His work is done, and he is now blest with peaceful rest. Oh, that I could have nursed him, that I could have kneeled at his bedside and heard his last whispers of mother, home, and friends! This is my sorrow, that I was not by his side while he fell asleep. I know that your heart is breaking. I wish that I could say a word to comfort you. Little did you know that his farewell was forever. But he shall be standing at the beautiful gate waiting for us. We shall soon join him, where farewells and adieus are sounds unknown. We will submit to the Master's will, saying "Not ours, but thine be done. What I do thou knowest not now, but thou shalt know hereafter.'

> "Sleep on, beloved, sleep, and take thy rest;
> Lay down thy head upon thy Saviour's breast;
> We love thee well, but Jesus loves thee best."

Everything of Mr. Lapsley's shall be taken care of, and if there is anything special you would have me look after, it will be my pleasure to do so.

I beg to remain yours to serve,

W. H. SHEPPARD.

His brother Robert gives me this little note, which makes for us an appropriate closing page:

"The most vivid and precious memory I have of Sam is that of his face and voice as he played and sang with me Mrs. Crowdson's exquisite words, 'Oh, for the peace that floweth as a river,'¹ with the music as written below. Where he got the music I do not know, as I never saw it in print. He would say, and we now see it was prophetic, "This always carries me forward to the Congo.'"

1. Oh, for the peace that flow-eth as a riv - er! Mak - ing life's
2. "A lit - tle while" for pa-tient vig-il keep - ing, To face the
3. "A lit - tle while" the earth-en pitch-er tak - ing, To wayside
4. "A lit - tle while" to keep the oil from fail - ing, "A lit - tle

des - ert pla - ces bloom and smile,   Oh, for the faith to
storm and wres-tle with the strong,   "A lit - tle while" to
brooks, from far - off foun-tains fed,   Then the parched lips its
while" faith's flick'ring lamp to trim: And then the bride-groom's

grasp heav'n's bright hereafter, A-mid the shadows of earth's "little while."
sow the seed with weeping, Then bind the sheaves and sing the harvest song.
thirst forever slak - ing Be-side the ful-ness of the fountain head.
coming footsteps hailing, We'll haste to meet him, with the bridal hymn.

¹The words are in Gospel Hymns 1, 2, 3, and 4, p. 181. The music I copy from pencil MS. of Sam's.

www.ingramcontent.com/pod-product-compliance
Lightning Source LLC
Chambersburg PA
CBHW030637030726

47497CB00006B/1836